A SHADOW FROM A DARK PLACE

by

Rory McQuaid

ISBN 978-1-914933-62-2

Dedication

'To the memory of my lifetime Muse, Pippa.'

Published by: -

www.i2ipublishing.co.uk
i2i Publishing, Manchester.

You can never be sure to know,
the one you are sure you do know. (Anon)

Chapter One

Blue smoke from the barrel of Lieutenant Brock's X90 snaked a lonely path up through rancid air. Spyda's body slid down easy over peeling skins of discount paint coated with scant enthusiasm over the last fifty years. The back of his scalp remained splattered head high on the wall: a sickening trophy in a sick environment. A brass bullet case rang empty as it bounced twice on cold stone and rolled with a hollow ring into dark shadows.

"Close call, Lieutenant!" Brock cracked an empty smile. Sergeant Grady Da Silva chewed on the silent reply; saw nothing more than piercing green eyes levelled across a dank, derelict warehouse. They weren't eyes of envy.

A dark shape sprang from the shadows. Brock spun round, squeezing hard on the trigger. A black cat rolled in dust, dancing its final mortal tango under a hail from the X90. Covering green iris with mirror sunnies, Brock clucked a wet tongue:

"There goes his ninth — let's get some fresh air, Grady — leave this mess to the blood wagon."

The mess, a ten-cent fart-breathed drug dealer slumped heavy on cold concrete, had bought himself a one-way ticket to a similar temperature. Chopper blades pulsing overhead excited a polluted atmosphere.

*   *   *

Roasted coffee rang in an unwelcome day. Yawning wide, Brock rolled a lazy body across crumpled bed linen, flicked the Coffee-Maid *off* switch, spun the top off a rye bottle, took breakfast with *Jack* and slaked a dry mouth. *Talk to me* flashed light blue on the handset. Brock reached out, flipped off the mute switch.

"Lieutenant . . .?"

"Yeah, what is it Grady?"

"Treat ya' to breakfast, Boss?"

"I've already had breakfast."

"Yeah right! I'll order steak 'n' eggs, see you in five, don't let it get cold. By the way, the captain's been callin', said he couldn't reach you."

"My phone was off, same as always when I'm asleep — Jerk! What a prick he is."

"Yeah well, he needs to talk — somethin's up."

"Such as...?"

"Beats me, he didn't say."

"Okay, Grady, thanks."

"See ya' in four, Boss."

Reluctance teased hard muscle into tight jeans. The bathroom mirror, once a reflection of better days, returned back nothing less than fatigue. Brock winced, rinsed out a stale mouth, threw on a loose jacket, filled a shoulder holster and flicked on the answer phone. It sang out its song as Brock sprang open the apartment door.

"Brock — Brock, I need to talk - Now!"

"Sorry, I'm not here right now. You know what you can do." Brock loved that message, beamed a smug smile and pulled the door shut on the captain's expletives.

*   *   *

Grady watched Brock saunter a sad path across a lonely street. He called the waitress over and ordered fresh coffee. Warm air shadowed the Lieutenant into Macey's diner.

"I just reset my watch again for the fourth time, Boss." Brock cracked a cold smile, brushed off the hard plastic seat pan on a steel tube chair.

"Sorry, Grady, duty called."

"So what'd he want?"

"Didn't wait to hear, didn't want to miss breakfast with my ol' buddy," Brock clucked a wet tongue and cracked a wink to the sergeant.

"Yeah right! Moneys on you've already had breakfast with *your* old buddy." Grady smirked a wry smile, poured fresh coffee.

"Any I.D. on the Leather-Jack?" asked Brock, didn't look up from lukewarm eggs. Grady didn't turn but sprang cautious eyes towards the full-width wall mirror. A white male, clean cut, early forties, muscle in all the right places, sitting alone at a table by the street door nursing a coffee, flicked a casual thumb through the pages of a news sheet.

"Search me, never seen him before," said Grady, "looks a little camp, could be on a pick-up."

"At nine-thirty in the morning?" queried Brock.

"Don't tell me you've never felt horny this early, Boss?"

"Yes I *have* Grady – when I wake up next to a pretty girl."

"*Moi aussi*, I'm right behind you there, Boss." Brock raised one eyebrow, broke out a warm smile.

"I sure as hell hope not, Grady."

Brock chewed hard on tough steak, swallowed tepid coffee, set the cup down and focused stern eyes across to Da Silva.

"How long have we known each other, Grady?" With a mind churning hard behind furrowed brows Grady thought deep, sipped hot coffee and spoke as he filled Brock's mug with a fresh shot.

"Eight years in the Specials, and seven in Covert."

"Eight in Covert," corrected Brock.

"My-my, how time flies."

"So it's sixteen years we've known each other, Grady."

"Glad to see the coffee's working, Boss." Brock's plaintive smile side-balled the comment.

"So why the *hell* do you still call me Boss?"

Grady polished his plate with a crust of rye bread as he shrugged mischievous shoulders.

"I guess it's because you look less of a boss than anyone else I can think of – Boss."

"What's that supposed to mean?" asked Brock. With a sly grin below a head of jet-black thinning hair, Grady shrugged heavy eyebrows.

"What d'ya want me to call you – Lieutenant Brock? Makes us sound as if we're in the fuckin' army corps."

"I have a name, Grady. What's wrong with using it?"

"Disrespectful – don't want to get too familiar now do we?"

"So how about I call you Sergeant Shiney Da Silva all the time?"

"Sergeant Grady Da Silva," corrected Grady. Brock chuckled, sipped coffee, muttered:

"Yeah — okay Shiney."

Grady flicked telling eyes at the wall mirror.

"Heads up, the Leather-Jack's on the move." Green eyes flashed a path through a miasma of fried cholesterol and followed black leather out the door. Taking the advantage, Grady plucked cold fries from a messy plate.

"Smell somethin' bad, Boss?"

"Maybe, Grady... talking of bad, let's go see what Captain Clod wants."

Scraping back chairs over a tiled floor they stood to leave. Grady dropped a bill onto the table, flipped his grey fedora onto his head and blew a kiss across to Macey; coquettish, she winked back long lashes, puckered ruby lips, picked up plates and revealed a length of white thigh as she stretched a lithe body over a table to wipe off smears. Beaming back his own coy smile, Grady stroked a brick-square jaw and held the door for the

Lieutenant. On an impulse, Brock scooped up the news sheet off a lonely table and headed out into the ambiguity of another irksome day in Covert security.

Fast food wrapping, empty beer cans, caked pools of ketchup and drying vomit littered the gutters of a friendless street. Empty doorways, never without a grime-clad body slumped bloody of eye clutching a bottle, wreaked of stale sweat and urine. The rancid scent of poverty hovered in the air, shameless as a hungry vulture. Hope was nowhere on offer.

"Maybe we should've used transport, Boss?"

"There's nothing like a little fresh air to clear the mind, Grady."

"Yeah right — an' if you don't mind me sayin': this kinda perfume ain't *nothin'* like a little fresh air."

Two blocks further they stepped over low chains into Sujo's Used Auto Lot. The office door was left ajar to compensate for what the air-con could no longer manage. They flashed I.D. at a nonplussed desk clerk and walked into a dank back room empty as a hobo's aspirations. Grady clacked back tired concertinaed doors on an ancient elevator and pressed a shiny button in a begrimed switch panel. Worn and tired as an old camel lifting a heavy load under the desert sun, the elevator clanked and rose from its comfortable base.

"Ya' think we're headed for a ball bustin', *Loot*?"

"*LOOT!* . . . What the fuck, Grady!"

"Just shootin' options, Boss," Grady beamed a smile and sidestepped a soft fist.

"One more ball busting won't make a lot of difference, Grady — believe me; I can personally vouch for it."

After groaning up a slow passage the elevator jerked to a halt and rang top floor at the second. Grady racked back the door and held it open; Brock stepped out into a cheerless corridor. LePage's office lurked at the far end, every bit as inviting as the beckoning finger from a proctologist. Tight knuckles rapped out a rhythm on a loose frosted glass door pane stamped in black with LePage's name and rank.

"Yeah, come in," growled the door. Grady spun the door knob and entered first. He crossed a torn square of well-worn brown lino, which could have once been either red or blue, then shuffled his feet on a floor of bare pine boards. He raked two chairs back from under a desk far too large for the small office then sat, resting two-twenty pounds against a wicker back chair; tired wood joints creaked out an ominous warning. Grady chewed gum. Arms folded and ankles crossed Brock leant back against the wall, didn't take a seat, but glared a dark message across to LePage.

"I don't remember asking you to sit down, Sergeant Da Silva," scowled LePage.

"Did your granny die, Sir?" returned Grady.

"What?" LePage screwed up his face in bewilderment.

"I was wondering where you picked up these old chairs from, Sir." Stretching out his legs, Grady lent back, cracked a tenon joint and looked stone-faced at LePage whose taxi-door ears burned scarlet east and west of a barren scalp. LePage rose from his office chair, moved across to the window, turned his back and took a deep breath expecting another knife blade. It didn't come. Insolence had lost impetus. From behind a phoney guise of self-control, LePage homed in on Brock.

"Good work on the east-side drug bust, Lieutenant."

"I couldn't have managed anything without Sergeant Da Silva, Sir." Nodding in fury LePage pursed white lips. The elusive comeback evaded him *again!* "Spyda was loose change, Sir. We missed the big bank roller," concluded Brock. LePage growled into his window:

"One more piece of vomit scraped off the street is a step in the right direction, Lieutenant." With malice festering in his soul he spun round to Brock. "And let me tell you: the good people of this nation will be glad to hear of it. Let's not forget our purpose here . . ." He underlined his statement with iniquitous, narrowed eyes and lips pursed tight as a cat's asshole.

"I take it you don't walk to work, Sir."

Evil eyes flared, staring poison tip daggers. LePage, bent low, turned his head to one side, pushed both hands deep into long pockets and focused to Da Silva.

"And what may I ask would be your point, Sergeant?"

"Nuthin' much, Sir, I was wondering if you'd seen first-hand how well the street cleaning program is working out."

"When the streets are cleared of the drug dealing filth and lawless scum contaminating our city, I'll be only too pleased to walk to work, along with the rest of the community. But the fact is, Sergeant Da Silva: we're crippled with crime-ridden anarchy brought about by corrupt politics, corrupt politicians and corrupt industrialists. And it's those facts, coupled together, Sergeant – are what really stink!"

"Well let's not forget the Virus and its outcome, Sir. The politicians weren't responsible for it but they sure turned big bucks over because of it," added Grady. The mood turned a murky shade of black, sombre as the result of a paddle-stick stirring up mud in a stagnant pond.

"But what the hell," added Grady, "I guess it's given us a job, Sir — Da Silver linings an' all that crap?" Grady shrugged heavy shoulders below a complacent smirk. LePage stared blank; turned to the grubby window and gazed out, focusing on nothing, then sucked his lips back onto his teeth and drummed his thumb in an open palm. Again, that elusive answer he so desperately needed dissolved swift as a drunk's promise. He rallied:

"Special Force has picked up Jute Malone ..." LePage, paused, spun on a heel as if he was auditioning for the lead part in Swan Lake. Brock smiled, conjuring up a bizarre vision of LePage in a Tutu.

"She's on The Island. I need you to interrogate her, Lieutenant. Take Sergeant Da Silva with you. Maybe Malone can lead us to this elusive bank roller you talk of."

"Malone's heavy baggage, Sir, I doubt she'll sing a song for sixpence," said Brock.

"Nor for a pocket full of rye, Lieutenant, which is why I'm sending you two to pay her a visit." Brock slow-nodded, dragging a wet tongue over dry lips.

"I guess it's good to see we finally got *one* blackbird baked in the pie, Sir," added Grady. Wide-eyed in surprise, Brock turned to Grady.

"What...! And I always thought you had a deprived childhood, Grady."

"Nah, not me — depraved not deprived, Lieutenant."

"That figures..." chuckled Brock, then turned to LePage. "Is there anything else, Sir?" Pulling a tired face into a blank frown LePage clasped his hands behind him, turned back to his favoured view, drew a deep breath through flared nostrils, bounced his Adam's apple and spoke in a hurried voice, pitched a minor third up from his regular key.

"A car will pick you up tomorrow morning at nine — don't be late – Meeting over!"

Grady welcomed the exit stressing loose chair joints as he pushed his two-twenty pounds out of a creaking chair.

"Wait outside please, Sergeant," barked LePage, voice laced hostile. Grady narrowed his eyes in question across to Brock, shrugged heavy shoulders and covered thinning black hair with a grey felt fedora. He left the room whistling a soft atonal melody. Teeth clenched, hackles up, LePage slow-walked across and pushed the door shut. Holding a tight palm flat on the door stile for a few seconds, he filled his lungs before he spoke. "Sit please, Lieutenant." Shrugging in reluctance, Brock took the empty seat, didn't appreciate the tone on offer. LePage paused, nodding in thought he moved slug-slow across the room and focused out again into a bewildering eternity through the dingy window. With his hands clasped behind his back, he tapped a nervous foot and cleared his throat with the sound of a stoker shovelling coal. He paused in thought before he spoke:

"Tell me, Lieutenant – do you trust Sergeant Da Silva?"

"Trust him…? He's my brother, Sir."

"Yes, metaphorically speaking I'm sure he is. However, let's say – how much would you trust Brother Cain, Lieutenant Abel?"

"Where the fuck is this going, LePage?" Brock stood in a fury, kicked back the chair. LePage turned, faced Brock, narrowed black accusing eyes and scowled:

"I heard a whisper."

"Fuck you! You know what they say about whispers. Let me take a wild guess here — this is fucking personal."

"It was quite a loud whisper, Lieutenant," said LePage, ducking the accusation.

"Sergeant Da Silva has worked alongside me for sixteen years, Sir; I've never once had cause for a moment's doubt about him or his loyalty. His manner may seem abrasive to some, but he makes up for it many times over in other ways."

"A well-established plant grows from a very small seed sown long before, Lieutenant. I'm asking you to watch your back." LePage paused, sucked his teeth, spoke back into the grubby window pane: "I've heard he's a plant!"

Narrowed eyes stared evil green at something distasteful. Without doubt LePage was an easy person to loathe. The overhead fan clanked out its tired old rhythm through an otherwise strained silence. Brock scowled:

"Will there be anything else — Sir?"

"Not for now. Thank you, Lieutenant," growled LePage sucking at his top lip. Folding his arms in frustration with tight lips, he glared down at a grubby floor. Brock left the door groaning on rusted hinges.

At the far end of the corridor, Grady's heavy frame leant back against the wall filling the corner outside the elevator. With a flick of his wrist he snapped his phone shut, didn't finish his conversation. Brock wrestled with the devil.

"What's with Captain Clod?" asked Grady. Chewing gum he avoided Brock's gaze.

"Nothing much, usual bullshit."

"Be careful, *Loot*, don't forget: there's a nasty rumour goin' round you might catch hearing aids from listening to ass holes."

"Yeah, thanks for the advice, Groucho. Don't call me *Loot!*" With a cheeky wink, Grady beamed a wide smile at his boss.

A shadow from a dark place slunk heavy across Brock's soul.

*   *   *

Chapter Two

Candy sweet lips nibbled on Brock's ear; gate crashed a disturbing dream. Green eyes sprang wide in the gloom of a shaded room. The tang of sweat generated from sex hung in the air heavy as an October mist over still water. Brock sprang from the pillow.

"Fuck! What time is it?"

"You tell me, sexy?" purred honey lips. The spunky raven-head played tender circles with manicured nails down Brock's back searching for the replay button. The coffee maker read eight-forty. Brock cursed for cancelling the wake-up alarm, spun off the bed and dialled Grady, praying the call wasn't headed for voice mail. Grady's phone rang six before pick-up.

"Grady."

"Right here, boss."

"Pick me up at my place, I'm running late," said Brock fumbling with shirt buttons.

"What's her name, Loot?"

"Well whatever it is, Grady, it's not fucking *Loot*."

"Not anymore she won't be doin' today that's for sure – see ya' in five, Boss." The phone buzzed dial-tone.

Brock dialled Securi-cab from the house phone; ordered a ride for the girl. Still full of desire, Brock's green eyes of envy followed the girl's sensual ballet as she strode naked across to the shower room. Brock clucked a wet tongue. Lust was about to disappear with sweat down the shower drain. Duty called!

*   *   *

The road to the chopper pad skirted the south side of the city down to the checkpoint of the twenty-four-seven curfew zone. A National Security Force combat vehicle flanked their ride.

From the helipad, an N.S.F. chopper flew Brock and Da Silva to a large expanse of bare open ground on the island; a place once home to deciduous trees and shrubs, but now planted with a matrix of anti-personnel mines and blockaded with rolls of barbed wire. A central concrete structure dressed with weeping rust bleeding copious as a running sore in barren flesh was the sole sight of relief in the man-made dust bowl; although relief was not a term its inmates were inclined to use. They nicknamed the place the Calcutta Crypt: nothing ever escapes from a black hole.

The chopper hovered before landing on a roof pad in a cloud of dust above the high-security holding prison. Brock and Da Silva were met on cold concrete with a matching societal indifference. The Covert Security Force: a necessary evil, garnered little respect amongst both patriots and criminals. If the C.S.F. were to succeed in their mission to clear the streets of killers, rapists, drug pushers and general lowlifes, there would be no medals awarded, for they themselves were killers — or to be more polite: 'exterminators of the anti-social elements in a threatened society'. Operating under a free rein, they were responsible to no-one, and blind eyes see nothing, especially when turned the other way. They were used as snakes to kill rats, and when there were no more rats the snake problem would have to be addressed. This was the sad new world of Brock and Da Silva: licensed exterminators.

A faceless man in an empty suit led them to a place where the sun would have once shone and would still do so if it weren't for the construction of twenty-five-foot-high retaining walls. Following the slothful steps of the prison guard, Da Silva trailed Brock down a cheerless staircase into the lower bowels to a place where incarceration ensured nothing animal or mineral would ever shine again.

Confined in cell thirteen behind bars, Jute Malone cuddled a cold heart in a lonely room. There was no window. The sole means of light came from one bare mesh-encased bulb active for only twelve hours a day, leaving the remaining twelve in total darkness. In a repetitive miserable monotony for those incarcerated, night became day, became night, became day, became night, ad-infinitum. A wretched existence only death could trump.

Known as the Snow Queen, Malone — a cold-blooded mass-murdering psychopath responsible for causing untold misery and degradation from the far end of a needle — had survived life amongst the sewer rats by flaunting an erotic countenance as she plied her trade, and in consequence from spreading her legs whenever something flaccid arose.

Clung tight as body odour to a hobo, Grady tailed Brock into the Snow Queen's hell. Green eyes smiled a cute love song through an iced atmosphere down to a sad figure clutching not even hope in a dirt-filthy corner. At the sight of human empathy, Jute Malone lifted the corners of her lips and smiled a passion as she rose cute as Libra from a chilled floor. Brock's instinct registered code red, saw nothing other than a spitting Cobra, but reached out a hand and cupped Malone's jaw. Hot lips kissed a cold heart. Brock's hand wandered, explored a pounding breast and teased soft nipples to hard. Jute Malone relaxed. Black lashes closed slow over sable eyes, ruby lips cracked and breathed a suffused moan. Tight in a leather glove, a knuckled fist sprang from nowhere, split Malone's nose wide and knocked her to the ground. Brock stepped back, drew black leather across wet lips and spat down at Malone. Grady stepped in. Malone hawked venom through a bloodied mouth: "I thought all this good cop, bad cop shit was crapped out with the fucking dinosaurs!"

"So it was, sweetheart, so it was! This is bad cop, bad cop – an' you're the bad lady," growled Grady licking his own leather wet over tight knuckles. He stepped up to the fray.

*　　　*　　　*

Shaking a head in frustration, Brock rattled the change tab on an empty coffee vendor, rolled green eyes, blew out a deep breath and tossed a pristine cup into the trash can.

"So what've we got, Grady?"

"A whole lot more than you're hoping to get out of a rusted coffee machine, Boss! We got a pretty beat-up songbird, a few names, and a long ride back to sanity," he racked his brows. Crouched low over a wash basin faucet he rinsed his hands, flushed his face and ran a comb through thinning black locks.

"Remind me to get the relatives of her many thousands of victims to send flowers," said Brock.

"Well, it's a dead cert she won't be gettin' any from her lovers, Loot!"

"Certainly not from the mortuary slab, and that's where *you'll* be soon if you keep on callin' me Loot!"

"Sorry, Boss."

"Brock'l do me just fine – it's my name. So who's Speed, and what do you know about him?"

"I know enough to keep away from him, Boss."

Brock pursed tight lips, shrugged eyebrows, blew out a heavy breath and racked tired eyes across to the big man.

"He's our first call."

*　　　*　　　*

Five blocks south of Macey's diner the Chan Woo twins drove Brock and Da Silva in a C.S.F. camo-paint combat vehicle through checkpoint three into the Toxic Zero-Zone: a two-mile wide ring of dust and dereliction contaminated from Zyclon 606: a powerful nerve gas first used in desperation to combat the virus and then to counter the effects of its antidote, but in the end — after all else had failed — it was employed as a deterrent to suppress the ensuing riots during the late twenties.

Dredged through the ruins of a once civilised society, a chain-link fenced corridor topped with barbed wire led down to a cluster of wretched shanties, pitiful hovels and squatter camps at the outskirts of a place termed the Outlander Zone, shortened for convenience to the O-Zone; Hell would've been a better name, but would be far too kind a moniker for the sprawling township housing the criminal element who had evaded extermination and were now banished from the city's Affluent Zone to this faraway place well away from sight and mind, abandoned in a move once comparable to the exile of lepers from an anxious society, left to fend for themselves in squalor and filth. Undesirable was now their colloquial term: it was not a dissimilar moniker to their namesakes from previous centuries. Nothing much ever changes — times were still tough *but only for some*, mused Brock.

The ride raised a wake of dust and litter, didn't slow for either stop streets or lights, none of which were relevant, for there was no need on an empty road to despair. Mutant breeds of hungry mongrel assault dogs roamed in packs on hard pads through bare streets devouring the endless supply of rotting human corpses, or at times live ones if they weren't smart or quick enough. Wild dogs, a saw-toothed deterrent, unbiased to colour, creed or status and more effective than any police force could ever be, kept the opportunists and desperate anti-social dregs away from the security and comfort afforded in the affluent A-Zone city populace: an exclusive community of the un-vaccinated languishing in their home sweet homes, safe in isolation behind high barbed wire-topped boundary walls. Howling cries from hungry dogs in the downtown suburbs had replaced the long since faded howling from police sirens. Nowadays there was no toss up as to which was worse: the dogs were the front runner on all counts with the added downside if you happened to tread in something nasty.

Brock stared out into decay and ruin playing a bottom lip with a forefinger and thumb and turned to Da Silva.

"You're coming up to forty-two next birthday, Grady, it's about time you found a nice lady and settled down, get yourself out of this stinking cess-pit occupation."

"I've already tried, Boss," Grady sighed, clucked his tongue, "major grief…"

"Maybe you tried the wrong girl."

"Nah, poor girl – she tried the wrong guy." Grady stared a blank look through black-tint glass as the combat vehicle drew closer to the mark in the condemned ruins. His vision merged into the O-Zone reflecting the sad analogy to his own life. "Sure want to get out of this shithole though. I don't know which is worse, but I do know which is more dangerous," he said, reflecting on the question of dogs versus the police. Brock missed the point, chuckled and ruffled Grady's hair.

"It's no way to talk about your lady, Grady."

"Fuck you, Lieutenant!"

Acrid smoke from burning tyres, the sole means of waste disposal, billowing despair through the twilight flagged the township's welcome. The C.S.F. Riot Wagon slowed at the outskirts with the wary caution of a blind man reaching down into a snake pit to recover something precious he'd dropped.

"Pull off the road up ahead Boo, we'll walk the last fifty yards and make our way around the back. No need to hand Speed a calling card."

"Sure thing, Lieutenant, buzz when you need us." Boo pulled the Riot Wagon into an empty lot. Stone and brick dust spat from studded tyres in a skid halt.

"Ready, Grady?"

"Ready as I'll ever be, Boss."

In the fading light of a hot day, deep shadows from low buildings spread across a graveyard battlefield, an area now nothing more than barren earth and rubble since commerce went east in the aftermath of death and social unrest spawned by the Virus and its constant mutations. This was followed by the subsequent rise of the YUNGEN ZYKLON KULT: an anarchist movement climbing to prominence after the murder of a city judge who freed a terrorist under a loophole in the Human Rights Act back in March 2027.

A small act in retrospect but an action which took an overstressed western civilisation already at odds with the deadly virus and the misery caused from the effects of an untested vaccination spiralling into a dark age of anarchy and dividing the social classes even further at a grave cost to humanity.

Tight as a flea on a hound dog, Grady shadowed Brock into the back streets behind Crack City. Brown eyes, savage, set in blood-veined pods colluded in the dark depths of a grimed alleyway. Nostrils flared, matted hackles rose on filthy black skin, communal vermin, desperate, moved in for the kill. Brock flipped off the safety, swung round at the first movement, took down two in a short burst. The X90 kicked again, spat dum-dums at the dumb in the dark. Grady let loose with the Street Sweeper, emptied the full twelve-round mag of heavy shot into brown eyes and howls from dark shadows. Crouched low, staring into the silent blackness he clipped on a fresh mag. He didn't blink or whistle.

Dust settled as the sound echoed away. Wild dogs whimpered; dragged bloodied limbs into dark corners. The stench of cordite cut through the rank air of deprivation.

"Wild dog packs stretchin' out these days, Boss," said Grady, chewing gum.

"Yeah I guess — so must be their food chain, unless they were here for another reason."

"Another reason…? Ya' think we've been set up?"

"No, it's not what I think at all, Grady. I'm sure of it! Buzz the twins. Let's get out of here."

Gravel and road dust spat from the two wheels left in traction as the Riot Wagon raced the corner. Doors sprang wide ejecting the Chan Woo twins trigger ready. With his six-two frame poking above the dust cloud, Grady shook his head, signalled the negative.

"Sorry guys, show's over. Let's head back to the city," said Brock, thumbed the safety and climbed into the wagon.

"What about Speed, Lieutenant?" asked Grady.

"He was never here; whoever let the dogs out is also long gone. A little bird sang a song, and it wasn't Jute Malone – She's lost her voice."

Grady stared out into a bleak wilderness, spat his gum into the dirt and began to soft-whistle his tuneless melody. Brock wrestled with a confusion of thoughts throughout the return trip. *'Maybe LePage was right. But if Grady was a plant, why then would he put himself in danger? It doesn't make any sense.'* It had become obvious Brock needed to be more careful, maybe needed to organise a covert set up – but right now could think of nothing more comforting than a serious leg-up from 'Jack'.

*   *   *

Bingo pounced at the smell of burgers as Brock walked into the apartment and placed a three-fifty-seven along with take-out food and the news sheet onto the low table.

"Down boy, there's plenty for all of us. Heidi, call off your dog before he licks me to death." Heidi took a break from running fourths on the piano and whistled the dog.

"Food smells good, Lieutenant."

The formality didn't bother Brock; it made the little girl feel in high company. Poor kid, she sure needed it.

"I'm going to take a quick shower, sweetie; it's been a long day."

Ten minutes later Brock came out of the bathroom towelling wet hair, threw on loose clothes, poured three fingers of bourbon and sat down to eat.

"A burger for Bingo and Thai for us. What were you practising there, sweetie?"

"Nothing much, I was limbering up for Saturday night. Are you still coming?"

"A date with my favourite girl — try and keep me away. How's your momma doing?"

"She's fine, working too hard as usual, but she's okay."

Brock set the food out on the low coffee table. The hungry dog's drooling tongue dangling from the side of its panting jaw hung down dripping like a roll of red stair rug hung over a wash-line in a rainstorm. Brock laid the burger down on the floor. Bingo wolfed it down in two bites and sat doe-eyed looking for more. Brock patted his head.

"Come and eat Heidi, you can carry on with your practice later. Bingo has started and finished without us. You really ought to teach your dog some manners, sweetheart."

"You're sounding bad as my momma." Heidi spoke with a smile, turned her head in the direction of Brock's voice. She closed the piano lid, and with one hand stretched forward she crossed the room, felt for comfort and took a seat on the sofa.

"Rice and noodles in front of you, soda to your right. Chopsticks or a fork?"

"I'll take a spoon. It's easier." Brock smiled into black glasses shrouding blank eyes and made certain the little girl didn't fumble anything, which she never did.

"Did you catch any bad guys today?"

"No not today honey, maybe tomorrow."

Brock pushed away a full plate of food, lifted a jigger of *Jack* off the table, relaxed back into the sofa and flicked through the news sheet scooped off the empty table at Macey's. At the foot of page five, four words and a phone number had been scrawled in red Gel pen. Brock stared deep in thought at the scribble before scratching notes, then, perplexed, tossed both pen and pad onto the low table and dialled Grady.

"Hey, Grady, call round tomorrow first thing, there's a few things bothering me I need to run by you."

"Sure thing, Loot — what's wrong with Macey's?"

"She can wait. I need your full attention right here, not on her cute little butt. Let's make it around nine-thirty."

"You got it, Loot."

"*Grady*," growled Brock.

"Sorry — *Boss*."

Sat back into the sofa Brock thumbed red and tossed the phone down onto the coffee table then jollied up the empty jigger with another two fingers of bourbon. Heidi fingered major scales then ran thirds and fifths on the piano. The landline rang in five-four time. Heidi picked up the rhythm, broke into a vintage Brubeck bass line in E flat minor. Brock got up, sauntered over and picked up the phone.

"Brock here, speak to me."

"Good evening, Lieutenant, please tell Heidi it's time for her to come on up now; I've run her a bath."

"Sure thing, Mrs Wiley, will do right away."

"How's her practice going?"

"She's going to do you proud Saturday night for sure, Ma'am."

"For both of us I'm sure. Thank-you and goodnight, Lieutenant."

"Night, Ma'am." Brock cradled the phone.

"Honey your mama's calling."

"Five more minutes – pleeeese, Lieutenant."

"It's your choice, sweetie. Take it from me; a cold bath isn't much fun!"

Sat in solitude with *Jack* for company, Brock took a pen and sketched out a game plan on blank A4, circled Grady's name with red ink in centre page, ran lines to satellite circles of recent hits and shake downs, particularly those which had left the rails. Not much added up or made any sense. Deeper thought would be needed. The soft sound of running fourths up and down the keyboard intruded, Brock wished they wouldn't but saying nothing blew out a deep breath and ran fingers through black locks, then reached for the phone and stabbed the numbers for the department directory. The call picked up after one ring.

"Lieutenant Brock here, CSF 51, I need a run-down on a phone number."

"Please hold, Lieutenant." Listening through silence, Brock tapped itchy fingers and waited for the voice ID line check.

"You're clear, Lieutenant. Go ahead."

"Six-three-six, five-nine-zero Q Y." Again, Brock sat through silence and reasoned it to be a whole lot better than piped digital music.

"Sorry, Lieutenant the number is NLIU: no longer in use."

"Do you have any info on when it was last in use, or who it was registered to?" Brock listened to the clacking of keys, tapped fingers in five-four time and waited.

"It was last registered to, 'Lewis *Lulu* Mbangang' in downtown district three, back in twenty-thirty-eight, nearly ten years ago."

"Nothing since . . .?"

"No, Sorry..."

"Okay, thanks anyway."

"It's my pleasure, Lieutenant." Brock reached for the bottle, poured more bourbon, pressed red and dialled the department I.D. Information Division.

"Lieutenant Brock, CSF 51, I need to run an I.D."

"Please hold, Lieutenant." In the wait for voice I.D. clearance, Brock listened to more stilled silence.

"Okay, Lieutenant, go ahead please."

"Lewis Mbangang, AKA: Lu-Lu, only known address: district three." Using the phonetic alphabet, Brock spelt out the name and listened again through silence, doodling Mbangang's name in red capitals at the top of the A4. The lieutenant didn't have long to wait.

"Lewis 'Lulu' Mbangang: male, North African origin, mixed race. D.O.B. September 12, 2001. N.F.A: no fixed address. Possession and distribution of a dangerous substance, three arrests for murder, two of those victims were cops, no convictions; six counts of assault with a deadly weapon, no convictions; robbery with violence and suspected arson on a public building, also no convictions. He was deported to the O-Zone May 2037 for raping a minor. There's more if you need it, Lieutenant."

"No thanks, it will be enough for now. Goodnight, Ma'am."

"Glad to help. Goodnight, Lieutenant."

A rap sheet as long as a wedding speech and yet no convictions; something about it sure stinks. Seems someone, somewhere needs to keep him breathing – Who, and why? mused Brock.

Heidi closed the lid on the Steinway, moved up behind Brock on the couch, squeezed supple hands on tight shoulders, then bent and kissed the crown of Brock's head.

"Night, Lieutenant."

"Goodnight, sweetie, want me to walk you up?"

"No, I'll be okay. Thank you for dinner."

"It's my pleasure, sweetheart."

"Catch you tomorrow?"

"You bet!"

Heidi felt her way to the door. Brock tapped teeth with the Gel pen, then flipped it onto the foolscap and mentally drew a blank. A tired body sank back into a tired sofa; blank eyes stared up to a blank ceiling. The screw top on a fresh bottle of *Jack* spun off way too easy. Brock poured out a serious measure, slunk across to the Steinway, lifted the lid, ran agile fingers over an old friend and teased out vintage *Monk*. A lonely night meandered into an all-too-familiar haze.

*   *   *

Chapter Three

The doorbell sang long at the third ring. Brock stretched with a heavy yawn, rolled off a snug bed, threw on a gown, ruffled wild hair, slunk across the room and flipped on the shower before answering the door. Grady followed two take-out coffees into a shaded room; tainted with the tang of alcohol, it rang sombre and soulful as a country tune.

"Nine-thirty, Boss."

"Thanks Grady. What *would* I do without you?" *Sarcastic!* Grady chuckled to himself, set the coffee down on the low table between an empty bottle and a glazed over portion of Thai. He sat, hung his hat on one knee, slackened his tie, grinned and asked:

"Late night, Boss ...?"

"Maybe, I don't remember," said Brock, wandering into the sanctuary of the bathroom.

Whistling a soft melody, Grady stood and tossed the empty bourbon bottle and take-out leftovers into the trash can. He threw back the shades. Sunlight flooded the room. A beam of light shimmered down through a mess of airborne dust preparing to settle on the Steinway. Brock called out from a hot shower:

"Make yourself comfortable, Shiney – be out in five."

"Now where have I heard that before?" muttered Grady. Searching for comfort he took the best option on a tired sofa. His attention was drawn to his name circled in red on a sheet of scribbled foolscap on the low table in front of him.

Towelling wet hair and trailed by a cloud of steam, Brock, clad in jeans, a loose shirt and a heavy hangover came out of the shower room. Grady didn't look up from the foolscap.

"Seen that name before, Grady?"

"Sure — I've been seeing it all my life."

"Smart ass! Try Lu-Lu Mbangang.'

"What kinda' name is Mbangang?"

"A bad one, Sergeant."

"Him or her?"

"Him — with a rap sheet as long and dirty as the towel roll in a whorehouse bathroom."

"So what's our connection?" asked Grady.

"Maybe nothing, but the name connects to a phone number written on the news sheet I took off the table at Macey's where the Leatherjack was sitting."

Grady pulled the news sheet across the table, studied the scribble at the foot of the page, massaged his jaw and took slow eyes up to Brock.

"Somethin's gettin' a little ahead of me here, Boss."

"You and me too, Grady." Three words set out in the shape of the letter T, were connected by a central letter S in a heavy circle. To the left of the S, the word *deep* was written. Vertically down from the S, was the cryptic word *nug*, and to the right was the word *loot*.

"Looks as if someone's doodlin,' Boss — while speaking on a phone I'd guess."

"Yeah, I thought the same thing. But it bothers me."

"*Loot*, you mean?" asked Grady.

"Yeah – *Loot*, it's fresh off the press. For me it sticks out plain as a boxer's chin a split second before the ten-count."

"You think he was tuning in to our convo, Boss?"

"Maybe, but if he was I didn't see him on the phone doodling."

"How do we know it's his news sheet, or even if it's his doodle?" asked Grady.

"We don't," answered Brock.

"Writing looks effeminate, Loot. Maybe could've been left by someone else. What's *nug* mean?"

"Search me, Grady." The sergeant pulled the foolscap back across the table, stared down at his name circled centre page in red. His bull neck flushed red. He blew out a heavy breath.

"Is there somethin' I need to know, Lieutenant?" Grady didn't look up from the table.

"I know you as well as I know myself, Grady, and I trust you more than anyone else I know."

"Same goes for me, Boss."

Brock threw down the damp towel.

"Someone put out the word you're a plant."

Grady blinked damp eyes, nodded his head slow.

"And you, Lieutenant? What do you think?"

"If I thought there was ever a grain of truth in it, Grady, we wouldn't be having this conversation. This stinks of a set up."

"Who by, what for...? LePage... the bastard!" scowled Grady.

"Maybe — I think I was meant to find the news sheet. But the word *loot* bothers me — and so does red Gel pen. Not a thing everybody uses much these days." *And there's one right here on the table*, mused Brock.

"I hear you, Boss, you're right — *Loot*, that's fresh off the press. You think we've been bugged?"

"Could be, maybe at Macey's, who knows?" said Brock.

"It wouldn't be Macey, Lieutenant, I know her too well."

Brock smiled at the big man.

"Sure, Grady. I understand — a blind man going over the falls in a barrel couldn't miss out on that one."

"Where does Mbagn ... Mbang, what the fuck's his name fit in?"

"We'll find out soon enough, I'm sure. But for now let's play their game, pay out a little rope; let someone hang themselves," suggested Brock.

"We're not detectives, Boss — there's no Watson and Holmes crap for us, we're nothin' more than plain ol' street cleaners," Grady shook his head in confusion, "so why all the cloak n' dagger bullshit?" He shrugged heavy shoulders. Brock threw on a loose bomber-jacket over a shoulder holster.

"Search me, Grady. Let's go get some breakfast."

"Sounds good, *Loo'* — uh, Boss — my call."

* * *

At ten-twenty between breakfast and lunch shifts Macey's was half empty, or — depending on your thought pattern — it was half full. But who the hell cares anyway, it sounds every bit as ridiculous as 'yes and no' as an answer? Brock took a corner seat, not their usual window table. Macey brought across mustard and ketchup pots along with cruets of salt and pepper and set them down with cutlery.

"What's it to be, guys?"

"Two specials, pretty blue eyes," said Grady.

"Flattery don't get you a bigger portion, Sergeant," quipped Macey through a wry look.

"I've spent enough time on my knees at Sunday service to know that's no lie, honey." Grady flinched as Macey rapped her order book on his head.

"You ain't doin' so bad, Sergeant." Macey wiggled a cute butt across the diner taking her tease back behind the counter. Salacious eyes followed sweet curves all the way.

"Seems to me she's got first-hand knowledge on you, Grady."

"Yeah, we hang out a bit now and again."

"Sounds to me you've been hanging out a lot more than a bit, Sergeant?" Grady smiled, flushed red, checked the salt and pepper pots and felt under the table. He looked up and shrugged.

"She's clean, Boss. Trust me."

"I do, Grady, believe me, I do."

Casting a hungry eye over Brock's left-over fries, Grady chewed on a slice of rye, licking his lips hopeful as a hound with eyes on the Friday night barbecue. Brock dabbed salty lips with a bright tropical print serviette which seemed a shame to blemish, then pushed the half-finished plate across the table.

"Thanks, Boss. What about Mboongong?"

"Mbangang," corrected Brock, "I was thinking, maybe we should take a discreet trip into the O-Zone, put out a few feelers — check out the lowlife," Brock shrugged, "It's about all we got right now."

"Okay, sounds a plan, Loot. Got any idea where to find this guy?"

"Scum rises to the surface, Grady. If he's still breathing he'll be on show somewhere."

"Maybe Jute Malone could help us," suggested Grady.

"I doubt it; our little jailbird has lost her voice. She was found hanging from a beam in the exercise room yesterday morning, and she sure wasn't doing physical exercise."

"I was always a little wary of exercising for a healthy lifestyle myself, Boss."

"Pity you didn't share such profound knowledge with her when you had the chance. Keep eating those fries, Sergeant."

Macey crossed the diner, cleared empty plates and ragged the table top.

"Anything else, guys?"

"Not for me, thanks," said Brock. Grady cleared his throat, held Macey's arm.

"Macey, d'ya remember a few days back, a guy in black leathers, sat over by the door?"

"Sure I do. I can never remember a face but I'll never forget a tip."

"He tipped you big?"

"I wish!"

"Seen him before?" asked Grady. Macey shook a mess of red curls over freckled shoulders.

"Mm-mm, no never did, why?"

"Maybe nothin' but do me a favour: if he comes in again, call me."

"He looked a little gay, Sergeant; don't tell me I got competition?" Macey flipped trimmed eyebrows in question above cute blue eyes.

"Not with such a pretty little butt you ain't." Grady teased her, wrapped a playful hand around her waist and squeezed tight flesh.

"Not so long ago I could've busted you wide open with a case of sexual harassment, Sergeant Grady Da Silva," she teased.

"Well I gotta' tell ya' – there's somethin' in my pants bein' harassed right now."

"Well don't let it bust out right here in my diner – save it for later, Sergeant."

"Okay, somewhere around seven thirty good for you?"

"Don't be late," she spoke back over her shoulder.

Brock, leant back with folded arms and frowned across to Grady.

"What?" asked Grady.

"You're a dark horse, Sergeant."

"*Stallion*, she says."

"Lucky girl!"

*   *   *

Squinting through dust on a grubby windshield smeared dirty by bad wiper blades after a brief shower of fine rain, Grady pulled the jeep away from the kerbside and made a U-turn.

"Drop me at Sujo's, Grady. I need to check in with Captain Clod. You go on down to archives, see if you can dig up anything at all on Mbangang, or on any of his known associates. With mucus stinking rank as him there's got to be a lead somewhere."

"There's a lot of mucus stinkin' rank as him in the O-Zone, Boss."

"You're on the big money there, Grady. Maybe you should play the horses, treat yourself to some screen wash and a new set of wiper-blades.

*   *   *

Chapter Four

Sujo's Auto Lot endowed as much welcome as a trial run in an open coffin. One step away from a condemnation order the auto lot was an undercover front for the Covert Security Force. Summer weather rolling down the tracks would leave a thick film of dust over the show models until the late summer rains thundered to the rescue in three months' time. As a rule footfall was low; not many punters bothered to visit the auto lot, but when they did it wasn't to make a purchase but rather to use the bathroom: a daunting experience traumatic enough for them to vow never to make a return visit. In future they'd use the bushes in the alleyway: it was a whole lot more salubrious.

The deadpan security clerk didn't bother looking up from the private channel on his computer as Brock flashed I.D. It would be a rare moment if he did. Brock took the stairwell at the rear of the back room. It was quicker than the elevator but had a strong smell of bad things; no doubt courtesy of the clerk what with the bathroom being a tiresome drag up to the top floor.

LePage's office was set on the second floor, one step up from the miasma along a corridor which might have looked homely had it been graced with a fresh coat of paint, carpets, and a wide view out over a sun-kissed beach. In stark reality, it had a run of bare floorboards, a stale smell and a flaking paint name board at the top of the stairway with: *Captain C. LePage. C.S.F.* etched in a lustreless, yellowing cream paint, below which, a wooden arrow hung on nails pointed off to a door at the far end of the passageway.

Brock slunk heavy steps along the corridor and paused at the far door; had always wondered what the 'C' stood for in LePage's name stencilled in black on obscure glass. Brock assumed it could only be for Clod, or maybe it was for a more suitable four-letter word. Brock smiled, rattled knuckles on the glass and entered. LePage was standing at attention at his favourite place. He didn't turn.

"You got my message about Malone, Lieutenant."

"Yes Sir."

"No suspects?" barked LePage into an innocent windowpane.

"I'd be very surprised if there were, Sir," replied Brock, wondering what the fuck it was he found so interesting staring through grimy glass out into an empty lot.

"Any more thoughts on Sergeant Da Silva, Lieutenant?" LePage didn't turn from the beguiling comfort of his window.

"I've got him under close surveillance, Sir, Macey's on top of him; she'll let me know if anything comes up."

"What? Who's Macey?" LePage did his ballet thing, spun round on a heel and sprang an eyebrow above a coal-black eye.

"She's feeling him out, Sir. But don't worry she's keeping it all very close to her chest."

Brock sucked in cheeks, suppressed a smile. LePage nodded, his mind in a fog he dredged his memory bank, feeling sure he'd missed something — again!

"Good, very good, Lieutenant, keep it up."

"I'm sure she will, Sir." LePage cast a quizzical eye back to Brock.

"Macey, Sir, she's keeping a firm grip on things."

"Yes . . . yes, quite," said LePage, lived up to his nickname, played with his ear lobe, took a deep breath and said: "You'll be pleased to know you will have some serious action going down in the O-Zone South-side Saturday night. I want you to strike hard, scrape up some scum. You will lead in the riot wagon with Sergeant Da Silva and the Chan Woo twins. You'll be joined by four other units from District Five." Brock winced, felt bad at letting a little girl down on her special night. *Duty calls. Shit!*

"It sounds a big hit, Sir."

"It will be, Lieutenant, I'm counting on your unit. There will be a briefing at sixteen hundred on Saturday. Don't be late." Brock held a tight tongue and asked:

"Is there anything else, Sir?" LePage sucked in his cheeks, patted his hands behind his back, lifted his chin and growled into a grubby window:

"No, nothing more for now thank you, Lieutenant." Brock turned for the door. "And Lieutenant . . ."

"Sir . . . ?"

"Let's keep this from Sergeant Da Silva until necessary," he spun on a heel, focused a sly glare from coal black eyes and said: "The less he knows the better." Brock replied nothing and turned to the door glad to leave. Treading tentative steps to a bitter-sweet waltz in a minor mood down a lonely corridor; Brock didn't feel good about having to veto Grady.

After a long and tiresome day spent chewing the end of a pencil in the CSF office to catch up with report forms, Brock took a Securi-cab to Macey's for an early nightcap. As dusk fell, small talk rallied between shots over a friendly bar. Without seeming obvious, Brock wanted to pump Macey about Grady, but knew Grady wanted nothing more in life than to pump Macey himself. Rather leave it there, he was no plant, he couldn't be . . .

As the shutters came down Brock pushed a big bill across the bar and slid down off the bar stool.

"Goodnight, Macey, keep the change."

Driving through light rain to a heavy date, Grady passed Brock pulling the door shut on the liquor store; he reversed and powered down the side screen.

"I got a lead on Mbangang, Boss." Relieved to shelter from the rain, Brock climbed in the passenger side, shook off wet hair blithe as a damp hound and rested two bottles of bourbon into the foot well.

"I thought you had a lead on a hot date, Grady."

"I have Loot, seven-thirty, half an hour away."

"Well, she's a lovely lady, don't be late."

"I appreciate such good advice from someone of your high calibre, Boss. Thank you."

"Fuck you, Grady!"

"Best leave that to her, Boss." Grady chuckled to himself as he blazed a wet trail down a dirty street, pulled in and scuffed the curb outside Brock's apartment.

"Got time for a quick sun-downer, Shiney ... shoot the shit about Mbangang?"

"Quick one, Loot, don't wanna' be late now do I?" Grady ducked a chin punch.

Leading the way into the apartment, Brock ignored the flashing blue voicemail and reached for two lonely glasses keeping company with an empty bourbon bottle in an otherwise barren cupboard.

"What did Captain Clod have to say about me, Boss?" Brock smiled: there wasn't much you could hide from Grady.

"Yeah, he asked about you."

"What did you tell him?"

"I told him all about your sex life. He seemed very interested."

"What! You're shittin' me."

"No, not you Grady, I was shittin' him. Now, tell me about Mbangang."

"He's still very much alive, Loot; high on crack, low on morals, running rackets for deadbeats in downtown O-Zone."

"Any faces we know?"

"Yeah, a whole lotta' them: Teko Mix, Zozo Sub, Suni Shaw and a fucking psycho called Kobra: calls himself King Kobra, also known as Kooky Black Rat." Grady paused. "Kobra's an acronym, boss."

"Thank you, Grady; I did pick up on that."

Sat at the low table, Brock wrote down the list of names on blank foolscap.

"Where the fuck do they get these names from?"

"Sure I dunno', Loot; could be from the old-time movies or left over dregs from the internet after it crashed? Go read the graffiti on every wall in the O-Zone; those guys leave their callin' card around same as hookers used to in phone booths."

"Yeah I guess so," said Brock. "The whole internet fuck up sure had a lot to answer for, I wasn't sorry to see it go down in cyber flames."

"Me neither," said Grady, "we're back into the caves again now. Be draggin' the girls round by their ponytails soon. Maybe I could even re-invent the wheel, make myself some *real* money!" Brock smiled at the sergeant, sipped rye, tossed wild thoughts through an active mind in a quiet moment. Grady whistled soft.

"Anything on Speed?" asked Brock.

"No, nuthin' Loot," Grady tapped his finger on the list of social misfits and said: "but a buck to a bag of donkey crap he's in there somewhere." Brock nodded, drained the jigger, massaged a tight jaw and worried a lower lip.

"Someone gave us the lead, Grady, who and what's more – why?"

"Search me; I ain't no Sherlock Watson, I'm just a plain ol' street sweeper."

"Yeah well, it's about time you got on down to Macey's. Sergeant, pull out your broom pole and do some serious sweeping up down there." Grady chuckled, drained his glass, set it down on the low table and lifted his two-twenty pounds up from the sofa.

"Call me if you need to, Boss."

"I won't, wouldn't want to interrupt a beautiful friendship. If you need *me,* I'll be in Jackie's bar later."

"Sounds to me like a good way to tidy up the day. Goodnight, Loot."

"Grady!" scowled Brock as the door latch clicked shut.

Brock smiled, drained a glass, leant forward and drew red circles around the names, scrawled *Saturday night* across the page then sank back into the sofa, tapped teeth with the pen and felt bad for not telling Grady about the hit on Saturday — *Fuck LePage!*

An empty glass cast an empty shadow, cried out for a refill. As Brock poured two fingers into a jigger a key turned in the door latch.

"Hi, Lieutenant."

"Come on in, sweetheart." Heidi turned a radar head, cocked high, tuning for sounds.

"I thought I heard the sergeant."

"You did, he left a few minutes ago — hungry?" No answer came, but a broad smile spoke loud.

"Pizza okay?"

"Sounds good, thank you, Lieutenant." Brock dialled Franco's, ordered two Calzone take-outs, one with fries and a soda.

"Did you practice today?" asked Brock.

"I came down and did three hours this morning after my momma woke up."

"Will you do more tonight?"

"Sure, if it's okay with you."

"Yeah, you're welcome. I have to go out later so feel free to help yourself."

"You gonna' catch some more bad guys?"

"No, not tonight, not unless they're in Jackie's bar."

Revitalised under the rose of a hot shower watching another day circle the drain, Brock winced as an imperfect Mozart piano sonata limped along to its coda. The door buzzer sang out putting Mozart on pause: Wolfgang could stop turning in his grave for a while.

"I'll get it," shouted Heidi, she jumped up at the aroma of fresh baked pizza. Brock, trying hard to digest bad thoughts towelled wet hair in a steam-filled room, checked a tired face in the mirror and figured some things would take a hell of a lot more than a four-cheese Calzone to improve.

*   *   *

Low light shone crystal radiance through ten polished shot glasses filed out in line on an empty bar top in Jackie Olson's saloon. Brock watched beads of rain cascade down window glass, felt the warm tang of rye cascade down a welcome throat.

"Bad night for some, Lieutenant."

"Are you talking about the weather, Jackie?" Brock turned on the barstool and connected with sad eyes across the French polished bar top.

"Take your pick," said the barman buffing glass, "never known it so quiet; seems as if we're in another fuckin' lock-down way back from the old days. I wouldn't want to go back to those days; the damn vaccine and an inept government terrorised and killed far many more than the virus ever could." More from habit than need, Jackie wiped a damp chammy over a pristine bar. "Don't usually see you in here so early, Lieutenant," he said, checking himself — he nearly said: *sober*.

"Well, it ain't so quiet over in my apartment, Jackie. I got some heavy piano practice going down tonight; the little girl's got a big night on Saturday." Jackie nodded, said nothing, saw the promise of another lonely night in his bar brewing on the horizon.

"Where's Sergeant Da Silva — lost your shadow, Lieutenant?"

"He's over at Macey's."

"What's this, he taking his custom someplace else now?" asked Olson. Brock slid down off the barstool, took a double over to the baby grand and smiled back to the barman.

"She's prettier than you, Jackie."

Nimble fingers ran up a chromatic scale, came back down the keyboard and settled into a soulful melody. Olson switched off the wallpaper muzak, sat back, polished glass and listened.

Outside, the gentle rhythm of early summer rain sang out its own soulful song.

*   *   *

Chapter Five

The sound of a new day permeating up from the resonance of road traffic roused Brock. A tangle of bad dreams faded like discount wallpaper under strong sunlight. Green eyes blinked a reluctant welcome to a golden dawn boring a rousing path down through the bedroom window. A flood of sunlight high-lit two flies as they sprung off dusty netting, buzzing the wrong side of a fly screen in their eternal search of exodus.

'Good to see it's not only me, who can't work out life's conundrums,' mused Brock, then clucked a dry tongue and tuned in to a distant songbird leading the dawn chorus. The rhythm of filtering coffee invaded a moment of reverie. *'At least it isn't the damn phone.'* Brock pulled tired linen back up over a tired face. A wealth of troubled dreams lay in wait beyond a semiconscious mind. Brock drifted rudderless under a quixotic daze in a sea of confused thoughts until the phone rang. Cursing with a deep sigh, Brock reached out to answer sending an empty bottle rolling off the bedside stand. It fell on the floor but didn't smash — maybe it was an omen; could be it was going to be a good day. Then Grady's voice intruded, breaking the moment subtle as a bugle call in a maternity ward:

"Lieutenant . . ."

"I need a fucking holiday, Grady."

"That sounds the best kind to me, Boss." Drawn into a change of mood Brock blew out a chuckle.

"What is it, Grady?"

"The Chan-Woo twins walked into a lead welcome last night." Brock sprang into a dirty day.

"What, where ...?"

"Right here, Boss, in Jackie Olson's bar."

"No way, you've got to be kidding; I was there myself last night."

"I guess you must've left before someone decided to call last orders, Loot."

"*Grady!*" scowled Brock.

"Sorry, Lieutenant – Boss."

"Anyone else hit?"

"No, I guess it was a quiet night."

"Not for some, Grady," Brock sipped lukewarm black coffee, "pick me up in five."

"Breakfast, Boss?"

"Sounds good, the twins won't mind if we keep them waiting a while. Not this time, that's for sure!"

*   *   *

In a grime-filthy street cooking under a burning sun after a brief shower, a thick mist of vapour rose from the tarmac dancing sweet as a troupe of angels on hot coals. Jackie Olson stood in front of a virgin fresh plyboard hoarding, brushing a mess of shattered glass from flagstones into a damp gutter.

"I hear you finally got some custom, Jackie," said Brock, striding out across the deserted street.

"That kinda' custom I can well do without, Lieutenant."

"I hear you. Let's go inside, Jackie – tell me all about it." Cuddling his twelve-gauge Street sweeper Grady checked the street for trash before he shadowed Brock and Olson into the dimly lit bar-room. In the sober light of day, a sensitive nose might still be able to smell cordite under the tang of cheap scent and the out of hour smack of stale alcohol. Olson racked up three shot glasses, spoke as he poured.

"After you left last night, Lieutenant, I cleared out a couple of barflies and was ready to close; then, in walk two girls – pretty – could be working girls taking a break I guessed," Olson shrugged, "whatever – I needed the business, so I stayed open. They sat right down there at the end of the bar," he motioned down the bar with his eyes, "lookin' very pretty and *very* sexy," he turned back to Brock, shrugged a silent coda.

"Ever seen them before?" asked Brock. Jackie shook his head.

"No, never did, but they looked every bit the same as maybe a hundred other hookers hanging out in late-night downtown bar-rooms. Anyway, fifteen, maybe twenty minutes later, in come the twins asking for you," Olsen racked his brows at Brock, "I told 'em you'd left a while back."

"Do you think the girls heard you?"

"I guess so, unless they were deaf: the muzak was still on pause and no-one was singing."

"Go on, Jackie," said Brock.

"I serve the twins a couple of stingers and figure it's turning out to be a busy night. Boo makes eyes at the hookers, felt lucky I guess, smiles big time at the girls." Olson, sucking his teeth looks down the bar then back to Brock.

"Did they smile back?" asked Grady.

"They sure did – With a sawn-off twelve-gauge!" Jackie spoke through a plaintive smile.

"Then what?" asked Grady.

"Then nothin,' I was down under the bar," Olson shrugged, "the twins took their exit through the window – backwards."

"And the girls?" asked Brock.

"Through the door I guess, *ladylike*. I didn't see – I was still cuddlin' the floor."

"Thanks, Jackie," said Brock and looked up above the bar.

"That thing work?" Olsen followed Brock's gaze and shook his head.

"Nah,' hasn't done for years. Never thought I'd need CCTV these days, not with you guys around. The two-bit system was only good for catchin' nose pickers even when it did work."

"Notice anything unusual about the girls, Jackie – apart from the twelve gauge jewellery?"

"No, nothing, Lieutenant: good bodies; average height; blond hair both of 'em, real pretty, spunky, dressed horny as hookers. What more can I say?"

"Hear any small talk, names – those kinda things?"

"Mm-mm," Jackie shook his head, "nothing I can recall. Didn't really pay 'em much mind the way my takings are going." Olson shrugged and laid open hands flat on the table: "Candy-coated treats are a little out of my price range right now, Lieutenant."

"I hear you Jackie. Did you notice their vehicle?" asked Brock. Olson shook his head, looked to the door and sucked his teeth to conjure up a memory.

"No vehicle. They came in a cab, a yellow Securi-cab, stopped right outside the door."

"How'd they leave?" asked Grady.

"Couldn't see, I was still kissin' the floor behind the bar." Olson ragged the bar top and frowned, "ain't any profit in it for me bein' a hero."

"Thanks, Jackie. Call me if you can think of anything else."

"Sure thing, Lieutenant." Olson wrung out his rag, wiped the pristine bar again.

Brock walked to the end of the bar, picked up a dead buzzer lying amongst empty shell cases. Cheap red lip-gloss smudged the tip on the lucky buzzer. Grady, soft whistling craned his neck over his boss's shoulders and shrugged his shoulders in question.

"Narrows it down to ninety-five per cent of all hookers," concluded Brock.

"Some lead!" replied Grady.

"Yeah, let's pay Securi-cab a visit."

"Sounds good, 'Loot – enant."

On the way out, Brock's cell phone rang.

"Brock here…"

"Brock – Brock, is this you, or is it your *fucking* answer phone?"

"It's me, Sir. But you can leave a message if you want." Silence fumed loud.

"Take Grady and get down to Olson's bar. We had an incident there last night." LePage rattled out orders sounding spent as a stuttering auctioneer with a bad hangover.

"We've just left there Sir – you want us to go back again?"

"What?"

"Are you okay, Sir? Did you forget to pay your early call account?" Brock winced at the sound of heavy snorting.

"My office right away, Lieutenant Brock, I need a full report." The phone clicked dead. A welcome silence rang in Brock's ear.

"What's the story, Boss?"

"The captain invited us for coffee, Grady. But first off, let's drop by Securi-cab."

*   *   *

Duzi Olifi tapped lazy feet under *Boso-phones* to a mindless pedal-point rap. He didn't look up as Grady tailed Brock into the cab hire office. Brock flashed I.D in a dim room to a dim mind light on content but heavy on chemical influence.

"We need info on a cab hired last night," said Grady. Duzi raised a predictive forefinger with the silent message: *'Not now man, give me five.'* Grady shook his head in mock disbelief. With a muted chuckle he strolled around the back of the cheap office recliner and cupped a playful hand at the back of Duzi's skull, then, slammed a surprised face down hard onto the desktop. Rap swung out a song from hot ears as Grady yanked bloodied flesh up by dishevelled dreadlocks and bent down close to Olifi's ear. He spoke soft words:

"You were asked a question, crap-head."

"Fuck! You could've busted my fuckin' nose."

Again, Grady rammed Duzi's face down onto peeling varnish – this time one hell of a lot harder.

"Okay, crap-head, now so as we won't have any more disputes about the state of your fuckin' nose, let's get back to the question. Two girls took a ride with Securi-cab to Jackie Olson's bar around eleven thirty last night, where was the pick-up?" growled Grady.

"FUCK! I dunno', shit man! I wasn't on duty then." Olifi spat blood, wiped a bloody nose on his shirt cuff. Grady gripped dreadlocks.

"If you ever took lessons in P.R, you shit-sucking bag-head, I'd ask for your fuckin' money back."

"Okay – okay, give me a minute – fuck man!" Olifi raised passive hands, spun round to the computer screen, dripped blood over the keyboard.

While Duzi played the keys Grady pulled open the desk drawer, lifted out a large plastic bag, tipped its green organic contents out onto a filthy floor and tutted aloud.

"This looks worth a five-stretch down in the O-Zone, would make you feel right at home with the rest of the fuckin' deadbeats." Olifi's head retreated into his shoulders dreading what was coming next. He reasoned it wasn't a good day to be a smart-ass, then spluttered:

"A call box on the corner of Seventh and Broad, a chick called Suzi Vango dialled it in,"

"Who was the cab driver?" asked Brock.

"I dunno' – they're all private-hire guys." Plastic keys flew in all directions as Grady rammed Duzi's bloodied face into the keyboard.

"You're a slow learner, crap-head."

"FUCK! – FUCK YOU! Bakta, Ali Bakta, it's his cab, a yellow Ford sedan." Olifi spat out words through a bloodied mouth drooling spit congealed with something green and nasty.

"Address …?"

"A shakedown on Prince Street, big house on the corner of Parkway; that's all I know, I swear." Brock smiled a triumphant look to Da Silva and motioned eyes to the door. Grady grabbed a hand full of dreadlocks and stuffed rapping earphones up bloody nostrils.

"That should help to stem the bleeding." He patted Duzi's cheeks as they left.

"Suzi Vango? Ring any bells, Lieutenant?" asked Grady, rolling down the sun screen in Brock's apartment.

"I'm sure she does to lonely hearts, Grady, but it's my guess her name's as elusive as the run down on cheap lipstick."

"Yeah, I hear you. So what are your thoughts, Loot?"

"My thoughts are you should stop fucking calling me *Loot,* Grady."

"Sorry – Loot – enant."

"Brock'l do me fine thank you, Grady. It's my name."

"Okay, but it don't seem right, Boss."

"Try it, Shiney, could be you'll get used to it. Anyway, I don't think the twins were the hit."

"You think the hit was maybe meant for us, Boss?"

"Could've been, or maybe someone's trying to tell us something."

"Tell us something … like what?"

"Beats me," said Brock, "never was much good at cryptic crosswords."

"How about the cab driver, he must be worth a touch?"

"We'll check him out after a hit of coffee. But for now let's go an' see captain Clod."

In a quiet moment of solitude, Brock wondered: *if the hit wasn't for the twins, who else knew I might have been in the bar? It was a short list for sure. And what was it Grady said about 'a good way to tidy up the day'?* A cold shudder rattled down a troubled spine. On the other, hand Brock reasoned it may have been nothing more than a coincidence; doubtful, but possible – same as a big lottery win with similar odds. *Trust no one, live longer?*

*   *   *

The boundary alert flashed red, a rare event for a warning system with scarce positive function, or one that was indeed ever switched on. LePage scowled dark eyes into his surveillance screen, sucked in his cheeks and buzzed Brock and Grady through security. He moved a chair across into the store room, leaving only one chair available for the lieutenant. He positioned himself in front of his smutty window and waited for the knock. Overhead, the rusted fan groaned and clanked out its mindless rhythm counting down the hiatus. After the knock, LePage made a slow count to ten before he would speak:

"Come!"

Grady walked in first, pulled the lone chair out from under the desk, handed the seat to Brock then walked around to LePage's recliner, sat and stretched out in comfort. LePage's neck burned scarlet along with his ears, his eyes narrowed, bored an evil message. Grady's ice-cold stare played game, set, and match as he sucked on his tongue and studied his nails. LePage, forever the runner-up, turned back to obscured vision, massaged closed eyes, blew out a frustrated breath and spoke into his window:

"So tell me, Lieutenant: what do we have."

"Two dead Agents, Sir."

"Any leads?"

"We're working on it, but I don't think the twins were the mark, Sir."

"What makes you so sure, Lieutenant?"

"Well, the twins don't usually frequent Olsen's bar, so, why someone would be lying in wait for them seems a mystery to me." LePage nodded in acceptance, sucked his teeth, and digested the possibilities.

"So – what, or who, were they waiting for do you think, Lieutenant?"

"Maybe they weren't too keen on the service, Sir. Jackie Olson's getting a little slack these days," put in Grady. LePage lost it, slapped down hard on the back of his recliner, swung the seat around.

"Are you aware of my standing in this outfit, Sergeant Da Silva?" Grady smiled cosy-cool up into an angry face.

"Why don't you fart and remind me, Sir." Already electric, a strained atmosphere kicked into high voltage.

"I think we're getting a little *off track* here, Sir," said Brock, stood erect, tried to ease the tension. LePage's tight embouchure could've blown a high 'C' an octave above Armstrong's best. Caustic stares froze in chilled air. Grady leant back into fake leather studying his manicure. LePage drew in a deep breath, narrowed his eyes, threw his hands in the air and scowled:

"We've kept these streets clean for more than ten years, and now this – murder of our own agents in our own backyard," growled an angry man spitting venom. Brock needing to defuse the tension, spoke slow and calm:

"As you well know, Sir, we're not detectives. We've a licence to keep the streets clean no matter what; and keeping them clean is what we'll do. We'll find the killers, Sir. Trust me. It's what we're good at," said Brock.

Nodding in thought but not agreement, LePage pinched his lips tight, bored evil eyes down into the back of Grady's neck; then, turned back to his comfort zone through a grubby window.

"Wait outside will you, Sergeant." Grady stood, spun the recliner, tossed his fedora over thinning locks and left the door ajar as he left. LePage, fuming red staring out at nothing patted hands behind his back.

"He's a good man, Sir – a very good man," offered Brock. LePage nodded into grimed glass, a nervous nod; but again, not in agreement.

"He'll need to be on Saturday night, Lieutenant; you'll be shorthanded now without the twins. I'll pull in a unit from G five," he spun on a heel and glowered down a smug look to Brock:

"If of course – that would be okay with you, Lieutenant?" he lifted his eyebrows in a mock question. Brock shrugged, uttered nothing, and then asked:

"Will there be anything else, Sir?" LePage turned to his window before he spoke:

"No, nothing for now but be sure to let me know as soon as you find out anything at all."

"Yes, Sir," said Brock, opened the door to leave but paused as LePage spoke.

"And Brock – fourteen-hundred – Saturday – don't be late! With his back turned LePage missed a middle finger reply.

*   *   *

"I guess we missed coffee, Lieutenant." Sat back in the side seat, Brock smiled across at Grady, turned up the A/C and said:

"Pull over at Macey's, we'll grab a take-out." Tight-lipped and agitated Grady gripped the wheel hard, held down the horn as he cut in front of a crawler.

"He's an asshole, Boss – he don't deserve any respect."

"I'm not saying anything, Grady; but maybe you shouldn't cut him up so bad."

"Now there's an idea, Loot – enant," chuckled Grady.

"I do agree with you though, he is an asshole," said Brock, spoke soft.

"I need a coffee, Loot."

"Me too, Grady, sure you don't just want to take another peek at Macey's butt?"

*　　　*　　　*

Graffiti-clad plyboard blocked out any light, which in a perfect world might have shed a glimmer of hope to the ground floor apartments at the corner of Parkway and Prince Street. In the front yard an area strangled with weeds and heavy evidence of a dishonest lifestyle, a discarded, brown-stained mattress nestled deep in a spread of overgrown grass. Grady thumbed on a filthy bell buzzer in a row of ten. It offered little promise. The only buzz came from a hoard of blowflies dancing in the thermals over decaying food in a rust-eaten trash can.

"Let's check around the back, Lieutenant," suggested Grady. As he spoke a sash window rattled up overhead.

"You guys looking for Johnny B?" Brock stared up to a pretty girl in a tired old face. She could've been a sad fourteen or the wrong side of forty, it was hard to tell.

"Ali Bakta – we need to pay him some cash," offered Grady.

"He ain't here – I can take it for him."

"Yeah I'm sure you can, sweetheart, but I don't think you can give us what we're hopin' he can. When d'ya last see him?"

"He ain't been around today; could be he got lucky last night."

"He usually gets lucky on a Thursday night?" asked Grady. The girl shrugged, spoke nothing.

"Where does he hang out?"

"In the fuckin' crapper," said the girl, slammed down the sash. Grady turned to Brock.

"Nice neighbourhood, Lieutenant."

"You're right on the money there, Grady. Let's not forget to wipe our feet on the way out – ach, sorry, Shiney, there go the Marx brothers again. I guess you're beginning to rub off on me. I think we should go and pay your buddy Duzi Olifi another visit." Confused, Grady frowned a question. Brock smirked a smile, explained:

"Maybe we can pick up the tracker on Bakta's cab."

*   *   *

Earphones tangled with matted dreadlocks as Duzi Olifi jumped up, kicked his chair away and braced himself. Cold steel from an unsteady hand flicked down behind his back. Worried eyes ricocheted around a scruffy room, narrowed to focus over a thick wad of surgical plaster. On the desk a squadron of flies buzzed over stale crusts of pizza; parodied it to an aerial dog-fight scene over a desolate landscape way back from the world war one movie 'Hell's Angels' by Howard Hughes. Grady flicked his brows in welcome, took off his hat and straightened the brim before he spoke:

"Good to see you've swept the floor, crap-head; nice to see ya' keepin' ya' nose clean."

"Sit down, Duzi; I won't let him hurt you, not unless you screw me around," said Brock.

"Thanks, I'll stand," said Olifi, wide-eyed, slow chewing gum as he watched Grady sheath his hands in black leather.

"Suit yourself." Brock leant back onto dry-wall lining strung with a matrix of shoddy wiring papered over with dog-eared posters of Bob Marley – the Soothsayer. A light bulb hung naked from a knotted cord, offered little hope for enlightenment. Sucking teeth Brock looked across to Grady, hoped a similar situation wouldn't soon apply to Olifi.

"Bakta didn't find his way home last night," said Brock.

"He's a big boy," replied Olifi.

"Then you shouldn't have any trouble finding him," said Brock. "I need you to run a security tracker on his vehicle." Olifi tensed. His lip quivered, muddled brain cells fought for higher ground; he groped for words. Grady straightened, took his hands out from his pockets, pulled black leather gloves tight.

"Okay, okay – Give me a minute." Olifi typed in a code to the GPS, then folded back the top sheet of a jotter, scribbled a location on a blank page, tore off the sheet, passed it across to Brock.

"Been parked up there all night, must've got lucky."

"Thanks – Smart boy!" said Brock.

"The corner of Main and Green, that's industrial isn't it."

"Yeah, down by the city recycle plant: hooker territory," replied Grady, changing down gears, "not far from where Bakta made his pick-up."

Summer dust clouded in the wake kicked up from the rear twin wheels of a city dumpster. Grady eased off the pedal, powered up the side screens and kept his distance.

"Follow that truck, Sergeant, he's going our way."

"You've been watchin' too many old-time movies, Loot – enant."

"I don't watch old-time movies, Grady, but to be honest, it's nothing more than a sad reflection of my underactive sex life."

"Can't help you there, Boss, I'm sorry."

"*You're* sorry!" Grady swung a left into Green Street, pulled past the dumpster as it turned into the city yard, then took a left into Main and pulled up at the kerb.

"Don't see a Securi-cab, Lieutenant."

"Never one around when you need it, Grady."

"Ain't that just the truth? I guess he's moved on. Who the hell would he pick up around here anyway?"

"It's my guess, Shiney – someone's picked him up."

"Boss?" questioned Grady. Brock nodded across to the rusted crane with its electro-magnetic grab hovering over a waste compactor.

"Let's drive into the yard and take a look, Grady; it looks to me as if somebody's been helping Bakta with some packing. And it wasn't for his holiday!" Grady reversed up, pulled into the yard.

Clad in fluorescent yellow, steel-tipped toes and a black look, a hard-hat slapped an aggressive hand on the side screen and pointed outside to the street parking. Grady pushed him aside with the door as he swung it open and flashed his Covert-Security I.D.

"We're looking for a Securi-cab."

"Try Main Street, buster, one passes by every few minutes." The sound of a freight train smashing into a church bell factory rang through the air drowning out Grady's reply as the Magnetic crane dropped a ton of scrap iron into the jaws of a hungry compactor. The hard-hat turned and walked away shouting orders to the driver of a heavy truck, then sprang back spooked as a threatened Springbok in lion territory; he fell and crouched low in blackened dirt as the front tyre of the heavy truck burst in front of him. He turned to Grady and dropped his jaw. Leant back lazy on a fuel bowser wearing a smug look above folded arms, Brock looked forward to Grady's gambol.

"I didn't catch your name," said Grady, snugging the fifty calibre back into his shoulder holster.

"You crazy bastard!"

"You'd be surprised at how many people have called me that," said Grady.

"You could have fucking killed me!"

"Now don't you go giving me ideas, crap-head – do I have your attention now?" The hard-hat looked around, checked his standing and blew out a deep breath.

"Come into my office."

"After you, Loot."

"I admire your style, Grady."

"Best tell that to the ladies, Boss."

Roby Douglas had his name stencilled on the door to a shabby trailer serving as his office. Inside, it was too filthy to serve even as a Mexican chicken coop; stinking from both stale beer and stale sweat it was a toss-up which was stronger. Naked pin-ups papered the walls, most with phone numbers scrawled across sensitive areas. A corner waste basket overflowed with empty beer cans, take-out wrappers carpeted the floor. As a total shithole, his office ranked five-star.

"Take a seat," offered the hard-hat.

"Don't insult me, I've thrown better away," said Grady. "If I were to get forensics down here they may find more than just sump oil dripping out from under your compactor, which would mean a twenty-year stretch down in the O-Zone for you, *and,* your operation. Sing me a song, crap-head. Make it something I'm gonna' want to dance a jolly-jig to!"

Roby Douglas threw his hard hat into a corner, ruffled a grimed hand through lank greasy hair and slunk into a seat. Leant back in the far corner Brock scribbled the flat side of a pencil over the jotter sheet Olifi had given them at Securi-cab, then dialled caller I.D.

"I was told to crush the cab, nothing more," pleaded Douglas.

"Did you check the trunk?" asked Grady.

"Why should I have?"

"Twenty in the O-Zone could be a good reason. Who sent the order?"

"I don't know. It came in over the phone."

"What is this: a fucking pizza take-out?"

"I only work here, nothin' else," exclaimed Douglas.

"Just following orders, yeah right: *'Mein Ober-Gruppen-Stormen-Fuhrer.'* Who holds the franchise? I need a fuckin' name, crap-head," growled Grady.

Douglas blew out a reluctant breath, said:

"Silo Holdings Incorporated trucking; they're who I work for."

"Cute acronym – bad choice." Grady pulled out his fifty calibre. Brock snapped the phone shut and said:

"Ludovic Mercowitz ring any bells?" Douglas froze. His face bleached white as a Hollywood smile spoke volumes behind tight lips. His eyes narrowed, his jaw dropped, made him look as if he was auditioning for a part in the remake of a Charlie Chan movie.

"Ludo Mertz, I should've guessed," said Grady. "Mister legal fucking loophole!"

Douglas stumbled over his words. "I ain't nothin' to do with this shit; I'm just trying to turn a buck, same as . . ."

"Same as Ali Bakta – the poor guy out there squeezed into a tin suit, probably with half his head blown away," said Grady.

"I had nothin' to do with no hit. I swear," pleaded Douglas, ran his tongue over dry lips.

"Call Mertz, tell him Bakta's *'packed for a long holiday.'* And while you're at it – tell him you're gonna' take the weekend off also," said Grady with a smile. Douglas stalled. Grady cocked back the hammer.

"Dial crap-head."

"I don't know the number," pleaded Douglas.

Stood in shadow back in the corner Brock called out the number. Grady span round; raised a questioned eyebrow. Brock held up the jotter sheet. Ludo Mertz's number with the time frame and location of Olsen's bar stood out embossed under pencil. Brock shrugged:

"I played a hunch; looks as if someone called the cab to take out the twins from the Mertz office."

"That would be a *very* careless mistake, Lieutenant."
"Not for us it isn't, Grady. Dial Douglas!"

*　　　*　　　*

Duzi Olifi would have been more pleased to see an old flame he hadn't seen for a few years crop up with a pram full of multiracial triplets who'd mirrored his looks than he was to see Grady's shadow cross back over the office threshold.

"One last favour, bag-head; now are we gonna' take the easy route, or do you wanna' jog uphill?" Olifi winced as he tried to twitch his nose, then nodded the affirmative, said:

"Let's go easy."

"Smart move, Duzi. Okay, I need a printout of all Bakta's pick-ups and drops over the last month. Let's get to it, bag-head. Anytime right now is good for me," said Grady kicking a space clear underfoot. Olifi danced fingers on his brand new keyboard.

*　　　*　　　*

Macey's eyes sparkled when she saw Grady waiting to cross the street; she brought over an extra coffee cup and set it down on the table. Brock smiled a *thank-you*, said:

"Bring something greasy with fries, Macey. Make him feel at home."

"Same thing for you, Lieutenant?"

"No thanks, not right now, maybe later."

Grady breezed in through the door tossed his hat crown down onto the table, patted Macey's rump and stretched out in the window seat opposite Brock.

"You were right on the money, Loot. Bakta *was* Ludo's runner; nearly twenty call-outs from the Mertz office over the last month alone."

"Same drop-offs?"

"No, Boss. Most were into the city, uptown beach side."

"Any address?"

"No, only the general location."

"Any return trips or pick-ups from the location?" Grady shook his head, winced as he swallowed hot coffee.

"So what do you think, Boss?"

"It's my guess Grady: Bakta was dropping *something* off, rather than *someone*." Grady milked his coffee, drained his cup and digested the thought.

"Drugs…?"

"Could well be," said Brock.

"D'ya think Ludo Mertz could have been Spyda's bankroller?"

"I'd put money on it, Grady."

A fork rang a high 'A' concert on a stone floor as Macey leant across Grady to set the placemat. Brock bent and picked up the fork, handed it to Grady. Macey snatched it from Grady's hand.

"I'll get you a clean one, honey."

"It's okay don't bother; your floor's cleaner than the damn table, an' that's about as clean as a hungry dog's bowl," said Grady, ducked his head into his shoulders as Macey's order book slapped down on his crown.

"It's a lot more than I can say for your damn dining table Grady Da Silva," said Macey. Brock leant back on a squeaky seat, laced both hands together behind a nodding head, and with a smiling face spoke to Grady with a cheeky smirk:

"Sounds as if you've been havin' a little medium-rare rump steak treat of your own across your dining table, Grady." He blushed purple; poured himself fresh coffee.

"No, it's nothin' wild as that, Lieutenant; she comes around for a little late-night pizza now and again."

"Never heard it called *pizza* before, Sergeant." Grady smiled, said nothing, winked across to Macey stood grinning behind the bar. He tried to recompose his standing, it didn't work; it was a lost cause. Brock, forever tactful, changed the subject.

"So why was Bakta rubbed out? Looks to me as if someone was being careful in trying to cover tracks; it's my guess Grady: *that* someone was Mertz."

"Could be, but then why did he rub out Bakta. What for – it doesn't make any sense."

"Okay, maybe we should go an' ask him, Grady."

"He'll be a tough nut to crack, Lieutenant. His place is tight as a fortress, full of lemons and lobos, *and*, he knows the law – he writes the fuckin' stuff."

"I hear he's partial to hookers," said Brock.

"He sure is, Boss. I hear he also likes to play nasty games with them, slap them around, those kinda' things," he took a slug of coffee, looked serious across to his boss, "and so I've heard, sometimes a whole hell of a lot worse." The espresso machine howled out from the bar; undeterred Brock nodded in thought and said:

"Maybe he had something on the two hookers who perforated the Chan Woo twins... well, I think I may just have something he might want. Call up Sherri; she owes us a few favours, ask her to make a date for Mertz tonight with a couple of her girls, make it a special treat, birthday, surprise promo pleasure, something along those lines."

"Boss . . . ?"

"Do you need Sherri's number, Grady?"

"No, it's okay, I – I got it . . ." he studied the floorboards. Brock smiled, Grady flushed bright red with eyes wide as a schoolboy's caught with his pants down behind the girl's shower room.

"Just so's you know, Loot: her girls are way out of my league; their meter ticks a little too fast for my wallet."

"I hear you, Sergeant, yours and mine too. Make the call, Grady."

"Rump steak, full house with fries." Macey set a steaming plate down in front of Grady. Brock stole a fry, smiled up at the waitress.

"Maybe I'll have the steak too, Macey; medium-rare, easy on the fries."

*   *   *

Chapter Six

Ludo Mertz, basking in the privacy of his ostentatious marble-clad en-suite bathroom, sunk back a heavy shot of bourbon before powdering his grog blossom nose; bloodshot eyes rolled lazy in red lids as he sank back into pink chintz to savour the chemical buzz. Black silk embroidered heavy with gold lace and light in taste draped in ruffled creases from puny shoulders down over a cholesterol-enhanced gut. A copious dose of aftershave, reeking from dense pockmarked cheeks cut through the fug of dope, masking nothing either way. He wore slippers he should've given to his wife; if indeed he still had one stupid enough to put up with him.

Ten minutes later a lithe forefinger tipped with a ruby red varnished nail stabbed on his bedroom door buzzer, setting off a tasteless nasal clang of classical digi-muzak vibrating a warning through equally tasteless décor inside the Mertz Empire. Straining heavy cellulite across his bed, Mertz blew a silent whistle at the sight accosting him from the CCTV security screen. With eyes bulging like organ stops, and a hungry tongue gripped in his teeth, he thumbed a red button on the bedside table and sprang the door catch. High-voltage sex pushed open the door and cat walked into his bedroom. Drooling deviant lust through coal-black eyes set far too close for elegance, Ludo Mertz found it difficult to blink.

"Hi, Sylvie – *who's* your new friend?" Mertz sleazed the question through brown-stained teeth every bit alluring as a row of condemned houses in a downtown suburb for the impoverished, then, dragged a yellow-furred tongue over bloodied-mauve lips. The stunning Thai/Euro blonde exuding animal lust stronger than the top shelf of a shady bookstore pushed the door shut and flipped the latch onto lock.

"Good start, cutie. Come on over here, show uncle Ludo your wares."

Lines of skunk coke lingered on the glass top dresser; Sylvie indulged, took two lines, one in each nostril. The Thai girl licked a wet, seductive tongue across bright red lip gloss as she pulled a high gloss black patent belt slow through a loose silver buckle. Black leather dropped to the floor, draped loose around patent black stilettos. Carnal lust pouted, permeating erotica through black gossamer silk.

"I see you're not a natural blonde, sugar." Mertz cuddled his fast-growing erection as he ogled her glistening crotch. Sylvie dropped tasteless clothing to the floor, pushed Mertz down onto the bed, slapped him hard and took him in her mouth. Mertz closed his eyes and groaned in ecstasy. The Thai girl climbed onto the bed and rose up above Mertz, flaunting lust fertile as a nubile goddess in a carnal triple X-rated fantasy.

"Come here, sugar, let me get a closer look at your tattoo." Mertz pulled her up onto him, she straddled his chest, dragged a wet tongue across the tips of her top teeth. Mertz's hand wandered, caressed black lace, moved to explore fresh damp territory after brushing a thumb across the serpent and dragon tattoo: a work of art scrolled in red, showing a long fired tongue on her upper groin, stretching out to reach the more sensitive part of her anatomy. She teased, pushed his hands away. A yellow-furred tongue, stretched to its limit from the mouth of Mertz, drooled, strained hard, but failed to taste utopia. Again she teased, pushed his hands up high, reached behind her back, sprung open her small clutch purse and dangled shiny cuffs in front of his face. Pouting ruby lips she flashed emerald bedroom eyes and clamped his wrists to the metal bedpost.

"I fancy where this is going, sugar," enthused Mertz. Sylvie took the cue and clamped his ankles to the foot of the bed.

"Take me to perverts' paradise girls, I'm all yours." The Thai girl pushed Sylvie off the bed and turned back to Mertz. Casting down a wicked smile she pulled off her blonde wig and shook her head; straight raven black locks fell lank over silken skin onto sculpted shoulders. Mertz scowled, his dark eyes twitched — she grinned. Loosing blood fast, a confused erection throbbed down in a sudden prolapse, now bright red only from gloss lipstick it wilted back down to the starting post.

"You fucking bitch! I thought I recognised you from somewhere: you work for that asshole LePage." A tight fist snapped on Mertz's jaw. She reached again for her clutch purse. Mertz tasted gun oil from the barrel of a three-fifty-seven invading his mouth, commanding silence.

"Shhhhhhhh…" A red-manicured forefinger stood to attention in front of a scarlet pout. A matching manicured thumb cocked back the hammer, underlined her threat.

"Let Grady in on your way out. Thanks, Sylvie."

"You fucking bitch! I thought you were …" The gun barrel pushed hard up into the roof of Mertz's mouth, forbade further diction.

"I know what you thought asshole, but you really shouldn't let your dick do the thinking. Things ain't always what they seem; you should know better, you being a lawyer an' all." Beads of sweat broke out across Mertz's top lip; anger flared but remained trapped firm behind coal black eyes. She pulled the weapon from his mouth, pressed it hard into the bridge of his nose. He gawked up in panic and didn't blink from the wrong end of a gun barrel. She smirked:

"Smart boy, Ludo!"

"What do you want?" he pleaded, hoping she'd say money.

"Information."

"About what…?"

"Let's start with who called the hit on the Chan-Woo twins, and why?"

"I don't know nothin' about no Chink hits." Mertz lied through gritted caps for the last time before they fell bloody to the floor, didn't bounce but left a red stain on thick white pile.

"Wrong answer, Ludo – try again." Her gun hovered for a second strike; Mertz spat blood through split lips at the impact; fresh blood and something nasty dribbled from his nose.

"Fuck – Fuck you, Bitch. You're dead meat!"

"Sound's rich comin' from where you're sittin'… you gonna' get me canned up same as you did Ali Bakta – is that what you reckon, asshole?" With a vicious swipe, she back pistol-whipped him, split open his nose and twisted his balls hard. He screamed in unison with classical digi-muzak as it chimed its fanfare. Mertz thanked his lucky stars. He shouldn't have done, the CCTV screen set at his bedside revealed his worst nightmare: a digital image of Grady Da Silva cuddling his twelve-gauge Street-sweeper. Manicured fingers buzzed him in. Grady's heavy frame filled the bedroom doorway. Mertz's face was not one of a warm welcome.

"You okay, Loot?" Grady stood, looking awkward, took a deep breath and dragged a nervous tongue across dry lips. Brock, naked except for scant black lace stockings and a red velvet choker sat astride Mertz on the bloodied bed with a cocked three-fifty-seven pointed at his sweat-drenched forehead.

"He's having a problem with his memory, Sergeant."

"No kiddin' …'an' I'm havin' a fuckin' problem with my eyesight'… an' him bein' a lawyer," Grady tutted aloud, "that's bad, Loot." Shaking his head in mock disgust he wandered into the en suite, crashed around in the cupboards and came out with a handful of pink flowery plastic shower caps.

"You've been a pretty careless boy, Ludo."

Mertz gawked up at Da Silva, furrowed his brow, the gun barrel in his mouth barred further question. A potent fear strong as foot odour from the unwashed, radiated from deep-set coal black eyes. Grady pointed to the ceiling, gave a sick smile and whispered:

"No smoke alarm," he tutted, "bad move, Ludo!" Moving closer to the bedside, Grady, shook his head in mock disgust, flicked an ancient Zippo under the shower caps held out high on the tip of a back-scrub brush. Brock clamped her hand over Mertz's mouth. Flaming balls of molten plastic rained down onto Mertz's bare chest. Muffled screams from his writhing body straining in cuffs triggered terrified eyes to plead for mercy; but after a lifetime dealing in drugs, murder and corruption, he deserved nothing less. Grady moved the flaming shower caps aside, let molten plastic drip down over the skunk coke. Brock removed her hand from Mertz's mouth. He begged for pity and cried out:

"Okay! Okay, I'll talk, I'll talk – Enough! Call him off me." Brock patted his cheek.

"Clever boy Ludo." With a cheeky wink, Grady soft-whistled his tuneless melody as he stretched over the bed head to straighten a signed Jeff Koons print of the maestro locked into his Italian porn star wife, then, leaned down close to Mertz's ear and whispered:

"Talk, asshole!"

"The call came from uptown," blubbered Mertz.

"Let me guess – uptown beach side?" said Brock.

"It's all I know, nothin' else," pleaded Mertz. Blowing out a deep sigh Grady slow shook his head, re-fired the shower caps, hovered flaming plastic over Mertz's flaccid groin area. Brock muffled howling screams with silk-sheathed feather down and waited for Grady to finish his taunt.

"Okay … I'm gonna' remove the pillow, this time I'm expecting to hear a clear-cut answer – last chance asshole, and no bullshit," warned Brock. She lifted the pillow slow from Mertz's face. He snivelled for mercy, shook his head. Grady picked up fresh plastic shower caps, grinned and thumbed his lighter. Mertz got wise.

"The call came from the Y-ZEE-KAY. I don't know any names. I swear to god," whimpered Mertz.

"The Y-ZEE-KAY... You gotta be kiddin' me," said Brock, "they went down twenty years back."

"No...! No, Yungen was never caught, you must know that. He's regrouped, got new blood."

"What – who with – Give me names," demanded Brock.

"I don't know, I swear," pleaded Mertz. Grady buried a gloved fist hard into Mertz's face.

"Then take a wild guess, asshole." Grady flipped his Zippo under pink plastic. Mertz, screaming, writhed in chains as flaming drops of plastic trailed up towards flaccid flesh between his legs spread wide.

"Okay, okay, okay!" He panted fast and deep. "They're gonna' . . ." Then with a raw crack loud as a thunderclap from hell, the bedroom door lock exploded sending metal and wood shards flying into the room. Hot lead sprayed through the door. Crouched down tight in the mayhem, Brock rolled off the bed, fell hard onto soft pile. Grady racked and fired the Street-sweeper into the turmoil. Mertz's head danced a leaden jig as his jaw parted company with his face, followed by the cap of his head splattering copious bloodied matter over silk feather down. Pumping heavy-gauge shot across into the door and through the surrounding stud wall Grady's gun blew off the upper door hinge. He ducked down, trigger finger ready. Something heavy rolled down the stairs. In the brief respite he called out:

"You okay, Loot?"

"Yeah, I'm fine, Grady, never felt better in a long while – Thanks for asking!" she looked down at what was left of Mertz, sucked her teeth... Nothing doing there!

"Let's get out of here, Grady." He met her eyes, jumped across the bed, tossed a stunner through the door and gawked down at Mertz, whose next move would be to the city morgue. Grady kicked out the fallen door, tossed another stunner down the stairwell into darkness and grabbed Brock's arm.

"Come; let's take the fire escape." He pumped the Street-sweeper into the sash, threw a silk blanket over broken glass, took her arm and helped Brock through the window.

"Go on down, I'll cover. The wagon's on the corner." Pumping shot back up at nothing Grady clanged heavy boots on iron steps down the fire escape and buzzed the wagon door open as he jumped the last eight feet to the ground, rolling as he hit the blacktop. He didn't drop his gun. Brock gave cover from behind the passenger door. She took the side off an inquisitive face poking a gun through the open sash. With heavy-gauge shot Grady blew out the front tyres on the three cars standing in the parking lot, jumped in the wagon, swiped the starter and burned rubber. He sunk his head into his shoulders as the rear screen shattered from gunshot. With his foot flat to the floor he took the corner on two wheels.

"You okay?" asked Grady as he raced through the gears.

"Yeah … Thanks Grady."

"It's bin' my pleasure," said Grady snaking the wagon down the road.

"GRADY …!"

"Boss …?"

"Keep your eyes on the damn road; give a girl a little privacy here. What the hell's wrong with you?"

"What's wrong with me…? Adrenaline's pumping testosterone big time, an' I'm sittin' next to the most beautiful naked sight I ever laid my eyes on – an' you're askin' me what's fuckin' wrong…?" Grady shook his head. Brock blushed, made a hopeless effort to cover her nakedness.

"If you were any kinda' gentleman, you'd offer me your shirt," she said coquettish pointing her gun at him. He clucked his tongue, checked the rear view, stabbed the brake pedal, pulled into the kerb and climbed out of the cab. He pulled sweat-drenched denim over his head; took one last long look at sexual poetry, and with great reluctance tossed his shirt across the cab.

"It ain't no gentleman would offer you his shirt, Loot; more like a fuckin' idiot if you don't mind me sayin' so." With a smile wide as a cabaret crooner's vibrato she recovered chastity with his sweaty denim.

"As I always said: you're the least likely *Boss* I ever met." Grady conceded with a wicked smile. He climbed back into the cab, the fallen hero. She faked a soft punch on his jaw.

"You're a gentleman, Grady. Make no mistake."

"Mistake's all mine." He racked heavy brows, "always has been."

*   *   *

Tire rubber scuffed grimed kerbstone outside Brock's apartment. She reached into the glove box and tossed the big man her key.

"Open the door, Grady, throw down my robe, wouldn't be right for the neighbours to see me runnin' loose in nothing but black-lace stockings and your sweaty shirt."

"No, that particular pleasure's reserved only for me," he said from a smug grin.

Peering through dusty blinds in Brock's apartment, Grady checked up and down an empty street, saw nothing of concern. He set his weapon down onto the coffee table, poured out two tumblers of Jack and relaxed back into fake leather. Brock ran the shower. Sat back on the soft sofa, Grady chewed hard on twisted thoughts, drained his glass, filled another, listened to tumbling water and wrestled with the devil. Water hammer rattled out a fanfare on ancient pipework as the shower turned off. Lifting his head out of his lap, Grady waited. Brock exited the bathroom clad with a scant towel draped loose over damp flesh. She held out his shirt.

"I'll run this through the washer."

"No, it's okay. I'll take care of it," he murmured. A coy face smiled. She tossed his shirt across, then crossed the room, plucked the tumbler off the low table, took a heavy slug as she sat astride Grady's legs, wrapped heavy manicure around his bull neck, looked deep into his eyes and soft-whispered:

"Ya' know, Grady – you're the one and only guy I'd jump back across the fence for."

The moment buzzed electric, lifted the bandstand, lust hovered somewhere way above passion and stepped up into a red danger zone.

"An' I'd be right there to catch ya', Loot." With a racing heart, Brock breathed heavy. Green eyes, lucid, shining bright as sparkling emeralds in bright sunlight, gazed deep into Grady's soul. Losing its scant grip, her towel slipped and fell loose to the floor. Grady stared down at erect nipples on firm breasts. Below a flat midriff, damp pubic hair glistened an enticing invite. Impulse leant her body forward. Grady's pants vibrated. He swore to himself, pulled out his phone, shrugged heavy shoulders:

"Fuck it – Sod's law, can you believe it!" Sad eyes smiled across a naked carnal landscape, but in truth he welcomed the hiatus. "No point in spoiling a beautiful relationship for a few minutes of pleasure?" he shook his head, racked his brows and shrugged heavy shoulders. He thumbed green to go from Macey's number.

"Talk to me, sweetheart." His face, not long ago flushing bright under the mask of passion, now drained to a stony white. "Who is this?"... The dial tone answered. Grady's lip quivered, his expression voiced loud but he spoke nothing audible, couldn't, his mouth dropped open, blank eyes stared up to Brock.

"Grady – What is it? Tell me..." Before he would speak, Grady battled to swallow the lump in his throat. His chin dropped to his chest, he looked up to Brock through welling eyes, slow-shook his head and uttered:

"Macey's been hit!"

The drive side door of the wagon scraped an arc across slab stones as it swung over the paving outside Macey's diner. With her three-fifty-seven cocked, Brock shadowed Grady into the diner. Water trickled from an open faucet, whispering a haunting rhythm through a stilled silence. Grady Da Silva howled out aloud; a desperate soul in search of a miracle he vaulted over the counter and kicked open the two-way swing door into the kitchen. Macey sat spread-eagled with her head stretched back over a tall wheelback chair. Blank eyes stared up to the ceiling. Her throat cut wide open smiled a gruesome story. Spooked at the intrusion, a blowfly buzzed a drunken circle, landed back on dead flesh and re-staked its claim. Stood distraught in a pool of Macey's blood, Grady knuckled his jaw with a clenched fist. He looked to Brock through welling eyes. Nothing but pure empathy rallied back.

"Why . . . ?"

There was no answer for Brock to give; she could do nothing more than slow-shake her head. Then, she spoke soft words, almost in a whisper:

"I'll handle this, Grady. You go, I'll call it in. Nothin' you can do now – go." Sad eyes welled; he nodded, not in affirmation and bit his lower lip. He looked down at Macey, took her in his arms and kissed her chilled lips, pulled her head into his chest, hot tears dropped down onto her fiery red hair. He stood, filled his barrel chest under a shirt smeared with her blood and left the room.

'God help somebody out there,' Brock whispered to herself.

*　　*　　*

Chapter Seven

Cocooned in a tight web of frustration, Captain C. LePage, at best a distasteful character, fumed in silence as he tapped the ball end of a sharpened pencil into an empty palm. He paced the floor over a small island of time-worn lino; an area well accustomed to being paced upon in the middle of bare pine planking. In exasperation, he snapped the pencil in two using only his right hand. He glared down at Brock, who sat resolute in her chair. With a rough hand, he spun his chair round, sat and leant a scrawny bodyweight across his desk. With white lips pursed he braced himself, rested his chin on arched fingers and didn't blink evil eyes as he spoke to Brock in a quiet, but stern voice full of venom.

"We're supposed to be keeping the streets clean from the stench of human vermin, the reeking odour of social filth, and the stinking dregs of a wretched humanity. Now all of a sudden we've got a fucking all-out war on our hands." LePage threw his hands in the air, popped his eyes and growled: "What the fuck is going down, Lieutenant?"

Still harbouring silent thoughts about Macey, Brock shrugged, could offer nothing back above disdain.

"Ludo Mertz?" growled LePage up into the air to the almighty. Evil eyes burned, then rove down to focus on Brock. LePage's head sank into his shoulders. He sat reminiscent of a tortoise under threat; questioning fingers sprang open like blooming flowers under strong spring sunlight. With vehemence, he continued his rant at her: "One of our top lawyers – murdered; two of our best agents – murdered, all within twenty-four fucking hours. This is a bad dream. Please tell me I'm not hearing this?"

"Mertz was running drugs, Sir. He was bad news."

"Ludo Mertz – a drug runner – tell me: who says so?" The chair creaked aloud when Brock, uncomfortable in its confines stretched her body taught. She folded her arms, looked him square in the face and glared contempt enough to freeze dragon breath.

"He kept bad company – Sir, the Chan-Woo hit came direct from his office, a fact we discovered from our recent Intel – Sir."

LePage screwed up his face, clenched a fist, searched for words as he raised his eyebrows.

"I hope this is something you *can* prove, Lieutenant?"

"We're not in the business of proving things, Sir. We're here to clean out grime from the drains and nothing more. Ludo Mertz was grime, Sir; no question about it. Now we need to find his supplier and who he was supplying to," she shrugged a blank look. LePage troubled a weak jaw, rolled his chair back, stood and returned to the beguiling solace of his grubby window. He pinched the bridge of his nose, blew a near-silent whistle through tight lips, glared down at her with disdain, and growled:

"Any leads?"

"Yes, a few, Sir."

"Names . . . ?" Skating on thin ice Brock shrugged, kept quiet about the Cult. She clutched at a straw.

"Lu-Lu Mbangang for one, Sir." LePage jumped as if he were dodging a brickbat.

"Where'd you pick *that* lead up from, Lieutenant?"

"His old phone number was written on a news sheet."

"What...! His '*old phone number, written on a news sheet,*' what the hell are you talking about...? Explain ..." demanded LePage.

"I picked up a news sheet from a table at Macey's diner. The suspect who left it there: a Leather Jack, didn't look right, something felt odd about him. I had a hunch," she shrugged and stared up to LePage, glared a look to cut diamonds and said:

"Lu-Lu Mbangang's phone number was written on the sheet. I followed the lead, nothing more."

"So! This suspect wrote the number, you think?" queried LePage from under the shadow of a doubtful brow.

"I guess so, Sir. Who else would have left it there?"

LePage hunched his shoulders, rolled his eyes.

"And what motive would you suppose this *mysterious* suspect had, may I ask, Lieutenant?"

"Beats me, Sir, I think it was left on purpose for me to find."

"Well how about Macey? What makes you think she didn't write it – or in fact, anyone else who used the diner?" LePage raised his shoulders to his ears and spread his hands wide.

"Motive, Sir. Why would she? She had no reason to." With both hands pushed deep into long pockets rattling loose change, LePage bent forward over her in his stock intimidating stance of a question mark and smugged a quiet question to her:

"Then may I suggest you go and ask her, Lieutenant?"

"That would be a little difficult, Sir."

"Difficult?" questioned LePage flicking his head with one eye half shut as if he had a tick.

"Right now she's kissin' a marble slab, Sir – someone cut her throat."

LePage polished his scalp, paced the office and puffed air through tight lips.

"Fuck! This gets worse every minute." Desperate as a moth seeking sanctuary, LePage turned towards the light, ran his hand over bald skin, massaged his neck, turned and sought solace through his grimy window. Outside the tainted pane a spider began to spin a silken thread around a struggling fly, which, for a fleeting moment kept LePage's attention. He clasped his hands behind his back in a stance as if he were waiting to be cuffed and led to the gallows.

'*If only,*' mused Brock, rolled her eyes in hope at the thought.

"Did you see the phone number written the moment you picked up the sheet?" asked LePage in a passive voice spoken into the window. He tapped a heavy foot, his head bounced in unison at one-forty beats per minute.

"No, Sir."

"Well – when then, Lieutenant?" barked LePage, spun on his heel, glared a look of disdain same as he would to a hobo with his hand out singing a Christmas carol on a mid-summer day.

"I don't remember, maybe a day or so later."

With both hands still pushed hard into his pockets, LePage bent over her, furrowed his eyebrows and drew in a breath as if he was preparing to shout. But instead– he growled:

"Well, where then? At Macey's; in your apartment; in some or other seedy bar or deadbeat diner that you and Da Silva choose to hang around in … where may I ask?"

"In my apartment I guess, Sir."

"So the news sheet sat in your apartment for one or two days, before you bothered to look at it. Is this what you're expecting me to believe, Lieutenant … surely not?" LePage stared in bemusement, slow shook his head, worried his lower lip with his top teeth.

"We've been very busy, Sir," said Brock, now visibly irked at the line of interrogation.

LePage pursed his lips, nodded, paced the floor, span around and fired a volley at Brock.

"Who else had access to the news sheet in your apartment before, you *bothered* to read it?" Her mind went straight to Grady. She said nothing but knew deep down LePage harboured similar thoughts. LePage narrowed his eyes, bounced his head in a slow rhythm and asked:

"By the way, where exactly *is* Sergeant Da Silva today?"

"He called in sick this morning, Sir. I gave him the day off."
LePage raised his brows, glared down his nose at her with the
pained look of a man who'd sucked a lemon. Nodding a
doubtful head, he turned back to the window. Outside, the fly
had stopped its struggle. The spider moved in for the kill.

"Was the Leather Jack your tail, Sir?" asked Brock,
knocking LePage off balance.

"What … my tail? If he was, I can assure you he would not
have given you an open lead with all the courtesy of a rank
amateur," replied LePage.

"I did not mention the mark was male, Sir."

"No, Lieutenant you didn't. It was an assumption on my
part." A hue of red flushed his face, he sucked his cheeks in.

"Assumptions can be dangerous, Sir."

"As can a plant, Lieutenant," he rallied. She answered
nothing; wondered if she could kick his sorry butt hard enough
to help him out through his shitty fucking window.

LePage stretched his neck, lifted his chin and pursed his
lips as he watched the spider start to truss up the fly. He smiled,
didn't look to Brock as he spoke, slow and in question.

"Tell me, Lieutenant Brock — was the Mertz hit anything
to do with Covert Security – perhaps there's something about it
that I should know?" he spoke with accusing emphasis, turned
as he pushed his hands deep into his pockets and rolled his eyes
at her over the top of steel rim glasses. Brock kept her cool,
didn't lose composure despite the provocative line of
questioning.

"If you're asking if my unit was responsible for killing
Ludo Mertz, Sir – the answer is a definite negative." LePage
massaged the back of his neck, sucked teeth, stared down to the
floor and drew a circle with the toe of his shoe. He took in a
sharp breath before he spoke:

"Then let me put it this way, Lieutenant," he brought an acid stare straight into her face. "Was Covert Security implicated in any way at all with the Mertz hit?"

"Not to my knowledge, Sir."

"So you say you know nothing at all about the hit?"

"Nothing other than it was two shots to the head and one to the chest from a heavy calibre suppressed handgun," she gave him a smug look and added, "all the traits of a pro-hit." LePage glared venom to Brock and raised his eyebrows in question.

"Police homicide report, Sir: Grady has connections," Brock volleyed, answered the silent question.

"I've read the report, Lieutenant. It also says, shots were fired at the possible assailant from inside the room," he paused and folded his arms, "there was no gun. So, it looks as if someone left the room in rather a hurry." He held a deep breath and glared at her over wire frame glasses.

"So Mertz was not alone, Sir," Brock parried not in question but in statement.

"No, he wasn't, Lieutenant. He was handcuffed to the bed, and whoever was with him, left without her clothing."

"How very careless, Sir. I know he was partial to hookers, or so I hear."

"Hookers with a twelve-gauge, so it would seem. It looks to me as if it was a set-up, don't you think so, Lieutenant?"

"Maybe they were the same two hookers who took out the twins, Sir. Could be he had blackmailed them to commit murder. It would be a good enough motive to take him out."

Brock shrugged a visual coda to underline her reasoning. LePage took in and held a deep breath. Lost for words, he hadn't thought of such an angle. He turned to his window; watched a gecko climb the pane, and with a flick from its long tongue, it swallowed the spider. The fly buzzed free.

"Are we done here, Sir?" asked Brock. LePage, gazing out of the window ignored the question, then said:

"Two more bodies were recovered at the scene: Sunni Mhaus, a trigger-man, and a muscle brain called Klint, both employed as security by Mertz."

"Well, it sounds an open and shut case to me, Sir."

LePage questioned Brock with heavy eyebrows.

"The hookers set Mertz up, the hit-man pulled the trigger," she shrugged at the possibility. LePage tensed his body taught; sprang his eyebrows high on his forehead.

"So why then didn't the hookers pull the trigger themselves? If they were the same two who took out the twins, they were certainly capable, and what would be the hitman's angle? And why, would they then shoot him?" ranted LePage, spread his hands in question.

"Who can figure out the motives and methods of the drug world, Sir? Anything's possible in such a degenerate mindless cesspit." LePage gave a slow nod, bit his bottom lip, then slow-wiped the windowpane clean.

Other than the monotonous clanking rhythm from the fan, the room fell into a stilled silence. After a long pause, Brock cleared her throat and spoke:

"Are we done, Sir?" LePage nodded a silent affirmative, didn't turn from his window.

"I'll see you at sixteen hundred tomorrow, Lieutenant. Please don't be late." Brock stood, made for the door.

"And, Lieutenant Brock," LePage, turned on his heel as he spoke:

"Sir ...?"

"Thank you, Lieutenant."

"Just doing my job, Sir, nothing more." LePage turned back to his window.

"By the way, does Sergeant Da Silva still favour his twelve-gauge Street-sweeper?"

"He does, Sir – when the need arises." LePage gave a rare facsimile of a smile; the first for a very long time.

Brock closed the door without a sound as she left.

*   *   *

Chapter Eight

Grady's phone picked up at the third ring.

"Hey Grady, you okay?"

"Yeah ... yeah, I ... I'm fine, Loot," replied Grady, convinced no-one.

"Want me to come over?" she asked.

"Nah, it's okay. I may take a walk later." There was a vocal pause, in which she could only hear breathing.

"Grady . . ."

"Yeah . . . ?"

"About last night . . ."

"Don't go spoilin' a beautiful moment for me please, Loot".

"It was beautiful for me too, Grady . . . Maybe we should've carried on?"

"Loot . . . ?"

"Well then at least you might start calling me by my name and stop calling me, *Loot*."

Grady cracked a soft smile; a heavy moment rose up from the dark depths of a deep well.

"Why don't you come on over, I'll order a take-out, we can share a bottle. It ain't a night to be on your own, Cowboy." Brock finger twiddled black locks through a quiet pause – waited.

"Thanks, Loot. I'd appreciate it."

"Thai okay?"

"Thai's fine."

"Don't let it get cold."

"Now where have I heard *that* before?" he chuckled.

With eyes closed tight, she let her head fall back onto the sofa and smiled, but at what, she couldn't say. She slow shook her head, drew a deep breath, held her bottom lip in her teeth, thumbed red and dialled Franco's take-out.

Twenty minutes later, dressed in a midnight blue suit, a black silk open-neck shirt without a tie, and two-tone loafers, Grady followed the delivery guy up the steps to Brock's apartment. He paid the guy, took the food boxes and rang the bell. Brock sprang the door and tweaked her nose as she did so.

"What's this Grady – you got a new job?"

"Yeah – it don't pay great but the tips and life expectancy are pretty good." She cracked a warm smile.

"It's good to see you Grady. Come on in, take a seat I'll fix you a drink."

After they'd eaten and exhausted small talk, she leant across the coffee table and recharged Grady's jigger. He hungry -eyed her unfinished take-out trays.

"Help yourself, Grady – I'm done." She was glad to see he hadn't lost his appetite.

"I don't want to talk shop tonight but there's a whole lot going down here, and not much of it adds up to jack shit," said Brock. "We've got a lot of dead bodies, a lot of live questions and not a lot of answers; all for which I don't understand. But right now I feel something is headed our way – and I'm not so sure it's gonna be a welcome thing when it arrives."

"I hear you, Lieutenant."

"For Christ's sake, Grady we're off duty, it's Maddie now."

"Sorry – It's habit I guess." Through a damp haze, Grady stared deep into sparkling emerald green eyes. Something had changed in the metabolism between himself and Brock, maybe for the better or maybe for the worse, who knows? He sure didn't. Without doubt she was stunning, and he'd been let through an unspoken boundary into a very private space: an area he didn't understand, and maybe never could. His ears burned, his eyes welled.

"I think maybe I should leave." Aware of the tension she backtracked, needed to get human. She ruffled Grady's hair and faked a punch at his big square jaw.

"I wouldn't want you to go, Grady, stay — for me." She cracked a cute smile, "it's okay, you can call me whatever you want."

"I'm sorry, Loot. I guess I'm a bit cut up about Macey."

"No kidding — sure you are."

"Ach...! I guess it goes with the job," concluded Grady. He rolled the jigger between his thumb and forefinger and stared into the golden liquid searching for answers. Welcome as a 'Taps' bugle call at Gettysburg, the door buzzer sang out, bringing Grady back into the moment.

"It's Heidi, not a good time; I'll get her to call back later," said Brock.

"No, it's okay. Let her in. I could do with a little song in my life," said Grady.

"You sure...?" He looked into her eyes, bounced his head in a silent affirmative. She sprang the door.

"Hi, sweetie, come on in." Heidi tilted her head up, radar scanned the room, flared her nostrils and sought the scent.

"Hello, Sergeant Da Silva, how was your take-out?" Amazed at the inner senses of the blind, Grady smiled a welcome to no-one.

"It was so good, sweetheart, I'm afraid there's none left, sorry. Want me to order you up some more?"

"No, it's okay thank you, Sergeant. I've already eaten."

"Then come play us a tune." The blind girl turned her head for affirmation towards where she sensed Brock was sat.

"Go ahead, honey, it would be just fine. We've got some work stuff to discuss so don't mind us. You carry on."

With one hand held out in front of her, Heidi navigated easy across to the piano, lifted the lid and practised a quiet sonata while Brock and Grady worked through their business.

"So who fingered Ludo Mertz and why?"

"As I said before, Loot - I ain't no Sherlock Watson, but maybe some other lowlife is moving in on his operation."

"It's possible, but why?" she asked, "Ludo's obviously well-established — or he was, so why not try and amalgamate, rather than start up all over again?"

"Who knows? What else? Money, power, I guess – I dunno," surmised Grady, opened his hands and sank his head into his shoulders.

"If we can track down whoever Mertz was supplying, and who is supplying them now, we might start to get some answers," she said, "or maybe even better, who *was* supplying Mertz and who *they* are supplying now."

"Tough call, Loot, it's a closed circuit. Moving merchandise up from the O-Zone without detection," Grady shook his head, whistled through pursed lips, "there's a tough call."

"Well someone's doing it. Let's start at the bottom."

"Duzi Olifi," said Grady, smiled bright eyes at the thought. She chuckled, played her chin, poured out another shot.

"Olifi's small fish but he must know something; we'll drop by and pay him a call tomorrow — early," said Brock.

"You okay with that, Boss … bein' early, an' all?" Brock gave Grady, *the look*, swirled liquid in her jigger then drained the glass.

"The hit on the twins I can understand – maybe; it goes with the job. But without doubt, something about it really stinks," she said. "Someone had inside Intel. Who, and how…?"

"You still think we were the real hit?"

"I do, Grady. But maybe it was nothing more than a ruse to make us think we were the hit; seems someone out there is sending us a message."

"A message?" he shrugged, "for what reason?"

"I guess we'll find out when we start digging."

Grady turned morose, dropped his look to the floor, didn't look up.

"An' Macey, Loot…?"

"Her murder really bothers me; it could *only* have been personal. Her sole involvement as far as I can see was in knowing us; or more so – you. Someone is digging down deep to the bone – but why?" Lost for words, Grady shook his head, ruffled his hair before he answered.

"Beats me; I can't believe she was involved in anything crook, not Macey, I would've known – Why...? What motive could *she* possibly have?"

"I trust you there, Grady."

"I'll check it out anyway," he said, "maybe check out forensics, see if they came up with anything."

"Thanks, Grady." Brock marked up a silent point, made notes on foolscap, drew a line through the blanks, added a question mark to the unanswered and ran a red ring around Duzi Olifi. Then she sat back, tossed the pen down onto the table and took a slug of *Jack*.

"How about LePage, how do you think he fits in?" asked Grady.

"You mean his thoughts, or do you think he's in on it?" queried Brock.

"Take your pick," remarked Grady. She slow shook her head, didn't look to him as she spoke:

"I wouldn't be so sure he's clean. There's something odd about him bugging me, but I can't put a finger on it. I don't know, Grady . . . I didn't tell him what we found out about the cult but I sure pressed a serious button when I mentioned Lu-Lu Mbangang, and I'm pretty sure he knows we were at the location when Mertz was hit. How? —you tell me . . ." *Trust no-one, stay alive,* mused Brock.

"I'm still trying to get past that myself," said Grady, bounced his brows. Coy eyes met across a charged atmosphere. Brock smiled, tweaked her nose.

"Let's move on, Cowboy." Grady took a slug of Jack, leant back into the sofa. A slack spring twanged a low 'C'.

"Right now everything is suspect, we've got some action going down tomorrow night; let's see what it brings."

"Action – Where?" asked Grady. Forever aware of security, Brock turned to Heidi who was having a struggle of her own with a difficult passage, then looked back to Grady and scratched out on the foolscap: *we're gonna' hit Mbangang, the O-Zone, south-side.*

"Check the fingering there, Heidi." The little girl checked her Braille sheet then ran the passage perfectly.

"Thank you, Lieutenant."

"You're welcome, sweetie."

"A big strike?" asked Grady.

"I don't know – there's a briefing tomorrow at fourteen hundred."

"You need me to come?"

"No, it's okay. I'm sure you got plenty things of your own to do."

"Yeah sure." Grady looked to the floor, sighed and jollied up their jiggers.

Heidi ran two octaves up a melodic minor scale, closed the lid on the Steinway and slid down off the seat. Grady clapped. The little girl moved across in the direction of the clap.

"Thank you, Sergeant. Will you come tomorrow night with the Lieutenant and see me play at the concert?" Grady looked to Brock, and then to his watch, shrugged questioned shoulders. Brock nodded okay – had to, no choice.

"Sure, sweetheart, I'd like to very much to come an' see you play."

"I know *you* won't be late."

"Don't you worry: I'll make damn sure we *both* won't be late."

"You want a soda before you go, sweetie?"

"No thanks, Lieutenant, I'd better get off to bed. Okay for a final practice tomorrow?"

"Sure thing, I won't be here but you know your way around."

"It sounds just fine to me as it is."

"Thank you, Sergeant."

"Want me to walk you up?"

"No thanks, Lieutenant, I'll be fine."

"Okay. Goodnight sweetheart."

As the door snapped shut Grady eased his fifty-calibre out of his shoulder holster, placed the weapon down onto the low table, reached for the bottle, popped the cap, poured two more shots and relaxed back into the sofa. Brock closed the door and dimmed the light.

"Cute kid, Loot."

"Yeah' but a sad story. I'm told her parents were drug addicts, both died in the epidemic ten years back."

"Sound's a tough call — Blind from birth?"

"From very young I think. I don't really know it's all a bit vague; she doesn't talk much about it. I guess I wouldn't want to either."

"Sweet name, Heidi — sounds continental – French?"

"No, it's Swiss I think…yes, from Switzerland not France," she said.

"How old is she?"

"I don't know, about thirteen, maybe fourteen … I don't really know."

"Looks older …"

"Tough life I guess."

"An' the lady upstairs …?"

"Mrs Wiley? She's a foster parent. Doesn't talk a lot, pretty much keeps to herself. She's also got a slight foreign accent, could be Swiss also, but as I said, I've never really spoken to her much. She pays me her rent on the button every month, she's the model tenant." Grady clucked his tongue, drained his drink and stared into the empty glass.

"Maybe you should adopt her."

"Heidi...? Yeah' right," Brock chuckled at the thought, "great parent I'd make!"

"You and me both, Loot."

"Touché, Shiney." Brock, raised her glass, twitched her nose at the hiatus, felt maybe it wasn't a good idea for either of them as things stood to be alone together in her apartment with a bottle. *'Never a good idea to start something you may regret later and can't undo,'* she mused.

"Let's drop by Olsen's, get a nightcap and shoot the crap with Jackie." Nodding the affirmative, Grady had read her thoughts. Maybe deep down he felt the same way. He slugged back another shot, stood and rested his fifty-calibre back in its holster.

"Thanks for tonight, Loot. I sure appreciate it."

"It ain't over yet, Grady." Eyes met dulcet as two ships passing on a moonlit night with a vision lingering for a long time past decorum should allow; then the phone rang and broke the moment. Brock flipped on the call-back, sprang the door latch.

"Okay, Cowboy, time to go."

She slung her leather bomber jacket on over her gun and smiled as LePage ranted into the machine on their way out.

*   *   *

The morning sun, dogged by weak cloud cover, failed to break ground through thick dusty shades. Truck gears screeched in the street, instigating strong words and an angry horn, neither of which disturbed Grady; it was only the ringing of water hammer that roused him. He yawned, stretched out under a soft blanket on the long, tired sofa. Brock stepped out of the shower, ran the basin faucets and brushed her teeth. The door slightly ajar offered a scant glimpse of flesh; a sight which somehow seemed more erotic than the recent full-frontal Grady had been witness to. He savoured the twinge in his groin, a private moment.

"You awake yet, Grady?"

"I am now."

Dressed in close-fit black jeans and a loose cotton shirt, Brock came out of the bathroom, threw back the shades and drowned Grady's fantasies in a kaleidoscope of bright light.

"Jesus, turn the volume down, Loot," he shielded his eyes as he spoke.

"Bathroom's all yours, Grady; I'll get the coffee."

"You stay up all night?"

"Huh?"

"It's seven-thirty in the fuckin' morning; I ain't ever seen you up this early."

"We got a big day ahead of us, Grady."

"Yeah! Don't remind me."

Brock felt bad for the real reason she'd risen so early: to check Grady's call register on his palm phone before he woke. An action she didn't feel good about but somehow had to put her mind at rest. She poured him coffee, and spoke soft:

"We'll get breakfast on the way, I haven't got anything in."

"Have you *ever* had anything in, Loot?"

"You tryin' to be funny, Sergeant?" she asked with mocked contempt.

"No, not this early in the mornin' — my brain don't work so well yet. I'm still dancin' in the dark, tryin' to figure out shapes an' colours."

"Well, maybe a chat with Duzi Olifi will kick you into gear. But first things first: we need to find a new diner."

*   *   *

Chapter Nine

Breakfast at Skinny's Grill, a downtown diner in the Latin Quarter four blocks from Brock's apartment, was worth the find but could never match Macey's; and as far as Grady was concerned, it wouldn't ever. The waitress, attractive in an oblique sort of way, much in contrast to Picasso's portrait of Madame Z, was brusque but efficient. With her heavy set frame, she would make a good partner in a *tag* wrestling team and looked as if she could pump iron with the best of them and at a push double as the bouncer, although she *was* quite cute in her own mysterious way.

Brock paid the tab, left a good tip and strolled out with Grady from air-con comfort into the burning heat of a sun-baked street. She rolled down the side screen and breathed in a sweet dose of summer ambiance. It looked to be a good day.

"I love the summer, Grady. I don't care how hot it gets. It makes me feel so good."

"I'm right in line with you there, Loot."

Fifty yards from the Securi-cab office, Grady pulled the wagon into the kerb on a quiet back street. Brock slid mirror glasses down off her crown to shade her eyes as she stepped out from the wagon into bright sunlight. Heat from sun-burned paving slabs permeated the soles of her sneakers; she lapped up every moment of it.

It was way past early but footfall was sparse. Grady took the lead and trailed the sound of a ringing phone down to the Securi-cab office. Duzi Olifi was already in office stretched out on the cheap leather high-back office chair. He didn't say a word when Grady kicked open the door — he couldn't, not with his throat cut. Brock clucked a wet tongue.

"It seems we missed the worm, Grady. Close the door."

"Same M.O. as Macey, Loot." She nodded but voiced nothing, pulled the plug on the phone, rolled the office chair and

Olifi back to the wall and ran a computer search of Bakta's pick-ups and drops over the last six months. While waiting for the printout she scanned round the squalid office with a look of disdain; Duzi hadn't even been allowed to finish his beer. *'Not a good place to die – but then again, where the hell was a good place?'* she mused.

"As I said, Boss, I ain't no clever detective, but even I can see there's some strange shit going down here."

"Yeah, I hear you … let's get out of here, Grady. This place isn't good for the soul."

"Too late now to tell that to Duzi!" Grady bent and gave Olifi a gentle slap on his cheek. This time he didn't seem to mind.

Stepping out into brilliant sunshine from the murk and shadow of a dark room, they closed the door on Duzi Olifi.

"So where to now, Loot?"

With a vacant mind and a forefinger tapping her chin, she looked up and down an empty street, then massaged the back of her neck and sucked her teeth.

"Let's take a break and grab another coffee, I need to check out Bakta's pick-ups, there's gotta' be a lead there somewhere."

"Back to the diner, Loot…?"

"Sure, why not? It's a good a place as any I guess, and the coffee wasn't all bad."

"Drop me at the door, Grady, I'll order. You park the wagon around back." Grady eyed Brock, quizzical — got a smug smile back.

"Hunch?" she winked, did her nose thing as she climbed out of the jeep, strolled into the diner and dialled Jackie Olsen.

"Hey Jackie, it's Brock, how you doing, buddy?"

"I'm good, Lieutenant, what can I do for you?"

"Tell me: did Grady make any calls last night on your house phone while I was busy over on the piano?"

"No – no he didn't."

"Can you be sure, Jackie? Maybe you were serving someone at the time — or didn't see?"

"Sure I'm sure, Lieutenant: my house phone was cut two months ago; I can't afford to make the payment."

"Gee, I'm sorry to hear that, Jackie. Okay — thanks anyway buddy." Brock sighed, closed the call, turned to the counter to order:

"Two coffees please, miss." As she spoke, she looked up into the most beautiful blue eyes she'd ever seen, curtained in a pretty face by a fall of golden blond locks and a honey-lip smile cute enough to make a circuit judge chew on his gavel. Stunned to silence Brock couldn't speak; she dropped her jaw and kept her gaze a lot longer than decorum should allow. It was one of those brief moments in life powerful enough to knock you sideways for a few seconds and take you off to a beautiful place far away from the mundane reality of everyday life. She drew in a deep breath, collected herself, gave back her own polite smile, turned away and took a booth by the wall.

Sat back on faux leather, she relaxed into an intimate moment of ecstasy and indulged in a very private and long-forgotten fantasy. Emerald eyes strayed across to the counter, gave copious thanks to someone somewhere for the change of shift.

Floating slow as soft feather down falling in still air she came down from the clouds as Grady strolled in through the door.

"Find anything, Loot?" asked Grady, dropped his heavy body onto the bench seat opposite.

"I sure did! But nothing we were looking for," she danced her eyebrows across at the big man holding her lower lip in her teeth. Confused, Grady furrowed his brows, reckoned the day was still too early for positive thought after one more heavy night of way too many.

He started to soft whistle and search his mind for shape recognition. Brock tweaked her nose and leafed through the printout.

"There's a lot of pick-ups from the same area code – all late, out of hours." She scribbled down the code on a napkin and passed it across to Grady.

The waitress with the grace of a swan meandered across the floor with two coffees steaming on a tray and set them down on the table. Blow-torch blue focused to Brock, smiled and asked in a pseudo-Dietrich purr:

"Could I offer you something to eat?" Brock's answer was nonverbal – It could only have been; her smile spoke the answer. It wasn't a *no-thank-you* smile. Grady, out on the periphery oblivious to the moment checked his watch and big-footed a tender moment:

"Maybe later it's still early; we've only just had breakfast."

"Okay, guys, let me know if you need anything more." She turned, and with legs and body that should have belonged to a ballet dancer, sauntered her sultry body back to the counter. Brock followed her cat-walk all the way. Green eyes turned from lust to desire, then came back down to reality on planet Earth. She re-focused, expelled a deep breath, turned to Grady and pointed to the napkin.

"Check the zip code on your GPS, Grady; it could be a good place to start." He tapped on his cell phone, scrolled down, pressed go and handed it across to Brock. She studied the screen, then went back to the printout, tapped her lower lip with her finger.

"Well, well – what a surprise!" she looked up to Grady, "The city utilities yard, two blocks past Green Street further down Main."

"Now there's a coincidence," said Grady. "Where'd he take the pick-up, Loot?"

"Grady!" scowled Brock lifting her glasses.

"Sorry, Boss – Lieutenant," Grady shrugged an apology, she shook her head, tweaked her nose playful. With a mild hangover she welcomed the retreat behind the recovering comfort from shaded glasses and turned back to the printout.

"He didn't. He went back to his place," she said.

"Who called it in?"

"No recorded number from someone called Johnny," she answered. Cogs churned inside Grady's brain, he ran fingers over a stubbled chin and gazed up to the ceiling. Brock's mind was far away, focused somewhere else into an electric shade of blue.

"What was the name of the guy who the spaced out pretty little girl thought we were looking for at Bakta's apartment?" asked Grady. "Wasn't he Johnny, somethin' or other?"

Brock nodded in thought:

"Johnny B! Could well be. I think you're on the money there Grady, well done, Watson." She slid the printout across to Grady, looked up to the waitress for a refill she didn't need and didn't take her eyes off the girl as she ambled across with the coffee jug. The pretty girl poured a slow slug with a distinct provocation into Brock's mug. She spoke a silent message through blow-torch blue into emerald green, tweaked her nose pouted her lips and sauntered back to the counter. Preoccupied, Brock relaxed back into the booth, spoke to Grady without looking at him:

"See what else you can find, Detective."

While Grady was busy with the printout, Brock re-checked the recent call and message register on Grady's phone. Nothing was made the previous night after they'd discussed checking Olifi out. She switched back to GPS mode and slid his phone across the table —*Relieved!*

"The next trip Bakta made each time after the utilities yard pick-up was to the downtown central station at noon the following day. No recorded fare," said Brock.

"Yeah, I see that, Lieutenant. Johnny B our next call?"

"Bingo, Watson."

"So who hit Olifi, Loot?"

"Pointers would suggest it was someone who knew we were about to pay him a visit."

Brock shrugged, then added: "Could be nothing more than a coincidence. Guys sucking the gutter as low as Olifi live on borrowed time; maybe we just timed it wrong." She conceded with a shrug, "I don't know – whatever. It beats me."

Grady's eyes dampened, his body language turned awkward.

"I know what you're thinking, Boss – but I had nothing to do with it."

"Believe me, Shiney; we don't need to go there." Grady lowered his eyes to the table, chewed on his tongue.

"You know I'd never do anything against you, Loot — and I ain't no plant. Fuck LePage!"

Brock screwed up the napkin, bounced it off Grady's head.

"Let's go talk to Johnny B. Sherlock Watson. Go get the wagon, I'll meet you outside. I'll go and pay."

A flock of butterflies floundered in her stomach as she pushed her body up from the booth and strode tentative steps across into the blowtorch gaze from the pretty waitress.

*   *   *

Deep in shadow, the building on the corner of Parkway and Prince offered little in the way of hope to the needy but pure gold for the rats and blowflies. Peeling paint above the entrance might have once read *La Belle Maison,* but lost a little more of its identity as Grady rattled hard on the front door. Almost as in sympathy, flaking paint fell to the ground from a rotting wooden sash running up shabby tracks in a window frame above. The same pretty girl with scraggy hair peeked out in a state of hallucinogenic confusion and gazed down with sunken eyes hollow as an empty thought. With her mouth hung wide and a mind on permanent pause she uttered nothing.

"Johnny B, around?" asked Grady. Both the sash and her mouth slammed shut without comment. Brock and Grady stood in strained silence at the doorstep. It took five seconds of rising fury before Grady blew out a deep breath, put his boot through the door and trod heavy steps up a grimed stairway to the second floor. Brock shadowed him, kept her distance – Wise move!

Crying out for a lot more than paint, the door to apartment three hung ajar straining on worn hinges. With help from his heavy boot, Grady opened the door wide, following his fifty-calibre into the dank room. Bloodshot eyes narrowed and peered out from beneath a filthy bed sheet. A grubby body stirred bearing a stark resemblance to a well-documented corpse resurrecting itself from under a dirt-trodden shroud. But in contrast to the hero from the Bible, this one wore no halo.

"What the fuck is this?"

"Well, it sure ain't the Samaritans, crap-head. Are you Johnny B?" snarled Grady.

"Who's askin'…? You don't look or smell cop."

"Believe me, sunshine – you wouldn't want him to have to ask again!" said Brock, slow-shook her head and cleared a space to stand amongst a mess of soiled clothes, empty beer cans and cold half-picked take-out trash – Fly food. Johnny B's eyes, hollow as yellow holes in the snow darted back and forth from Brock to Grady faster than a competition Ping-Pong ball.

The pretty girl ensconced in chemical oblivion fired up a 'Lucky buzzer.' Blank eyes searched to focus through a miasma of smoke mingling through a mess of unkempt scraggy hair draped down around her shoulders; a visage similar to the sight of damp kelp drying in the sun over a barren rock. Her drooling mouth hung open wide as an empty grain sack and dribbled spit down over track marks on her arms. The purple hue of her body echoed the skin of a featherless chick, fallen from a high nest down onto cold concrete with its beak working open and shut in silence, searching for the security it once had but would never find again. After inhaling a deep dose, the pretty girl tripped back into the befuddled seclusion of her private world: a world plagued under a drug-filled haze promising nothing more than depleted brain cells and the certainty of a terminal misguided adventure.

"So whaddya want?" asked Johnny B in a phoney low baritone. Grady craned his two-twenty pounds over the wretched bed, pressed his fifty-calibre into a grubby forehead and spoke soft:

"An answer to my fuckin' question would be kinda nice."

"Okay! Okay, yeah – I'm Johnny B, so what, whadda' ya' want?"

"Good. Smart boy! Now let's keep this train of questioning on a positive track." Grady yanked off the filthy bed sheet, dragged Johnny B off of the mattress by his pony tail hair and slammed him into a tight corner.

"You always sleep with your pants on, crap-head?"

"You have a problem with that?"

"Not me – But she might." Grady motioned across to hollow eyes, whose mindless oblivion had caused her body to slide down the wall limp as a discarded rag-doll thrown from the hand of a bored child and set to rest on bare floorboards.

"Are we done now – got what you wanted to know?" asked Johnny B, sarcastic.

Brock closed her eyes, sighed, slow-shook her head. When she opened them Johnny B was cuddling the floor cupping a bloodied nose.

"Smart-ass," growled Grady.

"Fuck!" Johnny spat blood, felt for loose teeth with his tongue, stared up in surrender; figured the floor the best place to be for a while.

"What's your connection with City Utilities?"

"I work there at the sewage plant — so what?"

"It figures – smells to me you've been bringin' your work home; or maybe you've just been pissin' into the wind?" Grady looked round at the filth and squalor Johnny B and the girl immersed their life in; he shook his head.

"Ali Bakta a buddy of yours?"

"Yeah – used to be," Johnny shrugged shoulders, massaged on a slack jaw.

"What'd he run you around in his cab; pick you up; drop you off – those kinda' things?"

"Yeah, sometimes he'd give me a lift home after I'd worked late, 'those kinda' things.'

So what's this about anyway? Why're you houndin' me?" Grady ignored the question.

"So who gives you a lift now?"

"No-one, I walk."

"You should be careful, crap-head, there's some nasty people around after dark," warned Grady. He shrugged his eyebrows across to Brock, who scanned around the room and saw nothing obvious to warrant staying, except for to maybe help clean up this shithole with a bucket of fuel and a match. She nodded to the door, time to go.

Grady followed Brock down the stairs, didn't holster his weapon. At the foot of a grime-ridden staircase, Brock stopped at the mail bin, shuffled through the letters in a wealth of junk mail and then through those scattered across the floor.

"Maybe Bakta's got some mail, could give us a lead."

Grady quiet-whistled and waited, eyed the staircase, didn't look to her but asked:

"Find anything, Loot?"

"Mm-mm," Brock shook her head, then, stopped shuffling and turned to Grady. She held up a utility bill, raised her eyebrows and spoke out:

"Now there's a coincidence, addressed to Johnathon Booth: apartment five."

As Brock made the second-floor landing Grady had gripped lank hair at the back of Johnny B's head and marched him across the corridor to apartment five. He didn't stop as his heavy boot opened the door. Inside on a grubby table stood a weight measure; spoon scoops; plastic bags; a large box of white powder and small packs of crystal meth. On the floor beside a filthy mattress, an ashtray brimmed with the tips of dead buzzers. The place stank from stale dope, stale sweat, and a very stale dose of rank humanity. A choked expletive strained for altitude as Grady pushed the barrel of his fifty-calibre up into Johnny B's throat.

"Sing me a song, crap-head. Make it a good one."

"I'm just the transit guy, I don't know names or places, honest to god I swear."

"I'm sure with a little persuasion you can do a lot better than that, crap-head."

"Please, they'll kill me," pleaded Johnny voiced an octave up from his pseudo baritone.

"Maybe I'll save them the fuckin' trouble." Grady dragged Johnny over to the window, grabbed his belt buckle and pushed him backwards out through the window. Glass rained down shattering on the concrete below. Johnny's pants slid to his knees as he hung upside down.

"Okay, crap-head, I'll try again. How does the junk transit?"

"Fuck, you crazy bastard!"

"Don't tempt me, crap-head."

"Okay – Okay – It comes in life-raft pods through the sewer system from the O-Zone. I retrieve it; bag it; and deliver it, nothin' more."

"Who do you deliver to?"

"It's all I know, I don't know nuthin' else, you gotta' believe me. Fuck man! They'll kill me. Pull me up, *pleease*."

"Maybe you should have a chat with Frank," said Grady.

"Whaa...?" Johnny groaned in confusion.

Grady took the Zapper out of his pocket, jabbed it into Johnny's crutch and loosened his bowels with thirty-thousand volts. After his body stopped jerking, Johnny screamed the ravings of a wild man, cried out expletives through a flood of tears. Urine streamed down from his hair, something even nastier slid down his back.

"Feeling at home now, sewer-man? Now where's your drop-off?"

"FUUUUUCK! Pull me up. Please I'll talk, I'll talk, I swear." Dragging bare flesh over broken glass Grady yanked Johnny back in through the window.

"Don't waste my time sewer-man. Where's the drop-off and who's the pick-up?"

"I drop off at a left-luggage locker on central, I dunno' no names, honest I swear."

"Wrong answer, sewer-man; back over to Frank." Grady rammed Johnny back out through the window and stabbed the Zapper into his groin. Johnny's body convulsed. His backside emitted nothing more than a trumpet of hot, putrid air. His bowels rang empty and stank! "Talk, sewer-man or I swear to god in two seconds you'll be kissin' your stinkin' pile of crap down there on the concrete."

"Billy Clack, he's the pick-up – Billy Clack. *Please*, they gonna' kill me."

"Who does clack work for? Who's your mailman?"

"I dunno', I swear to god. Please, please, no more." Grady buzzed the zapper into bare flesh. Johnny B. convulsed in violent spasms, screamed loud, choked vomit through both his mouth and nose.

"A guy called Speed, he sends the stuff up from the O-Zone, I swear to god it's all I know – honest."

Grady buzzed the Zapper one more time but the tank was empty. He thought about dropping the snivelling creep down the two storeys but pulled him back through the window and cuffed him to an ancient radiator. Disorientated, bloodied and stinking, Johnny gawped around the room sitting awkward as he drooled a cocktail of blooded saliva, snot and vomit into his lap. He whimpered the sounds of a chastised puppy in a poor-boys' dogs' home.

"When I think of all the people who've suffered from the vermin smack of your whale-shit low morals, I can't help thinking you've got off light, crap-head. Now is there anything you've overlooked to tell me, sewer-man? Because you'd better fuckin' hope and pray I don't have to come back looking for you!" Blood-shot eyes, dazed and confused, rolled behind reddened lids. Johnny B stank.

Grady crossed the corridor, brushed dust off his jacket sleeve, flattened black hair down on the crown of his head, pulled his hat down and re-shaped the brim.

Back in apartment three, Brock scrolled through the call register on Johnny's palm phone. Slunk in the corner beneath the window, hollow eyes in a vacant body registered nothing; no-one was home and wouldn't be for a long time, or maybe never again at all!

Brock looked to Grady with a smile in her eye.

"Okay Watson, what've we got?"

"Well, we got a couple of leads, Boss. Speed's the mailman and a guy called Billy Clack's the pick-up," Grady shrugged, "seems we got a connection at the city utilities and the left

luggage at central. It's all beginnin' to fit together now, Loot."
Brock nodded slow as she scrolled down the phone.

"Speed and Billy Clack, I'll bet we got both their numbers
here, Grady. Let's get out of this shithole and get us some fresh
air."

Grady bagged the dope in a backpack, scooped up a left
luggage locker key from the table, looked down at Johnny B and
spat as a prelude to his advice:

"Some bad-ass bastard's gonna' miss this package sewer-
man, so I suggest you put some serious distance between them
and you, *'mucho fuckin' pronto amigo'*," growled Grady. He
thumbed the switch on the Zapper, checked the weak arc across
the prongs and smiled down to Johnny B.

"How about that sewer-man: you wore out my charge
pack!"

* * *

Chapter Ten

Summer road dust clouded in the rear-view as Grady swerved to avoid a feral cat. He spoke to Brock but kept both eyes on the road.

"Where to, Loot?"

"Huh? Oh … let's go back to my apartment," she said without thinking. Her mind was a million miles away. She powered down the side screen, needed something fresh; maybe something even fresher than springtime air in a cherry grove. Grady howled on the horn as a drunk staggered a two-step at the kerbside. The tri-tone broke her reverie. She fluttered her lashes, rolled up the side screen and turned to the big man.

"So tell me, Grady, how does Speed transport the junk?"

"He sends it down the sewage system packed in life-raft pods with a tracker. Johnny B fishes it out the other end at the city utilities yard."

"Classy job! Let's check out who else is in his loop." Brock keyed her phone.

"Lieutenant Brock here, C.S.F. 51, I need to run an I.D."

"Please hold, Lieutenant." She waited for a voice I.D. check.

"You think Billy Clack's on the register, Loot?" Grady gave a quizzical look behind heavy furrowed brows.

"If he's bona fide, he must be in there somewhere," she shot him a glance, "it's got to be worth a try." She turned back to her phone as a faceless voice spoke:

"Go ahead, Lieutenant Brock, you're clear."

"Billy Clack – I'm sorry, it's all I got," she said. Keys rattled at the other end of the phone, then silence.

"No, there's nothing at all on Billy Clack, nor William, or Bill. I'm sorry, Lieutenant."

"Okay – Try John Booth, apartment 5, Parkway and Prince." Keys rattled in her ear; she switched to speaker phone and rested the phone in her lap.

"Yep, he's here. Johnathon Booth, alias Johnny B. Small time stuff mostly, released with a caution for possession; out on licence as we speak, Lieutenant."

"Any known associates?"

"Hold the line please, Lieutenant … yes; I think I may have something here for you. William Slack, also known as Willy," the I.D. operator suppressed a snigger, cleared his throat. "I'm sorry, Lieutenant, excuse me. Anyway, William Slack, A.K.A Joel Marcus Gorman, European descent, bad pedigree; you name it: this guy was wanted for it. He went off the radar for a long time, supposedly turned up two years ago in the rear seat of a burn-out roasted to perfection with three slugs in his head; no previous traceable address, believed to have been once associated with Karl-Heinz Yungen, although nothing proven. I have an old mug shot, Lieutenant – Want me to buzz it to you?"

"Thank you, I'd appreciate it."

"No problem – If there's anything else …"

"No, not right now thank you. I appreciate your help."

"You're welcome, Lieutenant." Green eyes stared over low sunnies at Grady, spoke loud. He shrugged heavy shoulders, begged a question:

"I guess Slack could be mistaken for Clack through a mouthful of blood and snot, Boss?"

"Nice work, Grady. Keep it up."

"Thanks, Loot," soft whistling his atonal melody, Grady drove a slow path through a sunny day.

Brock's phone buzzed; she checked the register, sighed heavy, pressed green with reluctance and drawled without enthusiasm into her phone:

"Brock speaking – talk to me."

"Lieutenant, I need you in my office before the full brief this afternoon."

"Anything wrong, Sir?"

"No, I need an updated progress report."

"Okay – one o'clock good for you, Sir?"

"See you then, Lieutenant. Don't be late." The dial tone buzzed in her ear. Brock thumbed red, puffed out hot air, muttered to herself, *"fuck you, ass-hole."* Grady beamed a wide grin, turned up the air-con. She rolled her eyes and sank back into her seat.

"Just what I need, another head fucking from LePage," she turned to Grady, "Okay, pull over. Here's what we're gonna do." Brock scrolled through the call list on Johnny B's phone; stopped at Billy S.

"This looks a maybe." She passed the phone to Grady. "Ring this number. You'll come up on his screen as Johnny B. If it's Slack – you're ready to make the drop – Play it by ear."

"I won't sound anything like that ass-hole, Loot."

"You'll sound more like him than I will. Make the call, Grady." He shrugged, pressed green. The call buzzed only once.

"Johnny! Where the *fuck* have you been?" Grady burst into a lengthy cough.

"I'm sick, Billy, real bad," Grady groaned, coughed heavy into the receiver.

"Keep your sick shit away from me you fuckin' sicko. I want my merchandise – NOW!"

"Okay, okay – I'll send a runner, *cough…cough…*"

"Better be there soon sicko; or bein' sick is gonna be the least of your fuckin' problems."

"Gimme an hour, *cough…*" The phone buzzed dial tone. Brock gave the slow hand clap; flashed her lashes to the big man.

"Grady, you've got hidden talents. I'm very impressed."

"It ain't a patch on your hooker rip-off, Loot, if you don't mind me sayin' so."

"I guess you ain't gonna let me forget that in a hurry are you, Grady?"

"Not a chance – just lookin' forward to the re-run." Brock leant across and pushed Grady's hat down over his eyes.

"You owe me buster – I should've charged you." She scrunched her face. "Okay, let's head back to my apartment and cool your libido down with a cold beer."

*   *   *

Brock threw open a window in her lounge in a futile attempt to draw in fresh air and dilute the thick scent lingering in the shadows from another heavy night; an intrusion dire as an uninvited guest festering on the sofa after an all-night party. She took in the sweet tang of honeysuckle from the gardens below and wondered why in all the years she'd lived in the apartment she had never noticed such a pleasure before. She left the window ajar, smiled to herself, pondering how much else she'd missed in her total preoccupation with her work. Maybe it *was* time now for a change.

On the wall behind her Steinway hung a limited edition signed print of Andrew Wyeth's painting, OVERFLOW: a work bequeathed to her from her late mother, who had a love for fine art. For the first time in a long time, Brock stared at it with a deep passion, saw much more in it now than she'd ever seen before and began to realise how much she also loved beautiful things. She turned back to the sight of Grady relaxed back on the sofa with his feet up on the low table. He caught a beer as she tossed it to him from the ice-box. With a soft sigh, she slunk back into the sullen mode of reality.

In the privacy of her bedroom, she made a quick change into blue-jean cut-off shorts, sneakers and a loose tee-shirt to give her thirty-two years a spunky youthful look; a deception her body didn't need. Then, she emptied the dope into a bin liner, emptied her trash can into the backpack and buzzed the mug shot of Willy Slack across to Grady's palm phone.

"Okay, Grady, here's what we do: I'll make the drop, you shadow me and watch for who picks it up. Remember – it's an old mug shot, but he can't have changed his looks too much. Don't do *anything*, follow him, but stay back and check where he goes. Then call me and nothin' else – Understand."

"Yep, you got it, Boss."

"I mean it, Grady. You don't do *anything* else."

"Sure thing, Loo… tenant."

"I'll catch a cab to LePage's office; call me as soon as you get a result, okay?" Grady nodded the affirmative. "Okay, let's get going."

"You ain't taking a weapon, Loot?"

"Sure I am, Grady – I'm taking you."

*   *   *

Chapter Eleven

Central Station: no longer a hub for intercity travel after the advent of the virus has been relegated down to a no-star squalid flop-house on a downhill slide for the homeless. Abuzz with perspiring bodies and their respective scent under the sweltering noon heat, it offers little attraction for the tourist; if in fact there were still such a thing these days what with nowhere much to go. Overflowing litter bins long past desperate need of a service agent in a broken society vomit out their contents onto the surrounding floor. Skulking in the shadows, drug addicts and drunks mirror a similar state of affairs. The clapped-out air-con hadn't run for five summers, and probably wouldn't ever run again. It's the way it was these days post-virus in the downtown station.

Brock mooched a casual body across the faux marbled concourse to a line of graffiti-clad left luggage lockers; Grady shadowed at a distance. At locker #B15 the key turned easy in the lock. Inside the locker, a grubby dog-eared envelope had been tossed back into deep shadow. Scanning round before she would remove the envelope, Brock saw nothing of consequence other than Grady lurking in the shadows. She loaded the backpack, relocked the door and sauntered across the station concourse into the main entrance of the ladies' room, once a sanctuary for the gentler sex but now an area requisitioned for use by hookers and dealers to ply their trades; each offering nothing at all gentle about sex. She rinsed her hands to the rhythm of a desperate soul groaning out a climax in the stall behind her. What a hell of a fucking life – literally!

She checked her phone, pausing a few minutes before scanning outside. The last seasonal rain shower began to spit out a warning on stone paving slabs. She slipped straight out of the western side entrance into a busy street, skipped past a parade of deadbeat hopefuls sat on cardboard luxury glaring scorn up at the menacing clouds, then lost herself in the crowd content no-one had followed her. She hailed a cab and rode to the Park-side Hotel and took a liquid lunch at the bar, paid for by a *Patsy* who had a lot more hope than he had looks or luck.

From the Park-side taxi stand she took a cab to LePage's office. The rain shower was on pause, leaving in its wake a low curtain of vapour rising from the blacktop as bright sunlight poked its nose through the clouds and flooded the stage. It was Twelve fifty-three. Grady still hadn't called.

A roll of thunder cued a heavy fall of driving rain as she stepped out of the cab after it had pulled up across the road from Sujo's. She got soaked to the skin in the short run for shelter. Under cover from a dripping awning at Sujo's entrance, she shook the ponytail out of her hair and mentally kicked herself into gear. She trod slow and unenthusiastic steps up the stairway and made a reluctant move along the grubby corridor for what she expected to be nothing more than another very unpleasant session of discord in her life. If hostility could exude an odour, LePage's office would be rank with the stench big time. She didn't bother to knock.

Once inside, she kept her cool with little help from the rusting overhead fan, whose blades, in desperate need of oil and a damp cloth, continued to groan out an endless morose rhythm. It offered little to enhance the dour surroundings of LePage's office. Clung tight to her body, her sweat and rain-soaked tee-shirt offered a cheap voyeuristic thrill for the roving eyes and probing imagination of LePage. Well aware of his glare, Brock folded tight arms across her chest, then, with a seductive feminine and provocative Hollywood tease befitting the young Lauren Bacall, she stripped off her sunglasses, allowing unencumbered emerald eyes to bore a smug complacence through LePage's veil of reticence. His ears glowed bright, along with his libido. He took a deep breath and asked:

"Did you enjoy your run, Lieutenant?"

"Sir?" questioned Brock.

"You look as if you've been for a run – Most untypical of you I'd have thought." LePage motioned a finger to Brock's casual attire. She gave him her best *fuck you* look.

"I've been working, Sir – Undercover."

LePage nodded, pursed his lips. Foxy eyes from under furrowed brows glared a prurient seduction as he mentally undressed her.

"Yes. I'm sure you have – Once again!"

She parried back hard with a belligerent stare, let the side-swipe dance in the dust and refused to take the bait.

"You wanted to see me – Sir?" scowled Brock rattling LePage's psyche. 'Or *did you only want to ogle my tits?*' she mused and sucked her cheeks in.

"Yes, Lieutenant, I would be grateful for a full update on your recent movements; and in full detail, those concerning Ludovic Mercowitz, if of course, it's not too much trouble."

"It's all in my report, Sir; didn't you read it?"

"Yes I did read it, Lieutenant: very interesting, brief as it was."

Brock returned nothing, remaining sat in a blank silence intruded upon only by the overhead fan playing out its jaded rhythm as two flies buzzed each other slaloming through the blades. LePage held his lower lip in his teeth, then paced the room sucking on a lukewarm coffee cup, then turned to his window.

"Lu-Lu Mbangang!" He voiced aloud from nowhere as he spun round on a heel expecting a reaction from Brock – None came. "What do you know about him, Lieutenant? I notice you failed to mention him in your report?" LePage bored a volley from dark eyes in an attempt to now probe *her* psyche. She moved nothing but her telling eyes as she held his glare through her brows.

"No need. There's not much I can tell you about him, Sir, other than what's on his rap sheet; and, for what it's worth, in my opinion the world would be a far better place without him taking up space in it." *And that goes for you too, you slimy creep,* she mused. LePage turned back to his window. Paused in thought, he tapped his foot.

"A particular pleasure no doubt for many, which may be coming his way a little sooner than he thinks, Lieutenant."

"Sir …?"

"Mbangang's tonight's hit: him, and his whole stinking, outfit."

"With a rap sheet as long as he's got, I'm surprised he's lasted this long, Sir."

LePage nodded to the window and filled his lungs with a deep breath inhaled through his nose before he would speak.

"The reason he's lasted this long, Lieutenant is quite simple: he's been working undercover for us ever since his exile to the O-Zone."

"Working for *us,* Sir; in what capacity?"

"It would seem now to be nothing more than to further his personal agenda."

"Why wasn't I informed of his involvement?"

LePage turned from the window, glared a steel gaze at her through narrowed eyes and uttered nothing in return. She didn't rise to the bait but said:

"I take it then – you won't be giving him a reference, Sir."

"No I won't, Lieutenant. But tonight you will." LePage lifted his coffee cup in a mock toast and said: "He's tonight's brief, for both you and Sergeant Da Silva." Coffee dribbled down LePage's chin, blemishing his shirt at the mention of Da Silva. He drew a tissue from a box on his desk, blotted the dirty mark and made it worse.

"Difficult to remove coffee stains, Sir, best get your shirt cleaned by a professional. It's a good job it wasn't expensive."

Contemptuous eyes scowled at Brock from under a furrowed brow, his ears glowed red as he drew in, and held a short sharp breath behind pursed lips in a desperate search for a slick evasive wisecrack. But a blank mind capped in a skinned dome covered with a thin smattering of hair succumbed to the challenge.

"Thank you, Lieutenant; I'm sure I shall manage."

"I'm sure you can, Sir. It's not difficult," patronised Brock with a smug grin, then asked:

"Has Mbangang been feeding us bad info, Sir?"

"It's possible, Lieutenant," he spun round to face her. "Why do you ask?"

"It's a feeling I get, Sir. We've stepped on a few marbles lately; I can't help thinking someone's on our case."

"What – perhaps a plant you mean?" he asked, taking his turn to be smug. Brock twitched her nose but it wasn't cute. She rolled her eyes, didn't make contact.

"I've had Sergeant Da Silva under close surveillance, Sir. He's clean, believe me."

"I prefer facts, Lieutenant Brock," scowled LePage. He swung his mock leather recliner around, sat and positioned himself at his desk in a direct line across from her. "Our job is to clear the streets of social filth; stop the gangs before they start and eradicate the drug lords in order to allow good citizens to walk safe in crime-free streets. Do I make myself clear, Lieutenant?"

'What an ass-hole!' she mused, shrugged tired eyebrows, drew a deep breath and turned her gaze to the door. 'Tell me something I don't know!' She glared back at him hard.

"Are you disappointed with my results, Sir?" Leant back in his chair, LePage rested his chin on arched forefingers and lifted his brows.

"On the contrary, Lieutenant Brock."

"Well, Sir, my efforts are all in direct collaboration with Sergeant Da Silva."

Frowning, LePage fingered his forehead, paused before he spoke.

"What does he know about tonight's mission?"

"Nothing more than we'll be working late, Sir."

"Nothing more…" snapped LePage.

"No, Sir. Nothing more," bluffed Brock wishing she hadn't revealed the location.

"Good," said LePage. He stood, swung the seat and moved back to his coveted window, didn't turn as he spoke in a high voice: "The location has changed, Lieutenant."

"And the hit, Sir…?"

"The same: Mbangang. It would seem he moves around quite a lot, for reasons best known only to him."

"May I ask how you're aware of his movements, Sir?"

"Yes, Lieutenant, you may well ask," he turned and scowled at her with a look to freeze hot coals in Hell.

'Ass-hole!' She mused.

LePage fumbled in his jacket and tossed an envelope across to her.

"Here you will find the co-ordinates and any information you will need for tonight's hit. Study it and tell no one. You will have four armoured vehicles to accompany you, each manned by two Agents from Special Force. *You* will be heading the hit. Good luck, Lieutenant Brock." As he turned to his window, her phone rang, she saw Grady's name in the call-log register.

"Excuse me, Sir. I need to take this." LePage pursed his lips, tapped a foot below an iced stare, worried his finger and cracked a knuckle. She thumbed green.

"Go ahead, Sergeant."

"What's all this *Sergeant* crap – you getting back at me now, Loot?" Brock lifted her eyes to LePage but said nothing. LePage folded his arms and tapped an impatient foot.

"The rat took the bait," enthused Grady.

"Did you recognise him?" she asked.

"He looked as if he was the grand-pappy of the guy in the photo."

"Was he alone?"

"Yep."

"You follow him?"

"All the way home, Loot."

"Nothing else…?"

"Nope, nothing else, just as you said, Loot."

"Okay, Grady, nice work. Pick me up at Sujo's."

"Shall I bring the bag of dope up, drop it off with LePage?"

"Yeah, you may as well. We're done with it. Catch you later."

Leant back against the wall, LePage furrowed his brow and stared at Brock over folded arms. She thumbed red on her phone, gave LePage a complacent look:

"That was Sergeant Da Silva, Sir. We have a break on a new drug ring, right here in the city."

"Is this anything to do with Mercowitz?"

"In some way, Sir, yes I think it could be."

"Any names, Lieutenant?" he queried, spun his chair round, sat back in the seat, tapped his teeth with a pencil waiting for her reply.

"We're still working on it, Sir."

"I'll ask again, Lieutenant," he glared a hostile volley across to her and growled: "Any names . . .?" LePage pushed, wouldn't let go. Brock threw out a bone.

"Joel Marcus Gorman, Sir." Dark eyes bored across the desk. LePage tossed his pencil onto the desktop, leant back and swung in his seat.

"Impossible – Gorman's dead."

Black locks shook a *no* over sculpted shoulders. "Not so, I'm sure it would be very convenient for him if we were to think he's dead, Sir; but my information tells us he's very much alive."

LePage ground his teeth, fingered a worried jaw, stood and turned back to his comfort zone.

"Anyone else?"

"A guy called Speed – He's the mailman. Also a few ten-cent faces: pick-ups and runners only in it for a quick buck."

"Who's the bank-roller?"

"Could be Gorman, Sir," bluffed Brock. LePage shook his head slow, beamed a wide grin, pulled his brows together.

"Nice try, Lieutenant," he leant forward over her and sneered, "now tell me who you really think it is?" She licked dry lips, sucked her tongue, avoided his stare.

"Well there's a nasty whisper, Sir, unconfirmed of course, that the Y-ZEE KAY is reforming."

"Yungen?" scowled LePage with a look on his face as if he'd sucked on the wrong end of a toilet bowl brush.

"It could be, Sir. Too early yet to tell; but let's not forget – he was never caught."

"Yes, I'm well aware of his elusive record, Lieutenant." He levelled his eyes, challenged her with a hard stare.

"I thought you didn't succumb to whispers?"

"I don't, Sir. Or whisperers."

LePage pinched his nose together, released air through a tight lip embouchure.

"Well then, why would the Cult reform? It doesn't make any sense, their revolution's long over. They achieved their aim. We haven't heard from them in years," he threw his hands in the air.

"Achieved their aim…?" she questioned, "did they, Sir – really? And tell me, what exactly *was* their aim? Society's been split in two ever since the first Covid vaccine debacle back in the mid-twenties. You were either pro-vaccine, or anti-vaccine, washed up on one side or the other with little choice in the matter; a nation divided. Look what happened to the people who were terrorised by fear into taking an untested vaccine. It's all about control, untold health problems, a screwed-up reproductive system, a fucked up DNA and a de-funked immune system, with no come-back at all from a group of slimeball rogues and politicians who made untold fortunes from unfounded scare stories to a meek, gullible, and desperate public. And what's left for those poor ostracised bastards now: condemned to a life of misery from a contaminated body and doomed to an early demise in the O-Zone, and far beyond; or, existing in a life of squalor with no hope or wealth with nothing more than a heavy dose of crime, filth and a thankful death to look forward to. They can't come here with the privileged elite, and what a fucking joke that is, it's far too dangerous for their health to mix with us. The wealth and health such as it is prospers only here in the A-Zone, and don't forget: we have the lifeblood of a seaport. If he's still alive, that's exactly what Yungen will be gunning for. It's an opportunity too good for him to miss, Sir." Brock stared hard through a wall of silence, then, added: "It's our job to stop him!"

LePage glared through the murk at his window, slow-nodded, pursed his lips and inhaled a deep, sharp breath through his nose.

"Get Sergeant Da Silva up here *now*...I want a full report from you both on the present situation – RIGHT AWAY!"

"Well there's some good news for you, Sir – Sergeant Da Silva's on his way here as we speak."

*   *   *

Chapter Twelve

"Captain Clod – What an ass-hole!"

"Don't tell me you've only just worked that one out of your butt, Grady?" Brock smiled smug, tore open the envelope from the left-luggage locker. Tucked inside were a few small bills and a scribbled note in serious need of a script editor.

"He's got a bad attitude. I don't need his bullshit," growled Grady.

"Forget him, Grady; he's not worth the grief."

Grady drove a fast track through a slow summer day. Brock studied the brief note,

"I think maybe we should pay your grand-pappy guy a visit. I've a feeling he might be a good touch for some info."

"You think he's the next link in the chain, Loot?"

"Could well be. Okay, let's drop off at my place first. I need to get out of these sweaty clothes."

"Shame, I'm kinda warmin' to the fragrance," pleaded Grady. She wrinkled her nose, slapped the letter on his head.

"Shuus' ... Pervert!"

*　　*　　*

Running-fourths in E flat major fan-faired them in, as Brock sprung open her apartment door.

"Hi, Heidi."

At the sound of her name, the little blind girl stopped hammering on the keys and soft-closed the lid.

"Don't stop, sweetie, we won't be long. I need to make a dry change and freshen up."

Brock kicked off her sneakers, tossed the note from the left luggage locker onto the coffee table and tipped a wink to Grady.

"Check it out, Sherlock, see what you think. There's coffee set to go in the machine or a cool beer in the ice box. Help yourself, I'm gonna jump in the shower."

"Okay, you want coffee too, Loot?"

"Sure, why not – but spice it up a little."

Showered, re-clad and refreshed, Brock stepped out of her bedroom, picked up a coffee from the low table, jollied it up with another shot of bourbon and took a healthy slug. Heidi sat talking to Grady on the sofa. At the bottom of the scant sheet, Brock could see Grady had scribbled out Willy Slack's address in red Gel pen. She opened the change of location order for tonight's hit; read it, shook her head, put it back in its envelope and dropped it back onto the coffee table. Looked across to Heidi and blew out a deep frustrated breath.

"Somethin' wrong?" asked Grady.

"I'm sorry, sweetheart," said Brock. Heidi turned to the sound and tone of Brock's voice, guessed what was coming.

"It's okay, Lieutenant, I understand. You've got to work." *'Cute kid.'* With bitter-sweet eyes, Brock turned to Grady, shook a sad look, kissed Heidi on her crown, didn't speak but sent a telepathic message of love.

"Stay here and practice, honey, I'll be home as quick as I can," but knew deep down she wouldn't be – She rolled her eyes to Grady and shook her head.

"I've gotta' make a call." She went into her bedroom and came out two minutes later shaking her head to Grady.

"No go . . . *Fuck LePage!*"

*   *   *

"Okay, Grady, ten twenty-two, Capri Heights, you know the way, let's go an' see just how *slack* Willy really is!"

Thirty-five minutes later Grady pulled the Jeep into the Capri Heights parking area, a cheerless place where more store trollies than cars filled the lots. Taking up space beneath a *'No*

Waiting' sign, a rusting hulk from the early thirties sat forlorn on bricks; now bedroom cosy to a hobo it was going nowhere – and neither was he.

Inside the sixteen-floor tower block they passed through a drift of smoke from a cigarette smouldering in a cut-down bean can at reception. An empty welcome on an empty desk from an empty mind. They rode the elevator up to the tenth.

"Looks a little more upmarket than Johnny B's shithole, Lieutenant, I guess we must be creeping up the chain."

"It's Brock, Grady – Call me Brock."

"Sorry, Boss —'*Brock*'..." Grady shrugged his shoulders and shook his head. "Just doesn't sound right?" he pleaded.

Tight knuckles rapped hard on ten twenty-two. Grady growled at the door:

"Room service . . ." No answer came. The door wasn't on the catch. With a soft hand (uncharacteristic for Da Silva), he pushed the door. It swung open, not being locked or even on the safety chain. Inside, drawers were turned out, clothes were scattered everywhere, with a mess of empty Pizza-boxes and beer cans strewn across the floor and a plastic bag taped over the smoke alarm, it all stamped a grim depiction of the occupants. A porn flick ran in silence on the wall TV screen showing a black-lace stocking-clad starlet attempting to coax flaccid flesh back into action; a half-baked clip which would have been better off left on the cutting room floor. Room ten twenty-two stank heavy from stale sweat, stale urine and a stale lifestyle. A table lamp lay smashed on the floor.

'*I guess it mirrors the usual state of the occupant,*' mused Brock. A buzzer sporting long ash smouldered in a coffee-stained saucer.

"Looks as if Johnny B could very well be this guy's valet; I wonder if anybody was hurt in the explosion?" Grady smirked as he wandered across to check out the bathroom.

Out on the balcony taking in a welcome dose of fresh air, Brock gazed out across the city, then further out over blue-water bay. Glistening white super yachts clad with Burma teak decking complimented with bright polished stainless steel and the promise of luxury, danced a graceful aquatic waltz in a rippling turquoise sea under a blazing sun. An exclusive world fit only for the elite. Brock smiled and lowered her gaze back into grim reality.

"I guess he went for more Pizza." Grady rattled a box of stale crusts next to his head.

"No..." She shook her head and spoke back over her shoulder. "He took a swim!"

"What?" He joined her on the balcony, strained his eyes way out into the blue sea. She tousled black locks over her shoulders motioning down with her eyes. Grady followed her gaze down ten floors. A body floated face down, leeching red into the sparkling turquoise pool. Slack Willy had skipped his last fandango.

"Holy crap! There goes our 'missing link'," conceded Grady. Brock nodded back to the near spent buzzer still smoking in the filthy saucer.

"Yeah and looks as if we've just missed it. Lets' check the room, Grady, look for a cell phone, notebook, anything to give us a lead."

After fifteen minutes of searching, other than a pungent evidence of a bad lifestyle, nothing of any use transpired.

"I'll check with the house phone register at the phone company," suggested Grady, "it might turn up something."

"Okay good idea," she said as she picked the pocket from a Levi jacket sporting a tan corduroy collar strewn on the floor. She bounced her brows, held up and rattled a set of car keys.

"We'll check his car, but first let's go down and sound out the desk clerk, check on the house CCTV, maybe see if we can catch who his swimming coach was."

In a grubby office wreaking a strong odour of bad things, Brock flashed I.D. to a sleep-eyed security guy behind the check-in desk. Bent over the desk with his head nestled in folded arms, sullen and in desperate need of a hose down, the filthy desk-clerk, who's sallow countenance looked as if he'd made his living selling far too much of his soul to the blood bank, didn't stir. Grady stepped forward and twisted a dirt-grimed ear – hard!

"Wake up Snow White." Two half-opened eyes gawped back with the lifeless cold grey pallor of those in a dead fish. The clerk dribbled into his lap as he lifted up his head and snorted a copious dose of snot into his brain. Grady patted him on the cheek:

"Have a good trip, genius?"

The house closed circuit TV produced nothing other than a lot more porn. Contact leads from CCTV cameras dangled down loose as a donkey's dick in an empty paddock. Grady slapped hard on the desk and poured a mug of cold tea into the desk clerk's lap.

"Go out an' clean your pool, ass-hole. Someone's left a turd in there!"

Down at the car park, their choice was obvious: a beat-up Ford with a smashed headlamp in a banged-up fender. A lucky dice hanging from the rear-view and the absence of a wiper blade from the passenger side confirmed any doubt. The Ford winked as Brock beeped the key fob. Inside, beyond the rancid stench from stale smoke, body odour and a degenerate lifestyle she found not much more than empty beer cans, used condoms, and grease-ridden take-out trash. Set in the drive side door panel she dug out a cell phone, its battery was too dead to power up the phone. *No problem,* she mused, and slipped the phone into her pocket. She scanned around the car park, shook her head and shrugged; nothing other than evidence of heavy drug use and a sorry lifestyle with an inevitable end had come to light. Grady closed the trunk: also nothing useful. Brock tossed the keys onto the floor pan and closed the door.

"Let's go, Grady, we've got a heavy night ahead of us after we've checked in with the Clod."

*   *   *

On the drive back to her apartment, Brock wrestled with the black monkey. It would seem every time she got a lead it led to another dead end, and more often than not, at the end of a dead end was a dead body. Who knew they were going to visit Willy Slack? Not many for sure. She thought about the info sheet she'd left on the coffee table. If Grady *had* made the call while she'd showered and changed her clothes, Heidi would not have seen him but would have sure heard him. No, it couldn't be Grady. If it was: why wouldn't he have used his own cell phone? Why take the chance? Could be she reasoned: it would be too obvious, and much too easy to check with the directory. He may be many things, but he's not stupid, nor is he a plant. He couldn't be? A chill shuddered over her spine, tremored down her back.

*   *   *

Back at her apartment, she checked the call register on her house phone. One call *had* been made around the time they were there. She called the directory, gave her passcode and asked for info on to who the call was made. The phone rang back after two minutes. A polite voice told her the call went to an unlisted number, probably a *burner* phone. The chill in her spine lingered; keeping bad company with the black monkey. She went into her bedroom and plugged Slack's phone into a charger. Grady called out to her from the sitting room:

"Want me to call up directory and check out Willy Slack's call-log from his room phone?"

"Yeah, but don't use the house phone, I think it's bugged; maybe both bugged *and* tapped," she spoke as she came back into the sitting room.

"Bugged, how come?"

"Beats me – I'm getting a strange feeling about it," she replied, then plunged herself into deep water without a life vest.

"Grady, you didn't make a call earlier on my house phone did you, maybe to one of those heavy-breathing numbers?" – *'Hated herself'*

"No, why would I, Loot? I got my own phone right here."

"No, I thought not — it's okay, Grady, I think someone's tapping into my phone."

"I'll make a call, get it scanned."

"Thanks, Grady. I'm gonna get togged up for tonight, make yourself comfortable, there's half a banana in the cool box if you're hungry."

"Thanks a lot, Loot – watch you don't take a skate on the skin when you come back out."

"You're all heart, Shiney."

"So they tell me but believe me, I sure never meant to be!"

*   *   *

Chapter Thirteen

Two hours before midnight on a hot humid night under heavy cloud cover across a starless sky, four military-grade Jeeps kicked up a thick dust cloud tailing Brock and Grady in their covert security semi-armoured combat vehicle. The convoy travelled East through the dank, dusted corridor into open scrubland leading to the hit location in the O-Zone. The unit of ten combatants fully armed and briefed rode two-up in five vehicles. A derelict fuel station, long since disused, fronting an abandoned scrap yard set skulking in a natural hollow of barren waste ground was their target. Drone survey reported neither site was occupied by anyone other than the suspects. Brock thumbed the handset:

"Okay guys, this should be a textbook surprise attack. Follow the plan as arranged at the briefing and nothing should go wrong. We're a mile now from the contact point; lights out, night vision on and keep alert. When I give the signal, follow the buffalo-horn plan as arranged: vehicles one and two, horn around to the right, three and four, horn around to the left. Take your positions as given at the briefing. Sergeant Da Silva and I will take the centre line. At the first flare, fire your stun grenades and C.S. Gas through the windows of the gas station as per the briefing. This should clear the area. Take prisoners if you have to but shoot to kill if needs be ... Negative that, shoot to kill on sight! These guys are bad news and are sure to turn nasty if we give them half the chance. Good luck crew, but I doubt you'll need it – we're not expected at their party. I'm sure I don't have to tell you to check your weapons. Any questions – over," none came. "Brock, over and out."

"You okay, Loot?"

"Yeah, I'm fine thanks, Grady. I'm not a great fan of these large-scale ops, too much and too many to rely on and way too much to go wrong. I much prefer it when it's only us."

"I'm right with you there, Boss."

"Yeah, thanks, Grady."

In the stifling heat of the night, sweat leached from her pores, ran down her back and into her seat pan. She mopped sweat from her brow in the humid air. Grady felt her pain, clucked his tongue and looked up to her:

"Somethin' else buggin' you, Loot?"

'*Fuck, this guy's psychic*', she mused, but decided now was not a good time.

"Yeah, maybe I'll run it by you later."

"Ok-ey' – Lieutenant Brock…" With a heavy smile and a heart to match, she turned to Grady, ruffled his hair and tweaked her cute nose.

"If you really must know: I was worried about leavin' my hooker gear at the Mertz place – figured I might be needing it again soon!" She flicked coy eyebrows at the big man brightening a dark moment. Lustrous eyes, eager, sprang back to her.

"I sure would want to help you out there, Loot," said Grady racking his brows.

"I'll bet you would, Shiney … I'll bet you would!" She tweaked her nose, turned back into the moment. Sweat trickled down her body soaking her heavy combat clothes.

"It looks *very* quiet, Grady," she spoke with a hushed caution as they moved in close to the mark and sat tense in the stilled silence of an overcast night.

"Hmm – Maybe a little *too* quiet, Loot?" said Grady slow-whistling a tuneless melody through a mouthful of gum. He dragged a sleeve across his sweating brow and would give a month's salary for an open window.

"I don't see any lights or signs of life anywhere," she said, massaging her neck and wiping damp hair from her vision. "Something about this doesn't smell right."

"You think we should abort …your call, Loot!"

A mind in doubt played a worried chin. She shook her head, blew out a heavy breath.

"No. It's too late to pull out now. I wouldn't want to be hit on the run," she ran her hand through damp locks, "open the roof, Grady; set me up with the fifty-cal."

"You got it, Loot."

She climbed up into the station behind the fifty-calibre. Perched ready, she felt a little cooler in the windless night air. She wrapped a black bandeau around her head to soak up sweat and keep the hair from her eyes. Searching for movement, she scanned through night vision glasses into the bleak, dark landscape, but could see nothing of interest or worry; but that in itself caused her to worry. What bothered her most was the absence of any sounds from nature. '*Maybe not so unusual in such a barren landscape,*' she mused, but in truth, she didn't believe it. There was a very bad smell about it all; a smell as if we're about to tread in something very nasty she reasoned. She called down to Grady:

"It's my gut feeling we've been set up."

"Okay … then let's get ready to shoot our way out, Loot. It won't be the first time…"

"Let's hope it's not the last…" she said and cocked the fifty-calibre. She keyed the handset:

"Okay, Guys, quiet now, change of plan; it's a Red Alert. I think we've been set up, it could be a trap so keep your eyes peeled." *Thank god for electric vehicles,* she mused.

"Roll forward, keep quiet and take up your positions. Stay alert, fire at will, and to kill! Over."

The moment she thumbed off, two bright deafening explosions from out on the horns lit up the sky and kicked both lead vehicles cartwheeling skywards in balls of flame. Before they'd hit the ground Brock had pumped hundreds of rounds from the fifty-Cal into the derelict building. Grady snaked the semi away from their position seconds before an I.E.D exploded right where they'd been sitting, showering them in dust and debris. A rocket-propelled grenade spat from their rear found its mark in Jeep number three.

"THE BASTARDS ARE BEHIND US, GRADY! SPIN ROUND, NOW!" She screamed into the handset: "ABORT, ABORT! ALL UNITS, ABORT NOW, REPEAT, ABORT NOW, OVER!" Grady spun the wheels, snaked a passage through scrubland kicking up dust and gravel to make a more difficult target. A rocket grenade roared up into the sky as Brock raked near six-hundred rounds per minute of armour-plated gunfire from the Heckler-and-Koch fifty-calibre into bright gun flashes emanating from low in the dirt. "THEY'RE DUG IN GRADY, GO...! LET'S GET OUT OF HERE, WE'RE SITTING DUCKS!"

Snake swerving, the crew in the remaining Jeep were sweeping the area with Napalm from a high-power flame-thrower. A lone figure engulfed in flames rose up and ran screaming to nowhere before collapsing in the dust. Brock ended his misery with the fifty-calibre. Raking lead across the landscape, Brock gave cover to the Jeep as they retreated leaving behind them; a sea of fire; six dead Agents; three wrecked vehicles and not a sign of Lu-Lu Mbangang. Grady gunned the motor. A dust cloud rose in their wake. Brock thumbed the handheld.

"Agent vehicle four, situation report, over."

"Agent Cox, vehicle four: my partner's bleeding from a stomach wound and we're losing power fast, our electrical system must have taken a hit, over."

"Copy that, Agent Cox. Keep up close. We'll stop up ahead and pick you up. Keep a good lookout and be quick. Will you need assistance, over?"

"Negative, I think we can manage. Agent Cox over and out."

Brock scanned around with night vision glasses searching for a safe drop point. At the hit objective behind she could see nothing of concern; saw only black smoke clouding from the burning glow in their wake.

"Okay, get past those trees, Grady; there's a clearing between them and the next copse, pull over if you can, I'll cover with the fifty-calibre. Be ready to kick up dust as soon as we get those guys on board."

"You got it, Loot."

"For *fucks sake*, Grady!"

"Sorry, Lieutenant – Brock." She bent down and slapped Grady's cap off.

"It's Maddie, smart-ass!" Beaming a smile he blew her a kiss and skidded the combat vehicle to a halt in the clearing.

The two Agents dumped their Jeep. Agent Cox dragged his partner across to the semi. Brock pumped lead from the fifty-calibre into their stricken Jeep.

"Let the motherfuckers try and fix that back up an' runnin' in a hurry, "she growled. In a white blinding flash, the gas cylinders from the flamethrower gun pack exploded as she spoke and disintegrated the Jeep in a fountain of flaming steel. She winced from the heat on her face, kept cover with the fifty-Cal as Grady hauled the Agents into the semi.

"Go Grady, let's get out of here!"

Putting distance between themselves and a ball of flame, Grady drove hard heading back to the A-Zone. Brock shaking with adrenaline in a body drenched with sweat, collapsed back in her seat and closed her eyes. She felt lucky again; figured if she was a black cat she'd have been dead long ago. She thumbed the hand-held to call for the blood wagon.

"It's been a tough day, Grady."

"Be a tougher one tomorrow, Loot."

"No doubt about that, Shiney." Brock danced an eyebrow, spat out the window at the thought of LePage.

*   *   *

Chapter Fourteen

In an atmosphere cold enough to chill hot thoughts down to ice cubes, Brock sat in contempt silence. Overhead, the rusting fan groaned out its cheerless rhythm, marking down the seconds to a further bout of mental and verbal conflict. LePage drew in a deep breath and exhaled through pursed lips before he spat out with vehemence:

"Talk to me, Lieutenant." LePage, an angry man oozing charm acrid as the puss from an erupting boil, didn't turn from his window. Provoked by frustration, Brock glared up at the back of his head, looked for a good place to bury the hatchet ... then growled:

"It was a fucking set-up ... Sir."

LePage span round on a heel; with both hands pushed deep into his pockets he bent forward in his intimidating mime's mimic of a question mark.

"A set-up – huh! Do please *explain*, Lieutenant?"

"We walked straight into a trap. They were expecting us, knew our every move all the way down to our pre-organised positioning. They must've been tuned in to our airwaves. How – who the fuck knew?" She asked, glaring up into angry eyes with her own angrier eyes of thunder.

"We lost six good men and four of our best vehicles," ranted LePage, "so I ask you again, Lieutenant: explain to me how this could be? Who already knew the details?"

Again he bent forward over her and growled into the crown of her head:

"Sergeant Da Silva perhaps?"

"As I'm sure you are well aware, Sir – he was not at the briefing so could not have known any details until we closed on the location." Shuddering at a thought, Brock winced inwards, remembered the written orders she'd left open on the coffee table. She slow-closed her eyes, chewed on her bottom lip and flushed red. *'No way... It couldn't be; he wouldn't, not Grady ... no, no, no?*

LePage turned; standing erect he held tight lips. With both hands deep in long pockets, he stretched his neck and glared down over glowing cheeks at her.

"So, you still maintain Sergeant Da Silva could not have been a party to it, and what's more – *not* a plant?"

"He put his life on the line along with the rest of us, Sir."

"Was he wounded?" scowled LePage.

"No, Sir, neither was I — not physically anyway."

"How very convenient, don't you think, Lieutenant Brock?"

"Sergeant Da Silva was in the truck, driving, behind armour-plate, Sir."

"Ah... Again, Lieutenant – How very convenient!"

"Three vehicles were blown to pieces, Sir. Six Agents died; it could've as easily been us who took the hit. If it wasn't for Sergeant Da Silva's quick thinking we'd have both been blown to pieces from an I.E.D."

"Yes, but you weren't, were you, Lieutenant? In the one vehicle very different from the other four, you both escaped completely unscathed."

"Well, I think you'd better drag your sorry ass down to the vehicle pound and take a good look yourself at what's left of our combat vehicle. IT'S FUCKING RIDDLED WITH BULLET HOLES!" *'Asshole!'*

LePage shuddered, turned back to the mysterious comfort of his window. Angry ears twitched, glowed red east and west of a balding scalp. Slow nodding his head, he sucked dry lips back onto his teeth. He didn't turn, but scowled:

"Thank you, Lieutenant. Please send me your report – *IN FULL!*"

Brock stood, dearly wanted to shoot the bastard. She left the door swinging open as she strode out into the corridor and took the stairway down to the car park. The black monkey clung tight to her back as she slunk heavy steps across to the Jeep.

"How'd it go, Lieutenant?" asked Grady holding the door for her.

"Let's just say: last night was a fucking cakewalk," she smiled coy green eyes at him.

"I need a drink."

"You got it, Loot"

Jackie Olsen swept on a dusty carpet, then, dusted out through the door into the street. He stepped aside as Grady followed Brock into the bar.

"Wow! You guys been up all night?" Jackie read volumes in the silent answer from Brock's face.

"Two Jacks Mr. Olsen, make it large ones."

"Comin' up..."

"New window looking good, Jackie," small talked Grady.

"Yeah – it looks a hell of a lot better than you two guys do, that's for sure."

"Well, we look a helluva lot better than we feel if it's any consolation believe me! Bring a bottle over, Jackie; we'll take a soft seat in the booth."

"You got it, Sergeant."

A moment of reverie slunk past as Grady watched Brock quiet-moan, open-mouthed with her eyes closed as she raised her arms; hard nipples staked their claim in her shirt as she stuck out her chest and stretched her neck up over tired shoulders against the rear leatherette of the booth. She relaxed her body and turned to Grady.

"Okay, Grady, what've we got?"

"It's more a question of what ain't we got, Loot?"

"Too many questions, Grady; some bastard out there is checkin' on our every move. I get the impression that same someone is using us to bring down the drug cartel migrating up from the O-Zone to right here in our own backyard. And there's only one reason for that I can think of . . ."

"To start up another cartel?" offered Grady.

"Yeah, you're right on the big money there, Sergeant."

"Yungen," suggested Grady.

"Also right on the money; but so far not even a sight or a sound from the bastard. It doesn't ring true," replied Brock digesting a bad thought. Glass chinked a high note as Grady re-charged their glasses with golden liquid.

"The bastard hasn't surfaced, Loot; and there's not even any talk of him from anyone, other than a few whispers from the vomit down in the dregs; which as we well know could be nothin' more than a heavy dose of bullshit."

"Mm-mm, yeah I agree," Brock, sucked her tongue aloud, "maybe it's all a blind alley. Or could just be – that's what someone out there wants us to think, and this could all be nothing more than one great big ruse."

"So who do ya' think tipped off Mbangang?"

"There's only one way to find out, Grady."

"Boss ...?"

She flashed her lashes. "Let's go an' ask him! Finish our drinks first, then I need to check Willy Slack's cell phone; maybe we can get some info from there." Brock picked up her glass, strolled over to the dusty Grand, lifted the lid, ran up the chromatic scale and meandered into a sultry blues.

*   *   *

A dog's paw scratched out a welcome on her entrance door as they climbed the last few steps to her apartment.

"Bingo, take it easy with my paintwork, buddy."

Fingering the tonic over three octaves, Heidi stopped hammering out scales and turned to the sound of the door opening.

"Don't stop sweetheart, it's only us. Help yourself to a drink, Grady. There's beer in the cooler or coffee in the machine." She wandered into her bedroom and left Grady watching coffee percolate in the kitchen.

Relaxed back on her bed, she closed her eyes, homed in on an electric blue vision and relished a private moment of solitude. She unwound, fantasized, savoured a cloistered thought until Heidi hit a dissonant chord on the piano and broke the moment. Brock took a deep breath, opened her eyes, shook her head and sprang back into reality. She picked up and checked the recharged cell phone. With a heavy frown, she stared down at the phone, rolled off the bed and strolled out into the main room, looked quizzical at Grady and stretched out her hand, palm up cradling the phone . . .

"It's been wiped..." she uttered, looked to Grady but questioned to no-one with her eyes. The black monkey clung on tight.

"Check if the unit's directory service guy can source the number," suggested Grady.

"Okay; I'll give it a try but don't hold your breath."

She ambled back into her bedroom, sat on the bed and went through the usual security rigmarole and waited... Five minutes later her phone rang.

"Lieutenant Brock, this phone was lifted from a bag in the Mall two weeks ago. I'm sorry, I couldn't get much from it, but there *were* six calls recorded to one number in the O-Zone, along with many more to a local take-out, and uh-mm ..." he cleared his throat, "and some to a local escort agency."

"Okay, thank you. Any info on the six to the O-Zone – Agent Grant, isn't it?"

"Yes ma'am, let me see...Yes, six calls to a phone registered to a Rupert B. Dibble."

Brock suppressed a snigger. "*Dibble,* really? Any address, Agent Grant?"

"Yes, I have the address right here Lieutenant." He relayed it across to her. Brock scratched down the address on a notepad.

"Thank you, Agent Grant, much appreciated," she closed the call. The smell of fresh-brewed coffee lured her back into the main room.

After giving the matter some thought, she shrugged her shoulders and mused: *'What the hell, if he sees it now, we'll be leaving soon anyway – then it'll be too late to do anything. Bad thoughts Maddie,' . . . Ashamed!* Without more ado, she tossed the notepad onto the coffee table for Grady to see. *'He couldn't be a plant. No way, not Grady, he's my buddy, I've known him too long. Could be it's just some bastard trying to put a wedge between us… Fuck LePage!'*

"Rupert B. Dibble," roared Grady, "who the hell has a name bad as that? Please don't tell me the 'B' stands for, Bear," he nearly rolled off the sofa clutching his stomach.

"I guess we'll find out when we get to number 15 Spring-Valley Mews," Brock grinned and tipped a wink. She sipped hot coffee laced with bourbon.

"Spring Valley Mews – sounds cosy."

"Yeah, Sergeant, cosy as a cushion on *Ol' Sparky* – You drive, Grady."

*   *   *

Fifteen Spring Valley Mews lived up to all expectations, and then some. A festering terrace of rundown, near derelict wood-clad shacks, echoed a stark resemblance to the decaying sparse tooth grin from the mouth of a deadbeat hobo. The sole colourful vision on offer, although fading in its cheerless surroundings, was a red bell wire hanging from a hole in the door jamb of number 15. Kicking out a clear place to stand, Grady stepped up to the plate, standing amongst a mess of bursting bags of trash, hooch bottles and beer cans long since deplete from intoxicating comfort. He fist-hammered on the door. Grey paint mutated many summers ago to khaki, compliments of Mother Nature, flaked, surrendered, and rained down onto the doorstep. It was the best and sole reply he would get from number 15.

Number 17 was an empty shell with ply-board windows and a caved in roof, but two doors away at number 19 a fierce argument polluted the atmosphere. Having ended a lengthy service as a moth's paradise, a pair of dreary drapes did little to muffle the dispute. Grady walked over and rapped loud on the door, cut off the argument, then shuffled his feet in the silent stench of poverty. After a pause fraught with tension, a lone voice called out:

"Yeah, whadda ya' want?"

"You've won the lottery, Sir."

Feet shuffled on bare boards; the door snapped open a little. A grog blossom nose peeked through the gap.

"How come, I never did no lottery?"

"You *are* Rupert B. Dibble, aren't you?"

"What? Nah, not me – never heard of him, wrong house!"

As the door started to close Grady stabbed his foot in the doorway and slammed into the door with his shoulder, knocking the guy flat out. Grady stepped in over the threshold. A forlorn-looking girl in a leopard print skirt, obviously tight enough to limit the blood supply to her brain, stared at Grady through two bruised and blackened eyes. Her jaw dropped open revealing the few teeth she still had left. Lucky girl – or was she?

"Okay. Thanks for inviting me in," said Grady, "now, I would like to know … who lives, at number fifteen."

"Who's askin'?" Grady took a deep breath, looked down at the deadbeat, slow-shook his head, sucked on his teeth, closed his eyes and spoke in a hushed growl sounding rough as a rake dragging over heavy gravel.

"Ya' know I'm gettin' kinda tired of hearing that answer, buddy." Cautious eyes blinked, stared up at Grady's twitching two-twenty pounds of body bulk. A slow mind thought quick, raised a hand in surrender; didn't want to prompt yet another beating from a stranger's knuckled fist in this violent, desperate society he'd been unfortunate enough to wash up in.

"Okay, okay – It's a big guy called Speed." Grady nodded a *'good boy,'* lowered his head down close to a terrified ear burning red and smacked a playful palm on a quivering cheek.

"And where, would I find this, *big guy called Speed? –* Sing me a song, dog breath."

Dragging a wet tongue across dry lips, dog breath paused for a moment, tossed the odds and then, thought better of it.

"Try 'MAMA KOOL'S' Pool bar and Pleasure centre, down on main. He hangs out there most days doin' business."

Grady turned to Brock, shrugged, spread his arms hands palm up. He turned back to the canary.

"Thanks for your help, Sir. Maybe you *should* do the lottery, give this shithole a coat of paint – if only you could win big enough!"

"Don't tell anyone I told ya," pleaded dog breath, hid his face, stayed down low.

"Mama's the word," drawled Grady, dropped a wink down to the guy and said: "Give your lady a cuddle for me, but this time don't make it so tight around her throat." He turned to his smiling lieutenant and bounced his brows. – *Looking good!*

"Good work, Sherlock Watson," drawled Brock leant back on their vehicle with arms folded and legs crossed in a ray of bright sunshine. Emerald green eyes sparkling bright below raised sunnies threw a complement to the big man.

"No wonder Speed changed his name – no contest." chuckled Grady. "Hey – You don't really think the B really stands for Bear do ya', Loot?"

"You've missed your vocation, Sergeant."

"Yeah'– how's that?"

"You could've turned a fortune writing Christmas jokes for table crackers," she snapped out a wry smile: "Let's go an' get us some *pleasure,* at MAMA KOOLS."

A thick dust cloud blossomed high in their wake as Grady drove down Main: a dirt-laden street polluted with a decaying mess of tin shacks draped with corroding satellite discs, rusting hulks of cars jacked on bricks and hungry mange-ridden hounds with corrugated flanks skulking in shadows scrounging for nourishment. The whole place was nothing more than a colossal monument to squalid decay and poverty. Brock scanned the area through the side screen; immune to such things way beyond her control, she frowned, relaxed back in her seat, closed her eyes and reflected back into the far distant past, searching for any moment when she might have enjoyed something close to pleasure herself. It was an empty thought.

Grady skirted potholes, drunks, and stray dogs all the way along the dirt road to the clip joint at the pleasure centre.
Agent Grant picked up the call from Brock. She relayed her call sign and waited in silence for voice recognition.

"Okay, Lieutenant, go ahead."

"I need any info you've got on a Rupert B. Dibble, of fifteen, Spring Valley mews, a shanty in the O-Zone. I'm sorry, I don't have an area code," she chuckled at the irony.

"No problem, Lieutenant."

Marking time, she drummed her fingers as she wandered her gaze around the derelict landscape; a region burdened with despair and pungent misery spawning low-life scum bad as or even worse than Speed, washing them up with the rest of the dregs around the high tide mark in the O-Zone.

Stargazing, she sat back, took her eyes out of focus, fantasized off to a far better place in the hue of blowtorch blue.

The red bell flashed on her phone, broke the moment. She picked up.

"Okay, Lieutenant. – Rupert B. Dibble, A.K.A, *Speed,* highly intelligent, IQ way above normal, but a rap sheet longer than a wedding speech. I'd read it out to you, Lieutenant but its early afternoon now and I'd appreciate getting home before dark." Brock smiled to herself; warmed to this guy. "I think you should be extremely careful in dealing with this particular person, Lieutenant."

"Thank you, Agent Grant. I'll call if I need more information. You have a good night."

"Thank you, Lieutenant. You too," but somehow, deep down – he feared she wouldn't.

*   *   *

A rusted strip board of flashing lights, having long since lost their virginal glow, graced the entrance doors into MAMA KOOL'S. Nailed on the door, a hand-drawn sign cautioned: *Heaven's free, but in here you gotta pay.* Grady, first across the threshold, pulled out and dusted a barstool, sat down his two twenty pounds and ordered a drink across a rough-sawn wood top bar, long since alienated with help from a damp rag. Brock strolled through the door one minute later. Discreet eyes motioned to a lethargic body sat in a wall alcove at a small steel-legged, glass-top table, which didn't look as if it was accustomed to being ragged clean too often either. She threw a tactful wink back to Da Silva but didn't really need to: the mark was as obvious as a moustache on the Mona Lisa. Two non-matching chairs crying out for paint chaperoned the non-matching table. Brock drew out the empty chair, looked down at a whiskey-soaked lump of muscle and asked:

"Mind if I sit?" Speed's head bounced up, snapped out of what seemed a semi-mindless coma. He brought his stare straight into a magnetic pair of stunning green eyes. His jaw dropped.

"Is this my lucky day or what, oh-pretty lady?" he drawled, then moved his slow gaze from her bright eyes down to a chest throbbing with a hard heart behind a snap button cotton shirt. Craning his heavy bulk across the table, Speed strained his attention through the glass-top down to her crotch.

"WHOOA...!" The sinister sight of a three-fifty-seven, cocked and pointed at his own crotch smacked him across the cheeks like a slap from a wet fish. He recoiled back.

"You sure got my attention, pretty lady."

"Smart boy!"

"Still breathin' above the dirt so far – so, what can I do for you, pretty lady?"

"You can stop callin' me, pretty lady for a start."

"Okay – then how about I call you, Lieutenant Brock?" Showing no surprise or emotion, she didn't blink. Cool as shower water in a flop-house, Speed slow-stroked his chin and stared into her eyes with a visual sense she found hard to explain. She rallied:

"That'll work, Speed – Or should I call you Mister Dibble, or maybe you'd prefer Rupert?" His face boiled somewhere between thunder and confusion, then surrendered, smiled and relaxed back into passive compliance. Long thin fingers similar to those of a Bass Fiddle player continued to easy-massage on a stubbled chin. He drew in a short sharp breath and cocked out a small laugh.

"You're a tough lady . . . Who sent you?"

"Nobody sent me."

"Then, how'd ya' find me?"

"Started off with a guy called, Johnny B," she answered. With his mouth open he nodded slow and didn't take his dark stare from her,

"I take it you an' your shadow over at the bar, didn't come across Johnny B at the annual general meeting of the local golf club?"

'This guy's sure got some I.Q. Not the usual dumbo. Be careful, Maddie,' mused Brock.

"No, we didn't. But my shadow *did* show him a few good swings."

"Yeah, so I heard – maybe a few strokes too for Willy Slack?"

Nodding her head slow, Brock smiled at the touché.

"Mm-mm . . . no, that wasn't anything to do with us. Willy went over the bar with a breaststroke with an over-enthusiastic cuddle from his handler. He took an impromptu diving lesson. I guess you could say: he made the hole-in-one."

Speed nodded, lifted the corners of his lips, worked his chin, didn't take his cold-eyed stare from her diamond-sparkle eyes.

"So, I'll ask again… What can I do for you, Lieutenant Brock?"

"Information – I need some information."

Speed bounced an eyebrow, got bright of eye and asked:

"What's in it for me?"

Brock stared inward at a cold thought and dug deep.

"How about we agree to leave you alone, keep off your back; don't point any hardware your way?"

Speed leant back, laced his fingers behind his head, looked across to the bar and saw a dangerous man raise a glass – and then an eyebrow. Speed leant forward, massaged pursed lips and asked:

"How do I know you guys are for real?"

"For one simple reason: – we haven't splattered your brains all over the wall yet." Speed nodded slow, lifted his whiskey jigger, drained the contents, slow-rolled the liquor around in his mouth, carefully placed the glass onto the table and lifted his eyebrows.

"Can I get you guy's a drink?"

"Sure… why not?"

Speed led the way into a small tasteless backstage office, decorated in a cut not unusual for the O-Zone, which is either a very low cut or no cut at all. In a room at best lacking sensual gratification, Brock rested her body down with care onto a broke-back plastic chair. Grady stood, turned down an offer of an upturned beer crate. Despite the overt austerity, copious golden bourbon flowed into sparkling cut glass. Leant back in his creaking chair, Speed raised his jigger.

"So … Whadda we got, Lieutenant?"

"Karl-Heinz Yungen. What do you know about him?"

"You should know more about him than I do," answered Speed.

"And why would that be?"

"Well, for one thing, he's living the high life in the A-Zone, not down here with us in this shithole."

"In the A-Zone – Where?" shot Brock back, furrowed her brow. Speed snapped out a laugh, said:

"You tell me; then we'll both know."

"I think Yungen's fixing to take down your operation, Speed."

"The way I see it, you're not far wrong there, pretty lady. And, as far as I can see, he's already got you guys workin' it out for him."

"How do you figure that?"

"Well it seems to me, you've been rubbin' my guys out all the ways up and back down the line."

"We're just doing our job, nothin' more. We work on info and feedback – do what we're told; it's nothin' personal," she said. "It's my gut feeling there's a plant somewhere along the line fuelling their personal agenda. We've trod on too many rakes to think otherwise." She sipped her drink, stared at him over her glass.

"Bingo, pretty lady!" cheered Speed, raised his glass, "between you an' me, I hear that plant's high up in your operation; wants to cash-in on the takeover when it happens."

Grady shuffled loose feet, spoke loud.

"Got a name for that plant, big guy?"

"Not yet – But I'm working on it."

"What about Lu-Lu Mbangang," suggested Brock?

"Lewis Mbangang's ten cents, he's clocking up borrowed time," replied Speed.

"Where can we find him?" asked Brock.

"Hangs loose above a clip joint, corner of third and seventh." Speed drained his glass, stared a hard look into nowhere, then added: "run down muscle bar, sumpthin' along those lines."

"Thanks, Speed – we'll be in touch."

"Lookin' forward to it, pretty lady."

"I'm sure you are – Mister Dibble."

*   *   *

Chapter Fifteen

After sweating through a ten-minute drive in the fading light of a hot July day in a deadbeat shanty town, Grady pushed open a rust-eaten corrugated steel door at the disused clip joint on the corner of third and seventh. The door wasn't locked and probably never had been. The foot of the door groaned in protest scraping a path across broken concrete, then jammed solid halfway. Inside the cavernous, dark, windowless room, strewn with broken chairs upturned tables and broken glass, the sight greeting them resembled the aftermath of a bar-room fight from an old cowboy movie. With guns drawn to follow the theme, Grady shadowed Brock into the clip joint. Sharp eyes peered into the gloom, bright eyes glowed back red under the beam from a flashlight, rats held court in the shadows. The customary O-Zone fragrance of body odour and urine screwed up a face and brought tears to the eye. A light switch toggled up and down, didn't work, produced nothing; no surprise there.

"Push the door wide open, Grady let's get some more light in here." Grady used his heavy bulk against the door. It didn't put up much of a fight. A beam of sunlight cast low from the western sky shone bright, flooding across the floor revealing the true contents of the dingy room. The golden glow of sunset shimmering through the dilapidated clip joint made even 'MAMA KOOL'S' dingy bar room appear right up there in a class befitting the Taj Mahal. Brock took her stare through the gloom up to the rafters. She clucked her tongue; true as Speed had said – Lu-Lu Mbangang sure was *hangin'* around.

"Looks to me that someone's been showing him the ropes, Lieutenant."

"There goes that *cracker* humour again, Grady."

"It's my pleasure, Loot."

"Well, it sure wasn't *his*! Let's cut him down and check him out. We're about all out of leads right now."

"Do ya' think maybe someone found out he was a snitch?"

"Could be, Grady; but I rather think *someone* knew we were on our way here to ask him a few questions."

"No way, who knew? It was only you an' me, Loot; no-one else could've possibly known."

"I think my apartment's bugged – It's gotta' be!" She shook her head in disbelief at the big man.

Mbangang's body revealed nothing other than a dog-eared I.D, a long expired driving license and a very bad smell.

"Do you think Speed already knew about this? Or could be he did this himself, Loot?"

"If he did," she said, "then why would he tell us where we might find him? It doesn't make any sense. No, that's crazy." Grady shrugged, pushed his hat back on his head and contemplated down at Mbangang's corpse.

"Crazy psychopaths enjoy these kind of games."

"Yes, but I don't think Speed's a psycho, Grady. He's just one big, bad motherfucker who is about to lose his position of power; and well he knows it. Maybe we can use it to our advantage."

"Ya' think, Boss?"

"You got a better idea, Shiney?" Grady soft-whistled his tuneless melody, thought deep, then said:

"Speed told us Mbangang hangs loose *above* the clip joint. Let's take a trip upstairs – leave this mess for the rats and roaches."

Rotting wood creaked out a warning for the unwary as Brock and Grady trod tentative steps up the staircase to the top-floor apartment. Pin-ups of naked girls added a colourful aphrodisiac to the dingy walls shrouding the stairway. At the top of the stairs a door of bare plywood hung loose on rusted hinges. Deplete of a lock, latch or handle it swung easy as Brock pushed it open and gazed inside. She figured: *apartment* was far from an appropriate word to describe the sight confronting her.

"How the hell can someone live in such a shithole?" she uttered to no-one. A bed sheet, bearing a stark resemblance to the *Turin shroud,* covered most part of a filthy urine and sweat-stained mattress set loose on the floor; which on closer inspection looked a hell of a lot cleaner than the bed sheet.

"Could be this guy shops at the same store as Johnny B, Loot?" Brock raised her eyes. *There goes Groucho again!* Littered across the floor were enough empty beer cans to jam a junk-yard compacter. A rusted bucket in the corner offered nothing of value, just a very nasty smell. Filth-stained cast-off clothing, used condoms, syringes and spliff dog ends filled the voids between the beer cans. It all made a Tracey Emin installation of her *bedroom scene* from way back in the late nineties look five-star Ritz.

"I guess as a plus for Mbangang – it looks as if he's in a far better place now." She rolled her eyes, "let's get out of here, Grady."

"Wipe your feet on the way out, Loot."

"Grady!"

"I'm right here, Lieutenant," said Grady through a big smile.

"You've been watchin' those re-runs of the Marx brothers – *again!*"

"I gotta' get a little humour in my life now and then, Boss. It helps to keep me sane."

She smacked his chin, playful.

"You need a lady in your life."

*   *   *

The sun, crouched low, curtsied and ducked behind the horizon saluting a parting flash in a good day as Brock and Grady headed west back to the A-Zone.

"Where's all the money go, Loot? These guys don't have a buck to scratch their backsides with; so what gives?"

"Beats me, Grady, drugs are top dollar, the money's gotta go somewhere. Maybe we've been lookin' in the wrong place. Or maybe we've been *told* to look in the wrong place," she shrugged, "I just don't know anymore."

"We're hired to exterminate the vermin; we ain't paid to do no thinkin', Loot."

"Well, maybe we should start doin' some thinking."

"I'm right behind you there, Loot." Brock stared at the big man over a pair of imaginary lowered glasses,

"Careful, Grady!" she blew the big man a kiss.

*   *   *

Jackie Olsen racked up two shots as he checked his favourite customers strolling in through the bar-room door.

"Good to see you guys are still breathin'."

"You couldn't live without us, Jackie."

"I hear that, you're my best customers."

"Looks to me, we're your *only* customers."

"Times are tough, Lieutenant."

"Then have one on us, Jackie," Brock, tossed a big bill across the counter, "keep 'em comin'."

She took her drink, ambled across to the piano, lifted the lid, teased out some timeless Bill Evans and immersed herself into a semi-hypnotic state revered by only the most creative of musicians.

"She should be killing people with her piano playing not a three-fifty-seven," spoke Jackie across the bar.

"Piano playing itself kills the player, Jackie," answered Grady. "People love to listen to music, couldn't live without it, but won't dip into their pockets and pay a cent out to the poor guys creating it. If you ever want to get a great band together, go on down to the welfare office; there's great musos all lined up ready for ya'... Take your pick!"

"Yeah, you're on the big money there, Sergeant; I hear you loud and clear." With his broad shoulders, Grady aped an agreed shrug, rolled his jigger in his fingers, stared deep into the amber liquid, prophetic.

"Seems to me you can live off a three-fifty-seven, but not a Steinway eighty-eight; what a crazy world. Set 'em up, Jackie."

*   *   *

A potent sun had to raise high in the sky before it would permeate powerful enough rays through the defence of heavy shades to coax Brock from a state of slumber into one of conscious thought; positive thinking might not be far behind. Half-awake in the half-light she stared up at a blank ceiling, focused on a corpus of minutely coloured dots: blues, reds and yellows, which en masse reflected a dirty white. Her mind wandered back to 'Le Poseuses:' an artwork painted by the French post-impressionist Georges Seurat, over one hundred years ago. How many other eyes have ever noticed such a conundrum she wondered? *'How sad – but more so for who – maybe it's me!'*

She turned to the bedside table, looked across to *Jack*; he returned nothing back beyond an empty stare. Yawning wide in protest at the thought of another day in covert security, she stretched out her lithe body, rolled out of bed and drifted across into the shower room with scant enthusiasm for the day ahead.

With both hands pushed hard against the shower wall, her head bowed, she stood and let steaming water cascade down over her body. Locked in rapture, she didn't move until the doorbell sang out its unwelcomed request. She flipped the shower off, wrapped her body in a loose towel, trod a wet trail to the front door and peeked through the spy hole. Stood outside in a miniature optical vignette, a smiling Sergeant Grady Da Silva held up two take-out coffees. She sprang the door; he stepped inside, grinned as he checked the not-unusual sight of the voicemail flashing blue on the side stand.

"Don't you ever sleep, Grady?" The sofa groaned as he sat down. He smiled and sent her a wink.

"It's ten-fifteen, Loot, get dressed, I'll treat you to breakfast." He nodded across to the flashing blue, lifted his brows.

"Clod's on the warpath."

Steak and eggs pleaded mercy from a hot plate at Skinny's diner. Without enthusiasm, Brock fork-picked at the food, turned to the coffee; she needed caffeine not protein. In a stance similar to a lost soul praying for a miracle, she kept her head bowed low, and with a blue mood in a blue day stared into her lap.

"What does Clod want?" she asked and gazed a blank look across to Grady whose hang dog eyes focused down to her plate. She nodded him an *okay*.

"Help yourself. I'm done."

He swapped his empty plate for her near full one.

"I guess he wants a rundown on yesterday's movements."

With her mind elsewhere, Brock nodded slow in acknowledgement, Grady shovelled in protein and gazed into curious green eyes.

"How did he know about our movements, yesterday," she asked?

"Beats me, Boss; I didn't tell him – did you?"

"No, I did not."

"More coffee, guys?" asked the waitress. She hovered a coffee jug and a cute smile over their table; her magnetic persona broke into a melancholic thought pattern. Brock smiled back, slid her cup forward. Revitalised now from her blue mood, she found it hard to take her eyes from the radiance of such a beautiful face — a countenance of purity with a saccharine innocence she should never lose.

"Yes, thank you," said Brock.

With his mouth full, Grady shook a *no thanks* and chewed steak. The waitress filled Brock's cup, flashed her lashes, then, with the grace of a Mozart flute sonata, cat-walked a cute body back behind the counter. Grady took no notice – but, to indulge in such pleasure, it was relished with passion by green eyes of envy. A forbidden fantasy, hidden well, faded at the speed of melting ice. In no hurry, Brock turned back to Grady ploughing his way through cholesterol into a further state of obesity.

"Ya' know, Grady, I've been thinking about what Speed told us yesterday . . ."

"Speed the psycho, Loot?" Brock smiled at her sergeant.

"Okay, psycho he may be, but in all seriousness, after what he said about a plant high up in our unit, and the fact Karl-Heinz Yungen may be somewhere here in our midst, I think *maybe* we should heed his words and start looking in our own backyard instead of clearing out an open path for the next cartel to operate in."

"D'ya think we *can* believe him?" queried Grady, shrugging questioned shoulders.

"Right now our choices are a little thin on the ground," she concluded. He nodded in reluctant agreement.

"I hear ya' Loot."

"You didn't much warm to him did you, Grady?"

He looked up, stopped chewing.

"Warm to him? – Why the fuck would I warm to such a piece of degenerate crap?" he shook his head, carried on chewing steak.

"Because he's not stupid; far from it," she answered. "I think he might be able to help us solve a lot of questions no-one else seems to want to answer; especially now as his business is circling the drain."

"Okay, I hear you," he used his aggression to slice steak. "Maybe I'll send him a fucking get well-card after I've beaten the shit out of him."

Brock laughed out loud, shook off the black monkey, sent a sweet smile across to the big man.

"I love you, Grady Da Silva." She twitched her cute nose at him, shrugged off the blues. He smiled back, looked down to the floor looking embarrassed. His ears glowed in a light red hue as he slow-reached into his pocket and slid a gift-wrapped package across the table to her. He didn't look up until he'd finished chewing, then, swallowed hard. She looked to him in question, held her tongue between her teeth and froze, didn't move. He spoke nothing. Head down, he stared up to her through his eyebrows and nodded down to the package. Tentative, she picked it up, unwrapped the packing and drew out a long black velvet-covered box etched in gold. Green eyes, mystified, gazed across the table, saw back only glowing red ears. She looked down to the box, sprung its lid, stared down at the contents: a beautiful gold watch. She said nothing, couldn't; but spoke silent words from moist green eyes as they soft-sparkled a powerful message across to Grady.

"I wanted you to have it, Loot – I bought it for Macey; she never got to see it."

Overwhelmed at the thought of Macey, his eyes welled, echoing with Brock's. She rose from the table, walked round and hugged him hard, ruffled his hair, kissed the crown of his head.

"Grady Da Silva; I've never had *anyone* do such a beautiful thing for me." Tenderly she cupped his head in her hands, stared deep into his teared eyes. "I love you, Grady."

He could only smile, well aware of the intimate ambiguity of such intimation.

"You know, Loot – I wish I could do more, an' take you away to a far, far off distant place, somewhere a long ways away from all this crap we've got goin' on down here." She smiled, looked him in the eyes and feigned a playful slap on his square jaw.

"You're solid gold and diamonds, Grady. Thank you," she smiled through damp eyes. "Talking of *crap*, let's go see what Captain Clod wants," she dangled her watch in front of him, bounced her eyebrows: "no excuse to be late anymore!"

* * *

The grubby window pane reflected back nothing but anger as LePage growled and spat venom into the sad pane.

"YOU'RE LATE!"

"Why, what did we miss?" tested Grady. The smart answer was hiding somewhere high up in the ether, far too high for LePage to reach, even with Grady's metaphorical boot up his backside. LePage drew in a long slow breath, held it as if expecting it to raise him up into a higher divinity. With scant civility in mind, Grady kicked a chair round, sat down hard and cracked a tenon joint. Brock, to remain aloof chose to stand. With folded arms below a cold stare, she leant back against the wall as distant from LePage as she could manage.

"I did not ask you to sit, Sergeant."

"You didn't ask me not to – Sir." LePage pursed white lips glaring back up into the ether. Fuming in silence he turned to Brock.

"Why was I not informed of your mission yesterday before you *chose* to go into the O-Zone without the proper authority and relevant clearance from me?"

"It would seem you already knew about it, Sir."

"Already knew about it – what are you talking about, Lieutenant?"

"As far as I know, Sir, myself and Sergeant Da Silva were the only ones who knew about our *trip* into the O-Zone. We were following up on a hunch," she shrugged her eyes. "We didn't have time to come back and fill out a request form for permission. So – who told you, Sir?" She glared a volley of iced daggers across the room.

"As head of this department, Lieutenant Brock, it is my job to know. It is not *your job* to question me. Do I make myself clear, Lieutenant?" A soft song of snoring cut through the chilled atmosphere; Grady, smiling, with his chin in his chest had his eyes shut. LePage fumed; turned back to the comfort zone of his window and barked into the sorry pane: "Wait outside will you Sergeant — NOW!"

Grady scraped his chair back, reshaped his hat brim, stood and ambled across to the door. He turned and said:

"No coffee and cookies for me today thank you, Sir." He slammed the door behind him as he left.

With both arms folded and a foot tapping at one-eighty beats per minute, LePage seethed and ranted into his window.

"That man is insubordinate to a fault." Fury massaged a tight jaw. Glaring venom into the back of LePage's head, Brock voiced nothing. Her blank face volleyed back only contempt. LePage eased his temperature, turned from his window back to his desk.

"Sit down, Lieutenant."

"Thank you, Sir, but I prefer to stand." LePage nodded with pursed lips, scratched the back of his neck and stared down to the floor. He began to walk round in a circle, but stopped as he realised the confines of his office.

"I would have preferred Mbangang to have been questioned before his demise, Lieutenant."

"It was the sole reason we went there, Sir."

"So, did you not question him before you killed him?"

"We didn't kill him, Sir. Someone else had killed him before we'd got there."

"What? Who? Who killed him?"

"I have no idea, Sir."

"Was Sergeant Da Silva there first, or did you arrive together?"

"I don't think I appreciate your implication, Sir."

"No, I'm sure you don't, Lieutenant. But I'm trying to find out the truth as to what actually happened."

"You can read it in my report, Sir."

"Hmm . . ." LePage drew a sharp breath. "Please file your report at your earliest convenience, Lieutenant."

"Are we done – Sir?" asked Brock. LePage rose from his desk, turned to his window, tapped his foot and answered nothing. Conjuring up a vivacious thought, Brock wondered should she start to snore, figuring if she did, he might throw her out. She smiled, perished the thought, he wasn't worth it. What an asshole!

Sporting a boiling red face of thunder, LePage spun round to her. He looked as if he'd fallen asleep under a sunlamp. He growled at her:

"Have you still no thoughts about a plant, Lieutenant . . . Sergeant Da Silva, perhaps?"

"No I haven't, Sir. But there is definitely someone on the take. I'm sure of it." With a muscle straining to lift an ugly eyebrow over piercing black eyes on a scarlet face, LePage could well have been the perfect portrait model for Francis Bacon in his heyday. Drawing in a deep breath, he turned back to his comfort zone and spoke into his window without turning back to her.

"I see you have a very nice watch there, Lieutenant. It looks, *very*, expensive."

"I wouldn't know, Sir. It was given to me by someone *very*, special." He slow turned his head round to her with a look of disdain. Avoiding her watch, he narrowed his eyes, nodded his head with menace, pursed his lips and looked as if he was preparing to blow a double high top 'C' on a sousaphone. Then, he turned, glared through his faithful ally back out into the comfort of the outside world in the car park.

'What the fuck does he find of any interest in an empty car park?' She mused.

"Thank you, Lieutenant," he snapped out, bereft of compassion.

And fuck you too! She thought. Wished she'd shouted it out aloud.

She left the door swinging on a hinge as she stepped out into the welcome solace of the dingy hallway.

*   *   *

Leant back in the reclined car seat with his grey fedora perched over his face, Grady feigned a snore as she opened the Jeep door.

"So I guess you really *were* tired?"

"Yeah – tired of his bullshit, Loot!"

"I'm pretty much the same way myself, Grady." Glaring back up to the dank office window she hated her thoughts, but nowhere near as much as she hated the one thing in particular stood behind the grimy glass discharging an anti-social odour rancid as the puss from festering boils on the anus of humanity.

She climbed into the Jeep, closed the door, rolled down the side screen, laid her head back and closed her eyes. She spoke soft, almost in a whisper after exhaling a heavy breath.

"I think I should put in for a transfer."

"A transfer . . . to where in the hell?"

"Who knows? We're already in hell, Grady." She turned a radiant face and smiled to the big man, waved her watch in his face.

"Look at the time."

"Lunchtime?" he guessed, screwed his face up. "Let's go see Jackie Olsen."

As Grady drove the Jeep out of the car park she glared back up to LePage's office window and rolled up the side screen in a futile attempt to mentally erase the dissonance.

*   *   *

Chapter Sixteen

The X-90 kicked to the left. Empty shell cases rang down onto a stone floor, bounced and rolled into shadows as Brock emptied the magazine in single-shot mode into a tight group in her target. Only one round went high.

"Nice work, Loot."

She lifted off ear defenders, tousled black locks and clipped on a fresh mag.

"Set me up again, Grady, looks as if I could do with the practice."

"Maybe you should use my twelve-gauge; you don't even have to aim."

"Ach, you know me, Grady, I need a challenge. Anyway if I were to be honest, I prefer my trusty three-fifty-seven. Okay, enough," she concluded. "Let's go grab a coffee."

"Now *there's* a challenge," quipped Grady.

Blowing a deep breath through tight lips, Brock slow-shook her head and flipped her eyes. "Fucking, Marx brothers *again!*"

The vending machine at the shooting range offered little source of enjoyment for the connoisseur; lukewarm coffee had a look and taste similar to muddy water from an out-back sheep-dip.

"Forget it, Grady; let's drop by Skinny's Diner for some decent coffee."

*   *   *

The pretty waitress flashed long lashes, real, not stick-ons, which for a fleeting moment mesmerised Brock until she realised her mindless finger was flicking at her lower lip with her mouth open. But she wasn't drooling – yet.

"Nothing to eat guys?" asked the cute waitress.

"No thanks, not right now, coffee will be fine," answered Brock, returning her smile, revelling in her cute-butt catwalk. She shook out an intimate thought and turned her attention to Grady.

"Ya' know, Grady, I've been thinking . . ."

"Yeah, I try that myself every now and again," he shrugged, "doesn't work out too well for me."

"Okay, Groucho, enough! No, I've been thinking about all the faces we've tracked down to interrogate, and why so many of them have been hit moments before we get the chance to sound them out: Olifi; Slack; Mertz; Mbangang . . ."

"Is this about the *plant* theory, Loot?"

"It's no theory, Grady, believe me. Most of those hits were ten-cents – except one."

"Mertz...?" offered Grady.

"You're right on the money, Shiney! You see, Grady – you *can* think when you try."

She toasted him with her coffee cup held high in the air. "Okay, the truth is: we never had the chance to check out his office, or his apartment."

"I was kinda' busy checkin' somethin' else out if I were to be honest, Loot."

She focused in silence over imaginary glasses, shook her head and blew him a kiss. He chuckled:

"Sorry, Lieutenant, you go ahead, I'm listening."

"So, let's go check his place out and see what we can find," suggested Brock.

"Guys crook as him, bein' a lawyer an' all don't usually leave too many clues lyin' around, Loot. Those kinda slime balls are much too shrewd."

"Nobody's one hundred per cent careful, Grady. Did you ever hear of a guy called, Wolfgang Beltracchi, the German art forger active around the turn of the century?"

"No, can't say I have; must've missed that one back at school."

"Touché!" she chuckled at him. "Well, he made many millions from forging paintings by famous artists and was always very, very careful not to get caught."

"And then . . . ?"

"And then Grady, one small slip sent him to the *tank* for a six stretch."

"How come …?"

"Well, he always used old materials to replicate the old masters. But one time he used a new tube of Flake white, which, although similar to the sort of white used by the old masters, unfortunately for him, contained minute traces of Titanium white – although it was not mentioned on the tube label. Anyway, he used the paint, along with others, to create a fake Max Ernst pastiche."

"So what?"

"Titanium white showed up under microscopic analysis."

"So what's your point, Loot?" asked Grady, furrowing confused brows.

"My point Grady: is that Titanium white hadn't been developed at the time Max Ernst lived. Therefore even someone as careful to cover their tracks as Beltracchi, can still slip up. So, let's go see if we can find some *Titanium white* in the Mertz place, Sergeant."

"Titanium white: sounds something the affluent powder their nose with," mused Grady aloud.

"Yeah, and I'm certain there's sure to be plenty of that kinda junk polluting the Mertz mansion. But first off, let's check to see if the crime scene's still active."

"Maybe we should call up Captain Clod, run it by him, save ourselves from another ball-bustin'."

"No, I don't think it's a good idea, Grady. Let's keep this one to ourselves."

"Okay, your call, Loot."

Sensual eyes flashed across to the cute one for a top-up.

"You appreciate art, Loot? You sure seem to know a lot about it."

"I love beautiful things, Grady," she spoke as the cute waitress arrived with the refill.

*　　　*　　　*

A nonchalant cop, shrouded heavy in lost hope and totally indifferent to a hum-drum day, stood guard behind crime scene tape at the entrance to the Mertz Empire. Had he left the coat hanger in his jacket when he'd dressed for his shift, he might have even had a chance to scare off old ladies. With a cute smile, Brock flashed I.D. The cop returned nothing, neither from his facial expression nor from his mouth: both rang empty as a transvestite's bra. She wondered if she might have got a better response if she'd have flashed him her tits. Maybe next time! After a deep sigh as if he was exhausted from over-exercise, the cop raised his arm to hold up the crime scene tape and made it look as if he was lifting heavy chain link. A blank face motioned them in, then day-dreamed back to wherever it was he'd been before they'd arrived. Brock felt the urge to check him for a pulse. *'Don't bother Lady.'* She shook her head.

"Let's check the office first, Grady. Although I doubt we'll find much. I'm sure the whole place has been turned over already."

"Could be, Loot, but let's not forget – *we're* looking for Titanium white here."

Indignant flies buzzed for altitude as empty file cases rattled out over rusted runners, angry spiders threatened forth their wrath, scurried into shadows. Books, ledgers, printouts and a confusing single black and white patent leather shoe minus its lace littered the floor. Most of the Mertz files had already been removed, along with his computer, phones and a paper shredder. A waste-paper basket revealed nothing other than a rotting banana skin, a torn porn mag and half a dozen empty beer cans. Skulking at the bottom of the basket, something brown and very nasty was best left where it was. An hour-long search produced nothing more than dusted knees and a strong thirst for coffee, or maybe something a lot more potent. Brock threw in the towel.

"Looks as if the place is clean, Loot."

"Not clean, Grady – Cleaned!"

"So we need to find out who by, it could give us a lead?"

"Maybe, Sherlock Watson, although I'll guess a buck to a bag of monkey's nuts, that particular track's cold as a penguin's asshole. Let's check upstairs."

The bedroom door hung loose at a drunken angle, fallen from splintered wood once home to a door hinge. A dried blood stain soiling the stair rug wasn't much of a warm welcome into the room. A cheap wall safe, the victim of a crowbar hung open empty as a cold heart, yawning wide as a Munch scream. Blood-sodden silk littered the floor alongside Ludo's slippers. Brock's hooker's gear she had left scattered across the floor as they'd made a hasty exit was nowhere to be seen. No surprises there; without doubt now serving as a comforter by proxy in the cop house locker room.

Another half-hour search produced nothing apart from the need to take a long hot shower.

"I hear coffee callin', Loot."

"Yeah, let's go, Grady." Brock stopped at the splintered door, noticed a small slither of black plastic amongst the splinters. She ran her fingers along the door head, stopping at a small hole the size of a bottle top drilled into the wooden frame head. Without turning, she held a hand out to Grady. Lacking any exchange of words he flicked his knife open and passed it across to her. She dug out the plastic wrapping and rolled it open, held up its small, but maybe invaluable contents to Grady. He bounced his brows, grinned a wide smile.

"Bingo! Pure Titanium white – good call, Loot." She tweaked her cute nose at him and slipped the SD card into her pocket.

Out in the bright sunlight, the cop's eyes, hidden behind mirror glasses now had a lot more life in them. He raised his arm as if he was expecting someone to sniff at his armpit and apply a social cure with underarm spray. He chewed gum in unnecessary contempt as he held up the crime tape for the lady. He didn't look at her. His whole countenance confirmed his personality had long since migrated south with the swallows for the winter. She should have flashed him her tits; but doubted he would've noticed.

"Should we ask this guy who cleared out here, Loot?" She looked at Grady and smiled:

"More chance of a hit asking him for an update on Einstein's theory of relativity."

*   *   *

On the drive back to Brock's apartment Grady sensed there was something wrong: she was unusually silent.

"You okay, Loot?"

"Yeah, I'm fine – I've been wondering: suppose my apartment *is* bugged – which would mean someone out there knows our every move. It would sure answer a few questions?"

"Yeah, I guess so, Loot."

"In which case: my computer could also be bugged, along with the house phone and my cell phone too. So maybe we shouldn't be checking this SD card in my apartment?"

"How about Jackie Olsen, he must have a computer," offered Grady. She shook black locks.

"No, Jackie's old school, he still communicates by carrier pigeon. And there's no such thing as an internet café anymore; they all got taken away on horse-drawn carts years ago."

"Maybe it's time we swept your place, Boss – I know a guy, very discreet. He may take some time but he does owe me a few favours."

"Okay, Grady give him a call. In the meantime we need to check out this SD card; times running out on us. Our choices are getting thinner than the knees of a cheap suit at a Sunday service," she smiled at the big man. "Let's pay Agent Grant a visit."

"Think we can trust him?"

"Who *can* we trust, Grady?"

"Beats me, Boss, but I guess you're right. You're always right. We've sure gotta' try somethin'."

*   *   *

The office on the third floor enjoyed an uptown view out over the bay. Everything else about it was a disappointment. Agent Grant opened the door to her. His Adam's apple bounced after a deep swallow at the sight confronting him. He flushed red.

"Come in, Lieutenant, it's so nice to put a face to the voice at last."

'*And one hell of a pretty one too,*' he mused.

"I need a favour, Agent Grant."

"And what sort of favour could I help you with, Lieutenant?" Hopeful eyes sparkled as bright as the inner vision flourishing from his groin; then, he sank back into dim reality as he caught sight of himself in the full-length wall mirror.

"A very discreet one Agent Grant." He offered her a chair and sat wide-eyed opposite her at his desk.

"Then I'm your man." His eyes widened, "Tell me: how can I help?"

"Could you check out an SD card for me? There may be nothing on it, but if there is, I'd appreciate a printout with no record either for the SD card or the printout."

Agent Grant took a nervous scan around the room, tucked his head into his neck, sucked his cheeks in and rolled his chair back. He stood and soft-shoed over to the door. With a light but steady hand, he pulled the door open wide enough to poke out his nose and check the hallway, then soft-pushed it shut as if he were closing the door on his dying mother. Brock wondered if he enjoyed old Bond movies.

"I'm sorry, Lieutenant. But everything here is recorded and filed in the system." He kept his voice low as a limbo dancer's backside.

"Who has access to it?"

"Anyone with proper authority, Lieutenant," he shrugged a hollow look.

"It's Brock, Agent Grant. Madeline Brock. Please – call me Maddie."

A red ring flushed around his neck; he could kick himself for not putting on clean underwear when he'd dressed for work.

"Okay, I'll tell you what – Maddie," he edged forward, a lot further in his mind than he managed in his chair and checked round behind him before he spoke in a low voice – a quiet voice, almost at a whisper.

"As a special favour," he paused, took another moment to scan the room, then bent forward in his chair and looked at her through his eyebrows, "I could run it for you on my home computer." He bounced his brows in eager anticipation.

'*Bingo!*' *Sparkling greens had worked their magic.*' She relaxed back into her seat and purred:

"If you could, I'd be forever grateful, you're very sweet," she dropped him a sultry wink. "You're on my Christmas card list, Agent Grant."

"It's Allan – You can call me Al."

'*Doesn't that just sound like a country tune!*' mused Brock.

She left him glowing bright as a sunset in a late September sky.

*   *   *

Brock sprang open the Jeep door. Grady flipped up his fedora and gave her the '*Look*'.

"Any luck?"

"Yep..."

"Well, how'd it go?"

"Let's say, I think I did a lot better than you'd have done, Grady." She cheeky winked him as she climbed into her seat. "Agent Grant says he'll work on it later tonight and we can pick it up tomorrow – that is if there's anything on it!" Grady filled his barrel chest through flared nostrils, raised heavy eyebrows and didn't ask. He fired up the Jeep and turned out into light traffic.

"Ok-ey, so where to now, Loot?"

"Let's go an' see your buddy about getting my apartment swept."

"No problem," said Grady, rubbing his jaw.

"Are you okay, Grady, what's wrong?"

"I got a bad tooth givin' me a problem."

"Ouch, sounds painful – I'll tell you what: you call your bug buddy, and I'll call my dentist, see if he can fix you up right away." While Grady massaged his jaw, she tapped keys on her phone, made the call. A warm sun peeked out from behind a dark cloud, glowed down a bright light in a dull day. She snapped her phone shut, tweaked her nose at the big man.

"Okay Grady, it's your lucky day – he can fit you in right away."

"Ahh, thanks, Loot, I owe ya'. We've got our first day off in a long while tomorrow, an' I don't fancy spendin' it nursin' a damn toothache."

She scribbled down the address for him on the back of her business card, passed it across and added:

"Don't be late!"

"I'm on my way. Want me to drop you off at your place first?"

"No thanks, Grady. Drop me at Skinny's Grill. It's been a long day, I'm hungry — I need something to eat."

*   *   *

Chapter Seventeen

A trail of discarded clothing strewn across the sitting room floor tracked a tell-tale path through into the bedroom. On a dishevelled bed, a sensual tongue slow-teased soft nipples to hard on a bare breast cupped in a tender hand. A naked body moaned in exaltation. The sensual tongue continuing its wet, erotic stimulation, licked a damp trail over shivering flesh down to a navel, circled slow, dug deep, teased and lingered a while, then step-kissed its way across a sexually charged body down to a serpent and dragon tattoo etched in red adjacent to a glistening black-haired pubic mound. A hungry mouth pouting lust pursed and kissed the red dragon's lips. Compliant legs spread wide, allowing the probing carnal tongue entry to the forbidden fruits of passion, delving deep, exploring and caressing a sensual body exuding both an intense and willing desire. The recipient body, eyes closed tight, began to throb, moaning in ecstasy. Her body pulsed as her back arched up from the bed. With her head pressed back hard into feather down her breathing panting hard began to race. She clenched her fists tight as the carnal tongue now charged with a deep sexual craving worked faster, harder, teasing, caressing, kissing sensitive flesh with a strong passion to enrich a climax. The recipient's mouth opened wide and groaned in ecstatic bliss as the explosive moment of an orgasm shuddered through her body with the vigour of a thundering express train.

Madeline Brock, having already lavished a similar carnal embrace to the willing girl, rolled the pretty waitress off of her, and over onto her back. Brock's hungry mouth went straight to the wet mound between the girl's open legs and began a deep oral massage and didn't stop until the pretty waitress closed her eyes, rolled her head back, gripped the sheet, arched her back and moaned in rapture at the climax of her second orgasm of the night. Both bodies, naked, glistening from sweat, spent of emotion, laid panting locked tight in each other's arms with eyes closed, sensual and replete.

The pretty girl, blissful, stared a passion deep into emerald eyes and whispered softly:

"I've never – ever, had sex so amazing in my whole life – Thank you."

"Don't you have a partner?" soft-talked Brock.

"Yes, a boyfriend," chuckled the girl. "Having sex with him is similar to being a horse in the Grand National: first off, the jockey pulls out his whip and mounts you, then at the crack of a starting pistol the traps open, and after a brief wild bang to the first fence the rider rolls off after the first jump, falls into an unconscious stupor and leaves me to run the course all by myself and cross the finish line with my panties down round my ankles; coming last – if I'm lucky!" She gave Brock a gentle self-effacing smile.

"And you – do you have a boyfriend or a partner?"

"No – neither," whispered Brock.

"What about the big guy I see you with at Skinny's; you seem pretty close with him?" Brock reflected her thoughts back to the passionate hug she gave Grady when he gave her the watch.

'I guess, 'passionate' it may have seemed to an onlooker;' she mused, smiling at the girl.

"No that's Grady, he's my business partner. I've known him for many years."

"What work do you do?"

"I guess you could say we're in pest control," side-stepped Brock but kidded no-one.

"You've got some pretty heavy equipment for pest control – Are you cops?" she asked, taking her gaze across to the three-fifty-seven staring out in blued gun-metal from atop the dresser.

"No, we're not cops. We both used to be, but not anymore. We work private now – security, I guess you could say."

The girl furrowed sensual fingers through Brock's hair.

"I'm so glad I met you."

"Me too, you're welcome to come here anytime – in more ways than one. I was thinking – tomorrow is Sunday, my day off – you can stay over if you want, I'll make the coffee." The girl smiled at Brock and kissed a passionate okay on her lips.

"What do you do on your day off?" she asked.

"Oh – relax mostly, get up late, play some piano, hang loose with *Jack*, those kinda things."

"Who's Jack . . . a friend?"

"I guess you *could* call him a friend; an old friend, a *very* old friend, we go back a long way." Brock, kissed the girl soft on her lips, trailed soft hands over firm breasts, then moved down a willing body to a sensual place and re-kindled lust back into a torrid fire.

*   *   *

A flaming ball in the sky, low in the east casting lifeblood aurora, flooded in through the window panes teasing open tender blue eyes. No more than a hands width away, emerald green, already awake, sparkled back a visage of passion and sent a telepathic caress to welcome blue eyes into the day. Sensuous lips pouted a kiss, spoke soft words:

"Is Josie, short for Josephine?"

Quiet words whispered back from the pillow.

"No . . . *Josette* . . . After my grandmother: she was French."

"It's beautiful – suits you. Do you speak French?"

"No . . . my mother did, but I never picked it up. There seemed little need living in an English-speaking environment. I do know a few words and phrases, I guess I could order a coffee if I had to." Staring deep into the pretty girl's eyes, Brock's lips radiated a soft rapture. Blue and green spoke their silent language, agreed on a further ride back into deep carnal ecstasy to welcome in the new day.

*   *   *

Neither Brock nor the girl acknowledged the house phone intruding the day. After the fifth ring, Grady broke through on voicemail infringing on their reverie.

"Hey, Loot, your dentist guy's a star, fixed up my tooth no problem. My guy's gonna come and sweep your place tomorrow mornin' early. We'll be there at nine — Are you okay Boss you've been awful quiet? Call if you need me, maybe catch you over at Jackie O's later."

The pretty girl brushed her hand through Brock's hair and tousled her ear.

"He called you *Loot* . . . and *Boss*."

"That's Grady, he always calls me Loot. It's short for Lieutenant. I hate it," she answered with a smile.

"And boss . . . ?"

"It's him being polite I guess. Fancy a coffee?"

"Sure, cream, no sugar." Brock rolled off the bed to make coffee.

"*Lieutenant!*'. . . Sounds really special," said Josie. Brock spoke back over her shoulder, smiling as she left the room twitching her nose at the pretty girl. "Ain't nuthin' special about it, sweetheart, it goes with the job." She strolled naked into the kitchen, called back to Josie: "You can take a shower if you want, I'll come and join you, soap you down."

After a long and memorable shower, Brock, towelling wet hair joined Josie on the sofa.

"Shall I order a take-out? I don't have anything in."

"No, it's okay. I'm not hungry – for food I mean. Will you play me some piano?"

"Sure," said Brock, "any requests?" Coy blue eyes sparkling from a naked body spoke volumes; such a carnally charged inference was a hard request to refuse. Brock teased the keyboard into life. A soft melody sang out a soulful love song before wandering deep into an esoteric improvisation in a minor mode; chords laced with colour tones: ninths over major-sevenths; sharp-fives on the dominant fifth; and tri-tone chords into a dazzling crescendo of atonal chromatics over a rhythmic pedal-point. A rare place only the gifted can tread. As Miles once said; *if you ain't lived it – you can't play it.* Relaxed back on the sofa, the girl yearned for desire across to Brock and did one of the two things she does best – Looked pretty!

A day laced with wine and roses passed way too quick, then the phone chimed, went straight to voicemail after two rings. It called the coda on a sweet and sensual day.

"Pick up if you are there, Lieutenant Brock – Hello – Hello. My office tomorrow morning, ten o'clock – DON'T be late!"

Josie screwed up her pretty face and said:

"Wow, I hope he isn't Jack. Whoever it is, he sounds a real creep, same as my boss."

"No, it wasn't Jack. But you guessed right – he is a real creep."

"Okay, Maddie, I guess I'd better get going; I've got the late shift tonight at Skinny's. Ahhg – I hate it!"

"Okay, will you call me? You've got my number." Pretty blue eyes nodded the affirmative, tapped her head.

"Locked away forever."

"Want me to call you a cab?"

The girl smiled, shook her head and said:

"We came in my car remember . . . You asked me for a lift?"

"Oh yes, of course. Sorry, I forgot. It all seems such a long time ago. So much has happened since then – nice things." Emerald green sparkled and beamed love.

"You sure did give me a lift, Josie!"

*   *   *

Olson's bar was buzzing, life was good.

"I see you got a busy night, Jackie."

"Yeah, not before time; holiday seasons comin' up, it's always busy around now. My guess is they've come to hear you play the piano, Lieutenant."

"I doubt it, Jackie – Barrel house Boogie's not my style." Pursing her lips thoughtful she looked down, rolled her glass around in her fingers.

"Why do you always call me lieutenant, Jackie? You've known me long enough now to call me by my name. I don't call you Mister Olsen." With a look to sculpt marble, she flipped her eyes up to meet his. He ragged the bar top and radiated a warm smile.

"It's respect, Lieutenant, after all – you *are* my favourite customer." She chuckled down into an empty glass, shook her head.

"You an' Grady – you guys are sumpthin' else. Jolly me up, Mister Olsen, and one for yourself."

Jackie charged her Jigger, raised his glass and chinked hers.

"You're lookin' good these days, Lieutenant; how about some piano, easy on the Barrel-house." She flashed Jackie a sultry smile, clutched her glass, ambled across to the keyboard, sat and played for nearly an hour. She transformed off into her private place, played sultry mood music for the sultry and the moody. Complimentary shots set out in line, sweet as targets at a funfair duck shoot collected on the piano top. Playing with her eyes closed in another world she noticed none of it.

As the evening mellowed, Grady wandered into the bar, small-talked with Jackie, then strolled over and leant on the Yamaha baby grand while she played. Glad to see her, he pushed his hat up on his head and smiled. Brock looked up, tweaked her nose, ran up a cadenza and hit the coda after a short final cadence and blew a kiss in a *comme il faut* pastiche scene straight from an old Bogart movie – without the cigarette smoke.

"I'd have brought you a drink over but looks as if you're gonna need some help with this little line-up you already got here," he nodded to the parade of Bourbon.

"Yeah thanks, Grady, help yourself. It's good to see you . . . It's always good to see you, Cowboy. Shall we take the booth?"

She poured the line-up into larger glasses, handed one to Grady and relaxed back into mock leather comfort. Grady set his hat crown down on the table and stretched back in comfort.

"How did your day off go?"

"A hell of a lot better without a toothache thanks to you, Loot. And you, what did you get up to? I didn't hear from you, I was gettin' worried, are you okay?"

"Yeah, I'm good. I got heavily involved with a knitting pattern for some baby clothes I've been working on."

"What! – get out of here," he frowned.

"I was in bed all day, Shiney."

"Alone?" he asked behind wide eyes. She raised her glass, answered with a bounce of her brows and changed the subject.

"I've been thinking, Grady: if my apartment *is* bugged, who could have bugged it? It's not as if I have a lot of traffic through there."

"Okay, think back: first off, who has been in your apartment? Maybe someone you don't know, or you think could've looked suspicious." She shrugged, shook her head.

"I can't think of anyone. It's mostly you, Grady – and I know it couldn't be you: you'd leave far too much mess."

"So, no-one else, utility workers, mailmen, those kinda guys, how about signs of a forced entry?" She shook her head, thought deep.

"Mm-mm. – No, no-one I can think of . . . Oh, wait a minute; yes there was one guy, a Mister Dodd: he wanted to buy my apartment, came in for a look around – cash buyer never gave me his first name. I've got his card back at my place. He owns all of the apartments in my complex except for my two. But I didn't see him doing anything or acting strange – he couldn't – I was with him all the time."

"Did he visit only once, didn't drop nuthin' off or leave you with anything before he left?" asked Grady.

"No, all he left was his business card. He's been hounding me about selling for some time now and came about three, maybe four times," she shook her head. "Anyway, it was all way back; I never thought any more of it. But it couldn't be him – why would he, what for?"

"How about upstairs, you own the apartment up there also. Did he look around up there?"

"I don't think so. I'll check with Mrs Wiley. But I don't think it could be him. What would *he* want to bug *me* for?" '*Trust no-one, live longer.*' The thought rattled through her soul clattered heavy as a cattle truck over a rusted railroad track. She bit her bottom lip, went into a dark place. Grady sensed her mood, changed the subject.

"You thinkin' about sellin', Loot?"

"No, I don't think so: buying my apartment has been about the only sensible thing I've ever done in my life. There's not been much else to spend my cash on, apart from a good piano. Anyway, how could I throw Mrs. Wiley and Heidi out on the street? She's been a great tenant in the year she's been here – never missed her rent once. No, I wouldn't throw her out, I'm not selling. But whatever, I'm sure it couldn't be Dodd. If there were a bug – why would he want to plant it in my apartment, what for? I can see no reason."

"Well, my man's comin' to check it out tomorrow and put your mind at rest."

"Thanks, Grady. Okay let's not let these drinks evaporate, otherwise I'll have to get back on that keyboard and break out some barrel-house." She tweaked his cheek, playful, lifted her mood.

Jackie Olsen planted heavy body weight down on the seat next to Brock.

"Thanks, Lieutenant sounding great as always. If you keep pullin' 'em in rich as this I'm gonna have to hire you full-time."

"I ain't pulled anyone in, Jackie. It's holiday time, nothin' more. Anyway, I see you're stretchin' out now with some new staff: you got yourself a nice new barmaid." Jackie looked across to the bar, beamed a sensitive smile.

"Yeah, she's my niece, Zowie: my sister's kid. Gonna be helpin' out when the goin' gets busy throughout the season," he shrugged and added: "She needs the bucks." He waved across to the bar, held up three fingers.

"So you gonna play me some more, Lieutenant, free drinks on the house?"

"No way, Jackie, forget it. You couldn't afford me, you'd go broke, buddy." She winked at him, clucked her tongue, got up and went back to the piano. The crowded bar room clapped encouragement before she'd even played a note. Jackie relaxed back in his seat. Zowie carried over a tray of three doubles and set two down on the table; Jackie pointed the third across to Brock, then sat back, listened to her play and slow-shook his head as he spoke to Grady:

"She's good, Sergeant." Grady chinked Jackie's jigger.

"No, she's not good, Jackie … She's fuckin' brilliant!"

*   *   *

Chapter Eighteen

Flaunting two coffees under a wide-tooth smile, Grady rang the bell at eight fifty-seven on a good-looking day; he was dressed to match it. Guessing who it was, Brock buttoned her shirt and sprang open the door. A smaller man, short on head hair but big on a midriff body fat large enough to excite a tribe of cannibals, waddled in behind the sergeant. He lifted his nose in the air and drew in a heavy breath before he spoke:

"Wow – Wild Rose! My ex-wife's favourite perfume," he spoke out aloud to no one, "I guessed she was having an affair when she took to using it – cost that woman her life." He chuckled from a satirical smile.

"How come?" asked Grady, curious.

"Guy she ran off with wasn't immune to the virus, turns out neither was she," with a sardonic grin he turned to Grady, "at least they smelt nice together on the marble slab."

"That's tough," said Grady.

"Not for me it wasn't; I got the house – and the dog."

"Sure is a familiar scent, can't think where I've sensed it before?" said Grady working his chin in question.

"It's my new perfume – *To a Wild Rose*. It came free with a six-box of red," Brock covered tracks. Grady took a deep breath, filled his lungs with the fragrant scent and said:

"Nice." He held out his hand to his buddy. "This is Charlie Malone, Loot, the sweep; no relation to Jute." He forced out a chuckle.

"Call me Bugsy, same as the guy who set up Vegas many years back."

"Okay, Bugsy, where do you want to start looking for bugs?"

"Already started, ma'am," said Bugsy, lifted a device flashing green in his palm.

"Let's go into my room, Grady, we need to talk, let's leave your man to his bugs."

She wandered into her bedroom; Grady shadowed her.

"WOW… Sure is a strong scent in here, Loot – Beautiful."

'*She sure is*', Brock mused, needed to change the subject but maybe not the sheets. She opened the windows – wide.

"I gotta see Captain Clod at ten," she said. "Did he call you?"

"No he did not. You know I ain't his favourite, Loot. I'll drop you off and wait in the Jeep if it's okay with you. I don't wanna spoil my day lookin' at that snivelling piece of crap. What d'ya' think he wants?"

"No idea, Grady," she shrugged, "he didn't sound too happy on voicemail, but then again – when does he ever?" She turned to the doorway.

"How you doin' out there, Bugsy?"

"Nearly done, miss, gotta do your *boudoir* next."

"Found anything, Bugs?" asked Grady. A flat open palm cradling a small magnetic device appeared through the door opening.

"Found this under a foot pedal beneath the piano. There's nothing else. The phone's clean and no bugs on the computer, but both of them could be hacked. I can check it out back at the office on my system."

Grady studied the bug in Bugsy's palm.

"You think this is active?" whispered Grady. Bugsy grinned and dropped the bug into Grady's coffee cup.

"Not any more it ain't."

Pensive, Brock folded her arms, cupped her chin in her hand, wondered about who the hell could've put it there.

"How far away would a receiver be, Bugsy?"

"Difficult to say, ma'am: depends on the quality. Maybe a pick-up in a truck, or . . ." he shrugged shoulders. "Who knows, could be anywhere out there in a circle of, five or six hundred yards. Maybe even a lot more if someone had big bucks?"

"Somewhere in this complex perhaps?"

"Yeah, I guess that's also possible, miss."

She tapped her foot, wrestled with the devil. The sweep finished his search in her bedroom; found nothing of interest other than a half bottle of *Jack* and some black lace underwear.

"How much do I owe you, Bugsy?"

"No charge, ma'am. I'm still working off favours for Shiney. Call me if you need me."

He passed her his card. She studied the embossed print and bounced her brows:

"Bug repellent! Speak of the devil: that sounds something I may well need." She flicked unenthusiastic eyebrows across to Grady. "Let's go and see Clod."

*   *   *

At nine forty-five, the rising sun blazing down through a dusty windshield from a cloudless sky held the promise of a good day. Not the same could be said for their destination. Grady drove a slow pace; he was in no hurry. Brock let her mind wander far away from any bad thoughts about where they were headed. She turned her thoughts to Josie and mellowed. She realized she had never been in love before, certainly not such true love as this; maybe puppy love at school but nothing since. Something was changing; she was determined it would be for the better. In her short life, she'd had far too much association with death, violence and conflict, leaving little or no room for neither love nor passion. Now, along comes this beautiful creature of pure innocence into her life, a violent life, a life buried deep in dark shadows, dealing every day with lowlife drug dealers, murderers, rapists and anyone else that morally stank. Sometimes to stay alive it would need for her to shoot first; how could she explain that if the situation ever arose? Opposites attract – she smiled at the ambiguity. '*She couldn't be any more opposite to me at all – but I can't let her go . . .*'

"Penny for your thoughts, Loot."

Brock looked up, shook her head and turned back into the moment.

"Sorry, Grady I was miles away."

"Not a bad place to be these days, Loot."

"So I *was* bugged. I knew it. That sure answers a lot of questions. Now we need to find out by who – then we may find out the why – or we might even find the plant?"

"Maybe we should've kept the bug active and set up a trap, Loot."

"Yeah, I did think about that; but I value my privacy."

Her thoughts drifted back to Josie. She feared what sort of lowlife had been listening in on Saturday night and Sunday morning. She closed her eyes, a chill ran down her spine, stopping at the image of Macey – her throat slit, it would seem for no other reason than to rouse Grady. She knew she *had* to keep quiet about Josie and shuddered at the thought of the possible consequences.

"You okay, Boss? You looked a million dollars early this mornin' – what's up?"

"Nothing, I'm bugged about the bug I guess."

"Talking of bugs, we're nearly there. By the way, how'd it go with the SD card we found?"

"Thanks for reminding me Grady – I forgot all about it. I'll call Agent Grant right away."

"Unlike you to forget – you sure nothin's wrong?"

"Sure I'm sure, Grady." She tweaked a playful nose but, didn't convince him, and smiled as she tapped her cell phone.

"Hi, Al, it's Maddie." Grady's head spun round as if he'd been swiped with a skillet from an angry spouse after coming home drunk with a flat wallet after a late Friday night poker club.

"Now I get it!" he nodded to himself. Curious: she looked round to him, furrowed her brows and covered her phone with her hand.

"Get what?"

"Wild Rose. He must sure be sumpthin' special. Lucky guy," Grady chuckled. Shaking her head she pushed his hat down over his eyes, put the phone back to her ear and listened to the agent.

"I didn't find anything useful, Maddie. Most of it was in code. Not really my speciality I'm afraid," said the agent.

"Sure, I understand – could you make a printout for me please?"

"Already done, Maddie."

"Okay to drop by and pick it up?"

"Sure, lookin' forward to it." She pressed red and mused: 'I bet you are!' Grady dropped his jaw.

"Maddie – Al – Are you *kiddin'* me?" said Grady.

"Let's say I've been kidding him. As I told you, Grady: I did a lot better than you would have managed. I don't think you'd have got too far wigglin' *your* fat ass in his face."

"Then maybe I need to try some of your perfume?"

"With your two twenty I doubt you could jump a fence that high, big–boy." She slapped his hat off.

*　　*　　*

After dragging her reluctant body up the grimed stairway and along a dismal corridor, she approached LePage's office with all the enthusiasm of a condemned sole slinking in chains across cold stone to a one-night-stand with *Old Sparky*. It was five after ten. She rapped twice – hard. He shouted her in. She entered into stilled silence, intruded on only by the dull rhythmic clunk from the overhead fan. LePage didn't turn from his favoured place. She didn't sit.

LePage stood with his back to her. She wanted to snore. LePage cleared his throat with the sound of a sack of coal being dragged over loose gravel, then scowled into the window:

"I have a mission, somewhat delicate for both yourself and Sergeant Da Silva. Suffice to say . . ." with a smug face he spun round on a heel to her . . . "not your usual mandate. Although I'm sure you'll manage. I've printed out the brief with times, places etc. for both yourself and Sergeant Da Silva to peruse over. You'll find all you need to know in the brown folder on my desk. Please ensure Sergeant Da Silva fully understands his purpose and standing in this assignment."

She lifted the folder off the desk. Didn't open it.

"May I ask what this is about, Sir?"

"Yes, you may, Lieutenant: a top government official is arriving later today, you are to escort him and his party to the Palm Beach Hotel, where you will ensure they arrive safely and are settled in comfortably with minimal fuss, using absolute courtesy and full protocol at all times," with a smirk he turned to face her. "Which, I fear may well pose a problem for Sergeant Da Silva. Let's say this will be a trial run for him and his future employment in this department. You are both to convey complete discretion at all times and are not to carry firearms under any circumstance; not even a Taser, you will not need them on this occasion. I do not want these people unnerved at the sight of firearms for no reason. So, it's not going to be one of your usual bar fights, Lieutenant Brock. There's a huge investment involved here for the good and future of our community. We cannot afford to give a bad impression and scare these people away. There are rooms booked for you both at the hotel. You are to escort the party back to the airstrip first thing in the morning after breakfast. You will be allowed an evening meal but absolutely no alcohol. Do I make myself clear, Lieutenant?" She returned nothing other than a complacent nod and the roll of her eyes.

"And the purpose of this visit *is* . . . Sir?"

He turned back to his window, smug.

"That is classified information on a need-to-know basis, Lieutenant Brock. Your need is not to know, but to read your orders and carry out your job in the satisfactory fashion required of you both at all times." With a face full of complacent superiority he turned from the comfort of his window, staring back at her with a look to freeze a corpse.

"Good luck, Lieutenant, but I doubt this time, luck is something you will need – only protocol and a lot of it." She pulled the single order sheet from the folder, scanned over it as if it were junk mail. Then, turned back to LePage and shuddered at the chill from his stare. She glared back evil eyes at him with nothing more exuding from her soul above pure disdain:

"Are we done here – Sir?"

In the epitome of the arrogant bastard he was, he turned back and scowled into his window.

"Good day, Lieutenant."

'*Asshole!*' She slammed the door on her way out.

*　　*　　*

Treading tentative steps down the stairwell, she paused in confusion halfway down. Thought: '*why us, and what's this thing about Grady?*' The whole thing stank. It's pretty obvious LePage disapproves of Grady, but if she were to tell him he's on trial, Grady would no doubt storm up the stairs and ram something nasty up LePage's backside – preferably his head. '*Maybe I 'should' tell him.*' She mused, chuckled to herself and lightened a dark moment. No, she decided not to tell Grady anything – nothing at all, no need – why rock the boat. After all, *babysitting* seemed no big deal. But why all the cloak and dagger crap?

'I need a coffee, preferably laced with a heavy shot of Jack, but just a straight twenty-four-volt shot would do right now,' she mused. She realised it wouldn't be a good idea to risk the chance of Grady seeing her with Josie. It would be obvious, even to a blind man shooting the rapids in a barrel that she'd recently tasted much more than just coffee with her. *'Isn't Josie on the afternoon shift though?'* she mused and figured she couldn't risk coffee in Skinny's if Josie *was* there.

"What's the rub, Loot?" asked Grady as she climbed into the jeep.

"Nothin' much – Usual crap. I'll tell you over coffee."

As Grady drove out of the parking lot he made a lot of enemies blundering his way into traffic with his hand on the horn and his middle finger to attention. Sat non-plussed, Brock read through the order sheet and worked backwards from the timeline. Sixteen-hundred hours was the downbeat, *'which is four in the afternoon for us mere mortals'*, then babysitting until nine in the morning, with another hour after breakfast to return the party to the airstrip, and then drop off the mini-bus. She checked her watch: time now: ten-forty-five probably get ready to leave at three. *'Which gives us around four hours,'* she mused.

Grady scuffed the kerb near Skinny's.

"Pull up right outside, Grady I need to check the menu before we order."

"Check the menu . . . you okay, Loot? When do ya' ever need to check the menu?"

"It's a joke, Grady. I need the bathroom – girl's stuff. I may need to go straight back to my apartment," she grinned at him . . . "Without coffee!"

"Oh, yeah, right, okay. Give me a shout when you're fixed up." He pushed his body back in the seat, tugged his hat down over his eyes and soft whistled.

The waitress inside wasn't cute, nor was she very pretty but the coast was clear. Brock waved Grady in. They took a booth by the window. Chewing gum in a brick-square jaw, the waitress ambled over, ragged the table clean and held her pen over a pad.

"What's it to be guys?"

"Two coffees please, miss. Where's Josie today?" asked Brock, casual.

"She's not on until two – late shifts this week."

"Okay, thanks." Grady leant back in the booth, folded his arms, gazed up to the ceiling and lifted his brows.

"Seems to me everyone's on first name terms today?" Cautious, Brock shrugged her shoulders, avoided the big man's gaze.

"Her name's Josie, it's written on her chest fob," she felt a flush rising, back-peddled, "don't tell me you haven't been staring at her tits, Shiney. I wondered where she was today, nothing more ..." she shrugged, looked the big man in the eye and said with a coy smile: "She gives good service." Wading into deep water without a life vest she needed to change the subject – and be fast about it.

"Okay, we've got to get suited up, looking smart and be ready to leave around three-fifteen. It's only pansy stuff, so no guns, we're babysitting."

"Since when have we *ever* had no guns as a brief? That *is* our brief, it's what we do."

"I said, we were *told* no guns, Grady. When have we ever taken any notice of that creep?"

The waitress arrived, set two coffees down in front of them.

"Let me know when you guys need a refill."

"Thank you, miss." The waitress tore off a pay tab, slapped it down on the table, then with the sex appeal of a parking ticket, she solo Rhumba'd back to the counter. It was one of those days without doubt.

"Babysittin!' – Are you kiddin' me?" groaned Grady.

"I wish I was, Grady, but it's all we're allowed to know; so bring along your bucket and spade."

"Where's the pick-up?" asked Grady. She shook her head, shrugged a *'don't know.'*

"I guess we'll find out later."

"All seems a bit vague if you don't mind me sayin' so, Boss."

The waitress lingered next to their table balancing a full tray of food for the next table over a capable arm.

"Lieutenant Brock?" she asked.

"Yes, miss."

"Call for you, ma'am. You can take it on the wall phone over by the bar."

Sat back in his seat, with heavy arms folded over a barrel chest and his thick black eyebrows high in question, Grady watched Brock squeeze out of the booth, walk over to the bar and pick up the receiver. She faced the wall and held the phone to her ear.

"Hello, Brock here."

"Maddie . . . ?"

"Josie . . . You don't know how good it is to hear your voice, sweetheart. How did you know I was here?"

"I asked Grace to call me if you came in. Can I see you?"

"I have to work tonight, right through until tomorrow morning. I'm at the Palm Beach Hotel, a security job. It sucks! I can call you later though. What time do you finish?"

"Not until ten. I can't get off early," she said, "I don't enjoy working nights. Skinny's not a good boss. He says he'll find someone else if I don't do as I'm told. He sounds every bit as bad as your boss."

"Nobody can be as bad as Captain Clod, believe me, sweetheart. Okay, I'll call you then."

The line snapped dead. She turned and stared into a pair of dark soulless eyes.

"Sorry, to cut you *off*, miss, but I need to make *my* call now."

With total disdain, she turned and checked his slender frame, up and down from his open-toe sandals and back up to wispy strands of thinning grey hair dangling loose above a smug look.

"I'm guessing you must be Skinny?"

"Yes, I am, and I'm the boss around here, and this: is *my* phone!" He enunciated his diction from the back of his throat in the misguided belief it would make him sound more important – It didn't work. Vigilant, she stepped back, put her hands on her hips, stared an ice-cold fury and gave him a mental: *'and so fucking what message'* with green eyes turned evil back into killer mode. When he saw her shoulder holster partially hidden under her jacket with the butt of a three-fifty-seven nestled inside, Skinny choked out a breath and sucked his lips back onto his teeth.

"I don't want any trouble, Lady," he pleaded with a voice now back up a fifth to his normal tone – or maybe even a little higher. As she reached into her jacket his face turned white and his eyes grew wide as hands in a fisherman's story; but it wasn't for her gun, she pulled out her business card and flicked it into his face.

"You won't get any trouble from me, but if by chance you do get any, I'm who you should call to sort it out; me and the rather large gentleman sitting over there in your booth . . . If of course – that's okay with you?" She burned her acid glare into his face. Skinny glanced across to Grady and muttered soft prayers under his breath. Grady stared a fiery wrath across to Skinny hard enough to give him a suntan.

"Sorry about this, miss, a slight misunderstanding, nothing more. Please don't bother with your tab."

She wandered back to the booth shaking her head. Life was sure getting complicated.

"What was all that about, Loot?"

"Ah, it's nothing. Just another face in the long line of assholes I guess we all have to put up with every day."

Blood flushed around Grady's neck. He stood and carried his coffee mug over to the counter. Brock closed her eyes, smiled and sat back with folded arms to enjoy what she knew was about to happen. Skinny looked worried, braced his body – he needed to. Grady reached out with his giant fist and grabbed Skinny by his tie and yanked him across the counter. Then poured a mug full of hot coffee over Skinny's head and bounced the empty mug on his crown to the rhythm of his speech pattern:

"I ain't got any manners, so I can't teach you none, but if you ever treat the lady like that again, fart breath – I'm gonna' stuff your fucking head into that popcorn machine until popcorns shoot out of your skinny fuckin' asshole – '*Com-fuckin'-prenez*', fart breath?"

Grady pulled the knot bone tight on Skinny's dripping tie and dropped him down behind the bar and turned back to Brock.

"Let's get out of here, Lieutenant, his coffee tastes of hair oil!"

*   *   *

"I didn't know you were such a wordsmith, Grady; all the way from the Marx brothers to Shakespeare: I'm impressed." She grinned climbing into the Jeep, relieved now Grady meeting Josie would no longer be a problem. But it looks as if they may need to find another diner.

*   *   *

On a lazy summer afternoon, at two-forty-five after an easy riverside lunch at a bar on the bay, Grady parked the Jeep in the department pound and signed out a ten-seater; a six would've done but none were available. Sat cosy in the front passenger seat, Brock opened the game plan, checked it through, and then told Grady to drive out to the city airstrip where they were to wait for the pick-up. Then she suggested:

"As we're early let's swing past Agent Grant's office and pick up the printout. It's ready."

"Will do, Loot. Was it him who called you at Skinny's diner?"

"Agent Grant – Yes, I told him we might be at the diner for a while," she said, felt bad about bending the truth.

"Okay, then. No funny stuff, Loot. We're on the clock."

"Well I'm not wearing any perfume, but I could give you a splash and you could go up for me if you want." She flashed coy eyes across to the big man.

"You want me to smell pansy sweet, Lieutenant?"

"Careful big boy," she racked her brows. "Don't forget who you're talking to!"

*   *   *

Chapter Nineteen

The twin-engine taxi plane burned rubber as it touched down on the tarmac in a westerly breeze and crabbed down the runway. It had landed fifteen minutes late, a full half-hour after Grady had pulled the ten-seater close up to the tarmac. Brock flipped up the brim of Grady's hat and pointed across to the plane. He dragged his feet down from the dashboard, muttered something distasteful and fired up the motor. The plane slow-taxied round and came to a halt. An eight-step side panel sprang open from the fuselage. A flight attendant in a smart uniform ushered two males and two females from the plane. Shading their eyes in bright sunlight they stepped down onto warm tarmac. In a move lacking protocol, a thick cloud of dust billowed in humid air as Grady pulled the ten-seater up alongside the taxi-plane. It wasn't a good start. Grady chewed gum, showed no remorse.

Introductions were brief as a kiss to a mother-in-law. The contingent brushed off dust, loaded their overnight baggage into the luggage compartment, and climbed into the cool solace of the air-conditioned ten-seater. The guys eyed Brock, Grady eyed the girls; then whistling his tuneless melody, Grady drove out from the city airstrip back out onto the highway and headed into the city. Brock rolled down the cab partition and turned around to the party:

"I have it on my itinerary you have a meeting in the conference room at eighteen-hundred hours, which to us mere mortals is six o'clock, correct?" She clocked four nods from four people. "Okay, after we check you in you can freshen up and grab a drink from the bar. Dinner will be served in the restaurant at nine. Sergeant Da Silva and myself will be on call for you if needs be . . . any questions?" Four heads shook a *no* in unison. She rolled up the cab partition, turned around, sat back and scanned through the printout from Agent Grant. Spoke as she did so:

"Okay, Grady, next stop: the Palm Beach Hotel, corner of west and eleventh. We've got a fresh bed waiting for us after we tuck this lot in," she looked up at him, tweaked her cute nose and added, "in separate rooms!"

He rolled bitter-sweet eyes, showed his teeth, drove on with the thought of a very boring and tiresome evening ahead.

"Well done, Loot, you're pretty good at all this stuff."

She popped a bubble with her gum.

"Wait 'till you see me stuff their heads into the popcorn machine!"

*   *   *

The Palm Beach hotel, built long before the virus came to check-in, was in its day a five-star extravagance fit to serve only the rich and the lovely. But now, with no A/C and a green-stained, stagnant pool fit for nothing more than a crab's home, the Palm Beach is way down the scale struggling for altitude somewhere above a one star; which could depend on the weather; the particular room you booked; and how big you are on giving tips. The rich are now all spent and the lovely have long since gone to seed. The dank hotel foyer exuded an aroma one step up from a French street-side pissoir, and is almost as welcoming; unless of course you needed to relieve your bladder. Having looked around the rest of the building, Brock figured the foyer to be the garden spot of the whole hotel. Brock's room was marginally better than Grady's; his was marginally better than the rear seat of his Jeep. Maybe that's the plus of being a pretty Oriental lady toting a three-fifty-seven. The Palm Beach, destined for reallocation as a hospital for the needy, will no doubt have to drop its one-star status. Poor bastards, then they'll really have something to complain about!

Relaxed at the bar, Brock browsed through the encoded printout from the SD card she had gleaned from the Mertz hit. She knew nothing about code-breaking other than what her cryptic logic might tell her but couldn't begin to discern any sense or logic from the confusing type on the sheet in front of her. Trying his best to enjoy a warm beer, Grady was not much help. He took his gaze out of his beer glass and spoke soft words without looking up.

"You okay, Loot?" She looked up in question from the printout, ran a wet tongue over her lips.

"Yeah. . . I'm fine, why?" she answered, stumbling over her words.

"You been actin' kinda strange lately, Loot – What's her name? Or maybe I should take a wild guess – maybe, a Wild Rose guess."

Brock flushed, dropped coy eyes down into her lap, avoided the big man's gaze and spoke soft words – almost in a whisper:

"Is it so obvious?" The widescreen smile he beamed back could melt the hardest of hearts.

"It is to me, Loot – and so far, only to me. I just hope it stays that way."

"I can't kid you, can I, Grady?"

"No, Loot, you can't. But keep her well-hidden, we can't afford to lose another waitress." Locked in on her damp emerald gaze, Grady didn't turn at the sound of voices stirring behind him, but said: "We're on, Boss – here comes the tea party."

She kept her smile on her sergeant, shook her locks loose and whispered soft words:

"Thank you, Grady." She slid off her barstool back into full protocol mode.

"And Loot . . ." She stopped – turned back to him. "She sure is cute," he raised his beer glass, racked his eyebrows to her and drained his glass.

Surrounded by far more chairs than bugs at a summer picnic, the long oaken conference table, set with glass water jugs and fake crystal tumblers grouped tight on time-worn silver plate, took up more space in the room than would a welfare queue; but, with more floor space than anywhere else in the hotel, the large room could easily stand it. Two local delegates joined the four horsemen and women for their apocalypse. Brock looked on in despair at what looked to be the start of a nightmare businessman's rehearsal for the first half of the last supper, with the late arrivals yet to come.

'Babysitting, this sucks!' Brock mused while Grady stood in the background soft-whistling, looking as bored as a shepherd counting his sheep. With formalities glossed over, the contingent scraped chairs back over glazed tiles and took their places. A briefcase lock snapped open. Slick as a hand of cards at a poker table, sheets of foolscap were dealt round to the party. Then with a feigned look of self-importance   the delegation settled down to business.

Stood back in the wings, Brock and Grady mirrored bored understudies at a school nativity, but when the lengthy discussion turned from the aftermath of the virus to the drug war, Brock's ears perked up. 'Is that why we're really here?' she mused. She also wondered if it had been a wise move to swop her three-fifty-seven for the smaller powered Glock 19 automatic tucked into her waistband. Time passed slower than a chess match on Valium.

At seven-forty-five p.m., Brock glared an uneasy eye at a serving trolley as it was pushed in through a swing door. Covered with a white sheet and manned by four guys dressed in white kitchen clothing topped with white Toques, the winds of doubt ran a chill down Brock's spine. 'It's not time for dinner yet, and why does it need four guys to push a trolley?' she mused. The body language and scruffy footwear alone told her all she needed to know. She went from green to amber to code red in less than one second.

"EVERYBODY DOWN, NOW!" she shouted aloud, spun round and checked across to Grady. Already on full alert, he checked her reaching for her gun. He dropped to his knee with his pistol aimed at the trolley. As the bogus kitchen workers tore off the white covering, all four scrambled for weapons hidden in the trolley. Rapid fire from Brock dropped two before they could cuddle a trigger. Startled by what was supposed to be easy pickings, the two remaining assailants sank back into the kitchen area spraying random automatic fire into the room. Momentarily frozen and slack-jawed with shock, two of the delegates, starred backwards with flailing arms from their seats, sporting some new red buttonholes in their fancy shirt fronts.

'Too slow!' clucked Brock. She rolled under the cover of the table for a better angle of shot.

"GET BACK AWAY FROM ME!" she shouted to the remaining delegates trembling, huddled together reminiscent of a flock of drenched lambs under a dripping hedge in a thunderstorm. She brought the trolley into her sights, emptied her magazine and clipped in another mag…*"Last one, better make it good!"* Creeping close along the side wall, Grady held out a stun grenade to her. She nodded. He gave a signal. She gave him cover. He tossed the stunner through the doorway. A split second after the explosion both Brock and Grady ran to the open door blocked with the trolley. They fired through at anything moving and made sure if it did move, it wouldn't ever move again. Brock's breach racked open on empty. Grady tossed her a machine pistol from the cart. She cocked the action – ready. A shot rang out from behind. Brock spun round. Out of the corner of her eye, she saw Grady go down. A rogue delegate rose up behind the table and fired his pistol again; three more shots, this time at her. Two went wild but her shoulder burned at the third. She recoiled, lost her balance and fell. Sat braced against the wall she lifted the machine pistol and emptied half its magazine into the delegate's body. With the flailing arms of a scarecrow in a thunder squall, he danced his last tango – but sad for his kudos, he was a hell of a long way from Paris.

"STAY DOWN! NOBODY MOVE OR I'LL FUCKING SHOOT YOU!" she barked out. With the machine pistol trained on the table, she backed across to Grady, reached behind her and tore open Grady's shirt. He'd taken a bullet in his upper chest close to his heart. He was losing blood fast. There was no need to check his pulse: his blood flow was obvious. Bleary-eyed security guards tucking in shirt tails peered round corners, keeping well clear.

"CALL A MEDIC! NOW!" shouted Brock. Security skulked back into the shadows, hoping they weren't seen.

Dense smoke had cleared from the kitchen. Kept low, she peeked around the corner; saw a pile of dead meat weeping blood slunked over smoking guns. From the trolley, she picked up a fully loaded machine pistol and turned back to Grady.

"WHERE'S THE FUCKING MEDIC!" she shouted, hoped someone was listening.

'He's still losing blood – and a lot of it,' she mused, clucked her tongue and bent down close to Grady's head, keeping her eyes trained on the table she spoke soft into his ear.

"Can you stand, Grady?" Now barely conscious he slow nodded his head but could utter nothing. She slung the machine pistol over her shoulder, flipped his lucky fedora onto her head and pulled his arm up round her neck. Single-handed she rattled a burst from the machine pistol across the table top; crystal shattered, shards of glass sprayed through the air, rained down thick as an Arctic ice storm, sheets of paper took flight through the air, wild as a flock of startled doves. She screamed out aloud:

"STAY DOWN! I'LL SHOOT THE FIRST BASTARD I SEE MOVING!"

Pumped with adrenalin, she staggered with Grady from the conference room, dragged him through the foyer and out into the street. No-one stopped her. A private SUV meandered in a lazy jog along the road towards her. Stood in its way still holding Grady up, she trained the machine pistol on the oblivious driver. He screeched to a halt at her feet.

"OUT NOW!" she shouted. Wide-eyed with his jaw on the floor the driver froze. Brock rattled lead through the front windshield to help him along with a decision. A terrified body sprung the door, dived into a hedge for cover; would no doubt need a change of plans for his evening, along with a change of underwear. She bundled Grady into the rear seat but could do nothing to stem the flow of blood. With the machine pistol slung from her shoulder, she jumped into the driver's seat and gunned the motor. Tires screamed, burned rubber as she spun a circle in the road.

The Medical Centre close by was enjoying a welcome lull until she arrived holding the horn down from two-hundred yards out. Smoking tires screamed up to the entrance. She sprang open the rear door. Grady, bloodied and semi-conscious half slumped out onto stone steps.

"MEDIC NOW!" she screamed brandishing the machine pistol. Nobody argued.

Seconds later a stretcher on a trolley wheeled Grady, now no longer conscious, away into intensive care. She stood inside the entrance doorway breathing hard with her heart beating up-tempo fast as a Buddy Rich drum solo. A white-faced medic stood paralysed in front of her, couldn't move; he mimicked a statue. With eyes wide open he didn't blink once, just stared down in terror at the smoking machine pistol slung over her shoulder. He cleared his throat, took a deep breath, wet his lips and spoke slow in a very high voice . . .

"Would you allow me to look at your shoulder please, ma'am?"

Brock looked down, realised her whole left arm from shoulder down to her hand was drenched with blood, dripping down from her fingers . . . It was blood that didn't belong to Grady!

*   *   *

Chapter Twenty

Hard-moulded plastic cloaking a steel tube chair offered Brock about as much comfort as would a Fakir's bed; but her emotions were too drained to care. A cautious medic approached from the intensive care unit. He looked down at Brock's bandaged arm, cleared his throat before he spoke.

"Lieutenant Brock." She nodded the affirmative. He looked into her weary, washed out eyes, said nothing but took a deep breath and exhaled slow through his nose.

"How is he . . .? Can I see him?" she murmured.

"I'm afraid it isn't good, Lieutenant. We're doing all we can but I don't think he's going to make it . . . I'm sorry." He spoke with a soft empathy reflected in his eyes. She stood, narrowed her eyes.

"Take me to him," she spoke not as a request, but as an order. He took a deep breath, thanked a deity somewhere up above she wasn't still holding the machine pistol lying behind her on a chair.

"I'm afraid it won't do any good, Lieutenant, he's under heavy sedation." Emerald green turned evil, she picked up the machine pistol, slung it over her shoulder, flashed her Covert Security Force I.D. in his face.

"TAKE ME TO HIM – NOW!"

The sterile intensive care room of the private National Security ward worked its miracles in a silence intruded upon only from the steady rhythm of a pulse register: a welcome signal of comfort telling her lifeblood was still pumping through Grady's heart. At his bedside, Brock stared down to his heavily bandaged body invaded by a matrix of pipes and tubes taped to his skin. Bags of blood and plasma hung around the bed emulating a ripper's wash-line in a waking nightmare. A bellowed-type apparatus pumped life into his lungs. His lucky grey fedora, she'd cast down onto a side table stared back up to her. It seemed to plead for help.

With a dampness welling in her eyes, she bent over him, ran gentle fingers through his hair, kissed his forehead and dropped hot tears down onto his cheeks. She pulled a chair forward, sat beside him and cradled his hand, a strong hand, one having saved her life on so many occasions now sat limp in her own hand. A soft voice came from behind:

"I'm afraid it won't help, miss."

"FUCK OFF!" Soft shoes made a tactful exit, tip-toed back into the distance.

Throughout the night she sat at his bedside, stroked his hair, squeezed his hand, whispered silly stories into his ear, tweaked his nose and slapped his chin, playful. Medics came and went, changed bottles, pressed buttons and did what medics do. She held on firm, was not prepared to let him go.

A bright dawn light from the early morning sunrise cast a rosy glow around the long shadows creeping deep into the ward. She was still awake, holding on tight. A medic came in and checked on the lifeblood machinery. He lifted a clipboard from the end of the bed and finger-scrolled down the readout.

"Good, he's responding. His vitals have stabilised. But let's not get too complacent, although I think we *can* say he's out of danger now, Lieutenant. He must have one hell of a constitution." Resolute, the medic stared down into the exhausted but nonetheless beautiful green eyes shrouded heavy in dark rings. The bloodied bandage on her arm and the machine pistol at her feet reflected the grim reality of her anguish.

"It's early days but I think he's going to pull through." He re-hung the clipboard and smiled to her with triumph in his eyes. Drained of energy but not of emotion, she looked back up to the medic, then dropped her head down to her lap. Green eyes welled.

"Can I arrange something for you to eat, Lieutenant?" Still bowed down into her lap she shook her head.

"No thank you, just some coffee please."

*   *   *

Despite not regaining consciousness, Grady was taken off most of the life support units and could now manage on his own. It was doubtful he would regain consciousness soon and probably wouldn't for some time yet after losing so much blood and being under deep sedation. But he was in good hands she assured herself. She leant across and kissed his forehead.

Low rays from the warm morning sun in a clear blue sky caressed Brock's jaded face as she stepped out into the well-manicured gardens of the medical centre. She closed her eyes; her ears homed in on a skylark high in the sky singing out its dulcet song. She could now appreciate what had enraptured Hoagy Carmichael to compose such a beautiful melody one hundred years before. She took in the sweet, rich sounds of the dawn chorus and cherished a time of the day she had never been much aware of throughout her violent and torrid lifestyle. But not even comfort from a tender warm breeze or the sweet sounds around could help soothe and carry away her troubles. She stood resolute. For now, above all else – she had a mission . . .

She hopped a cab from under the early morning shade of a king palm at the medical centre taxi stand, then rode the cab across to the Palm Beach to pick up her three-fifty-seven from the room safe. No-one uttered a word as she passed through hotel reception. Most avoided her gaze. The security sought cover. The same cop in the same empty suit stood behind the same empty crime scene tape at the entrance to the conference room. So this was his sole vocation? What a life! He chewed gum powering a complacent look straight through her. She gave him back her best 'what an asshole' look. He didn't budge; it was obvious it was something he'd gotten used to.

She rode the elevator up to her room.

*   *   *

Chapter Twenty-one

From the Palm Beach, she took a cab to the department pound. With the skeleton night staff still on call, it was early yet for the pound to be busy. A security guard fifteen minutes from the end of his shift dozed to attention in an office swivel chair. He didn't notice her walking through the barrier. She saw Grady's Jeep standing right where he'd left it: undercover in the shade of a candy-striped awning. She reached for the start fob hidden under the dashboard and drove to the barrier. She sounded the horn. The security guard shot out from his seat fast as the fairground human cannonball as he recognised her. With his face glowing scarlet and a hand quivering in salute, he raised the barrier. She winked and gave him a friendly wave. He smiled back a thank you. Still early, she drove out into light traffic and headed down to Sujo's Car Lot.

She pulled into the parking lot, saw only one vehicle parked there: LePage's black SUV gleaming bright on rubber under the early morning sun in his private parking slot. She'd hoped to have got there before he'd arrived and wondered why he was in so early. Breathing venom, she glared up to his grubby window, despised with a passion everything behind it. She scanned around at rusting chain-link, peeling paint from bare brick walls and the bland rear view of an advertising hoarding. *What the hell could intrigue him so much about a view into a car park, and an empty one to boot?*

Brock bypassed security unchallenged. The staff, late as usual, had yet to surface. She took the stairs avoiding the rattle of the lift. Her heart pounded at the far end of the dank hallway. Pausing at his door, she nestled the magnum into the rear waistband of her jeans. She took a deep breath and soft-kicked the door open; it wasn't on the latch. Long past succour from an oilcan, the grating of dry rusted hinges roused LePage. He turned; looking surprised he stopped from feeding papers into a shredder and lent back in his chair. He arched his fingers in prayer under his chin, lifted his brows over wide eyes, dragged a damp tongue over his lower lip and composed himself. Then, furrowed heavy brows, swallowed hard and drawled in surprise:

"Lieutenant Brock – I was not expecting *you!*"

She stepped into the room, replied with nothing other than a glaring, fired wrath through dark-ringed eyes. Stood back well away from him she welcomed the support of her three-fifty-seven. Blood leached through her arm bandage as she enunciated words slow and mean with a fired anger:

"It was a fucking trap – you bastard!"

"A trap ...?" he whined, shrouding his timbre in a feigned sigh of disbelief. He let her implication slide off his chin and drift off into the ether.

"Haa! – So you can now see, Lieutenant: it is way beyond proof, Sergeant Da Silva is without doubt the plant. I understand there were casualties and some deaths also," he said with a smug self-satisfaction.

"Sergeant Da Silva took a bullet in his chest and went down." She spoke without any emotion.

"I'm sorry to hear it, Lieutenant. I knew you were close. At least now he won't have to suffer the indignity of an inquiry and humiliation of a court martial."

She glared at him with a loathsome desire in her soul, wanting to cuddle his throat.

"I didn't tell him," she slow-scowled, showing no feeling above disdain.

"What!" he snapped back and raised a single eyebrow. His Adam's apple bounced a jig above a loose tie in a slack collar.

"Sergeant Da Silva knew nothing of the plan – Only two people knew the details ... You – and me." She glared daggers six inches deep into his scrawny chest. "So I know it wasn't me who made the call. No guns needed . . . You bastard!"

Clad with the mask of guilt, LePage stood, moved across to his window. His mouth, in a series of strange movements voiced nothing. His ears glowed red. His neck stretched tight as he pushed out his chin. His body language stiffened as his hand rode up inside his jacket and drew out a small automatic pistol. With the weapon cradled against his chest, he turned from his window and brought the gun up with her in its sights. With manic eyes turned evil, his face grimaced in a filthy sneer. She checked herself: had never known him to be armed, would never have been caught off guard had she not been so exhausted. LePage flicked off the safety, tensed his trigger finger, gave the sick grin of a madman and spat evil words through gritted teeth:

"Sad to say, Lieutenant Brock, your particular purpose on this planet has come to an end. What a shame you didn't meet a valorous death along with Sergeant Da Silva – as was planned for you both last night."

"So *you're* the fucking plant!" she spoke soft, slow, and low.

"Tut, tut, Lieutenant Brock, language please . . . not with your last words."

The chips were down, she had to keep him talking – bait him…

"Sergeant Da Silva didn't die."

"Oh yes he did. I had him shot!"

"No – he's not dead," she spoke slow, marking time, thought it too dangerous to reach back round to her waistband for her gun, but reasoned if she could spring to the right, counter-spring to the left and roll into him, she may have a chance. It looked a slim chance – she was exhausted and he was standing too far away with a loaded gun aimed at her chest. *'Talk … keep talking,'* she mused.

"Do you want to hear what Mbangang told us about you before he died?"

"You told me he was already dead," he scowled in disbelief.

"No, he'd been shot, but he made a deathbed confession – All about you."

"Tell me – I'm all ears."

At which point he raised his pistol up and motioned to his ear in a move trite and clumsy as that of a ham actor in an amateur dramatic ten-cent stage show,

'BIG MISTAKE LEPAGE!' She sprang to the right, countered to the left, rolled onto the floorboards, but ended up nowhere near as close to him as she'd aimed for. She reached for her gun. Her hand clasped the pistol grip and half-drew the gun from her waistband. But she knew it was too late. Caught off guard, LePage fired a blind shot at nothing, then, with the manic drooling grin of a madman, he spun and braced himself to re-aim. In the split second he took to steady himself, glass shattered behind him as a hollow-point bullet from a high-powered rifle exploded in his head. Surrounded in a red mist of blood and grey matter, his body lunged forward and slammed hard against the wall, cast off cruel and unwanted as a rag-doll thrown in a tantrum from an angry child. The remains of his mouth dragged a wide blood trail over dreary paintwork all the way down to the bare pine floorboards. Brock's jaw rang open, sparse as an empty cash register. Apart from the irritating clank of the rusting fan, an eerie hush rang in her ears.

LePage's comfort window now had a clear view out into the outside world, but only through a very small hole from which tiny cracks spidered to the edges of the pane, mirroring the arms of a soul released, reaching out for something but didn't know what. Mystified, she picked herself up from the floor. Keeping low she edged forward, kicked the gun away from LePage's hand and took a small vanity mirror from his desk. Stealing a slow path across the room she came up beside the window. Keeping out of sight she raised the mirror to reflect back the outside view, and slow-scanned around, stopping at the sight of a tall male figure, dark-haired, well built, clad in a black leather jacket, standing high out on the flat roof of the car lot. Without menace in his demeanour, he lowered a sniper's rifle. Confused, she made a slow turn and stood in full view to the window. The Leather-Jack acknowledged her, saluted, kept his gaze, then, after a warming smile he turned and disappeared from view.

Exhausted, confused and tired, she slunk her weary body down into LePage's office chair, desperate to make some sense out of her bewildering situation. She delved into her muddled mind for answers, anything at all to enable her to fit together the pieces of this crazy enigmatic jigsaw puzzle she had found herself a piece of. But she was far too drained in both body and soul for her mind to even start to compute. She closed her eyes. The fan droned on seeming louder now, invading her psyche. With both disdain and anger, she looked down to the torpid, disgusting corpse at her feet. Now nothing more than a pollution to the very soul of mankind, huddled in a crumpled heap on the floor in front of her, leaching blood and gore into a glowing red pool, mushrooming slow out across bare pine boards. For her, she thought it the most endearing moment she'd ever seen LePage; and very nearly broke into a smile at the thought. The three-fifty-seven gripped loose in her hand dropped down into her lap. She wished dearly she could have used it, but its barrel was cold. Revenge is sweet, but rare to attain.

Ambient light blinked in the doorway. A figure emerged from the shadows. She raised her eyes without moving her head. On impulse her hand twitched around the grip of her gun, but she couldn't raise it; she was deplete of fuel. Breathing heavy through her mouth, she focused at the figure now stood in the doorway. He spoke:

"Lieutenant Brock, it's such a pleasure to meet you at long last." The Leather-Jack stepped into the room, moved across to her and offered a warm hand below a warm smile, and said: "Major Randolph Falconer, special field-Agent, National Security force. Please – call me Randolph." He spoke in a perfect English gentleman's accent. Drained of energy she didn't have the wherewithal left in her body to even think straight, let alone shake his hand.

"I'm sorry it was such a close call, but you were in my line of fire. If I'd taken the shot I would have hit you also. I didn't want to take that chance. However: you obliged when you jumped aside."

She pointed down to the corpse at her feet, didn't move her head, but kept emerald green focused on Falconer. He stared back into her jaded face. She spoke soft in a slow tired voice as she light-kicked the corpse.

"How did you know about him?"

"Eventually through you, and then confirmed beyond doubt by the events at the Palm Beach hotel yesterday evening. He has been a suspect to us for a long time, you all were."

He paused, afforded her a polite smile before he spoke again:

But now it was time for us to take action – I'm only sorry it wasn't sooner." Falconer went across to a table lamp and drew a bug out from behind a felt cushion under its base. He turned back to her.

"I was listening in to his final conversation with you. I have to say, Lieutenant: you have my greatest admiration."

"Did you put the bug in my apartment?" she asked almost in a whisper from her motionless body.

"No! – No we didn't. We concluded you were clean, but still could not afford to take any chances and include you in our National Security operations."

"And Grady…?"

"Also clean." He nodded with a slight smile, aware of her concern. Dispirited, she dragged a damp tongue over dry lips, nodded lazy as she kept him in her gaze. Then exhaled a deep breath, sunk her chin into her chest and sighed. A tear rolled down her cheek and dropped onto her lap. Falconer, uncomfortable, searched for words, needed to break the moment.

"My team is on its way here as we speak," enthused Falconer. "They'll leave no stone unturned to find anything here we can use against him, or to help us with our investigations."

With deep empathy radiating from his eyes, Falconer stared down to her from his towering six-foot-three-inch frame. She cut a tired, exhausted, spent force, slumped back in a chair with blood weeping through her arm bandage, a cloud of dark rings enshrouding emerald eyes. Her face was drawn and her body language confirmed she was drained of energy; but still, there was something magnetic about her stunning him. He stepped forward, lifted her gun from her loose grip and held out his hand.

"Come – I think you could do with a decent breakfast – I'm buying."

He lifted her from the chair. She stepped over LePage's corpse and didn't look back.

At the door she stopped, reached out and turned off the fan. Now she could leave.

*   *   *

Displaying the flamboyance of a cock-pheasant, the five-star diner on the bay was way above her pay grade; but this time she didn't care – she wouldn't be paying. The Major led her past a saluting concierge, through a walnut-panelled foyer and into the plush hotel dining area. Placed with a sensitive acumen in the corner of the room, a piano player dressed in a white dinner jacket and bow tie, meandered artistic fingers over ivory keys on a gleaming black grand piano; not in a loud way but still with enough animation to allow discretion to private conversation. Tasteful artwork set in gilded frames hung in aesthetic opulence from the walls. High above, a parade of silver chandeliers hung from a formation of ornate floral plaster ceiling roses. French polish over rosewood tables reflected a kaleidoscope of light from the silver service cutlery. If you didn't enjoy the food on offer you for sure couldn't knock the five-star ambience of the members-only private club.

After a wade through thick pile carpeting across to a quiet green leather corner booth, screened for privacy by green pot plants, Brock rested her body down and for the first time in a long time collapsed back in opulent comfort. Falconer took the bench seat opposite. Seconds later as if transformed by magic, a bow-tied waiter appeared it would seem from nowhere holding a menu heavily bordered in embellished gold clutched close to his chest. He swallowed hard, coughed lightly into a rolled fist, lifted his eyebrows, and asked:

"Is there anything you would want me to get for the lady, Major Falconer?"

'*Like maybe a fucking ambulance!*' he thought to himself.

"Thank you, Jackson – please bring us both a decent breakfast and some coffee."

"Certainly, Sir, right away."

"Oh … and Jackson . . ." The waiter stopped, turned on a heel.

"Sir…?" The Major glanced up through his eyebrows, "and bring some brandy, two glasses. Make them doubles if you would."

"Certainly, Sir, right away."

Falconer turned to her, opened his mouth to speak but his voice was hi-jacked by two ravishing green eyes as they bored a path across to him mesmerising his gaze: *magnetic*. He closed his mouth and leant back into his seat, didn't blink from her visage.

'*Christ, she's fucking beautiful,*' he mused, thought of his wife and child, swallowed hard and cleared dark thoughts: '*tough call!*' He shook his head, ran his fingers through thick hair, smiled politely at her. Fumbled with whatever he could find to fumble with. But lucky for him: welcome as a cavalry call at a scalping, the breakfast setting was rolled out on a gold lacquered trolley with an inset green faux onyx tray and transferred to the table; closely followed by two glasses of brandy and two plates of steaming food from the breakfast buffet.

Although Brock had eaten nothing since her breakfast with *Jack* the previous morning, she still only pecked at her food. She sat back, drew her tongue across her lips, picked her eyes up from the table and spoke soft words:

"So, where to now?" Falconer smiled, relieved at the break in the hiatus. He lifted his glass, mocked a toast, and said:

"National Security will take over the C.S.F. office. You will be working in tandem with us from now on. I will replace LePage as your superior officer."

"In his office...?"

"Yes, in his office. But only until I've sorted through everything of relevance, then we will move out to N.S.F. Headquarters and close the C.S.F office down. Which I'm sure will come as a relief to you. And if may I add: not before time."

"And Sergeant Da Silva ...?"

"Yes, of course, we will certainly need him. And may I take this opportunity to wish him a full and speedy recovery. And while we are on the subject, Lieutenant – may I suggest you take a vacation yourself, charged of course to the department. We can arrange a meeting and have a full de-brief sometime next week, or whenever you feel fit enough to come back to work." With her arms folded over her chest she played her lower lip with her thumb and index finger, stared without emotion across the table at him, in silence. Then, in almost a whisper, she asked;

"Would you drop me back at my apartment?"

"Yes – yes of course."

Pensive, she waited before she would speak again; then whispered: "Thank you for breakfast."

He looked down at her near-full plate set next to an empty brandy glass.

"It has been my pleasure, Lieutenant Brock."

* * *

Chapter Twenty-two

Strained sounds from a limping Bach sonata breathed a sweet greeting as Brock slunk tired but welcome steps up to her apartment. Relieved to be home, she slid her key into the lock and spun the barrel. Canine scratching on the door, a receptive touch she sure needed, brought sunshine to her face.

"Don't stop," she called out to them both as she pushed the door open. Bingo, an effective early warning system, jumped up and tried to dry off his tongue on her face as she ruffled wiry black hair on his head. She laid her gun down on the coffee table, along with her door key and the sim-card printout. Then, with safety in mind, she picked up her gun and carried it through to rest on her bedside locker. Her bed beckoned, a refuge more inviting than ever, but first she needed to wash away the black and blues from the last twenty-four hours. She hung her head, needed to call out to Heidi, but if truth be known she'd rather not have to call out to anyone. She wanted nothing more than to be left alone and sleep.

"I've gotta' jump in the shower, sweetie. You carry on, it's sounding good: *'poor kid, sure needs encouragement from someone.'*

She stripped off blood-sodden clothes and tossed them down into the corner of her bedroom, then wandered tired steps from a bloodied, naked body across into the shower room. Head bowed and hands spread against the wall in the assumed position, a pose she had ordered to so many undesirables, her naked body stood poised in ecstasy beneath the shower rose. Hot therapeutic water cascaded down over her head, ran down her back. She craned her head back, let soothing water run into her mouth; then, frowned down to the stitches weeping blood in her arm. She felt great relief at watching a whirlpool of red water circle the drain, washing down with it many of the bad thoughts collected over the last twenty-four hours. A soft hand tapped on the door. Heidi called out:

"I'm going now, Lieutenant, may see you later."

"Okay, sweetie, you take care."

Not one minute later the doorbell sang out. Brock dropped her head and groaned little pleasure at the termination of her hot water massage. With reluctance she flipped off the shower, wrapped a loose towel around her dripping body and called out:

"Did you forget your key, sweetie?" She sprang the door and breathed in the rich scent of *To a Wild Rose.* Ice blue eyes met tearful green in elated harmony. Her wilted body, limp as a rag doll, fell forward into Josie's arms. Hugged tight in a tender embrace they savoured a long, lingering kiss. She pulled Josie in through the doorway and with a stab from her foot, kicked the door shut behind her. Leant back against the door Brock hugged Josie tight in her arms, buried her head into the pretty girl's shoulder. Tears rolled down her cheeks, she didn't speak – couldn't. Lifting her head she gazed into a radiance of twenty-four-carat splendour. Brock's soft voice said nothing aloud; spoke only volumes of passion through her eyes as she led Josie through the apartment to the sofa.

"I knew you were at the Palm Beach hotel," said Josie, "I was so worried when you didn't call." Sad eyes watched a trickle of blood running down from the stitches in Brock's arm. Josie gave a questioned look into Brock's eyes: "What happened? Tell me, Maddie."

Brock held Josie's head in her hands, looking deep into moist eyes.

"Sit down, Josie, we need to talk. I'll get some coffee." If she were honest: she needed a large slug of *Jack.* She hadn't slept in thirty hours and had come close to death at gunpoint on two occasions during those desperate hours.

"No, come here, sit, I want to look at your arm," whispered Josie, wondering what could have caused such a wound. Brock complied and went to her on the sofa. Tender hands took her arm, Josie puckered her lips and planted a sensuous kiss, then freed the towel, let it fall to the floor, licked damp moisture from a shuddering body alive and aroused by carnal thought. Breathing heavy through her mouth, Brock closed her eyes, soft-moaned, pulled Josie up from the sofa and led her into the bedroom.

An hour later they lay in a naked sweat on the bed, cuddled tight in each other's arms, sexually nourished. Almost in a whisper, Brock spoke tender words:

"You have no idea how much I needed that." With her hand still slow-massaging Brock's breast, Josie cracked a lascivious smile.

"You and me both, Maddie."

In a brief respite from carnal reverie, Josie caught sight of the bloodied clothes discarded on the floor, she scanned up to the menacing gun-blued three-fifty-seven lying dormant on the bedside table; then took her gaze back to the bloodied wound on Brock's upper arm.

"Were you – involved, in the incident at the Palm Beach, Maddie ...? Please say no."

Brock wouldn't lie but felt compelled to improvise on the truth.

"Only from the security angle: nothing serious."

"But seven people were killed?"

"So I heard," said Brock needing to change the subject.

'*So much blood-stained clothes,*' Josie wondered aloud as she gazed down at Brock's bloodied clothing.

"Most of that blood belongs to Sergeant Da Silva; there was a hell of a lot of broken glass." Josie's jaw dropped open below eyes grown wide.

"Is he okay?"

"Yes, he's fine, taking it easy, relaxing in bed. It's nothing a few Band-Aids and a bunch of aspirins can't fix." Sensitive in thought, Brock focused into the soft innocence of sapphire blue eyes, didn't want to say how many of those deaths had originated from the barrel of her own gun; or mention the fact she had narrowly escaped death by gunfire herself on two occasions over the past twenty-four hours; or that in truth Grady was all tubed up in intensive care fighting for his life – how could she? Prudence called for her to change the subject.

"How's the boyfriend?"

"I wouldn't know; I put that donkey out to pasture." Brock choked a smile.

"Atta' girl! How'd he take it?"

"I guess he's gone back to his porn mags."

Quizzical, Brock stared deep into the custom-made face of an angel, wondered how anybody could pump out satisfaction from a porn mag when such a pretty girl as this was on offer.

"My job took a turn, thanks to a little help from your sergeant."

"Whoops!"

"No, it's okay." Josie gave a cute laugh, ran her fingers through Brock's hair.

"The boss decided he wasn't much cop at customer relations, so he handed the grill over to his partner, a much nicer guy – *I think*. But I guess we'll see." Then she popped her forefinger on Brock's nose and added with a wide grin: "And – he sold the popcorn machine!"

Brock smiled at this beautiful creature's sense of humour, closed her eyes, God how she loved her.

"I want to meet your sergeant one day, he sounds a great guy." Such thoughts caused Brock to smile inwards, thinking of both the good and bad times she'd been through with Grady over many years. Emotions ran wild through her exhausted, hallucinating mind. In retrospect he was the only other person in the world she could say she had truly loved. Her eyes glazed, grew damp.

"You okay, Maddie?"

"Yeah – I'm fine." She digressed, changed the subject and held Josie in close.

"I was thinking – could you get some time off?"

"I guess – why?"

"I've been given leave for a while; been told to take a vacation all expenses paid. I thought I might rent one of those cute little rustic beach chalets out on the bay, way down South hidden in the wilds by the dunes. I thought you might – maybe come and join me?" Staring deep into emeralds, Josie said nothing. Her eyes welled; she chuckled out a small laugh.

"When do we leave?" Brock sighed back a great relief, a cute nose wriggled; she felt her body beginning to refuel.

"Let me call up and check." She reached over, tapped on her palm phone, scrolled down and checked on a number, rang and set a date.

"Seems they're pretty empty right now, it's not quite holiday season yet," Brock racked her eyes in hope, "how's tomorrow morning sound . . . Okay?" Josie smiled a lust back at Brock.

"Can I stay here over tonight?"

"Is there an idiot running the government?"

Before driving back to her room to pack a bag, Josie dropped Brock off at the medical centre. Under the heavy scent of antiseptic pervasive in his room, Grady was still unconscious and had not moved since she'd left him. Brock assured herself it was due to the drugs and medication he'd been given. Bent over his bed she whispered sweet-nothings into his ear, thought she saw his face twitch but realised it was nothing. She squeezed his hand, kissed his forehead, landed a soft playful slap on his cheek. With a tear and a sigh, she scribbled out a note, stamped it with a lipstick kiss and left it by his bedside. She asked the nurse to make sure he would get it when he woke up. It read: *Brought you a couple of sexy strippers, but I couldn't wake you up, so I ate them myself. Call me, Brock xx.*

In search of something fresh to flavour her lungs, Brock strolled out into radiant sunlight burning down onto the lawns of the medical centre gardens. Relaxed back, facing up to the sky she closed her eyes and let golden rays of solace from the blazing orb re-vitalise her body. Such simple feelings of atonement had been a stranger in her life for way too long.

The sun had climbed high in a blue sky since the dawn chorus had chanted its final melody for the day, having been rudely interrupted from the drone of an industrial lawnmower. Despite the intrusion from machinery, fresh-cut grass sparked a dulcet memory conjured from the sweet fragrance of childhood; a pleasant but distant thought, which to her detriment had been long since neglected until now. In an all too rare moment of reverie, she closed her eyes; let her mind time travel back to those halcyon days of innocence. Feeling dizzy on her feet she began to hallucinate and realised how tired she was, and in desperate need of sleep.

From the taxi stand outside the medical centre Brock hopped a cab to Sujo's Auto Lot. Shimmering under bright sunlight, two black National Security force SUV's with dark tinted windows flanked LePage's vehicle in the parking bays. She reasoned Falconer and his team would be sifting their way through files in the Covert Security office, but their quest for any skeletons LePage may have hidden was now their business and not hers, for she had no desire to step into LePage's office ever again. She climbed into Grady's Jeep, flipped the start fob out from under the dash, scowled up to LePage's grubby window, spat out into the dust and closed the door on a very bad chapter in her life. She fired up the motor and drove back to the solace of her apartment and the welcome comfort of her bed.

As she spun the lock and pushed open her apartment door the sole sound greeting her came from a dripping faucet.

Breathing out a sigh of relief she walked into the bathroom, tightened down the tap, closed her eyes and cherished the silence. Searching for comfort in solitude, she cracked open a bottle of *Jack* from the bedside locker, took a three-finger slug, and then another before sinking her weary body fully clothed into the sanctuary of soft mattress; then closed her eyes and fell into a deep sleep with the hope to venture into a world where she would dream only of beautiful things.

*   *   *

Chapter Twenty-three

Aroused from a near comatose slumber, Brock's inner senses flickered to life from the scent of *To a Wild Rose*. Emerald eyes blinked, sprang wide and held the sensual vision of a beautiful face curtained in a soft flow of golden locks. She saw an angelic image of innocence, pure enough to have taxed even the sculptural talents of Michelangelo. Her semi-conscious mind registered she was still ensconced in reverie with an alluring dream, as two pretty eyes warm and sensual stared back a passion she had never before shared with such rapture throughout her life. The rich aroma from French roasted coffee was dwarfed by *Wild Rose*. With reluctance, she drew her lids down over her eyes and asked:

"How did you get in?"

"The little blind girl."

"Of course . . . remind me to give you a key."

With her eyes still closed Brock ran her tongue over dry lips and mentally chastised herself in disbelief. She wondered what in hell she was doing running around with a gun blasting hollow-points at lowlife and filthy slime-ball drug dealers when she could have this beautiful creature in front of her all to herself. She figured it was now time for a change and should quit while she was winning, for to carry on with Covert Security it may well only be a matter of time before she drew the short straw. Events yesterday had brought it home to her how close she'd teetered on the edge, and twice in twenty-four hours. Yet, that nagging old Hindu proverb gate crashed her psyche pungent as a bad smell to the spirit in a crowded elevator: *'They who ride the tiger can never get off its back'*. The doorbell rang loud for her.

Blue eyes sparkled above her; Josie bent and kissed her lips. Sensual hands cuddled her head and said:

"Hungry? I ordered Pizza: four-cheese calzone, I hope it's okay."

"Sounds good honey, I'm starving."

Swathed in the rich, alluring aroma from *Wild Rose*, Brock wrapped herself in black silk oriental dragon print and wandered out to join Josie at the coffee table. They ate pizza off their laps, drank white wine and cherished a welcome moment of solitude.

"What time shall we leave in the morning?" asked Josie.

"Somewhere around nine, we'll pick up breakfast and supplies on the way. It should take us about two hours in a slow drive. I've got Grady's Jeep outside; I think we may need it where we're going."

"Doesn't he need it?"

"No, I don't think so."

"Thanks for coming Josie; it means such a lot to me."

"I wouldn't miss it for anything." Josie spoke through tender blue eyes. "Come and play some piano for me please, Maddie." Brock as long as she had life in her body could never resist such a radiant look. She lifted the lid on the Steinway, ran three octaves up and back down the chromatic scale to loosen up her fingers then teased out a progression of thirteenth chords before she settled into a stirring, enchanting melody in A Major. She improvised over the chorus, resolved back on the melody, then with a stunning crescendo of colour chords ending with the relative minor-triad under a ninth over a major seventh, eleventh under the thirteenth and the tonic in the bass, she sat back with her head bowed, then, beamed a smile across the room to a damp-eyed Josie sat spellbound in silence.

"So truly beautiful, Maddie. I've never before heard such passion in music. What was it called?"

"It was an exceptionally tender piece, written way back in the late eighteen hundreds by a guy called Edward MacDowell – I think he wrote it especially for you . . . It's called, 'To a Wild Rose'." With welling eyes, Josie went to the piano, hugged Maddie and dropped tender tears down over the keyboard.

"It was so beautiful, Maddie." Brock hugged her close, kissed her forehead.

"And so are you, Josie. Come – let's get naked."

*   *   *

The rich saline scent from sea air thickened in the atmosphere as the highway drive South from the city dropped in altitude to near sea level. Ten miles back in a desolate cove, they'd passed a derelict fish canning factory. Clad with corrugated iron running with rust and flapping loose in a light breeze it reflected a sorry sight; now nothing more than a target for amateur photographers and the expectant easel of the weekend water colourist. It was the first and the last sign of civilization they'd seen in a good while, until a hand-painted shingle with an arrow pointing off to the left told them they had arrived at the Echo Beach resort.

Sentried at each side with tall pines, the drive down a long dust track morphed into a stand of towering palms as the Jeep closed on lapping surf at the seashore. A reclusive sense of solitude was on offer. The track terminated at the entrance to a small gathering of log and shingle cabins spaced far enough apart to afford the occupants total privacy. For more than one reason Brock had rented the far cabin nearest the ocean. She trailed tire tracks in soft sand set below windblown rolling dunes, peppered with growths of sand couch and wisps of sprouting Lyme grass. At the far cabin, she pulled the Jeep in under green shade cloth. Their luggage was light. The only heavy thing Brock carried along with a crate of wine was her three-fifty-seven and a box of hollow-points; something she hoped she wouldn't need, but prudence trumped negligence: a defensive thought pattern saving her life many times over – maybe too many times! *'Time now to quit, it's gotta' be,'* she mused.

Stood on the porch leaching both sweat and craving under the ray of a hot sun in the flawless setting of an ocean backdrop, Brock cute-tweaked her nose, laced her hands together behind Josie's neck, pulled her close and kissed hot lips with a tender passion.

"Come sexy, let's unpack and then we can check out the bedroom."

Inside the cabin, décor was rustic but cosy. A large, open stone fire hearth shrouded under a black-steel flare-spread chimney stood dominant in the centre of the room. Entrance to a bathroom with a rustic shower but no bath was accessed through a bamboo door in the far wall. A small ice box and microwave sat on a cabinet top. A coffee maker on the small kitchen drainer was a welcome sight. Outside, provided under shade, a barbecue stood charged and ready for simple cooking if required; its shade was more to shield from the sun than from rain at this time of the year. Inside the main room, spacious under a low timber ceiling stood two cane easy chairs, a rustic table with stools and a double bed set against the far wall. Over which in case you forgot where you were, hung a large painting of a sailboat becalmed in the sunset on a golden sea. A colourful African Ndebele-crafted rug covered a section of bare pine boards. En masse, it offered a fairy book setting for the amorous. Brock draped her arm around Josie's neck.

"Hungry," she asked. Josie flashed her lashes, purred soft into emerald eyes, ran her fingers through Brock's hair and stared a sensual blue-eyed sultry passion.

"Yes – then maybe we can eat later.

*   *   *

Early evening shade drew a cooling breeze over the cabin complex. Soft flames from a fire glowed bright in the hearth of cabin number five, high-lit two naked bodies entwined together on the bed. The fire, an unnecessary requirement in the warm climate, afforded further visual comfort for the impassioned. They drank white wine and got drunk on love. A lot of each was on offer.

"I don't think I've ever been as happy as I am with you, Maddie. You've changed my life."

"Maybe I've opened a new door into another life for you, sweetheart?"

"Yes – a door into your life sounds better."

"It's been kinda' lonely in my life for a long time now Josie."

"Was there ever anyone?"

"No." Black locks brushed her shoulders as she shook her head, "no, never as intense as this; nowhere even close." Setting her wine glass down, Brock took Josie's glass from her hand and placed it on the side stand, cupped her hand round Josie's head, pulled her close, gave her lips a long and caressing embrace, ran tender fingers through her soft blond hair and hugged her tight. Split logs in the open fire cracked and popped out their private conversation, aloof to anything happening behind them. Leaping tongues of fire were not only active in the hearth. Two empty wine glasses kept stark company to a loaded three-fifty-seven on the dresser.

*   *   *

At the finish of a late breakfast, tanning hot flesh under a scorching sun high in the sky, two naked girls rolled in the dunes, played cute as kids in the shallows, splashing each other and swimming in the surf. Brock dove under a breaker, surfaced and swam out past the shallow breakers into deeper water. Josie followed, trod water next to her.

"It's so beautiful here, Maddie, just the two of us all alone."

"Yeah – all alone, except for the guy fishing up at the other end of the bay.

"You think he can see us?"

"I doubt it. I wouldn't think it would be his fishing pole he'd be wrapping his hand around if he *could* see us."

She splashed water at Josie and swam for the shore, shouted back:

"Come sexy, let's get some lunch."

Lounging in the porch swing seat, they feasted high on French Brie, crackers and black olives. Chilled white wine followed twenty-four-volt Columbian coffee. Life was good. Any thoughts of what Brock usually did in her day-to-day life had started to fade back into the distant horizon, far away behind her. But those dry thoughts, hard to swallow, would sneak up on her in dark moments, continue to regurgitate and stick in the craw of her throat. She reflected on Grady, wondered how he was doing. With any chance of a phone signal also way back past the distant horizon, there was not much chance of her finding out. She felt a sudden fatigue as the weight of the black monkey climbed on her back.

"Are you okay, Maddie . . . what's wrong?"

"Nothing, honey—I'm fine." She spoke with the conviction of a squirming politician caught with his dick in a place it shouldn't be. Josie stared deep into Brock's eyes, put her arms around her neck and pulled her close.

"It's okay, Maddie – I understand." Josie kissed Brock's lips soft and tender; Brock smiled back, did her nose thing, carved off another slice of French Brie and sat back in silence searching for answers far out beyond the distant horizon. Determined now to enjoy nothing more than a long life with someone she loved was a choice paramount to all else; a choice she figured to be not the only, but the most favoured way forward, and through hell or high water, she'd take it.

"Shall we take a walk along the beach later and see what the old fisherman finds so interesting on the end of his pole?

Hell, he's been out there frying under a burning sun for most of the day."

"Sure, why not? We could probably do with some exercise."

"Well, we sure are getting a lot of sexercise, pretty girl."

"Not so much of the *girl,* Maddie; I'm coming up on twenty-seven."

"You look as if you could take ten years off that, Josie."

"I wish! How old are you, Maddie?"

"Me? I'm thirty-two and still counting. But I'm feeling a hell of a lot younger since I met you, sweetheart." A sensual eye drew a lingered line under her statement. Unchained love smiled across to Josie and danced bright as a firefly around a flame.

"Come on gorgeous let's go see what the '*Old man and the sea*' has caught. Maybe we can brighten up his day if he hasn't hooked anything."

"I think we'd better put some clothes on first Maddie. We wouldn't want to give him a cardiac arrest on his last earthly erection."

Maddie tweaked her nose: "Whadda way to go: up to heaven with a smile on his face! What *would* Saint Peter say?"

"Probably tell him not to bring such a disgusting thing in here and take it down to that nasty hot joint down below," quipped Josie. Brock cracked a smile, shook black locks and went inside for her gun.

Josie watched Maddie coming out through the doorway tucking the magnum into the back of her waistband.

"Do you think you'll need a gun, Maddie?"

"No, I guess maybe not. It's been a habit for me over the last sixteen years – kinda hard to shake off. But I'll leave it here if you'd feel better about it. Not a problem, honey."

"No, it's okay. You go ahead if you think it's best. " Brock stared down at the gun. She bounced her brows and said:

"Tell you what. I'll leave the gun here. If he attacks us we'll smack him to death with wet fish."

"Well there's a lot more chance of him getting into heaven smelling of wet fish than with a huge erection."

"Very true, Josie, I guess the smell of wet fish is going to hang around in heaven a lot longer than an erection."

"Not if Michelangelo has anything to do with it, that's if he's still up there and hasn't been relegated down below for bad behaviour and sexual harassment on the disciples."

"If you keep this line of conversation up Josie, I'm draggin' you straight back to bed."

"Okay..."

"Okay what?" Josie spread her legs and grinned. Brock shook her head and shrugged.

"Okay then, I guess we could go see him tomorrow – If he's still there," soft eyes radiated across to Josie. "Hell Josie, you're so bloody cute!"

*   *   *

The next morning following a lazy breakfast, the two girls locked together in arms under a crystal clear ultramarine sky paddled ankle-deep through warm shallows along the shoreline beneath a burning sun to check out 'Hemingway's old man and the sea.' Despite feeling undressed without her gun, Brock saw nothing much in the way of danger in the secluded surroundings they were enjoying. Then again, she didn't see much in the way of danger either at the Palm Beach Hotel; or at one hell of a lot of other places if truth were known. Gripping his pole hard, the old fisherman waved as they approached. Two high-charged spunky girls in sawn-off denims and tee shirts tied high at the front way above the midriff oozing more sex appeal than a naked Bardot in her prime – he saw as a gift from heaven. His eyes went up into the clouds, thanked whoever the hell it was up there. From behind a coy smile, Brock thought how considerate they were not to have taken a dip on their way up and arrived flaunting a heavy dose of voluptuous enticement under scant cover from wet tee shirts. Poor guy, life can be so cruel.

"Hi, girls," he said, casting his line way out to sea a lot further than usual powered now by pure testosterone. They waded closer in the sparkle of a warm turquoise sea. The old fisherman grinned through a generous growth of grey whiskers terminating well before reaching the crown of his head: a vulnerable part of his anatomy, bare to the elements it burned and glowed red under the sun in tandem with another part of his anatomy not yet in the sun but for sure glowing red. His fantasies, long forgotten in the fading shadow of an unremarkable life, sparked and re-kindled. Once more he had hope. He reeled in...

Draped around each other's shoulders, cool and relaxed as battle heroes from a victorious conflict, the two girls stood thigh-deep in the shallows, exuding enough carnal power to condemn the celibate to eternal damnation.

"Caught anything?" asked Brock.

"A few – do you eat fish?"

"Yes, it makes a change from burgers," she replied. "Are you here alone, Sir?"

"Yeah – I used to come here a lot with my wife."

"She's not here?"

"No…" He cast out his line with a passion he hoped might hook a memory; then, relaxed back, gazed out to sea and spoke with a soft heart: "She died. The virus took her."

"I'm sorry."

"Thank you, I appreciate that." He beamed a warm smile to Brock. "I come here now for a few memories."

Before she would speak Brock felt it prudent to let such a comment float in the air for a while. The old fisherman took in the slack.

"Pretty nasty gash you got there up on your arm, miss," said the fisherman scratching at the side of his nose.

"Yeah, – Teach me not to go swimming with the sharks again in a hurry."

"I hear that!" he agreed.

"How long are you here for?" she asked, changing the subject.

"I came down for the weekend, I go back tomorrow, see my kids . . . Maybe take them some fresh fish if I'm lucky. How long are you guys here for?"

"We're also going back late tomorrow. Back to the big city," replied Brock. A dark cloud fell across Josie's face, her jaw dropped; blue eyes grew wide and sad.

"Anywhere around here we can get some supplies, we're all out back home, don't want to arrive back late with nothin' to eat," said Brock.

"Sure, get back on the highway and drive south for a mile or so, there's a store up on your left. It's not a big-city store, no fancy wines or frillies but you should find something to suit your tastes there."

"Okay, thanks. Well good luck with the fishing, Sir. Come, let's go sweetheart."

Wishing he was fifty years younger, the old fisherman reeled in his slack and pulled in his stomach. He watched without blinking as two themes for a sweet dream strolled back down the bay, wrapped in each other's arms. He shook his head, *'what the hell ever happened to youth?'* His line struck hard, then went slack – Shame, he'd fumbled life's curved ball.

"Back tomorrow, Maddie … why?"

"The only place we're going tomorrow, Sweetheart, is to the store to get more supplies."

"Don't scare me, I thought we were about to leave," whispered Josie's cute voice. "Poor guy, he's probably real lonely; no-one to talk to but the fish. But why tell him we were leaving, Maddie?" Providence wouldn't allow Brock to tell Josie the real reason she wanted to hide her away. *'Tell no-one, trust no-one, live longer!'* Macey paid the price. Brock wasn't prepared to lose Josie the same way.

"You know, Josie, in the security business it's not a good idea to casually allow people who you don't know what your movements are. Or even better: nor to anybody, to be really safe. You never know who is listening. I guess it's been another hard habit for me to shake off."

"You don't think *he* could be a danger to us do you?" queried Josie.

"No, I don't. But the danger is, you never know, honey. Trust no-one and you keep breathing. Anyway, let's not go there. Come on, let's get back, crack open a bottle and have some fun. I've got something I want to talk to you about."

*   *   *

Brock held up two bottles.

"Red or white, sweetheart...?"

"Let's go white."

Brock carried two glasses of Chardonnay out to the porch. The light golden liquid glistened through cut glass sparkling bright as a hungry tiger's eyes stalking prey in brilliant sunlight. Life was good. Sat back in the swing-seat with her arm cuddled round Josie, Brock focused her thoughts. High above still blazing full in the sky, the sun was burning down hard enough to crack rocks and grill skin off a rhino. The porch in shade was the perfect place to relax stretched out on the swing seat enjoying a cool glass of wine in a lush life.

"You said you wanted to talk to me, Maddie?"

"Yes," she turned and sent a tender smile into sweet blue eyes. "I've been thinking . . . since we've been here I can't remember ever being so happy. The thought of going back to the insecurity of a life *in* security, doesn't make me feel good. I've about had enough of it now, honey."

"It's a job, Maddie. What else would you do? – You could play the piano – sure why not?" Josie enthused.

"Sweetheart, you're so cute," she smiled at Josie's naïve innocence, "and then I can join all the other muso's and artists in the welfare queue. No, I don't think so. The security thing is all I've ever done throughout my working life, I don't know anything else. Maybe I should come and help you flip burgers at Skinny's." Josie stared down into her wineglass.

"You'd be on your own – I don't work there anymore."

Sad eyes looked up to Brock.

"Josie, what do you mean?"

"The new boss tried to hit on me, said I could only have time off if he could have sex with me."

"I'm so sorry, sweetheart. I shouldn't have asked you to come. It was so selfish of me."

"Are you kidding me, Maddie? Do you honestly think I'd have given this up for an asshole repulsive as him? He turned out to be every bit as bad as his partner." Brock chuckled at the thought, then suggested.

"Maybe I'll ask Grady to go look in on him."

"No need! The popcorn machine's gone now – remember?"

"Grady's quite a creative guy when he's all fired up. I'm sure he'd find something else to shove the guy's head into."

"No, it's okay. I was fed up there anyway. I need to find something a lot better than waiting tables. Anyway, now I guess there'll no longer be any need to get back in a hurry." She racked her eyebrows across to Brock.

"Well we'd better get some clothes on in a hurry; here comes Ernest," said Brock.

"Huh? Who's Ernest?"

"Ernest Hemingway: our old man and the sea – the fisherman guy."

"Maddie, what *are* you talking about?"

"Nothing, sweetheart, put some clothes on before he has a heart attack."

"Hi girls, I thought you could do with something fresh." The old fisherman held out a couple of big fish. Seemed a nice gesture on the face of it, but maybe he was trying out what could be his last attempt at smart-talk over a long and mundane life. Or maybe he was only being kind; which is probably more the truth.

"I've gutted them for you, ready for the barbecue . . . Enjoy!"

As the bearer of gifts and to emphasise his prowess with his pole, he slung the fish with panache over the rail, then turned to walk away and take himself back out from a brief, but exquisite fantasy.

"Thank you, sir, you're very kind, it's much appreciated," said Brock. As he turned to leave she called after him:

"Hey, excuse me, Sir. How about you come and share them with us as it's all our last night?"

Looking stunned, the old fisherman didn't know what to say, but sent copious thanks up to someone up in heaven – Albeit a bit fucking late!

"Thank you, miss, I'd sure appreciate it. My name's Jerry by the way." *So he wasn't Ernest.* Brock shrugged her shoulders, bounced her eyebrows at Josie.

"Pleased to meet you, Jerry, I'm Pastor Weston and this is Pastor Smythe; but you may drop the *Pastor* if you'd feel more comfortable. Rather call me Susie, and her Jaynie. Can I get you a glass of wine, Jerry? . . . I'm sorry, we haven't any cold beer."

"Sure, thank you. Wine's good, red if you have it – doesn't need chilling," he said with a feeling he'd wandered straight into a bloody convent and reasoned: *'the guy up there's sure got a sick sense of fucking humour!'*

"Jerry, would you know how to fire up the barbecue, we're a couple of city girls not used to this sort of thing?" Feigning helplessness, Brock shrugged her shoulders and spread her palms out in request.

"Sure, but I'll need a light," he said, and thought maybe a thunderbolt might arrive from somewhere up above. Who knows, stranger things have happened to him this week.

"Matches on their way with your wine, Jerry. Come, give me a hand please, Jaynie."

She nodded Josie inside and silent mouthed: *'Happy'*... and tweaked her nose.

"Pastor, Susie – Jaynie – what *are* you talking about Maddie?" asked Josie, her head bent over curious. With a face full of concern, Brock held Josie tight by her shoulders and gazed deep into those blowtorch pools of pure innocence.

"I only hope I never have to explain it to you, sweetheart, maybe one day I will – but I sure hope not. For now, what does it matter who he thinks we are? But it could matter, to someone, somewhere. I can't take that chance. I don't know who he is, Josie. You're probably right: he's nothing more than a very lonely old fisherman who isn't called Ernest, and who has lost his wife. I'm sorry to sound so vague, sweetheart. I would never let anything happen to you … Do you trust me, Josie?" Blond locks nodded.

"With my life, Maddie." Confused, Josie stared into Brock's eyes. With deep passion, Brock pulled her close, held her tight in her arms and hugged her hard.

"I'm so glad to hear it, sweetheart. Don't worry, thinking about it though – you should be Susie and I should be Jaynie: Susie suits you a hell of a lot better than it does me."

"How about I stay Jaynie and you are Tarzan?"

"Wouldn't be here if I *was* Tarzan, but if I was you could beat my chest for me, but not too hard!" she tweaked her nose, "let's go see how Ernest's doing... Sorry, I mean Jerry."

Fresh fish barbecued over a charcoal fire, along with the rest of the French Brie, crackers, wine and olives, hit the right note. Sad for Jerry nothing else was on offer.

"So what is it you two girls do?" *'Apart from looking so seriously, fucking gorgeous!'* he mused.

"We're both with the church, Sir. Here to spread the good word of the Gospel."

'That should put an end to any further enquiries about us', figured Brock. Wide-eyed and speechless, Jerry looked about ready to comb what was left of his hair, button up his shirt and get down on his knees. Instead, he picked his jaw up off the floor and stared straight across to Josie with a look to build a dream on.

"Well if you don't mind me sayin' so, miss – you *sure got* those Angel-eyes." Josie flushed red and looked down into the sand. End of convo on the subject figured Brock.

"What about you, Jerry, what do you do?"

"Not a lot more than hold my pole out to an empty ocean these days. I used to be in commercial fishing, drag-lining, deep-sea, those kinda things. But it all went down with the ship when we got hit by the virus way back," he shrugged it off. "Now I guess I'm busy just waitin' around . . ."

"We will pray for you, Jerry."

Shirt buttons stressed in the best shirt he could muster as he drew in a deep breath.

"Yeah . . . right!" Ready now for a long, wilting, and uneventful tramp back in the sand to an empty cabin, he slapped both hands down onto his knees, massaged his thigh muscles, took a deep breath and rose up onto his feet.

"Well, I guess I'd better get going, got an early start tomorrow. Thanks for the company and the wine. Goodnight ladies, 'bin a real pleasure to meet you both," he grinned and wondered if he would've had better luck hitting the Jackpot if he'd brought along five loaves to go with the fish. *Next time, maybe. What a Loser!*

As a parting gesture, Brock placed her hand over her heart.

"So long, Jerry, may God be with you." It was all too much, Josie couldn't contain herself. She dashed inside, shook her head in amazement as Brock walked into the cabin.

"Maddie – you really *are* something else!"

"So Grady keeps tellin' me, but I just don't believe him. Hell, Josie, Jerry was in for the long haul. To his credit, he's probably had one of the best *'if only'* moments he's ever had in his life. I'm sure with a few dramatized erotic embellishments it'll be a story he'll dine out on until his dying day. Anyway, there's a whole lot better things we should be doing, Angel eyes." Brock tweaked a cute nose at her.

*   *   *

Chapter Twenty-four

Glowing bright as guardsmen's buttons, the early morning sun slunk a slow path up the sky's backdrop, burning its way heavenward for yet another scorching day. Absolute comfort from shade on the porch was still about an hour down the line. Such is summer, and Brock loved every moment of it. Relaxed back on the porch swing seat soaking up a healthy dose of vitamin D, two girls swung, drinking creamed iced coffee from the cooler as they watched Jerry the fisherman chug his SUV out of the complex. A lonely soul with cherished memories wrapped tight around his pole, who had muffed the biggest catch of his life. Eager bar room ears would no doubt be titillated by a more lascivious account of his adventure, and why not, poor guy: we all need sweet dreams at some time in our lives.

Laid back in the swing seat with her mind meandering in neutral on a slow drift into a mood of somnolence, Brock gazed out to sea; a silent witness mesmerised by rolling surf lapping low on the shoreline, a recurring event ever since the very dawn of time without any sign of abatement, a divine blessing from Mother Nature. In contrast, she mused how brief and fragile life could be. The thought took her gaze across to Josie, relaxed back, eyes closed, soaking up the sun with her neck stretched over the seat back. A replicate image of Macey sent a shiver down Brock's spine. She snapped back into reality, shook black thoughts into the sand and reached for Josie's hand.

"Come, Angel eyes, let's check out this store."

A heat mirage hovered low, simulating shimmering water over the near-empty parking lot outside the country store. Brock drew the Jeep into shade under a lone Palm and cut the motor. Nonchalant as a couple of tourists savouring a sweet gift from Lady Luck, the two girls ambled lazy steps on a slow path across to the store. With her arm cuddled round Brock's back, Josie felt the three-fifty-seven tucked snug in Brock's waistband. She said nothing; let it ride.

Inside the store, the aroma smelt fresh as garden gloves picking sweet peas in the spring; and *Ernest* was right – there were no fancy wines. But there were now some frillies, worn with discretion by the two girls who drifted in through the open door; an enviable sight capable of conjuring up a dulcet dream to even the most troubled of minds. The counter clerk drew in his stomach, slicked fingers back through matted hair and regretted grey stubble on his chin.

From fully stocked shelves they collected fresh fruit, cheeses, home-baked frozen pizzas and whatever else might come in handy to complement an easy life. High up on the liquor shelf, Brock stared up to a not-so-easy past life. A bottle of *Jack* on offer stared back down at her with open arms. The black monkey climbed up her back, dug in tight. Below wide craving eyes, a damp tongue licked a slow path across honey lips as dark thoughts ricocheted off to a previous life; a life far too difficult to forget.

"Red or white, Maddie …?"

"Huh?" Brock, a soul lost in distant thought, turned to the sound of the voice, she shook off the black monkey and smiled a welcome detour into pretty blue eyes. Relieved!

"Let's take both."

"How long shall we stay, Maddie?"

"How long is forever, sweetheart? Put six of each in the trolley. We can always come back for more," she said with a smile, turned from *Jack,* walked away and forced herself not to look back.

The cabin cool box was small but efficient and she figured would be okay to store the cold stuff, but not too much of it. Forever prudent, she added a bag of ice to the trolley.

"I think we're done here, Angel eyes, unless there's anything else you want."

"No, nothing in here." Blue and green shared a moment. Brock smiled, blew Josie a lip kiss.

"Okay, Honey, let's go and pay."

The counter clerk rang up their goods and spoke as he did so.

"You here on vacation, ladies?" he asked. (*Friendly question.*)

"No, we're passing through on our way to the big city." (*Polite answer.*)

"Does the landline hanging on the wall work, sir?"

"Only if you feed it, miss."

"Okay thanks. Take the trolley out, sweetheart. I've got to make a quick call; I need to check on how Grady's doing. I'll meet you back at the Jeep."

Pensive in thought, she lifted the phone, fed the meter and dialled the medical centre. After the usual rigmarole she got through, but no-one would accept her call – blood relatives only. *'Hell, he doesn't have any. Same as me and most people these days,'* she mused. But they did tell her he was still under sedation. She thanked reception, hung up and strolled out into the sun.

Over at the Jeep, two pot-bellied muscle heads crowded Josie as she was trying to unload the trolley. Playing games with her, they pulled her around trying to get her to smoke dope. Infuriated to code red, Brock shouted out and ran over to the Jeep.

"HEY...! LEAVE HER ALONE!" The fatter of the two turned to face Brock and blew out a wolf whistle.

"Well look who we got here! Where's the party, Sexy Lady?" he drawled.

Not one second later, pot-belly felt the cold steel of a gun barrel pushed hard into his forehead. Green eyes bored evil: *the killer...* She cocked back the trigger. A wet patch grew in the guy's jeans around his groin, drained down his legs and filled his sneakers.

"FUCK OFF!" she barked. Stumbling back witless as a schoolboy after his first pint at the prom, pot-belly fell backwards wide-eyed onto the tarmac. Not a sound uttered from his mouth – it just quivered. She fired a round into the ground below his groin kicking dust up into his crotch. The rank stink of dope mingled with the smell of fresh excrement and urine assaulted the surrounding air. His partner turned and walked away – quickstep fashion. He didn't whistle.

"Get in the Jeep, sweetheart," soft-voiced Brock, went around to the drive side, climbed in and gunned the motor out of the store car park slowing as they drove the blacktop back down towards Echo Beach.

"I'm sorry, Josie – I shouldn't have done that."

"Why? – Did you want them to come to our party?" Brock chuckled out a small laugh.

"No, sweetheart I did not."

"Would you really have shot him?"

"I didn't need to."

"But would you have?"

"I would do anything to protect you, Josie. Let's consider him lucky he didn't make me take the choice." She didn't want to tell Josie that any drug-doped, lowlife scum of his kind were a target she was paid to eradicate and had a licence to do so. She craved to put it all behind her in another life, and hoped she could leave it there.

"I love you, Maddie."

"I love you too, sweetheart – Maybe a little too much."

*   *   *

Back in the solitude of the cabin complex, they spent a lazy day rolling in sand dunes, playing in the surf and doing all those crazy things people deep in love enjoy. Late in the afternoon as the sun began to cast long shadows over the sand, Josie, lying naked, dosed in a hammock strung across the front pillars of the cabin in the shade of the shingle overhang. Brock swung on the swing seat nursing a glass of wine, trying to decipher or make some sense of the cryptic printout from the Mertz hit. No luck, maybe it was too much wine. Maybe it was too much of something else. Or maybe it was all way too much of everything.

Two gulls screamed overhead as they tried to hijack a third bird from its catch. Josie stirred at the screeching sounds, yawned, stretched out her nubile body and rolled over to face Brock.

"What are you reading, Maddie?"

"I don't know, I can't understand it … It's all in code." Josie held her hand out.

"Can I see?"

"Sure, be my guest." Brock passed her the printout.

Relaxed back in the hammock Josie studied the sheet and swung in a lazy rhythm.

"It doesn't make any sense; looks to me as if it's written in a foreign language."

"I don't think it's supposed to make sense, not unless you have the code to decipher it," said Brock.

"Maybe it's Venusian algebra?" kidded Josie. Brock stared at her over the top of her sunglasses and drawled:

"Have some more wine, Angel eyes."

"Sure, why not, Tarzan." Brock soft-chewed her finger.

"I hope *that* ain't gonna' stick!"

Ten idyllic days of wine, women, and hot love passed by in seventh heaven, but they weren't counting. Their skins, tanned to a deep bronze had the healthy look of pure contentment from tender living. Apart from a few trips to the local store they neither mixed with nor saw anyone. They revelled alone in the shade of their private sanctuary making love, swimming in the ocean and rolling in the dunes. Life was just perfect.

*   *   *

With both arms full of bagged fruit, she backed through the doorway into the cabin, put the bags down and called out to Josie — no answer came. Bent low, she searched under the bed, thought maybe Josie was playing a game with her. She wasn't. She was gone – Panic! Brock ran through the cabin, searched outside, looked under the Jeep, saw nothing. She looked up along the bay, ran through the dunes but couldn't see her. In the distance, she saw a crowd of dope-smoking deadbeats playing ball games in the sand. *They weren't there before – were they? Where the fuck did they come from,'* she wondered. One group, staggering around in a stupor, was attempting to build a long wall of sand across the beach down to the water's edge. Realising she didn't have her gun, she panicked. Frantic with terror she ran to the crowd shouting out Josie's name, but still couldn't see her. The crowd grew thicker as she ran. Pushing her way through a mass of laughing bodies' no-one spoke to or acknowledged her. Now desperate, she noticed a fisherman stood in the shallows, *Jerry* — she ran to him, waded into the sea shouting, Jerry! Jerry! The fisherman turned, but it wasn't Jerry: it was LePage. He showed his teeth, wagged his finger and laughed at her. Floating on the surface she saw the rotting carcass of a dead crab; she grabbed it. Holding the carcass as if it were a dagger she waded into deep water towards LePage. His eyes grew large, bore a manic welcome from the sniggering, smug slob he was. He swung his pole around at her, hooked with the ugly, fearsome, rotted remains of a ragged tooth shark. Giant teeth flashed bright as diamonds in a gaping mouth as it closed on her, forcing her to dive for cover. She tripped; fell headlong into a raging whirlpool, her body spinning down into the depths . . .

Her eyes flickered – She woke up. Drenched in sweat with a racing heart, she turned to Josie, whose radiant body quiet at sleep lay wrapped in her arms beside her. With a sigh, Brock leant across and gently kissed Josie's forehead. Her heart slowed, she rested her head back onto the pillow, blew a deep breath, closed her eyes and relaxed back into soft feather down. With hands tender as kid gloves, she caressed Josie's soft blond hair; but not enough to wake her.

Mellowed, she breathed easy now, pushed her head back into the pillow and stared up into the roof beams. Daybreak still in its infancy had begun to glow on the horizon. Early yet, the dawn shadows soon to form would be cast long for some time to come. The remnants of an early morning mist had begun its cycle to dissolve back up into the ether. Birdsong had been a delight to wake up to; but now – there was only silence – Then she heard it. A sound: an unfamiliar sound alien to anything made by nature. Now alert and fully awake she cocked her head and listened — nothing! In the silence she couldn't make out what the sound had been but knew whatever it was: it didn't belong here. Forever vigilant, she took her gun out from under her pillow, kept quiet and listened – thought she could hear the sound of footsteps; not so easy in soft sand she reasoned. Who in the hell could know she's here? It could be nothing – but *'trust no-one, live longer: trust only your intuition.'* She shook Josie and spoke in a soft, but urgent voice:

"Wake up, sweetheart." Josie rose up in the bed.

"What is it, Maddie?" whispered Josie, rubbing her eyes. Brock rose slow from the bed, shook her head, raised a finger up in front of her mouth and gently eased the curtain aside with her gun barrel enough for her to peek out. From the small window in the cabin, her limited view was only from the East. She saw nothing. 'One chance in four: not good odds,' she mused as she bit her bottom lip.

"Get under the bed Josie, don't make a sound and don't move. Stay there whatever happens," she whispered.

"Maddie, I'm scared."

"Shhhh . . . it's okay, honey, get under the bed. Stay still."

Careful not to make any sound, Brock drew open the drawer on the bedside table, took out a box of hollow-points and emptied some slugs out onto the bed ready for a reload. The total absence of birdsong was warning enough; she knew someone was out there. And there may well be more than one of them. Then she heard light footsteps tap on the porch boards, creaking slow across dry, loose joints. They stopped at the door. Mentally she kicked herself, knew she should've locked the door. *Slack: bad move Maddie!* She aimed her three-fifty-seven loaded with six hollow-point slugs at the door, spread her legs, stood ready and cocked the trigger back; the sound of which prompted a voice outside the door.

"Don't shoot, Loot. It's only me – Room service."

"Grady Da Silva, what the fuck!"

Grady's heavy hand sprung the door open. His jaw dropped to the floor at the sight of naked flesh pointing a gun at him. With a sigh of relief, she grabbed her robe, wrinkled her cute nose, beamed him a welcome smile and gave a slow nod.

"Good to see you, Grady, you great big . . ." she shook her head, couldn't think of anything suitable enough to call him, but was sure glad to see his big fat smiling face.

"You too, Loot. Stunned at the sight, he couldn't take his eyes off her. He didn't wrinkle his nose, it wasn't cute enough. Although he did raise a smile as he closed his eyes and sniffed at the air.

"Okay, Josie – You can come on out now, sweetheart." Brock released the hammer and rested her gun down on the bedside table. Pure naked poetry rose slow from the floor.

Grady imagined he was witness to a tropical Passion flower sprouting on a cloud in heaven. Mouth agape he pushed back his hat – slowly and didn't blink.

"Wow!" Speechless, he could say nothing. When he did speak he spoke soft and slow, as he watched Josie disappear under the cover of a bedsheet.

"Sure am pleased to make *your* acquaintance, miss."

"Put it back in your zipper, Sergeant. She's taken – she's not for sale!" Brock smiled damp emeralds back to him, did her nose thing.

"I hope you've at least had the decency to bring us some take-out coffee. Step outside and enjoy the view, Shiney; let a couple of girls get some clothes on in here."

"Ok-ey, but I gotta' tell ya': no matter whatever beautiful view there is outside, even if it was the hanging gardens of fuckin' Babylon, it ain't even gonna come *close* to what I've just seen in here."

"GRADY...!"

"Okay, Sherlock Watson, how'd you find me?" She asked swinging lazy in the swing seat.

"Easy, Loot — Titanium white."

"How come?"

"My Jeep..." he pointed across the yard. She closed her eyes, nodded in surrender.

"Of course — the tracker."

"Yeah right, the Titanium white tracker courtesy of Bugsy. Ya' gotta' be more careful, Loot."

"I thought you'd still be in intensive care for quite a while yet."

"Signed myself out, couldn't stand the food, or the room service. An' I thought the reception at the Palm Beach was bad. Anyway, I sure gotta' thank you, Loot – you saved my life. An inch lower and it would've hit my heart, and then I would've bled to death for sure."

"It's all part of the job, Grady – it's what we do, remember." Cute eyes smiled across at him, "anyway I'm surprised he could've missed such a great big organ – must've been a lousy shot."

"It ain't so big, Loot."

"Don't kid yourself, Grady." Quiet in thought he looked down to the floor, spoke without looking back up.

"I thought they'd got you, Loot – when you didn't call, or contact me. It's the real reason I signed myself out. I had to come and find you – One way or the other," he shrugged his shoulders, danced his brows. "The Major came to see me, Major Falconer – told me about Captain Clod; seems you came pretty close to it yourself, Loot." Tactful, she shrugged it off, didn't want to talk about it.

"I'm sorry I missed not drawing a bead on such a piece of shit! Wanna' tell me about it, Loot."

"Maybe some other time, Grady." Sad eyes turned to Josie sitting quiet in the swing seat next to her. Brock spoke soft and tender. "I'm sorry, sweetheart." Josie wrapped her arms tight around Brock, dropped tears down onto Brock's shirt.

"Gee, I'm sorry, Loot – I figured she'd have known?"

"It's okay, Grady. Why don't you take your big foot out of your mouth, go inside and make us some coffee. Use the percolator, it's under the sink."

Brock locked her arms tight around Josie. Hugged her hard, never wanted to let her go. She spoke soft words:

"Sixteen years I've been doing this and never once have I given a thought about the danger. Before I met you I never had anyone I cared about, or anyone who cared about me. But now it's different. I couldn't imagine causing you any pain. It's why I never told you about what we really do. Ever since we've been at the cabin, I've come to realise how precious and delicate life is, and how precious you are to me. And that's why I've decided to throw in the towel, quit the job . . . I've had enough, Josie. No more . . ."

"Did you ever kill anyone?" asked Josie, in her sweet voice hardly audible.

"Yes, I did – I won't lie to you, sweetheart; but only the bad guys, the real bad guys. You can't imagine how bad some people can be, Josie. Drug dealers, murderers, rapists and all the lowlife scum who have no respect for human life or dignity, and anybody else who wanted to cause harm, pain and misery to the general law-abiding public. The legal system broke down long ago and it became our duty to save the courts a lot of money and keep the prisons empty. It was a job, honey, nothing more. Now I'm done." Josie hugged Brock hard.

"I love you so much, Maddie."

"I love you too sweetheart – I don't want to lose you."

"Coffee guys."

"Look out Josie, here comes Big-Foot."

"Sure is pretty here, Loot. How long are you guys fixin' to stay?" No vocal answer came. Grady read the only reply he feared from emerald green eyes, she knew she couldn't kid him. A light wash of rolling surf harmonized the silence. He looked out to sea, soul-searching.

"Major Falconer will need to de-brief us, Lieutenant," he turned back to her, *hopeful.*

She shook her head.

"No need to call me Lieutenant, or Loot anymore, Grady – I'm through."

Grady said nothing; saw only austerity reflecting from her eyes. He nodded slow in acceptance and looked down into the sand, then up across to Josie and into those beautiful blue eyes, sculpted in a pretty face of pure unadulterated innocence.

"I understand, Loot – I guess if it were me I'd also wanna quit. No doubt about it. I'd love to have had the chance with

Macey; but now I guess with my life bein' what it is — I can only think of revenge."

Swinging slow and easy, the swing seat sang out a soft rhythm holding Brock and Josie locked together in love. Grady sat on the step, a lost soul floundering in a sea of dissolute desperation. In the brief hiatus, he flipped his hat on.

"I'd best be off now." He picked himself up and turned back to her and asked:

"If I ain't to call you Loot anymore, what should I call you?"

"Maddie – call me Maddie. It's my name."

"Sixteen years I've been with you, Loot, way back from the cadets when you were nothing more than a kid. An' right up 'till now, I ain't ever felt right about callin' you that. It's about respect."

With a song in her heart, she looked at the great big tough figure in front of her, frightened of nothing who had fought alongside her, shared his grief with her, saved her life on many occasions and had been a solid rock for her to depend on throughout tough times. But now, she could see only the soft side of him, a side she had never really imagined could exist. Maybe he felt the same way about her.

"Don't go yet, Grady – Please stay. Hang for a while; have some lunch with us – if only for me?" He pushed his hat back, gave her a smile big enough to melt the hardest of hearts, and sat back on the step.

"Okay, you got it, Loot." She tweaked her nose and threw a black olive at him.

Chapter Twenty-five

Heavy tread tyres rumbling over compacted sand kicked up a thick cloud of dust at the entrance to the Echo Beach resort. The culprit: a large silver SUV dragging a loaded trailer rode into the complex and pulled to a halt at cabin number one: a spacious single-storey two-bedroomed four-berth. Brandishing buckets and spades two kids made up a family of four unloading holiday bags; they were not quiet about it, neither was their dog.

"Looks as though we've got company, Josie, here comes the Flintstones. Seems we're heading up to the holiday season. I guess we'd better get down to the store, call up and re-book the cabin while we still can. How long shall we book for, sweetheart?"

"I'm in no rush, Maddie. I love it here with you, I've never been so happy. Anyway, I don't have anywhere else to go."

"What are you talking about? What about your apartment?"

"I don't have an apartment; I rent a small back room from Grace in her apartment. Now I don't even have a job to pay for it. But she's okay, I'm sure she won't throw me out."

Brock let out a soulful sigh, ran her fingers through Josie's hair, pulled her close and kissed her in a tender embrace.

"Are you kidding me, Josette DuBois?" Brock looked on in dismay. "Okay, that settles it. Now you can come and live with me forever. Or until you get fed up with me."

"I would never get fed up with you, Maddie, but I can't afford to pay you, not without a job."

"Do you honestly think I'd charge you, Josie? My apartment is all paid for so there's no charge. There's only one problem." Josie's jaw dropped in question, soft blue eyes stared deep into Maddie's soul. Brock kissed the pretty girl's forehead, explained with a smile: "There's only one bedroom." Josie wrapped her arms around Maddie, hugged her tight.

"I love you, Maddie – forever."

"Don't cry, sweetheart. Come, let's get down to the store and make the call, then we can stock up with some more cheese and wine. And maybe a few more frozen pizzas and some iced coffee. How's that sound?"

*　　　*　　　*

Brock snapped the wall phone back into its cradle, blew out a deep sigh, raised sad eyebrows and turned to Josie:

"I'm so sorry, honey; they're all booked up for the whole month. I'm not used to this holiday scene crap, I've never bothered much with holidays in my line of business; come to think of it I don't even remember ever takin' a holiday. But cheer up, sweetheart; we're okay here until next Monday. That gives us another five days in the cabin, so let's sit back and make the most of it. You go choose the wine; I'll choose the cheese and pizzas."

On the drive back to Echo Beach Josie looked to Maddie, tentative she brushed her hand through Brock's hair and asked;

"Was that *Jack* I saw in the liquor section, Maddie?"

Paused in thought, Brock smiled, nodded slow.

"Yeah," she turned to Josie and smiled. "Yeah – that was *Jack*. Since I met you, he's no longer been my buddy – No need to be."

"And I was worried. I always thought it was Jackie Olsen. I thought I had competition."

Brock shook her head and smiled with tender eyes into the pure innocence of a pretty face.

"Not a chance, Angel eyes. You've got first place forever; like it or not!"

*　　　*　　　*

Back in the solitude of the cabin, they drank wine, made love, relaxed in the sun, swam in the sea and lived life as if there were no other. Stretched out on the swing seat, Josie lay on her back resting her head on Brock's lap and fiddling hair around her finger.

"Who was Macey, Maddie? Was she Grady's girlfriend? What happened to her? Did they split up?"

Aware she was headed into deep water; Brock filled her wine glass and took a heavy slug before she spoke.

"No . . . she died."

"Died! How ...?"

Brock took a deep breath, wasn't going to tell a lie.

"She was murdered, Josie."

Jaw dropped, Josie sat up on the swing seat and turned to face Brock:

"Murdered – why – who by?"

"We're not sure, honey; like I told you, there are some real nasty people out there. You'd better believe it. That's why I always carry a gun. I think she was killed because someone wanted to rouse Grady. I won't let the same thing happen to you. I promise you deep from my heart sweetheart you'll never leave my side not while I still have a breath left in my body. So that's why I'm through with it all and throwing in the towel. You're far too precious to me."

"I guess it's all beginning to make sense now, Maddie. Thank you for being so honest with me."

"I wouldn't blame you or stop you if you wanted to get up and walk away from me right now, Josie. I'd understand. I'd hate it — but I'd understand." Josie's eyes welled. She burst into tears and fell into Maddie's arms. Maddie held her tight, looked out into the deep blue ocean, saw no answers but knew she had to somehow stop the nemesis bestowed upon her. There was no choice left.

*　　*　　*

Laid back in shade from an unrelenting sun, the two girls relaxed in the swing seat eating pastries, cheese and fruit, washed down with twenty-four-volt Columbian. Josie set her cup down on the low table, ambled into the cabin and sauntered out with a sheet of paper and handed it to Brock.

"Sorry, Maddie, I forgot all about this; I meant to give it to you earlier." Brock, confused, stared down at the sheet and then looked back up to Josie in question.

"I cracked the code for you: simple!" Josie, shrugged out a cute smile, "It looks to me it might be a combination of numbers to open a safe." Frozen speechless with her mouth hung wide under a furrowed brow, Brock stared up at Josie, held her bottom lip between her thumb and forefinger; she spoke nothing for a long while, couldn't, then said:

"What — you've cracked the code — how?"

"Well, I enjoy cryptic crosswords so I guess I've got a cryptic mind. Anyway, first off: if you look for recurring letters, a single letter is easy as it will usually be an A or an I. But we don't have any here, it would be too easy. Two letters together will be two n's, o's, b's, etcetera; schoolboy stuff nothing more. Now, if you draw out two alphabets and use them as a slide rule until they make some sense of the letters written. Then we can begin to crack the code. So if we start our first alphabet at A, which is usual. Then using our slide rule and in this case start with an M under the A, and translate from there; a recurring X becomes an L and a recurring D becomes an R. So, they *could* stand for; left and right. Let's assume they do. So, as the rest of the letters don't make any sense in that idiom we have to look further. If we put numbers under the first line of the alphabet and translate to numbers instead of letters for the second and third letters, QN becomes fifty-five, so XQN equals left to fifty-five, DOT equals right to thirty-eight and XRU equals left to sixty-nine. So, to start at the beginning, first off: X-P means left times four, that's turns I'm guessing. Then turn to the first number, which is fifty-five. Then DOT-XO equals right to thirty-eight, times three turns. XRU-XN equals left to sixty-nine times two turns. They're my favourite numbers by the way! She smiled blue angel eyes, racked her eyebrows to a speechless Brock. Then it's back to zero. Spin back a little until the wheel stops, twist back to TQ which is eighty-five and you've cracked it. Simple – there's your combination to open a safe. But of course, you must know where the safe is in the first place to be able to open it." Brock, speechless – sat back in the swing seat and stared up to a Josie she never knew existed and drawled a slow question:

"What in the fuck are you doing flipping burgers, Josie?"

"I'm not flipping anything right now, Maddie," she shrugged shoulders, "do you fancy some RU-XN, but with maybe more than only two turns?"

*   *   *

Two nubile bodies tanned to deep bronze played silly games in the shallows. Beads of water glistened bright as diamond chips in sunlight on bare skin. Deep in love, the two girls hadn't a care in the world, until way off in the distance under a backdrop of rising dust, a two-tone red and silver SUV dragging a trailer gave an ominous sign of yet further intrusion into their private utopia. It was high week in holiday season so no surprises there. Enough supplies to equip a troop of Legionnaires were unloaded from the SUV to the accompaniment of a barrage of loud music. Trailed by screaming kids and a yapping dog lifting its leg on anything non-mobile, cellulite wobbled and tangoed down to the water's edge. Brock beamed a sorry smile of frustration to Josie.

"I guess it's not a bad idea for us to take a break for a while during the holiday season, Sweetheart. The agency says we're okay to rent again in a month or so," she tweaked her nose, "let's go get some breakfast." If truth were known what Brock in fact needed to do was to get a little closer to her gun.

For the two girls, five days of sun, sex and wine flew past quicker than a cheap toupee in a strong gale; a slow paddle boat to China would have been more to order. After a healthy breakfast and three cups of coffee followed by a final dip in the ocean, they packed and loaded the Jeep, cleared and closed the cabin.

They headed out past a mess of rowdy holiday makers sporting an over-generous display of cellulite turning bright lobster-pink as they stretched out worshipping the sun on gaudy sun loungers of a similar hue. No-one would be enjoying sweet dreams tonight for sure. Maybe it was a good time to leave. But then again, maybe it wasn't. Who the hell knows?

*   *   *

Brock drove a slow track along the highway, not in any rush, unlike the parade of vehicles crowding the opposite lane.

"Shall we drop by your room and pick up your things?" asked Brock. "Do you think we can get it all in one trip?"

"In one trip, Maddie – we could get all my things in the glove box!"

"I think I need to take you shopping, sweetheart." Josie smiled, reclined her seat and closed her eyes.

Up ahead before they hit the city outskirts, Brock pulled the Jeep over in a U-turn waking Josie from her nap.

"What's wrong, Maddie?"

"Nothing honey it's okay, we just passed a cute little fruit store," she racked her brows, "thought we might go back and buy something fresh, maybe take a break and relax a little before we get back to the city armpit." She headed the Jeep back South.

Rolling the Jeep across compacted gravel Brock pulled in under the shade of a towering Scots pine close to the store. It wasn't a big store by any means, but looked inviting; with powder-blue and pink clapboard complimented by similar coloured doors and windows, capped with a white painted slate roof, the cute little store reflected a vision from someone who had visited Bermuda and had left with fond memories – or perhaps they just had young children, one of each and a lot of discount paint. Whatever; the store looked a million dollars and a far cry from the rolling dull grey they were headed for back in the city armpit.

They bought fresh-picked strawberries, bananas and, not because they really needed any, passion fruit. Take-out coffee would have been a bonus if only the store had sold it; instead, they settled for third best: iced coffee from the cool fridge. Laid back on the grass verge relaxing in the sun gorging on fresh strawberries and passion fruit, they were in no hurry to leave. Josie looked across the road to a pretty fairy tale cottage standing in its own grounds.

"Such a cute little cottage over there, Maddie, it's got a signboard up let's go look, maybe the place is for rent; we could finish off our vacation there."

"Yeah, okay why not, sounds good to me." Wrapping casual arms around each other, they ambled slow across a quiet black top and ate strawberries in the shade of a large old pepper tree while they checked out the sign.

"No go – It's for sale not for rent. But I tell you what, sweetheart, I'll call up anyway and see if we could maybe get a short rental for a couple of weeks; it seems such a cute little place to hang out in for a while."

Now back in the land of technology and able to get a signal, Brock made the call to a very polite lady who told her how very sorry she was but needed to sell it, not rent it. *'You're sorry!'* mused Brock. Thanked her and rang off.

"Sorry, Josie, no go, she doesn't want to rent it out so I guess it's back to the armpit for us."

After driving north for another half an hour the scenery changed from warm sand, palms and greenery to a grime-ridden grey as they drove into the city suburbs along a street littered with trash, junked vehicles and a heavy dose of despair. A blind person wouldn't have noticed it but would have sure smelt the difference.

In the narrow street outside Grace's apartment, Brock pulled the Jeep into the kerb and cut the motor. A hungry dog, doe-eyed, hopeful and skinny, sat on the curb wagging its tail. Brock had nothing much to offer other than a smile and half a stale croissant. The dog wasn't fussy; he wolfed it down then lifted his leg on the Jeep's rear tyre. *There's gratitude for you!* Brock mused. She patted the dog's head.

The steep rise of stairs up to Josie's room was bare pine without carpet. Her small room to the rear of the apartment served to make the rental listed as a two-bedroom. A one-bedroom with a small storeroom would have been a more legitimate mark-up. Inside, Josie's room was as sparse as a last-ditch comb-over on a bald head. The room, empty apart from a small bag of clothes, a single pine frame bed and a wicker chair, on which sat a book of cryptic crosswords open at page eighty-three with a half-finished problem. The sight of which triggered Brock to think: if it had been a smoker's pipe on the chair, her room would have been a close facsimile to the starkness and paltry possessions in Van Gogh's cramped bedroom at Avignon.

There was not much else in the room except for a small wall mirror, a drawn blind over a small window and a heavy dose of austerity. A Trappist monk would have needed more space for his meagre belongings. A blowfly buzzed a bare bulb hung from the ceiling. Grace wasn't around.

Josie stripped the bed, zipped up her bag and left a note along with a sigh of relief. Before she closed the door Brock held her close, looked deep into her eyes and asked:

"Are you okay with this, Josie?" Angel eyes welled as she ran a dry tongue over her lower lip.

"You don't want me to come, Maddie?" Wide-eyed, she asked rather than stated. Brock looked down into that beautiful face of pure innocence, wrapped her arms around her, hugged her tight and stared into the stark emptiness of the room. She shook her head.

"I don't think I've ever wanted anything so much in the whole of my life."

*   *   *

Chapter Twenty-six

Brock was in no hurry. A light cloud of city dust trailed the Jeep along a grey street in bright sunlight. She bounced the kerb outside her apartment, killed the motor and ruffled Josie's hair.

"Welcome home, sweetheart, let's dump the bags then take a stroll across to Jackie O's, say 'hi' and grab a cool drink, there's nothing in the apartment."

They carried bags up the short flight of steps and into the entrance hall. Brock froze, noticed the door to the apartment was ajar. Why? – Red-alert! She rested her bags down, nodded for Josie to do the same. She wrapped a tentative hand around her gun butt, drew the weapon and listened... then called out in a soft voice:

"Heidi?" Silence – no answer came back. She motioned for Josie to stay still; then with the flat of her left hand eased the door open and peered inside. The sight of a bloodied corpse lying in a pool of blood in the middle of the lounge took her breath away. Bingo had been hacked to death. Blowflies buzzing the carcass were the sole movement she could see in the room. Treading cautious steps she followed her gun into the apartment and felt Bingo. He was no longer stiff in rigor but was decaying, cold, and smelt rancid. His tongue hung out; this time not in welcome but in distress. Laid in dried blood it was obvious he'd been dead for some time. She searched the rest of the apartment; all was clear. With a heavy sigh, she covered Bingo with a large bath towel before she would call Josie inside.

"Go into the bedroom, honey, and stay there. I'll check upstairs. Lock the door; don't open it for anyone, even if you think it might be me. It won't be – I have my key."

Out in the hallway, she called up the stairway for Heidi. No answer came; she didn't expect one. With the stealth of a Siamese cat she inched soft footsteps up the staircase keeping her feet to the outer edges of the treads to avoid any creaking sounds. At the top of the stairs she could see the apartment front door was also ajar, but she could not see inside. The pungent smell of death and decay permeated, spoke loud. She took a deep breath, reached forward and pushed the door with her gun barrel. In the lounge, Mrs. Wiley sat perfectly still with both arms taped to her rocker. Staring up to the heavens she uttered nothing, couldn't, not with her throat slit open. Red veins spidered over her body, busy as a road map. Her body cold and cheerless as gravestones in winter confirmed she'd been dead for quite some time, days if not a week or more.

No stranger to death Brock didn't panic, but didn't welcome the thought of searching Heidi's bedroom. Crouched down outside the door to Heidi's room she kept low, beneath a height which could offer a gun sight from someone inside. She slow-twisted the door handle then kicked the door open, rolled into the room and came up off the floor with her gun raised. Heidi wasn't there. Apart from a dishevelled bed and a stilled silence, the room was empty. She checked the rest of the apartment and found nothing more than morbid thoughts. Before she would leave, Brock stared down at Mrs Wiley; whose mauve-mouthed grimace for a bizarre fleeting moment, she mistook for a smile. Her eyes, wide open despite having glazed over still read terrified. Blowflies crawled from her mouth and feasted on the gash at her throat. Poor lady – she had nothing to smile about.

Back down in her apartment, Brock dialled Grady, asked him to bring the blood wagon and forensics to her apartment.

"Are you okay, Loot?"

"Yeah, we're fine. But we had a nasty welcome home present."

"Heidi…? NO!" he wailed.

"No! They've taken her, she's not here. There's only Mrs Wiley, same M.O. as Macey, and Bingo also in my apartment. Could you take care of it for me, Grady? I can't leave Josie here."

"I'm on my way, Loot." She thumbed red.

The tang of death hung heavy in still air. She scanned her room. It now looked alien to her; a place no longer her home. She went into the bedroom and wrapped her arms around Josie. Wide-eyed and frightened, the pretty girl sat tearful on the bed with a face white as the bleached bones of a long-dead romance. Brock held her close, kissed her forehead and pulled her up from the bed savouring her scent.

"Come, sweetheart – Let's get out of here," she held her tight. "Do you want me to take you back to your room?"

"No, I want to stay with you." Thankful, Brock closed her eyes, let out a deep breath and hugged her.

"Okay – then let's go across and check Jackie Olsen; maybe he can fix up something for us."

*   *   *

Jackie reached for the Bourbon as his favourite customer walked into the bar room.

"Nice tan, Lieutenant, you're lookin' good." She cupped her hand over the empty jigger on the bar top.

"Just a coffee please, Jackie. Make it black and strong." Jackie Olsen rested the bourbon on the bar top and raised his eyebrows; thought he was hearing things.

"Jackie this is Josie, Josie this is Jackie." Olsen held out his hand.

"Pleased to meet you, miss – A coffee, Lieutenant? – You okay? Want anything in it?"

"No thanks, Jackie. Straight black will be fine. What about you, Josie?

"Could I get a shot of Bourbon please? I think I need one."

"Sure you can, miss. I'll bring your drinks across to your booth." Jackie shook his head, confused. The girls took the regular booth by the baby grand.

"What now, Maddie?"

"We can't go back to my apartment, honey. Grady will get it cleaned up for us, but I don't think it will feel right living there now: bad karma. I'll check us into a hotel for a few days. Don't worry we'll be okay. I've got to make some calls now, sweetheart."

She took a deep breath, pulled out a business card and rang mister Dodd.

"Hello, mister Dodd? Yes. (Pause) It's Madeline Brock from apartments 106 and 107. Does your offer to buy still stand? (Pause) Good. (Pause) Yes I do, as soon as possible, something's come up. (Pause) Okay. I'll come to your office and sign the paperwork if you could get it ready for me. (Pause) Yes, when is good for you? (Pause) Yes, okay then tomorrow afternoon is good for me also. I'll see you after lunch. Thank you. Goodbye, mister Dodd." She thumbed red and turned to Josie.

"Now I guess we're both homeless. Don't look so worried, Josie, we could always go back and live in your room with Grace – only kidding, sweetheart."

"One black coffee no sugar, and one Bourbon. Are you sure you're okay, Lieutenant?" Jackie looked concerned, raised a brow as he set the tray down in front of them.

"Yeah, I'm fine, Jackie. My apartment was broken into while we were away on vacation. Grady's over there right now takin' care of it for me."

"Sorry to hear that, Lieutenant. Was anything taken?"

"Yeah – a couple of lives!"

"Wow! You sure you don't want that Bourbon?"

"No thanks, Jackie – I need a clear head."

"Okay, if there's anything I can do, you just let me know. I'm right here, you know that."

"Sure thing – thanks, Jackie."

*   *   *

At the stroke of six, Grady wandered into the bar, scanned round and walked straight over to Brock, didn't stop to grab a drink.

"Okay, I got the guys cleanin' up, Loot, but I don't think you should go back there tonight. If you *do* have to I'll come and keep watch for you, but there sure is a bad smell in there an' it's gonna' linger for quite a while yet."

"Thanks, Grady. We won't be going back there tonight or any other night. I'll check us into a hotel for a couple of days while I work things out. I've gotta try and find Heidi."

"Well, please don't make it the Palm Beach, Loot."

"Don't worry, I wouldn't be seen dead in there; nearly once was enough. No, I'll book something a little more up-market. Could you ask Major Falconer to give me a call, I might need a safe house for a while."

"Sure I can. He still wants to debrief us so I'll fix up a meet."

"Sit down, Grady, have a drink. Forensics will be a while yet."

"I ain't gonna' turn down an offer to sit with my two favourite ladies. Can I get you guys anything – another coffee, Loot?"

"No thanks – you okay Josie, want some wine?" Josie looked across to Grady.

"Coffee would be good please, Grady."

"Okay, comin' up guys."

Deep in thought, Brock drummed her fingers on the table top, held her bottom lip in her teeth and turned to Josie.

"I'll make a booking at the hotel, maybe the smart one down on the bay. Let's treat ourselves. Then I think we should go an' eat something – food I mean." She tweaked her nose to Josie.

"Later, Angel eyes!"

*   *   *

The Inn on the Bay was way up the list from the Palm Beach with a clientele that didn't look as if they would be carrying any heavy hardware – except for Brock. As a precaution, she had checked in under the name *Mrs. Wiley*, figured no-one would be looking for *her* in a hurry. *'Stay safe, trust no-one, live longer.'* Room four-twenty-five had an en suite with a large spa bath, thick fluffy towels to amuse your body, and a walk-in shower room almost as big as the bedroom at the Palm Beach. In the main room, a fully stocked mini-bar and a coffee machine were a welcome touch, along with a view across the bay from a cosy west-facing balcony. The cutlery was silver-plated, the china wasn't plastic, and the king-size double bed didn't feel lumpy as a sack of walnuts. But not dissimilar to high-end sex, it didn't come cheap. Brock dropped her travel bag on the luggage rack, opened the mini-bar and turned to Josie.

"Red or white, sweetheart – I think we could both do with a drink."

"Maybe I'll have a glass of white, Maddie; I think I've seen enough red for one day."

"Okay, what about some food? Shall we try the restaurant or do you want to give room service a shot?"

"How much is this all costing, Maddie? I haven't got this kind of money, and it's not fair for you to keep on paying for everything." Brock, deeply touched put her arms around Josie, stared a passion into those pretty innocent angel eyes and squeezed her hard.

"Please, don't even think about it, sweetheart. Until I officially throw in the towel, the Office of National Security will be picking up the tab. They owe me big time for dodging bullets and scraping grime off the streets over the last eight years; and in those eight years this is my very first holiday. So don't you worry your pretty little head and go and run a bubble bath for us. I've got to make a couple of calls and I'll order some food from room service. After our bubble bath we'll sit out on the balcony, relax, watch the sun go down and enjoy a good meal. What do you want to eat?"

"Let's decide in the bath," said Josie. 'Cute kid,' thought Brock.

Digging down deep into her soul for a positive attitude, Brock tried hard to keep up morale, but in truth she was worried about Heidi. She thought it a little strange there had been no contact from anyone with demands to allow her safe return; it didn't make sense, but then again what *does* make sense in the twisted minds of the criminal world? Talking of a safe return, she needed to find the safe Josie had cracked the code for. It could reveal something useful. The Mertz mansion was the most obvious place; maybe she shouldn't have stopped looking after they'd found the SIM card. Now she needed to make a more constructive sweep and check if they'd missed anything, perhaps get Bugsy in to sweep with his special equipment, it must be worth a try. She dialled Grady, ran the idea by him, thumbed red and joined Josie blowing bubbles in the bath.

*   *   *

Chapter Twenty-seven

Two plates of half-picked food sat glazing over on the balcony table. Neither Brock nor Josie had much appetite for food. No surprises there. Snuggled close together in the evening sun drinking white wine, they relished the view out across the iridescent waters of the bay as it reflected the golden glow of the setting sun. Nothing stirred in the shimmering water apart from the gentle wash from a commercial water and fuel supply bowser, painted with scant care from a more than generous coating of red oxide over flaking rust. Vomiting out a cloud of black smoke and listing badly, the decrepit vessel looked one step away from eternal rest as a crab's home. Despite the obvious handicaps, the crew still managed to ply their trade to those riding at anchor.

At the other end of the scale were the super-yachts; wallowing in a comfort to befit royalty they provided a coveted life of privacy, safety, and a copious dose of sheer luxury to the privileged few. A privileged few who neither knew nor cared anything of the plight of another 'unprivileged' few, working hard to keep a high standard of living ticking over in safety; at times even to the cost of their lives. Not much will ever change, mused Brock, and for sure not in her lifetime. But right now she was living her life with someone she loved, and not much else mattered.

"Are you okay, Josie?"

"Yes ... I guess it's been a rather unusual day for me." *'Poor kid, pretty much run of the mill for me,'* mused Brock.

"Well we can't change what has happened, sweetheart but we *can* learn from it. Do you fancy a stroll along the beach – wash away the blues?"

"Okay, sounds good."

"Okay, put some clothes on, Angel eyes. Let's go and grab us some quality time."

*   *   *

Strewn with sun-bleached loungers, sunshades and toasted cellulite, the beach front was a far cry from the idyllic time they'd spent in utopic bliss at the Echo Beach resort. Although sitting in early evening shade at a beach bar with a cool drink seemed a far better alternative to anything else on offer right now. Brock ordered a couple of highball cocktails.

Relaxed on tall barstools listening to low-key Salsa, the two girls watched the fading sun preparing to duck below the horizon. They stirred fancy straws in their drinks, laughed and talked nonsense in an attempt to erase bad thoughts from a bad day.

"Hi girls, get you another drink?" The lone voice invading their reverie came from a hopeful patsy well past maturity, but with one foot still deep in the throes of adolescence. He made hard work of holding in his stomach as he wandered over from a group of potbellied muscle-bound creeps sat on the beach sinking back beers under the shade of a heavy fug of dope.

"Not now, thank you," replied Brock, rolled her eyes across to Josie.

"Well, how about later up at my place?"

"No thanks." The mood turned foul.

"Somethin' wrong with me, Lady?" Brock turned on her stool, spoke with evil eyes, Romeo had sure picked a bad time!

"There might be in a minute, sonny!" The atmosphere iced over. The big barman broke in quick, spoke loud:

"Hey! Why don't you leave the girls alone, buddy, they ain't interested. Take the hint. Beat it, I'm warning you!" Romeo checked the barman's sturdy frame, spat at the ground, slunk back to his party muttering obscenities and kicked his pride into the sand.

The barman ragged the bar top.

"Sorry girls, it's usually quiet around here, but hell – I guess there's always one!" He stopped ragging the bar top and looked to Brock. "I recognise *you*, miss..."

"I don't think so, sir, we've never been here before."

"Yours is not the sort of face a man could easily forget, miss, if you don't mind me sayin' so – I work some evenings at the Palm Beach, I served you drinks at the bar. That clown over there doesn't know how fuckin' lucky he is!" Brock smiled back politely, pushed a bill with a big tip across the counter, slid down off her bar-stool and took Josie's arm.

"Thank you for the drinks, sir. Come Josie."

"You're welcome, miss – anytime," the barman beamed a friendly smile. As they walked away he looked up from her cute butt to the bulge in her waistband under her shirt. He shook his head, blew a cool whistle and ragged the bar top.

"See what I mean, Josie: you never know who is looking," *'trust no-one, live longer.'* Come let's get back up to the room, sweetheart."

As she closed the hotel room door her cell phone buzzed on the dresser. She snatched it up and thumbed green.

"You okay, loot? I've been callin' you for over an hour."

"Sorry, Grady. We took a sunset walk down on the beach. What's up?"

"I've fixed up Bugsy to check out the Mertz place tomorrow morning. Pick you up in the hotel foyer around ten, you okay with that? Oh, and by the way: Falconer wants to see us later on in the afternoon?"

"Yes, ten o'clock will be fine, but tomorrow afternoon isn't good for me, I already have an appointment – I've got to sign some papers and fix up some legal stuff. I don't know how long it'll take I may be quick but who knows? Ask the major if we can make it later or maybe the next day; and, Grady," she spoke soft and slow, "I'd appreciate it if you could do me a big favour..."

"Anything, Loot, you just name it – it'll be my pleasure you know that."

"Would you look after Josie for me tomorrow afternoon, I don't want to leave her here alone, but please don't let her know you're babysitting, I don't want to alarm her. Maybe come and have lunch with us and stay lounging in the sun on the balcony while I'm away?"

"No problem, Loot. Lunch sounds good."

"Did you tell Falconer we're goin' to check out the Mertz place?" she asked.

"No, I didn't. Do you think we need to?"

"No, let's keep it to ourselves; unless of course we find something. Okay, Grady, see you at ten."

*   *   *

Breakfast was continental: croissants, cheeses, yoghurt, fruit and coffee all set out on silver plate trays polished to impress all but the blind. But steak and eggs at Macey's on powder-coat tin would beat it hands down every time. Showered and dressed to drop jaws, two pretty girls breezed down the hotel hallway cool and sweet as a fresh zephyr winding through a grove of flowering cherry trees on a bright spring day. At two minutes to ten, they stepped out from the elevator into the foyer. Loafing back his two-twenty pounds of body bulk into polished leather on a three-seat Chesterfield, Grady sprang the surprised look of disbelief across to Brock. She lifted her arm, showed him her watch, blew him a kiss, strolled across, plonked her body down next to him and waited while he drank his coffee. He lifted his cup.

"You two girls want one?"

"No thanks, we're good, we've already had breakfast." Grady could read into that any which way he wanted to, Brock didn't care anymore.

"Okay to keep the Jeep for a while, Grady?"

"No problem. I've got LePage's company SUV: make the bastard turn in his grave." He mocked a toast with his coffee cup, tipped her a wink, "So, we go in style today. With pursed lips and a foxy eye, Brock stared in question at Grady; she could see his mind churning. She grinned at him, bounced her brows.

"She's coming with us to open the safe – if we can find it."

"I ain't said nothin,' Loot." Grady raised open hands in surrender.

"Oh yes you did, Sergeant Watson!" She pulled his hat down over his eyes and scrunched her face.

The drive to the Mertz Empire took a little over fifteen minutes in heavy traffic thinning to almost sanity as they passed into the more exclusive part of the city. The cop in the empty suit was no longer on guard and there was no longer any red tape to step through or duck under. The ancient ornamental front door, built to repel a heavy volley from musket fire was locked but not barred. Grady pulled a bunch of keys from his pocket, fiddled the lock and pushed open the door. Brock stared at him in a frown with questioned eyes. Grady smiled, rattled a bunch of keys in answer:

"Picked them up off his desk last time we were here, wouldn't want to leave them lying around, very careless — where d'ya wanna start, Loot?"

"Let's check upstairs first, same as good sex, start at the top and work your way down."

Grady drew a deep breath, let the carnal thought bounce off his chin and changed the subject.

"Ok-ey, Bugsy should be here soon," said Grady, "Maybe I should wait down here for him. I told him ten-thirty, it's ten-twenty five now."

"Okay. We'll start upstairs. Come Josie."

"What are we looking for, Maddie?"

"Anywhere there might be a safe hidden. It's a wild shot, there may not even be anything here but we have to start somewhere." Josie shrugged back a smug look.

"If I had a safe I'd keep it in my office, same as in the old-time movies."

"Okay then," said Brock, "let's go back down and start in the office."

In the dishevelled mayhem of Mertz's office, they knuckled on wall panels, checked in cupboards and searched under carpets but found nothing more than dust and roaches wallowing in the fading decadence of a wilting society.

Grady came down with Bugsy from a fruitless search upstairs, poked his head through the doorway and asked:

"Anything?"

"Mm-mm . . . no nothing yet, only the usual footprint of depravity." As she spoke a motor growled rolling a large mirror down the wall revealing a heavy cast-steel wall safe. All eyes turned to Josie sitting back smug in the office chair. She racked her brows:

"Buttons under the desk, two of them, one each side, same as in the movies – simple!"

Brock folded her arms and looked speechless into Josie's cute face, did her nose thing.

Grady pushed his hat back; Bugsy switched off his machine, shook his head and said:

"I paid a damn fortune for this scanner. D'ya wanna' job sweetheart?"

"Okay, Josie – let's give it a shot," said Brock.

Josie opened her notebook and read off the instructions she had written.

"Okay, start at zero, left four turns past zero, then stop at Fifty-five, the first number. Now spin right passing zero three times. Stop at the third time on thirty-eight. Spin left, roll back and stop at the second time on sixty-nine then back to zero and turn back slow until you feel a resistance."

"But it ain't open," said Bugsy. Josie rolled her eyes, walked across and tweaked the wheel back to eighty-five and the door fell open. Jaws hit the floor, three people slow-clapped in astonishment. It wasn't tight hot pants and a bare midriff from a pretty girl making jaws drop; she had one hell of a lot more going for her. It's just a downright pity she didn't know it.

Brock turned to Grady.

"Clear the desk, Grady; let's see what we've got here." They unloaded the contents of the safe onto the desk. Money, jewellery, papers, a ledger and six sealed bags of white powder, each probably one kilo spread out across the table.

"Okay guys, let's bag it and get out of here."

"One minute, Boss." Grady picked up the litter bin and emptied it into the safe then shut the door and spun the lock. "Okay, we're good to go now, Loot; you can wind the mirror back up now, Josie."

Bugsy ran his fingers through what was left of his hair and turned to Josie:

"If you ever need a job, miss, give me a call ... please."

Back at the hotel room they counted the cash, checked and itemised the jewellery but left the dope alone. Brock leafed through the ledger then passed it across to Josie.

"You've got more de-coding work here, sweetheart. You okay with it? I'll make sure you get well paid."

"No problem, Maddie. Would that be in money or in kind?" Brock gave her a cheeky smile:

"How about both..." She tweaked her nose. "Okay, let's order some lunch. Will you join us Grady?"

"Sure, why not?"

"Okay, I'll order up some cholesterol for you. Put the loot back in the sack and put it in the closet; we wouldn't want room service to feast their eyes on that little lot." Realizing what she'd just said took her mind back to the news sheet from Macey's. *'Loot'* – it might not have been a reference to her name at all. Now there's food for thought. Maybe she needed to check out the news sheet again from a different angle, but figured in all probability it was a cold lead and nothing more than a time-wasting ruse.

Grady cleaned off the plates from a lazy lunch, Brock checked her watch.

"Okay guys, I'd better get going. I'll call you if I get held up, Josie. I'll try not to be too long, sweetheart."

"Okay if I hang here for a while, Loot, I ain't in any hurry to get anywhere now we ain't gonna be seeing the Major today."

"Is it okay with you if Grady hangs for a while, Josie?"

"Sure why not, I'll teach him how to break a code?"

"Well, kick him out if he's a pain. Okay, catch you later, guys."

*   *   *

Chapter Twenty-eight

Out on the bay in shimmering turquoise waters, the crew of a small sail boat struggled with sheets to set a bright red spinnaker in a light wind. It was a lost cause; they were becalmed. A drift of blue smoke rose from the transom as the motor fired up. Idly curling a lock of hair around her finger, Josie watched the yacht limp back to harbour. She guessed the crew would no doubt have more fun finishing off the day's sail dropping anchor at the clubhouse bar and drinking a sailor's toast to wives and sweethearts.

Grady wandered out from the suite, squinted in the sunlight, shaded his eyes with black wraparounds and rested his elbows on the balcony rail.

"Can I get you some coffee or a cold beer, Sergeant?"

"No need to call me sergeant, honey, it's Grady... and thanks, I'd love some coffee."

Five minutes later Josie carried a tray of coffee out onto the balcony, set it down on the low table, relaxed back in the lounger and gave an empty shrug:

"I feel as if I'm back at Skinny's."

"Don't underestimate yourself sweetheart, you're far too good for those kinda' places."

She smiled into her lap. 'If only . . .' she mused.

Sat across at the low table from Grady, Josie explained about cryptic crosswords and how a similar train of thought had helped her work out the codes to open the safe. Then she spent some time with him on the ledger to explain it all further. A lot of work culminated in nothing more than a blank look on Grady's face. She realised she'd make more ground trying to teach a Kreen-Akrore tribesman deep in the Amazon rainforest about the complexities of algebra and multiplying fractions. Poor guy, he didn't deserve this. She needed to change the subject.

"How long have you known Maddie, Sergeant? – I'm sorry – Grady."

"Around sixteen years now, ever since she was a pimply kid."

"I bet she wasn't ever pimply."

"No, she wasn't. She was beautiful from the word go, getting prettier every day and still is."

"Did you ever date her?"

"No, I did not, much to my great regret. Never saw her with anyone else either, you know – not serious. Not until you came along. I gotta tell you, Josie – you sure mean a lot to her. I know her better than she knows herself and I ain't never seen her as happy as she is with you."

"What about Jack?"

"Well, you know, Josie – sometimes our job is real tough and it can get to you deep down; you had a small taste of it yesterday. If you don't have a soul to turn to, and I mean someone special in your life, it's easy to sink down low under a heavy cloud with a bottle to drown out your sorrows. Sometimes it seems to be the only way out. And a lot of the time maybe it is. I dunno, it beats me, I try not to think about it."

"What happened to Macey, Grady?" He crossed his arms, cupped his jaw, looked out into the bay, took a deep breath and wrestled with both his jaw and the devil. He blew out a long, deep breath, maybe to contrive a tactful answer; or maybe to console his emotions.

"Not sure I should be telling you this, sweetheart."

"Maddie told me Macey was your girlfriend, and she'd died. I'm sorry, Grady. I didn't mean to pry."

"It's okay . . . She was murdered. That's enough for you to know right now, sweetheart."

"Murdered! – Who by?"

"We don't know. But we do know there are some real nasty people out there who will stop at nothing to get what they want, even if it means getting to us by hurting the ones we love. It's our job to stop them no matter what. The drug world is a filthy, nasty business Josie, run by scum so low you couldn't suck 'em up with a dirty pond pump. So we do the next best thing and tread 'em into the dirt, right back where they belong. We're getting close now, an' they're getting worried. The countdown's tickin' an' they know it!"

"Is it why you're here, Grady: to look out for me … Did Maddie ask you to?"

"You're a bright kid, Josie; it's a yes to all three. It would mortify her to see you hurt. Didn't take you long to work it out, honey; easy as cracking the code for the safe I guess – she should've known."

"It's okay I don't mind. I feel a lot safer with you around. Although I'm glad there isn't a popcorn machine handy."

"You heard about that, huh!"

A cute face danced a cute jig, nodded a yes and chuckled: "He deserved it."

"What're you doing waiting tables, Josie?" Grady shook his head in a moment of serious disbelief.

"I'm not waiting anything anymore," she shrugged, "but I guess something will turn up."

"For a kid as smart as you it ain't gonna be a problem sweetheart believe me."

"It's very sweet of you, Grady, thank you." Again she felt the need to change the subject: "Don't you have anyone now, Grady?"

"No – I'm not really lookin; not after Macey," he spoke through a plaintive smile.

"Were you ever married?"

"Uh-huh, I did that once. Didn't work out too well for her – or for me either. But that was all a long time ago. She's happy an' married to some other guy now. I feel glad for her. She's a nice lady."

"No children?"

"No – no children, just me." He forced a coy smile, looked out to sea and stared into a painful vision from the past.

"Has she said anymore about leavin' Covert security?" he asked.

"Yes, I think she's serious about it."

"I didn't mention anything to the Major, figured it's best if she tells him herself. I'm sure gonna miss her!" His eyes stared hard away into nothing, let his mind do the work for a change.

A knock on the door broke the moment.

"Are you expectin' anyone, sweetheart?"

"No."

Grady stood, took his gun out of its holster, motioned for Josie to stay put while he soft-shoed across to the door. The peephole was black – masked as though someone had their thumb over the eyepiece. He beckoned Josie over. With eyes wide and a thumping heart, she came to his side. He whispered into her ear. She nodded and turned to the door:

"Yes, who is it?" She spoke in her best little girl voice.

"Room service, I need to clean the room, miss," answered a man's deep voice. The peephole, still blank, threw up a red card for Grady. He bent and whispered again to Josie. She nodded and spoke again to the door:

"Hold on a minute, let me put some clothes on." Before she'd finished talking Grady sprang the door. Two surprised eyes were staring down the barrel of a gun – a very large gun! Up close, the black hole the guy stared into looked a whole lot bigger than its fifty-calibre, and he didn't want to see anything coming down *that* barrel. Doubtful he'd have much time to see it even if it did. Grady grabbed a hand full of hair and with his gun jammed tight under the guy's chin he dragged the guy into the room. He swung the guy round and rammed a vicious knee up into his groin then threw a punch to his jaw hard enough to ring the bell at a fairground. Squirming on the floor dribbling blood, the guy gasped for mercy as Grady stabbed his boot into his throat and frisked him. He drew out a suppressed Glock 17 from a shoulder holster and a switchblade from a back pocket; other than those he was clean, apart from a lot of blood and spit drooling from his nose and mouth. Grady dragged him up by the hair, threw a glass of water into his face and spoke close to the guy's ear after he'd twisted it – Hard!

"Fixin' to do some room cleanin' with these, snot gobbler?" He held out the Glock and the knife under the hit man's nose. "Anyone else with you?" The guy dribbled blood over the carpet as he shook his head. "You wouldn't want to be lying to me, snot gobbler; that wouldn't be a good idea, not right now where you're standin' believe me."

"No – There's no-one else – I came alone," he spoke in short bursts with a plea in his tone. He shouldn't have bothered: there was no soft spot for him to hit. Grady brought his gun down with menace on the hit man's head, hitting a hard spot. Then, pistol-whipped him and drew more blood as his gun barrel opened the guy's cheek. Grady kept his gun trained on the trembling hit man while he checked the hallway outside. Nothing doing – he closed the door and turned back to the snivelling wretch, picked him up off the floor and threw him into a chair. Then looked across the room to a tearful Josie.

"Sweetheart, why don't you go out on the balcony, draw the blinds and turn up the music; I'm gonna' have a quick word with the cleanin' lady here."

Trembling faster than party jelly under the applause and hoo-ha from that well-worn birthday song, the hit man soiled his pants as Grady yanked him out of the chair by the hair, dragged him across into the bathroom and slammed him down on the crapper.

"Okay, snot gobbler, it smells to me you're in the right place now, so I'm gonna ask you one question and one question only; and I'll take my gun out of your mouth while you answer.

But you'd do well to remember: it's four floors down to get out of this place, and you don't wanna be takin' the quick route over the balcony. So – snot gobbler, now you're nice and cosy – One question – One chance – Who sent you?"

The hit man closed his eyes, spat blood as he spoke:

"I don't know his name; it was a contract from a guy in the Trafalgar Bay office block."

Grady holstered his gun, picked up the Glock and poked it at the guy's forehead – hard!

"Name...?" Bloodied lips trembled but gave no answer. Grady back-whipped the Glock into the side of the hit man's face, much harder this time. Bloodied teeth, broken, dribbled down his chin. With the Glock, rammed in hard and twisted under his throat drawing blood, Grady bent low and whispered into the hit man's ear:

"Okay, snot gobbler, last chance, just be aware: *your gun* won't make any noise – I need a name – now!"

"Sculley – Nelson Sculley. I don't know no more – I swear!"

"Who was your mark here?" growled Grady.

"I was contracted to terminate anyone in the room." A dark shadow shrouded Grady's soul. Thoughts of Macey clouded his vision. He sucked his lips back against his teeth, stood up and filled his chest:

"Well, let's not disappoint Mister Sculley." He squeezed the trigger, plastered blood, brains and the back of the hit man's head all over the wall mirror.

"That's for Macey, you snot gobblin' sack of shit!" He placed the Glock back into the limp hand of the hit man and went out into the main room. He called out to Josie:

"Okay, Josie, pack your bags we gotta' get out of here." She came in from the balcony with a face whiter than the canvas of an uninspired artist.

"Where's that guy gone?" she asked.

"He needed the bathroom." Grady dropped a nod to the closed door. "He might be some time!"

Stabbing keys on his palm phone as he drove, Grady dialled Brock; she picked up at the first ring.

"Where are you Loot?"

"At Dodd's office, I'm about finished, why? What's happened – *Josie?*"

"It's okay, don't worry she's fine, she's right here with me. We'll come an' pick you up. Don't use the Jeep, Loot, it's bugged. Don't go outside, keep in the shadows. Promise me, Loot."

"Are you okay, Grady, what's happened please tell me?"

"We had to leave the room. The bathroom needs cleanin.' Someone made a very nasty smell in there!"

*   *   *

Chapter Twenty-nine

The mid-July sun kept its promise for a fine, hot dusty day over the city; a setting in which most would choose to slacken off into a low gear, relaxing back and smelling the roses – but not Grady: in a racing fury behind dark glasses and an impending fear of loss he made a lot of enemies and traffic violations as he drove a fast-track to Dodd's. He kept Josie in close next to him and dialled Bugsy as he drove.

"Bugsy, I need a big favour right now, it's an emergency. I need you at Dodd's office, two-ninety-five River Street, A.S.A. fuckin' P. – I'll meet you there." He pressed speed dial — called Brock.

"Okay, Loot, how you doin' there?"

"Nearly finished, Grady what's happening? Josie – is she okay, please tell me?"

"She's fine, sittin' here right next to me blowin' bubbles with her gum, don't worry. We should be with you in about ten minutes," he held the horn down as he jumped red lights. "Wait for us there but don't go outside. I mean it, Loot, promise me!"

"Grady . . . ?" She heard him race gears in the fast lane with his hand on the horn and the Covert security siren howling. She sank back onto the sofa in Dodd's foyer with her head in her hands.

Bugsy was marking time at the kerbside as Grady scuffed the curb and skidded to a halt outside Dodd's; he jumped out of the SUV and checked up and down the street. It was a side street, empty as a flim-flam's promise; there wasn't a soul around. The Jeep, cool under the shade of a Jacaranda tree was parked further down the street. Grady checked the street again, and then spun round with his gun cocked and ready as a spooked pigeon flew out from an overhead balcony. Eagle-eyed, he scanned the street. No change, it was still empty. He re-holstered his weapon.

"Thanks, Bugsy – I owe ya'!"

"What's up, Grady?"

"Check the Jeep for me I think it's been bugged." He checked the street again, sprang the door for Josie and took her arm.

"Come sweetheart, let's go see the Lieutenant; leave Bugsy to do his business."

Josie ran inside and hugged Brock. Grady sank his two-twenty into the threadbare sofa, pushed his hat back on his head and explained to Brock what had happened back at the hotel. He left out some details in front of Josie, no problem: any elaboration was not necessary; from past experience, Brock could guess the details.

"It seems hotels ain't a healthy place for us to hang out in, Boss." Brock looked down to Josie, pulled her in tight. A black thought turned her stomach; this was much too close for comfort. Tearful, she looked into the big man's eyes.

"Thank you Grady – what *would* I do without you?"

"Just doin' my job, Loot, nuthin' more."

She tweaked her nose, pulled his hat down over his eyes. "Yeah, right ..."

He gave her a wide smile. Lifted his hat off and plonked it on her head, and said:

"Come; let's go see if Bugsy's found anything."

Shading his eyes as he stepped outside, he checked the street, saw nothing of concern and waved the girls out. Bugsy held up a tracker bug. It wasn't the one Grady had originally put there. He turned to Brock:

"Found this under the wheel arch, miss. That's how they knew where you were. But that's not all." He lifted the hood, pointed to an explosive device cuddled in tight next to the ignition. "That's only just been planted there, Lieutenant. Set to burn soon as you fired up to go." Brock looked to Grady then up and down the empty street and drawled:

"I wonder whose day that would've brightened up apart from mine." She wondered also how anyone could have known where she'd be now and able to plant a bomb in the Jeep. *'Trust no-one, live longer!'* She turned to Bugsy:

"Could you set it off?"

"Sure – But it'll make one hell of a mess."

"Okay guys pull your vehicles back out of the way and set it off," she said turning to Grady, "right after the explosion call our guys – and *only* our guys to come and clean the mess away. Then call the media station and give this report: *Lieutenant Madeline Brock, an operative from Covert Security and one other female, as yet unknown, were both killed in a car bomb explosion today in River Street,*" she turned to the sweep: "Go ahead, Bugsy. Do your business."

Windows shattered as a cloud of black smoke from the burning heap bellowed high into the sky, spooked birds took flight and debris scattered across the street. Grady drove a fast exit, turned the corner and drove into a bright afternoon sun. They were glad to be alive — once again.

"Where to, Loot?"

"I don't know, Grady, we're running a little short on hotels. Let's go and see Jackie Olsen, see if he can fix up something for us; maybe he's got a spare room out back. I'll give the Major a call; see if he's got a safe-house we can use."

"Okay, I'll drop you two off first then I've got a pressing appointment with a Mister Sculley down on the waterfront." Brock didn't ask.

Grady pulled up outside Jackie's bar, walked round and held the door for the two ladies.

"Thank you, Grady." Josie spoke sweet and soft as an ermine wrap as she stepped out of the SUV.

"You're welcome, sweetheart, anytime." The big man ruffled her hair.

*　　*　　*

Chapter Thirty

Set deep in the heart of gilt-edge real estate, the Trafalgar Bay office block stood six floors high of stainless steel, clad with half an acre of reflective glass grinning out like a beacon to wealth across the bay. Sculley's office high on the sixth languished in luxury beneath a mirror-glassed penthouse and a lot of hard cash. Grady rode the elevator up to the sixth.

Soft-whistling a tuneless melody, he trod lazy steps along a hallway carpeted in blood red, heavy pile weave, with a compass rose embossed in gold at great expense at every step to show you were headed south. The sole sound in the vicinity came from Grady's footsteps on thick pile crunching to the sound of footfall on a virgin snowfall. Draped along the walls hanging in heavy gilt frames, oil paintings depicting ancient naval battles gave validation to the nautical theme in complement to the name of the office block. At the far end of the hallway, Grady stopped at a door with Sculley's name scrolled in gold on a teak cartouche bordered with white Blanco'd marlinespike rope work. He didn't knock.

In the middle of reception stood a mahogany desk, trimmed with brass and not too much covering it; not dissimilar to the receptionist sat behind it chewing gum in a mouth custom made for pleasure. Dressed with a mission to mainline the flow of blood to male genitalia, she didn't look up from filing her nails. She wore enough make-up to cover up six of the seven deadly sins. The seventh: lust, was still on offer. She wore a cheap scent strong enough for a drunk to lean against and flashed long black lashes every bit as convincing as a female orgasm in a porn flick. She puckered rouge lips, blew a pink bubble with her gum, took her gaze up to Grady and popped her bubble.

"Help you?"

"Not unless you want to give my dick a quick manicure, sweetheart. I'm here to see Mister Sculley."

"You got an appointment or a hard-on, wise guy?"

"I don't need either, sweetheart. I've gotta feelin' Mister Sculley might be expecting me. I got a complaint about a cleaning job he organised back over at my place." Grady flashed his credentials.

"Who shall I say you are?" she asked, chewing gum to the sound of a hungry dog chomping back Friday night's leftover steak fat.

"Tell him it's a mister . . ."

"Mister what?" she asked, impatient, stabbing a file at her nails.

"Yeah, that'll do. Tell him a mister *what's* here to see him – Oh, don't bother – I'll tell him myself. Why don't you take the rest of the day off, sweetheart; maybe go out and pole dance around a lamp post, earn yourself some real money. I might be keeping him busy for quite a while."

Grady pushed open the door into Sculley's office, strode inside and bum-pushed the door shut behind him. He strolled across a very expensive royal blue carpet embossed with gold crossed anchors and ships' spoked wooden wheels. Sculley's office, decorated out in nautical memorabilia, was set to impress people as they walked in – Grady wasn't one of them. He took a seat in the visitor's chair and stared up to a large oil painting. It depicted a figure dressed in early-nineteenth-century admiral's attire; who, if you were to squint your eyes, may have looked close enough to be a much younger Sculley armed with a telescope, staring out from the poop deck of a one hundred-gun first rater into the wide blue ocean yonder. It boasted a self-indulged voyage into vanity straight from the myths of tinsel town. Sculley didn't speak as he leant across his desk to call reception.

Grady also leant across the desk – and brought his fist down hard on the desk machine. He spoke with a smirk:

"Don't bother. She went home." Sculley narrowed his eyes:

"Who are you? What do you want?"

"Some answers to my questions would be a good start."

"Who sent you?"

"Someone who you sent to clean up my hotel room recommended you to me," said Grady, running a tongue across his lips, "he's still workin' on the bathroom as we speak."

Sculley sat back in his chair, drew a deep breath and stared down at the remnants of his intercom.

"Keep your hands away from the table, fart-breath." Grady drew out his gun, "I wouldn't want to make a mess, an' add a touch of reality to your fancy painting sitting up there on the wall behind you." Sculley clasped his hands together in front of him and looked as if he was praying. Maybe he was – If he wasn't he sure needed to!

"What do you want, money – How much?"

"You haven't got anywhere near enough to buy me off, asshole," said Grady. He burned a wrath from his eyes with an intensity to peel the flock wallpaper right off the walls.

"So you're the guy who organises hits on poor little defenceless girls?"

"I don't know *what* you're talking about," blubbered Sculley. Grady bent low with venom in his manner:

"Okay, fart-breath, let's start off with Macey's grill, and to a cute little girl who had no quarrel with anyone." Sculley flushed a red collar around his neck below a screwed up chalk white face shaking harder than a mess of tripe on a busy butcher's chopping board. Sculley held a deep breath; two ears burning bright gave his silent response.

"So now I'm guessin' you know who I am," growled Grady. "I'm also guessin' you might be the man at the top of this here Trafalgar house, what with you bein' called Nelson sittin' up here on your plinth. But I'm also guessin' you're not the man at the top of the shit stinkin' drug deal contaminating this city," Grady narrowed his eyes, "wanna save your neck...? Give me a name…" *Silence!* Ears burned red flanking a sheet white face. "Huh, no, I guessed not." Grady palmed the hit man's flick knife, sprung the blade and thumbed the tip.

"Your man never got to use this today. So if it's okay with you – I'll oblige." Grady flicked his brows over evil eyes and said: "Open your safe, fart-breath."

"I don't have a safe."

"You know it's funny – I thought you might say that." Grady got up, strode around the desk, spun Sculley round in the office chair and faced him to the wall mirror. Then he picked an ornamental brass cannon off the desk and swung it hard into the mirror.

"How about that! I guess you didn't know that was there." He drew his gun. "Open it, fart-breath." Staring down the barrel of a gun gave Sculley little choice. He tapped in the code on the digital keypad, opened the door and stood back.

"Take what you want – all of it – just go," pleaded Sculley.

"Now what do we have here?" growled Grady, "it looks as if you got enough scooby snacks and black tar here to set a herd of elephants dancing a crazy conga all the way across the plains of Africa; and there's enough China White in there to powder your nose for ten lifetimes. If, of course, you hoped you were gonna be around for that long. And I see a *very* nice ledger nestled under those bags of coke – might make some very interestin' readin'. Sit back down asshole!"

Grady pulled Sculley's arms around behind the high back office chair and cuffed him. He sprang the knife, yanked Sculley's head back by his hair and dragged cold steel slow across the skin of his stretched throat. A dribble of blood rolled down Sculley's throat as the blade passed over his Adam's apple; he winced but said nothing breathing quick and hard below wide eyes of terror.

"This is how it must have felt for Macey, only a whole lot deeper, and much, much more painful. Still don't want to give me a name, fart-breath …? No – I thought not. Okay, let's take you on a little voyage. I hope it ain't gonna make you seasick."

Grady took a bag of cocaine from the safe and slit it open with the switch-blade. He yanked Sculley's head back, pressed his thumb and forefinger hard into Sculley's cheeks to hold his mouth open, then he poured neat dope into the mouth of another dope; then punched Sculley hard in the stomach to make him take a sharp intake of breath. He repeated this four times until the bag was empty. Then pulled out another bag and emptied it over Sculley's head and down over his body. Sculley bore a stark resemblance to a nightmare snowman with blood-red eyes, choking, spluttering, and puffing out white dust.

"Nothin's gonna bring Macey back, fart-breath," growled Grady, "but I'll see you in hell, motherfucker!" Teeth bared, he yanked Sculley's head back by the hair and ripped the knife across Sculley's throat; then plunged the blade deep into his skull and growled through gritted teeth: "That's for Macey, you shit-sucking, dope-swilling motherfucker!" He spat down at Sculley, retrieved his handcuffs, bagged the dope, the money and the ledger, straightened his hat brim, dusted his cuffs and strolled out into reception. The six deadly sins had long gone. She wouldn't be fulfilling the seventh again with her boss anytime soon, for he was sure never to be hard at work again.

*   *   *

Chapter Thirty-one

Idly whistling a tuneless melody Grady drove a slow pass along an empty street. The blacktop shimmered under bright sunlight after a light rain shower. He swerved to avoid splashing a feral dog as it lapped a liquid lunch from a puddle. Two blocks further on he swung a left into the street housing Brock's apartment, parked the SUV outside Jackie Olsen's and walked into a half-full bar room. He leant a casual arm on the polished counter and scanned the room. From the reflection of the full-width bar mirror, he couldn't see Brock. No-one took any notice of him except Jackie, standing behind the counter.

"Thing's lookin' up, Jackie – she out the back?" Grady asked in a low voice. Olsen leaned across the counter, spoke quiet as he poured Grady a shot.

"They're upstairs – back room."

"Thanks, Jackie," said Grady, slugged back the shot, dropped a bill and a friendly wink, lifted the mahogany counter flap, went behind the bar and out up the stairs.

Of the three doors on the landing one was closed; he knuckled a quiet rhythm on it.

"Loot, it's me." She opened the door, holstered her gun and pulled him inside. Josie, sitting quiet on the bed, gave him the best smile she could muster under the circumstances, but managed only to lift the corners of her lips below sad eyes. But she did give him a cute wave.

"How did your meeting go?" asked Brock. He handed her the ledger, she tweaked her nose.

"Good work. Seems we're makin' quite a collection of these. Where did you find it?"

"It was in another safe."

"How'd you open it?"

"I had some help from the owner – a mister Sculley: a *very*, obliging gentleman."

"I'll bet – Where is he now?" she asked. *As if she didn't know.*

"He's masquerading as a snowman with a bright red bib – and he's got his carrot stuck in his throat." Brock smiled, shook her head and didn't ask.

"Did you call the Major?" asked Grady.

"Yes, he's got a safe house for us," she checked her watch, "we could go there right now. I'll call him and he'll meet us there. Would it be okay, Grady? Can you take us – please?" He looked at her with big sad eyes and gave her his favourite smile.

"What a question, Loot, sure I can, no problem. I'll tell Jackie and meet you two out the back. Take a brolly, it looks like rain."

*　　*　　*

The drive to the safe house set on the city outskirts took twenty-five minutes in light traffic after they'd crawled through rush hour in the busy city centre. Stood lonely in its own grounds, the safe house, set behind a stone wall fronting high bushes in a well-manicured tree-lined street, offered top security. Under the shade of a *porte-cochere* in front of the small brick and clap-board building, Major Falconer sat in his Jeep. He stepped polished leather boots out onto fresh cut grass as Grady pulled up behind him. Dressed in his customary leather jacket, Falconer strode forward, held out his hand to Brock. This time she shook it. He greeted her, again in his perfect English gentleman's accent, spoken through a heart-warming smile.

"Lieutenant Brock, it's such a pleasure to see you again. Did you enjoy your break; I must say you're looking very well for it?"

"Yes thank you, Major. Such a pity it couldn't have been longer."

"Yes, I always ponder that thought myself on the odd occasion I can manage a few days away." Aroused at the scent of *To a Wild Rose,* he turned to Josie and inhaled a deep breath. Brock spoke:

"This is Josette DuBois – Josie, this is Major Falconer."

"What – an – enchanting name, French – Bonne journée Mademoiselle, c'est mon plaisir de vous recontrer." He took Josie's hand and kissed it. She lit up the garden as she flushed red. Grady leaned forward and whispered in her ear:

"I think you've made a friend there, Josie. If not a friend – certainly a hell of a fuckin' impression!"

"Come, let's go inside, I'll lead the way," said Falconer.

Brock followed the major feeling as if she was going on a guided tour of Buckingham Palace; if only the building was a thousand times bigger, covered in gilt-leaf and reeking of unearned privilege and a staled opulence. Inside, the décor was no comparison to Buckingham Palace or anyone else's palace if truth be known. But it was cosy, and as far as she hoped, nothing more than a temporary sanctuary.

"You'll be quite safe here, Lieutenant. There is an excellent security system with a safe room in the cellar if all else fails. Everything you need to know is in the folder on the bureau. There is a direct line to my office so you won't need to use your cell phone, which perhaps could give away your location. Here is a burner phone, untraceable, for you to make any calls you may otherwise need to make. The news channel has been giving out details of your *demise* so I doubt you will have anything more to worry about in that respect. I must say, Lieutenant: it was quick thinking on your part. I'm only glad I knew about it before I heard about it on the news channel. I take it Mademoiselle DuBois was the other person *killed* in the Jeep with you?"

"Yes, Sir, so as far as anyone out there knows: there should now be no need to bother us anymore," she didn't want to say: '*to hunt us down and kill us,*' in front of Josie.

"Yes, I'm sorry about the incident today at the hotel. Thank god for Sergeant Da Silva. What with the bomb threat and the confrontation in your apartment, it must all be quite a trauma for you. I'm deeply sorry."

"It goes with the job, Sir. I'm well used to it. Have you any leads on Heidi yet."

"No, nothing at all I'm afraid; it's all very strange I must say. I would have thought by now we would at least have heard about a ransom request," he didn't want to say she was in all probability dead. "Okay people, I must be off. I'll leave you to get settled in. Tomorrow morning I shall come over and we'll have a full de-brief, which would also include you Sergeant, if you wouldn't mind. Let's make it, shall we say zero-ten-hundred hours. I'm sure I don't need to tell you to check you are not being followed, Sergeant. There's coffee in the store cupboard and frozen food in the freezer. So please feel free to help yourselves. Okay, I think it's about all for now. I'll look forward to seeing you all tomorrow. May I bid you all a good evening." He shook Brock's hand; patted Grady on the shoulder, turned to Josie and kissed her hand. "Merci et bonsoir, Mademoiselle DuBois; á demain," he bowed as he spoke, then turned and left the house. He didn't click his heels. Maddie turned to Josie, pulled her close.

"You sure made an impression there, sweetheart; I can't imagine what he's going to do when he finds out about your de-coding and safe-cracking skills."

Grady pushed his body up out of his seat ready to leave.

"You gonna be okay now, Loot? I'll hang around for a while if you want."

"No, it's okay thanks, Grady, and big thanks for today I owe you big time."

"You don't owe me nothin', Loot. It was my pleasure, always will be, you know that. You look after her. I'll see you tomorrow, zero-ten-what-the-fuck-ever."

"Ten-o'clock, Grady."

"Yeah right." He flipped on his hat, pulled down his cuffs and strolled out into the early evening whistling a tuneless melody in a fading sunset. She called out after him ...

"Oh, Grady, could you do me one big favour: I need Josie's vehicle, it's the tan Ford in the underground parking lot under my complex. Maybe check it out with Bugsy first but I'm sure it's okay – wait, I'll get you the pass-key."

"I'll bring you a company Jeep if you want," he offered.

"No too conspicuous. Josie's Ford will be fine." She handed him the key, smiled and spoke soft words with her eyes. "Thank you, Grady."

Easy in her mind, Brock relaxed, pulled Josie close, hugged her hard and kissed her lips with a sensual passion.

"Are you okay, honey? I'm so sorry you have to go through all this. Is there anyone you can go and stay with for a while: friends or relations maybe?"

Sad blue eyes spoke a no. "I'm okay. I want to stay here with you, Maddie. Anyway, I feel as if we're in the old-time movies," she shrugged a half-believed smile under those big blue eyes.

"I've got to say, sweetheart: this is a hell of a long way from Hollywood. I've never thought of it that way myself, but yes, maybe a very, very bad movie," she shrugged her shoulders and smiled ... "hungry...? Let's go check the freezer, see if there's a pizza. We can get hot while it's defrosting."

Intruding on the warm glow from a copper dawn flooding the sky, a cloud burst broke and fell on parched land in a brief shower, enough to damp down the dust and nothing more.

Green leaves covered by beads of aqua-crystal sparkled bright as emerald broaches under the luminescence cast from the morning sun sneaking out with a warm smile from behind a blanket of cloud, its blazing heat would soon be sending a mirage of vapour cloud back up to the heavens. *'Mother nature's sure got the handle on perpetual motion,'* Brock mused, now awake and staring out through the East side window.

She rolled out of bed, left the cute visage of Josie sleeping and meandered into the bathroom to savour a moment of solitude in ecstatic bliss under the shower rose. It was eight fifteen on a bright summer morning. She towelled off and wandered into the kitchen, searched for something suitable for breakfast, then ambled out into the garden. Dressed in light cotton clothes she swung in the garden swing seat with her breakfast: a glass of white wine. She pondered down through the glass into a vision of the capricious dilemma engulfing her life, wondered if such a vision through alcohol was the only true answer to distance her from the violent world she inhabited. With her lower lip tight in her teeth, she stared up into the azure blue sky, clucked her tongue and poured the wine into the grass. She went inside, woke Josie and hugged her.

The clock read nine fifty-five; or Zero-Nine-Fifty-five hundred hours if you'd prefer, most don't care either way except perhaps the Major, who, true to form strode up the front garden walkway and tapped on the knocker. He pecked Brock on the cheek as she welcomed him in, left her hand alone. His face flushed as he retracted.

"I must apologise, I'm afraid it was most inappropriate of me. I'm very sorry. I was so relieved to see you safe and looking so well." She blushed as he rested his briefcase on the dining table.

"It's not a problem, Major. I don't meet many gentlemen in my line of work. Actually, if I were to be honest – it makes rather a pleasant change – thank you." Emerald green eyes smiled radiance in the privacy of the moment; she spoke soft:

"Please – call me Maddie."

His cheeks flexed, lifted the corners of his mouth. He looked as if he was going to take a bow, lay his cape down for her to walk over and shower her feet with red rose petals.

"It would be my pleasure, but only in private I assure you."

"I've made coffee if you would care for some."

"Coffee would be very nice. Thank you. Where is Miss DuBois? Has she left?" he sniffed the air as he spoke: "No. . . I think not."

"She's still here, Sir … I wanted to talk to you first in private for a few minutes."

"Certainly, I think I know what's coming, Madeline." He filled his lungs and said:

"Before you speak, Lieutenant, I want to commend you on eight years of exemplary service in a very difficult and dangerous job. Your total dedication to duty has not gone unnoticed, especially by me. I promise to honour and help you with any decision you may choose to make regarding your future." Sat in silence she folded her arms, worried her bottom lip with her thumb and forefinger, then, speaking almost in a whisper, she said:

"Recently I've had cause to realise how precious life can be. I feel now I'm living on borrowed time."

"I completely understand," he confided, "but I can't afford to lose people of your calibre. And I mean you especially Madeline. What I propose, is for you to come in out of field combat and work with me as head of Covert Security. National Security will amalgamate with Covert Security, and your experience in the field will be far too valuable to lose. We will always need new blood and they will all need training." She felt awkward, confused, wished it would all go away.

"Thank you, Sir. Would you mind if I thought it over for a while?"

"Certainly, of course Madeline, and while we are on the subject, may I enquire as to Miss DuBois' purpose here?"

"Yes, Sir, you may," she paused, looked up to him with an emotive passion in her gaze and said: "She's my lover." Two cherries and a raspberry rang up in Falconer's eyes. This time *he* took the pause, said nothing, but smiled and stood rocking on his heels. Mesmerised by those emerald green eyes for far longer than protocol would allow, he spoke out aloud, more to himself than anybody as he looked up to the heavens:

"Lucky Girl!"

The doorbell rang. Grady walked in and broke a tender moment with all the subtlety of a loud fart at a funeral. He carried in two bags of spoils and dumped the sacks down onto the dining table.

"I picked this little lot up from a drug bust yesterday, Sir, from a guy called Nelson Sculley at the Trafalgar Bay office block. Yeah, I know, Sir – What a moniker! Sounds great don't it. Anyway, there's enough cash and dope here to fund a small army and keep an opium den wheeling out halfwits until well into the next century; plus a ledger full of the names of contacts, dealers, pushers, suppliers … you name it. But it's all in code. And there's also the other ledger we got from the Mertz office safe, also in code, Sir, along with a lot more cash, jewellery and dope." Falconer stood in silence, shook his head as Grady emptied both sacks out onto the dining table.

"*Well done*, Sergeant. I'm more than impressed."

"We're getting' there, Sir. But it wasn't only me, far from it. I tag along in the dust behind the Lieutenant here. She's the primary, Sir; always has been."

Falconer looked to Brock, shook his head in disbelief as he picked up the ledger.

"We must see if we can get any of this de-coded as soon as possible. It won't be easy; it's a field we are rather short-staffed in."

"No problem, Sir, already done, most of it anyway from the Mertz bust," said Grady.

"What, how —who by – don't tell me you've got hidden talents, Sergeant? If you do have, I need to know about it, ASAP!"

"No, Sir, not me, it was Josie, Miss DuBois, Sir; she also worked out how to crack the safe, she's very, very clever, Sir. Ain't nuthin' to do with me I assure you, I ain't so clever, nowhere near it."

Falconer looked as if he were a man who had realised he'd forgotten to put his trousers on when he'd left home this morning. He stroked his jaw, composed himself and looked across to Brock.

"Call Miss DuBois in here please, Lieutenant, if you wouldn't mind."

Forever the gentleman, Major Falconer stood as Josie entered the room. He pulled out a chair for her at the dining table, took her hand and sat her down. Holding court at the head of the table, he stared at her in silence, massaging his chin before he eventually spoke:

"Where do you work, Miss DuBois? Are you with the Government – or are you with a private concern?"

"Neither – I'm between jobs."

"Well, who did you work for?"

"Skinny's Grill, I waited tables."

Falconer, pushing back hard in his chair didn't flinch at the sound of a cracking tenon joint. He looked as if he'd been slapped across the cheek with a wet Kipper. He turned to Brock; emerald eyes stared back to him with a look to stop a clock. Dumbfounded, he turned back to Josie, gazed into azure blue pools, then, with a slow nod turned his gaze again to Brock. Two and two suddenly added up to one hell of lot more than four. He massaged his chin again before he eventually spoke:

"Shall we take a few minutes, people – I need to talk to the Lieutenant if I may." He slapped his hands down in perfect unison onto the carver's arms, pushed his body up out of the chair, pulled his cuffs straight and strode determined steps out into the garden.

Brock followed him out in her own time.

"Tell me about Miss DuBois, Lieutenant?"

"I'm very fond of her, Sir."

"As I can see, Madeline; I can also see she is very fond of you, the feeling is without doubt mutual." Brock could hear only birdsong in the following silence, she licked dry lips to wet before she spoke:

"A short while ago I was nearly killed on two occasions in thirty-six hours; and on many, many similar occasions before; too many to even keep count. Yesterday I narrowly missed being blown to pieces by a car bomb, while Miss DuBois narrowly missed having her throat cut. And now we are both in hiding. It's enough, Sir. I won't take it anymore. I don't want to lose her – She's more than anything I've ever had or wanted." Falconer looked away into the distance, continued to massage his jaw and said nothing. Then, he turned and spoke:

"I understand, Madeline – only too well. Tell me: does she have any family?"

"No, Sir. Same as me, her family all perished long ago with the virus." Falconer sucked on his teeth. Nodding his head slow, he spoke without looking at her.

"If you wish, Madeline, I will put out a twenty-four-hour round-the-clock surveillance for you both, for however long it takes to clear away this drug scourge. It would seem, with your and Miss DuBois' help, an end to all this may well be in sight. I implore you to consider my offer and would appreciate it if you could persuade Miss DuBois to join us in our quest. I can assure you both you will be working together in complete safety. Please, take some time to think it over," he took her arm, "come, Madeline, let us go back inside and join the others."

The dining table covered in cash and jewellery looked like a good day for Lookout Farm, and the closing of a bad day at Tiffany's. Hard cash was piled high one end of the table, the dope heaped high on the other end and jewellery sparkled centre stage. Falconer went through the jewellery, broaches, bracelets, ear rings, high-end watches and much more. He itemised it all, along with the bags of dope and piles of cash.

"Miss DuBois, please show me the ledger you have de-coded." Josie opened the book and slid it across the table to him. Leant back in his chair he perused the ledger in silence, worried his ear lobe then massaged his chin and spoke to no-one in particular but to anyone who wanted to listen.

"There are a lot of very high profile names here, some in very high office."

"What a surprise," said Grady; *sarcastic!* "The scum who tried to take us both out at the Palm Beach a couple of weeks back were government officials in high office, Sir; and then there's LePage. And now we got a whole lot more assholes to deal with."

Falconer thought deep, continued to worry his chin. With a furrowed brow he turned to Grady:

"Sergeant – I shall allocate to you a team of twelve of the finest combat troops we have. I want you to round up every single name in this ledger. We will come down on them with the full force necessary to stamp out this scourge. I give you full authority and a license to use whatever means – and, I *mean*, whatever means you consider necessary to bring these people to justice, one way or the other."

'*At fuckin' last, a bugle call!*' thought Grady; and he's the one who's going to be doing the blowing.

"Do we have any idea who is the ring leader?" asked Falconer.

Brock answered: "We're pretty certain it's Karl-Heinz Jungen, Sir, the terrorist from the Y-Zee Kay active around twenty years ago. He was never caught and has since gone to ground and disappeared without trace. From information we gleaned during our recent operations in the O-Zone, we now believe he's hiding somewhere in the city, but so far haven't been able to track him down. He just hasn't surfaced. Our efforts to find him have always been hampered by an unknown entity. We learned from our interrogations there is a plant very high up in our system; which may well have been LePage. But myself I'm not so sure. I think LePage was in it for any eventual money he may have scammed, and not the power," she paused. "Karl-Heinz Jungen wants power," she sucked her tongue, "maybe we can find a lead when we de-code the ledgers. We've been clearing out the drains polluted with lowlife and drug traffickers from the O-Zone; I think we've nearly got it busted now, Sir. I'm pretty certain their whole operation has been taken over and moved up here to the city, where a new cartel is forming. So it's clear to me we have been used, possibly by LePage to clean out the drug cartel in the O-Zone; which, is the only reason we are still alive. LePage told me when he was about to shoot me before *he* was shot, that our services were no longer needed." She looked to the major with silent thanks. "This was why the attempt was made to kill us at the Palm Beach Hotel. It qualifies to me as proof of his involvement in the *coup d'état*. So with all the events over the past few days, it's clear to me someone is now trying to draw us out into the open – and kill us, Sir." She sat back and took a breath.

"Thank you, Lieutenant. A harrowing account indeed," said Falconer, bounced his eyebrows and took a deep breath. He turned to Josie: "Miss DuBois, would you consider a position at National Security? I can promise you will be well paid for your efforts, and I can assure you in such a position, you will certainly *not* be waiting tables." Brock beamed across to Josie, smiled through her emerald eyes and shrugged '*I told you so*' shoulders.

"Why don't you talk it over with the Lieutenant, Miss DuBois in your own time?" Falconer rested a comforting hand on her arm, "I will make certain you will be well rewarded for your assistance so far, and in whatever decision you may make for your future one way or the other. I'll look forward with anticipation to your decision."

'*Poor Josie,*' mused Brock. A month ago she was minding her own business flipping burgers and waiting tables, and now look – up to her neck in drug dealers and espionage.

Falconer started to load up the sacks, Grady helped him.

"Thank you, Sergeant. Is this all?" Grady looked up, stern -faced and glared at the Major.

"I don't want nuthin' to do with no dirty drug money, if that's what you mean, Sir."

Falconer realised his unintended *faux-pas* had hit a sour note. He backtracked, tried again in a different key:

"I apologise Sergeant. I'm sorry if you miss read my implication. It was not meant to accuse you of anything. I only wondered if you had any more leads on any pending drug deals."

"That's okay, Sir. No offence taken. I'm sure Josie will come up with plenty more leads to where this lot came from, and much, much more."

"Yes, I'm sure she will. I'm also sure whatever *spoils* you and the lieutenant had ever surrendered to LePage went straight back into the drug pool; I have little doubt about it. LePage never once informed me of anything ever gleaned by Covert Security. The money and spoils you have confiscated will go to National Security in order to fund the fight against the drug war. We will make the bastards pay for their demise; and I can assure you Sergeant: both you and the Lieutenant will be well rewarded for your efforts. And that means with clean money, I can guarantee you that. And I'm certainly not forgetting you, Miss DuBois. Give me a hand out with the bags please, Sergeant."

Falconer said his goodbyes in the manner well accustomed only to him and arranged to return sometime the following day to check everything was okay. At what particular Oh'-Hundred he didn't mention. Brock hoped it wouldn't be at the sparrow's O'-fart.

*　　*　　*

Chapter Thirty-two

Two baths the size of the one in the safe house could have comfortably fitted into the spa bath at the Inn on the Bay, and would still have left room enough for a Sumo wrestler and his opponent to perform a few holds. But in stark contrast, the safe house bath was cosy enough for the two naked bodies languishing in its bubbly confines to perform their holds, tight in each other's arms. Such is love.

"Do you think the major is serious, Maddie?"

"Sure – why not?"

"Well, why would he offer me a job in National Security with no experience or qualifications? It doesn't make any sense. I wouldn't even know what I would be expected to do."

"Things are not how they used to be, Josie. These days' people with your skills are in short supply, almost non-existent. So, you no longer need a ten-page reference endorsed by the old school tie, a stack of qualifications and yet still have to suck someone's dick to get a job. Nothing more than a clever mind is good enough for National Security; and you qualify hands down."

"What about you, Maddie?"

"I don't know, sweetheart, I can't make up my mind. I guess it would be a lot better to work in a safe environment," she shrugged a contemplative smile, "I wish there was something else I could do."

"Such as…?"

"I dunno – flipping burgers? Come, gimme a kiss Angel eyes."

*   *   *

Heavy rain beating out a steady rhythm on the bedroom window panes echoed the rapturous applause enjoyed by a solo virtuoso taking a bow as he made his exit through moth eaten dusty curtains back into the stark insignificance of reality. A sinister cloud cover grumbling away with the scolding rebuke of a tired old spouse threatening retribution shielded the rising sun. Low-down, playing hide-and-seek, the sun had yet to grace the stage with its seasonal commitment. A gust of wind rattled the window panes. Lightening forked, lit up the bedside clock face. It was seven thirty-eight. The following bolt of thunder would've woken Brock, as would the rattle of gunfire, but after a night of broken sleep she was already awake. Her muddled mind couldn't stop thinking about *Jack*: her one hit antidote to defuse life's traumata. To say life was complicated was an understatement; futile as saying it's a long way to fly to the Moon, Venus, or Mars. Across the pillow, the angelic sight of the innocent beauty fast asleep at her side worried her. Brock wondered what in hell she had let her in for — couldn't see her hurt, couldn't live without her. She shuddered, felt selfish. The black monkey clung tight to her back and took a strong hold. Her mood sunk low into the deep depths of a dark abyss. She'd gained small comfort from her car bomb ploy, which may have given her some breathing space in a coin flip world, but deep in the depths of reason and stark reality – who the hell knows?

'*Take no chances, trust no-one, live longer,*' ricocheted through her mind. That haunting thought had kept her safe negotiating life's tightrope, although she knew sooner or later she would be bound to slip and fall if she did not get out now. The clock was ticking. Thoughts of Heidi clouded her mind; she wondered if the little girl could still be alive. Rational thought doubted it, for if she was what sort of hell would she be going through? A vulnerable little blind girl all alone and who knows where…? If nothing else Brock knew she was contested to find her. After which she could start to reconsider her own future. But first and foremost she had to track Jungen down and serve him justice by the only way she knew how – From the barrel of her gun.

A hammer blow from a thunderbolt rattled the windows, gate-crashing a soft dream. Josie flashed her lashes, opened her eyes but didn't move her head. She felt sorrow at the sight of Brock's vacant gaze up at the ceiling. A tender hand reached out, stroked Brock's cheek.

"What's wrong, Maddie? Tell me." Brock turned to her with a sigh, took in the soft dusting of freckles at the bridge of her nose diffusing across into her cheeks; then took her gaze to the downy beauty spot on the left side of her face above those honey lips. A curious mind would wonder how she could look as stunning and beautiful as a fresh bloom in spring when she had just woken up; a rare privilege of very few, but to the bane of many.

"It's nothing, honey. The storm woke me up. Go back to sleep, sweetheart, it's still early."

Brock's answer was as convincing as a schoolboy fumbling his way through a bad card trick, and well she knew it.

"No... what's wrong, Maddie, tell me, you're worried – why?" Leaning over Josie's nubile body, Brock popped a finger on the pretty girl's nose, said:

"Ok-ey mind-reader, I'm thinking about the future – our future, something I've never had to do before. I don't much care about anything else now, only you sweetheart. I wish we were back in the beach cabin and could stay there forever, far removed from all this ..." she drew breath through gritted teeth, "but I guess that's nothing more than wishful thinking," *and right now that's about as useful as sound advice from the back end of a donkey,* she mused. "Come – let's get up early for a change; maybe go for a run before breakfast." At the mention of breakfast, Josie rolled her naked body over on top of Brock, kissed her with a seductive passion and probed her tongue deep into Maddie's mouth. Brock closed her eyes, rose up from a deep dark hole out into the bright and welcome glow of sexual ecstasy.

No doubt about it: a run and a conventional breakfast would have to wait.

*   *   *

At nine-thirty the doorbell sang out. Torrential rain had surrendered its onslaught. Heavy cloud cover had dispersed, allowing a burning sun shining bright to step up to the fold and vaporise the wet terrain back up into the atmosphere. Grady's face flashed up on the CCTV wall-mounted screen in the bedroom. Behind him in a rising mist of vapour Josie's Ford stood gleaming under the *porte-cochère*; he'd taken it for a wash and valet before delivery. He stood clean-shaven in the shade of his faithful grey felt Fedora. With a powder blue cotton shirt under an ivory blazer, midnight blue neck-tie, light shadow-stripe pants and white loafers, he felt good; and he looked it.

Brock slunk out of bed, slipped on her black silk dragon-print robe over bronzed shoulders and wandered across to the front door. She sprung the lock and let Grady in. Studying her back he followed her into the lounge.

"I much prefer your other dragon print, Loot. She turned, slapped his cheek, playful.

"Go and make us some coffee, pervert."

Looking cute as a nymph from a dream, Josie drifted out from the bedroom, barefoot with shorts and a snap-button shirt tied high at the front exposing a tight, tanned midriff: an unintentional tease but such sight left open to the imagination could well instigate a Bacchanalian riot in a Cistercian monastery. Glowing with a strong sense of gratitude, she beamed a smile across to Grady and said:

"Thank you for bringing my car over, Grady, it's very sweet of you."

"It's my pleasure, sweetheart. It's all nice and clean, smells a million bucks; same as you always do." He called out to Brock running a hot tap in the bathroom: "Late night, Loot?"

Black locks dripping soapy water peeked around the door jamb.

"No, Grady – Late morning, there's cholesterol in the freezer and eggs in the pantry if you need breakfast."

"Okay, thanks. I'm guessin' you've already had yours."

"Well, at least it was healthy. Take the hint, Shiney!"

At zero-nine fifty-nine, Falconer, clad in his customary attire strode up the driveway and tapped on the knocker. Whistling a soft atonal melody, Grady re-set his watch as the knocker struck three. Dressed casual in black close-fit jeans, sneakers and a loose snap-button stone-washed denim shirt, Brock sprang open the door. Falconer offered his hand; she took it, offered her cheek.

"Good morning, Madeline, I trust you slept well?" Captivated, he stared at her beautiful face much longer than he meant to, waiting for something, but wasn't quite sure what; then with reluctance he succumbed, checked himself, smiled and said: "Come, let us join the others."

Josie rose from the sofa as the major entered the room. A powerful scent rose with her. It wasn't the only thing rising or was disturbed as the Major inhaled another deep dose of feminine fantasy. Lucky for his disposition she'd untied her shirt front, let her shirt hang down loose – in stark contrast to *his* disposition. Or maybe it was unlucky, who knows? But so what — she's got the job anyway.

With formalities over, a brief flight into fantasy came down from the clouds, settled back onto planet Earth and formed a war cabinet around the dining table. Falconer sat with his elbows on the table and his hands flat together holding up his chisel shape chin below dark furrowed brows shrouding a strong countenance. He looked as if he were praying; maybe he was, but what for? A heavy silence hung in the air, dank as a rain-sodden mattress strung out to dry at a drenched and soulless camp park. Then, the Major spoke:

"On Monday morning at zero-seven-hundred hours, Sergeant Da Silva will lead a team of highly-trained combat agents to seek out and apprehend some of the names Miss DuBois has de-coded for us. We will start with the big names and, I regret to say, these *are* some very big names in our society. As I mentioned to Lieutenant Brock yesterday, Covert Security will now amalgamate with National Security and operate from N.S.F headquarters at the disused Black-rock military air base on the city outskirts. Black-rock is now a secure military-type base offering high protection to anyone employed there."

He sucked his bottom lip as he paused and flicked his eyes across at Brock … *hopeful!*

"Sergeant, you will accompany me back to the base after our meeting. We will set out a battle plan with your combat troops for Monday, which should give you enough time to prepare. We plan to hit hard and fast – Any questions?" In the following silence, Josie pushed forward the ledger with sheets of foolscap. With lips tight as a piccolo trumpet player, Falconer lifted his gaze to her, then in question back across to Brock. She pointed to the ledger, said:

"There are a lot more names, drop spots, bank account details and much more to keep you busy, Sir; courtesy of Miss DuBois." The major ran a finger down the foolscap list, chewed awhile on something soft inside his cheek.

"Thank you, Miss DuBois. Excellent work indeed – I'm most impressed, well done."

He breathed in Wild Rose as if it were a tonic to his soul. Maybe it was. If so it would be something only his wife would know; but then again – maybe she wouldn't!

"I see we have some names here from the police force, Lieutenant; which smells to me of a protection racket. Was there anything at all on Jungen?"

"No, not so far, Sir, but we're still looking. There are still a few things left to de-code, so I'll check it out as soon as Miss DuBois has finished de-coding."

Falconer drained his coffee cup; stood, scraped his chair back and soft bowed his head to Josie, took a deep breath and said:

"Splendid. Okay, thank you everyone. I shall leave you to it. Sergeant, would you care to follow me in my Jeep?"

"I'll ride with you if it's okay, Sir. I'll leave the Ford here for the ladies, my own Jeep's down in the scrapyard on its way to make bed springs and bean cans."

"Right, I think that's all, thank you people. May I have a quick word with you please, Lieutenant, before we leave?" Brock scraped her chair back over wooden floorboards making a sound similar to a no but followed him out onto the front lawn anyway. He took her arm as she joined him.

"Have you any more thoughts on my offer, Madeline?"

"Yes, Sir..."

He broke in: "Randolph please, Madeline. There is no need for formalities when we are in private conversation; call me Randolph – please."

"Yes, okay, Sir, thank you. I've given it some thought and feel I would at least want to help track Yungen down. We are close now; I feel I may have a lot to offer. I owe it to Heidi," she paused... "I'm not naïve, I know she is probably dead by now," she bit her bottom lip, took a deep breath, "but feel for my own sake, I must try and find her, or at least find out what has happened to her. I know if I *can* find her, then we can probably find Yungen. Then, I can make a solid commitment to you one way or the other. I'm sorry – It's the best I have to offer."

"Thank you, Madeline. You will have my full support at all times. I have set up an office at N.S.F headquarters for yourself and Miss DuBois. Please feel free to make full use of it, but please – take some time out first. You deserve it. Thank you again."

He pecked her on the cheek; to hell with the outcome.

*   *   *

"Fire up the coffee machine, sweetheart; I've got to make a couple of calls."

'*A heavy shot of Jack, or maybe even three shots to start, would be better*', she mused. She sat back, made her calls, thumbed red and joined Josie in the garden. Curled up in the swing seat under a hot revitalising sun they drank twenty-four-volt Columbian, enjoying the solitude, listening to birdsong and watching the grass burning brown under the blazing July sun.

"The Major's a strange guy, Maddie, is he for real?"

"He's old school, sweetheart. A perfect gentleman; something you don't come across too often these days. He's okay… I find him quite pleasant."

"Does that mean I have competition, Maddie?"

Breaking out a soft grin, Brock took Josie in her arms, hugged her tight. "No, Honey you don't, not even a bit of it, never ever – please don't think those things. It's a similar sort of feeling I have for Grady: a far cry from intimate love or affection. Anyway, he's married, so let's not go there." She smiled across into those cute angel eyes and wondered how she could ever even *think* of anyone else.

*   *   *

Chapter Thirty-three

Circular shadows cast around the base of towering pine trees stamped the mark of high noon in mid-summer; a good day for some. A small bright-coloured bird pecked on an even smaller bright-coloured berry hanging from a tree branch. Wild squirrels foraged for nuts among fallen needles under the pines, then sprang up rough barked trunks with their bounty to perform acrobatics over the bowers with a panache to shame an Olympian athlete. High in the far distant sky, a hawk glided lazy circles in the thermals in its eternal quest for food. A skylark, oblivious to all around, sang and performed its ethereal feathered cabaret way up high in a clear blue backdrop. Relaxed back on the garden swing seat on a hot summer day was the perfect place to enjoy such things, and to inhale the scent of wild roses. Shaded under the wide brim of a straw summer hat, Brock stepped out into the garden, joined Josie on the swing seat and passed her half an apple.

"Who were you calling, Maddie?"

"No-one special, sweetheart, I had to make a few final arrangements about my apartment. I need to get it cleared out for the new owner," she said. "Watch you don't burn, honey; the sun high in the sky is blistering at this time of the year." Forever mindful, Brock took her hat off and set it on Josie's head, then cuddled in next to her, kicked out a swing and chewed on her half of the apple.

"Was it Grady I heard at the door?"

"Yeah, he's come to pick up your final de-coding sheets for the Major. Come – let's go see if he wants to have lunch with us?" Clutching both of Josie's hands, Brock pulled her up from the swing seat and cuddled her on a slow walk through to the conservatory. It was a lazy kind of day – slow, carefree and hot.

"So, how's it going at Boot Camp, Grady?" He finished chewing his toasted sandwich, swallowed, then said;

"Not the same without you, Loot – it never will be." Sad eyes pleaded, looked up at her, he smiled, turned and poured more coffee.

"Why don't you come in out of fieldwork, Grady? You have a lot to offer training up the new guys. Let them all go out and get shot at for a change. We've done our bit for the cause many times over. It's time now for a rest, big guy."

He shook his head in affirmation: "It's all I know, Loot."

"Grady! Stop callin' me *Loot* – It's Maddie now. I don't want to be *Loot*, anymore," she smiled tender eyes across to him. He raised his coffee cup.

"You got it, Loot." She threw a grape at him.

*   *   *

Long shadows cast from tall pines inching a slow path from the west, stretched out like crawling claws across the well-manicured lawn. The sun prepared to bow down for its curtsey after another stellar performance throughout a long hot day. Yet even at this hour a homeless man could have still fried his purloined chicken eggs on the roof of a car. If only every day was this good thought Brock, but she didn't kid herself, knew fate had a wicked way of throwing a curved ball; she needed to make sure she wasn't around when it sought its target, for she knew only too well — just as you think you've cracked it, that intangible wizard up in the heavens has an uncanny way of rearranging your well-thought-out plans without caution or consultation.

She called out to Josie: "Red or white, sweetheart, let's crack open a bottle, relax, have a sundowner."

"A chilled white please, Maddie; far too hot for red."

"Okay, comin' up – Crackers?"

"Who's crackers?"

"I'm guessing we both are, sweetheart."

*   *   *

With the temperature still sweating its way up the scale, the evening was far too hot for closed windows. For comfort in security, Brock reasoned the CCTV and motion sensors should take care of anyone who felt it might be a good idea to make an unannounced visit in the wee small hours under the blanket of moonlight. Her three-fifty-seven loaded with hollow-points nestled ready under her pillow; an old friend in waiting, in case the tooth fairy got nosey and decided to drop by.

Since her bomb blast ruse, as far as anyone out there knew, Madeline Brock had been blown to hell. Tonight she'd been blown to heaven by her pretty little girlfriend lying at her side. A thin sweat-soaked cotton sheet was not the only thing cloaking two naked bodies; a heavy dose of sensual craving took first place. Sweat leaching from their pores was not only from the heat but more a product from intense carnal desire. Two hours had passed since they'd indulged in their final intimate encore. Now, a stilled silence, empty as the hollow fragment of a fading fantasy hung over them; but only one of them was asleep. Dark thoughts from a dark place in the dark hours are good only to darken the soul, and nothing more, mused Brock. During her past life in times of despair *Jack* would have been the perfect companion. But now he was no longer around and she couldn't call him up. Josie stirred, felt the pain, sprang awake and reached out.

"Maddie, what's wrong?" With a sigh and a tear, Brock stared into blowtorch eyes glistening vivid as sapphires in the moonlight. Staring deep into the quintessence of innocence, Brock could only reflect on what a complete fuck-up her own life had been. The lives she'd taken in the field of combat didn't bother her. They'd deserved everything they got in the rough game they'd played: a game with one winner and a terminal booby for the rest. This beautiful creature in her arms was one life above all else, the one life she cared for dearly and could not afford to lose.

"I don't think I'm going to take up the Major's offer, sweetheart." Josie said nothing, stroked gentle fingers through Brock's hair and massaged her ear.

"What will you do instead?" she asked.

"I don't know. I thought I could maybe go into corporate security, or something along those lines. God only knows I've got the experience."

"Okay then, there's your answer; now get some sleep, Maddie, it's the middle of the night. We can talk about it in the morning. Things always look so much clearer in the fresh light of day, especially after a serious hit of coffee to fire the senses." She ran sensual fingers through Brock's black locks; tender kissed her cheek, then rolled her naked body over and nestled herself in between Maddie's legs and kissed her lips in a long and passionate squeeze.

"If you think I'm going to be able to go to sleep now, Miss Josette DuBois, you've got another thing coming."

*   *   *

Green eyes flashed open to the sweet chorus of birdsong. Sparkling emeralds stared out across a nubile, tanned, sexual landscape over to a clock face showing the big hand had crept past eight-twenty on a bright sunny morning. It was Monday. It wasn't going to be a bright day for everyone; Grady and his SWAT team would be out there to make sure of that.

Whispering sweet nothings into her ear, Brock slow-teased Josie out from a state of quiescence, tickled her nipple erect with her tongue, then kissed and licked a sensual passage down a bronzed torso and circled her tongue around Josie's naval. She massaged on a damp pout. Josie breathed out a quiet moan as she slow-spread her legs. With a tongue now charged with sensual passion, Brock began a slow tantalizing trip south, teasing out a sultry zest for carnal desire. Then – her burner phone buzzed.

"Jesus, what timing, who the hell's that calling me this early?" 'Could be Grady' she thought, better answer it. She rolled off Josie and slunk pained steps across to the dresser, swore aloud and picked up her phone.

"Yes, (pause) yes, okay. Yeah. Give me an hour or two … Sometime around ten or ten- thirty. Okay (pause) Yes, thank you. I'll catch you then. Okay – Bye."

"Who was it, Maddie?"

"Someone looking for a dozing donkey in racing colours, sweetheart," she joked. "No, it was nothing honey; boring legal stuff about the apartment I need to sort out. You want coffee?"

"Come and finish breakfast first," whispered Josie in that sultry, *Dietrich* purr.

*   *   *

At nine forty-five; the sun still had a long way to climb. The day was already hotter than the front teeth of a dragon's mouth. Brock loved the summer and everything it brought to the party. To her, sunshine was the pure essence of life itself. Most people welcomed the diversity of the changing seasons, she hated them, would love it to be summer all year long. If only life wasn't so difficult these days post-virus, she would make a serious effort to move closer to a much warmer, all-year-round climate nearer the equator. But those dreams had all been trashed a long time ago in a now-defunct world. She doubted there would be any change in her lifetime. So live for today; there's time enough to die tomorrow!

Flashing back into the moment, she wondered how many people were now regretting ever being born as Grady helped them along in his inimitable way to confess their sins. She'd find out soon enough, but right now — there was something she needed to do.

"Finish your coffee, honey, there's something I want to show you." She pulled Josie up out of the swing seat and marched her out to the Ford.

"Come – you drive."

"What's happening, Maddie, where are we going?"

"When is your birthday, Josie?"

"October the fifth. Why?"

"Okay, so let's pretend it's October the fifth today. We'll take an easy ride out in the Ford and maybe grab a bite to eat somewhere cool in the country. We've had enough of being cooped up here all day, sweetheart. Let's take a day off, go out and have some fun."

They rode the highway south out of the city, took a slow drive through the outskirts, past the N.S.F base and out into the unspoilt sanity of a wide open country landscape. Ahead the road narrowed to one lane and lost its bordered walkways to grass. Wild flowers took the place from scatterings of trash and decadence littering every uncivilised area inhabited by the uncivilised footprint from humankind.

After a cool twenty minutes of easy driving Brock turned to Josie:

"Pull over up ahead, sweetheart, there's the cute little country fruit store we passed on our way back from the beach cabins. Let's grab a cool drink and a snack."

Josie swung the wheel over, pulled the Ford into the parking lot and rolled to a halt on slate chippings into the shade of a towering Scots pine. Stood in dazzling sunlight, the little store looked purring kitten cute, and homely as a seashell to a hermit crab. Inside the store, they bought fresh fruit, home-baked muffins and iced coffee from the cooler.

Checking through the wine rack, Brock chose an expensive bottle of red, picked up two paper cups from the take-out counter and paid the bill to the laidback owner, whose fresh face looked trouble-free and knew nothing about nightmares. Then, cuddled close, they strolled back out into the heat of the day.

Passing up the chance of rustic pine plank bench seating set in shade, the two girls stretched out under full sunlight on a manicured grass bank bordering the roadside. They mellowed in the heat drinking iced coffee and savouring home-baked blueberry muffins. Josie gazed across to the sold sign on the cute little house across the way; she scrunched her nose:

"Oh – how about that, Maddie, it's been sold. 'Scheew,' I guess it's just as well we didn't rent it out." Brock, relaxed back on cosy grass flicked her eyes open, raised her body up and came to rest on her elbows. She lifted her sunglasses and scanned across the road.

"Yeah, how about that. Let's stroll over and check it out; maybe congratulate the lucky new owners."

"We can't go wandering into someone's house, Maddie, it's not right."

"Don't worry, we'll tell them we're writing a thesis on cute country hideaways and theirs is the best we've seen by far. Anyway, it looks as if it's only the workmen there, honey, and those guys will probably be thrilled to see such a pretty girl as you, especially with your sexy midriff." Brock clucked her tongue, "make a nice change for them from slopping paint around all day and staring at the fat crack in the plumber's backside."

Locked together in each other's arms they ambled across the blacktop, gorging on fresh lychees. Construction guys were busy repainting inside the house. Gardeners were busy preening the lawns. A two-man team was busy installing a security system. They were all busy, until two spunky girls, laced together; cat-walked slow up the front garden path. Brock smiled to one of the workmen and asked:

"Hi guys – okay to go inside?" The painter, clad in white dungarees splashed with enough colour to guarantee him a shot at the Turner prize, gestured them inside with a smile wide enough to park a car in. Brock pushed the front door open and stood aside to let Josie enter. Tentative, she peeked in through the doorway. Two pretty blue angel eyes stared down at the Steinway Grand piano stood in the lounge beneath the Wyeth painting hung on the wall. Her mouth dropped open. Her eyes welled. She turned back to Maddie, who stood smiling, picked her up and carried her across the threshold.

"Welcome to your new home, Miss Josette Louise DuBois. You're now a fifty-per-cent part-owner."

"Maddie, I don't believe it. How could you do this to me; I haven't got any money?"

"Don't cry, sweetheart. I love you, Josie – that's more than enough payment for me."

"But How?" she asked, shaking her head.

"Easy — I got a good deal when I sold both my apartments for cash in the city, and I purchased this place for cash out in the country. It's small, cheap and cute. And I still have some cash to spare; not much, but enough to buy you a decent wardrobe, and maybe enough to spend another couple of weeks out on the bay in those sexy cabins." She smiled, racked her brows, let the thought hang in the air…

"Come here Angel eyes."

*   *   *

Chapter Thirty-four

Zero-seven hundred hours on the second Monday of July was not a good time for an early call for those in the top suite of the Goldstein Building on Riverside View as the entrance door burst open in splinters without someone bothering to knock first. Six armed assault crew clad in black, tangoed in behind Grady and fanned out in pairs through the apartment. Grady's heavy boot opened the door into the main bedroom. Roger Leighton-Smith sprang up as if a firecracker had gone off in his backside.

"What is the meaning of this? Who the hell are you? I'll have your badge you bastard!" Tight-lipped with a red face of thunder, Leighton-Smith reached across for his phone. Grady didn't stop him.

"Go ahead. Why don't you give your wife a call, asshole? She can have a nice little chat with the spunky young girl with the big tits lyin' next to you, and compare stories about what you can and can't do with your dick. I'm sure this girl with the big tits will have a lot more to say on the subject than Mrs. Leighton-Smith." Grady bent low and scowled: "In the meantime I'll be having a nice little chat with you about what you've been powderin' your nose with." Grady winked, dropped a smug grin.

"You have *no idea* who you are talking to. What is your name and rank?" demanded Leighton-Smith behind a heavy scowl in an attempt to reinstate his composure; but he went down on a par with Custer at the Little Bighorn, with his own not-so-big little horn.

"My name's *'Mister get your fuckin' clothes on pronto!'*" growled Grady, "or else I'll drag you out into the street by your fuckin' dick! And I can assure you – your dick won't be doin' any of *that* kinda thing again for a very long time. The only fun you'll be havin' is a backside massage in the shower at the Calcutta Crypt from the big guys servin' life there. An' believe me: some of those guys are sure guaranteed to make your eyes water. Get dressed, asshole!"

A bong fell and smashed on the floor as Grady pulled open the drawer in the bedside cabinet. He picked out a large bag of cocaine, along with a leather wallet and a small-calibre Colt automatic. He pocketed the Colt, flicked open the wallet and emptied its contents out over the girl with the big tits.

"Take a hike, sweetheart; watch out for those tits in the elevator doors." Then, neglecting his manners, he dragged Leighton-Smith off the bed by his hair. "Okay, Roger the Romeo, let's go take a look in your safe." Leighton-Smith, now passive in thought, slow-raised his hands up.

"Okay . . . okay," he scowled in submissive acceptance. "How much do you want?"

Grady fumed, swung the butt of his Streetsweeper into the sad, pleading but ugly face of drug dealing and corruption contaminating the city.

"Don't you go insultin' my integrity you shit-stinkin' dope-peddlin' mother fucker! Open the fuckin' safe before I forget my manners and turn nasty." Grady dragged him across to the safe, rammed his gun into soft flesh under Leighton-Smith's chin and bounced heavy brows over fearsome eyes. Leighton-Smith got smart, fiddled the dial, sprang the safe and stood back. Grady shook his head at a safe packed full of heroin, cocaine, crystal meth, money and another ledger. He racked back his Streetsweeper and turned to Leighton-Smith.

"Flap your arms, asshole," growled Grady.

"What ...?" pleaded Leighton-Smith.

"Flap your fuckin' arms like a bird – Now, asshole!"

Leighton-Smith, confused, made a weak effort to imitate a bird, then, furrowed his forehead, shook his head and spread open hands in question . . . "Whaa . . .?"

"I can see that ain't gonna' work out too well for you, Romeo," said Grady and turned to his team.

"Throw the bastard over the balcony."

"STOP! STOP! – Okay, okay I'll talk. What do you want to know," he pleaded as the team dragged him screaming out to the balcony. Grady stepped forward, grabbed Leighton-Smith's throat in a choke hold and spat into his ear.

"Don't try and fuck with me asshole; I'll leave that little pleasure with you and the big boys in the Crypt." He turned to his team.

"Take this piece of dog crap down. Mind he doesn't bang his head and hurt himself if he should happen to trip and fall down the stairs."

*   *   *

Skulking in shadow, two blocks back from prime real estate fronting the bay, the city police station was Grady's next port of call. Armed and dangerous, the SWAT team bypassed a frozen face behind a security desk and made their way up to the third floor. No one stopped them. They filed out of the elevator into a narrow hallway and stormed down a well-trodden pea-green carpet, curling back frayed at the skirting boards. A puce baby vomit colour coating the office doors was no compliment to the fading hue of the toffee brown, tobacco-stained paint, purple tinged, coated on grubby walls, copiously graced with rows of display photos of grinning policemen. An inquisitive mind might guess a blind man could well be responsible for the interior decor; but maybe it was nothing more than a sad reflection of the pitiful taste employed in most provincial buildings. The place reeked of everything but cleaning fluid. Behind the glass partition of the first office, a slate-eyed lady with an exploding mop of bleached hair sat aghast behind a loaded desk. Her ruby-lipped mouth gaped open, wide as Knievel's jump across the Snake River canyon. If she'd been thirty-five years younger and smiling, she could have easily been mistaken for a blow-up doll. The door at the far end of the hallway had the name Captain E. Cerrino stamped in black script on frosted glass. Grady didn't knock. Cerrino spluttered, dribbled coffee down his shirt front at the intrusion.

"What the hell is the meaning of this? Who the hell *are* you?" Cerrino sat thunder-faced in his chair, braced his body to get up, then lowered his backside down again slow; a movement mirrored by his jaw as four SWAT assault crew came through the doorway and filed out in line cuddling blued-steel behind Grady.

"Ya' know Ernesto – that's the second time I've been asked that very same question in the last hour," said Grady, "it must be somethin' in the air today," he flipped his eyebrows. Then, calm as a meditation group sat on the top of an ocean rock at the summer solstice, he whistled a soft tuneless melody as he strolled around behind Cerrino, bent down and spoke soft and slow into his ear.

"Karl-Heinz Yungen – Where is he?"

"I don't know who you're talking about," blubbered Cerrino. Grady gave a small chuckle:

"Well let's take a look and see shall we?" He leant across and picked up a cell phone off the table, scrolled down the contacts register, stopped at K.H and held it out in front of Cerrino's face.

"And who would this be then? Kebab House; Knuckle-Head; or perhaps it's King Henry the fuckin' eighth…? Take him down, Soldier!" The team dragged Cerrino out of his chair screaming retribution and frog-marched him to the door. Grady gazed down to Cerrino's empty chair and chuckled to himself.

"Well how about that – our inveterate police chief pissed in his pants!"

Six more top names were apprehended and taken by force to the N.S.F. headquarters at Black Rock for questioning. Many of them were executives and management from the city utilities yard. Roby Douglas stood high on the agenda and did not welcome a reunion with Sergeant Da Silva. A lot more names would no doubt be joining them in their concrete and iron-bar luxury throughout the following weeks.

Grady stood his team down, washed his hands, shaped his brim, straightened his tie and reported to the Major.

"Well done, Sergeant. We will let them stew a while before we interrogate them tomorrow. I'm sure you will want to oversee the interrogation yourself, Sergeant. Any sign of Yungen?"

"No nuthin,' Sir. Although I did get a contact number from Cerrino's cell phone which I think could well be used to contact him. Maybe we could get a lead on it; I've got a guy checking it out as we speak. But it's my guess it's a burner phone, so I think we should hang back a little until we get more info. I wouldn't want to warn Yungen off before we can finally nail him to the wall, Sir."

"Quite so Sergeant, as you wish. Perhaps you would inform Lieutenant Brock of your progress – keep her in the loop."

"Sure thing – anything else, Sir?"

"No thank you, Sergeant, nothing more for now. Well done again. Have yourself a good evening."

At a point well past its apex, the sun in the late afternoon at Black Rock was still burning hot enough to roast chestnuts on a baboon's backside. Grady, shaded under his light grey fedora, wore a light cotton ivory jacket and a duck-egg blue shirt over slate-blue pants complimented with tan loafers. He cut a dash. With a lazy stride, he wandered out into the sun, mopped his brow, felt his shirt front beginning to sweat-soak and figured there were a lot worse places he could be. He panned round to the iron-barred windows on the concrete Black Rock hotel V.I.P suite housing its new inmates. *'It might seem bad now guys, but you'll be longin' back for today with a passion when tomorrow comes around.'* He slacked off his tie and promised he'd treat himself to a straw Panama before the hot summer wound down. Soft-whistling his atonal melody he dialled Brock; got no answer. He tried her new burner cell; got a similar answer. Red alert started to take up a lot of space in the back of Grady's mind. He pulled his SUV out into the main road and headed for the safe house but was not yet in panic mode.

Fifteen minutes later Grady turned in and pulled up under the *porte-cochere* arched over the safe house driveway at the city outskirts. He stepped out from the SUV and scanned the area. Apart from two long rows of purple flowering Jacaranda trees and a stray dog in urinal paradise, the street was empty. The Ford was gone; the house was silent. He circled the house but saw nothing untoward: no broken windows or signs of a forced entry. He sprang the lock at the front door, disarmed the security system and followed his fifty-calibre into the house. A search of the rooms revealed nothing of significance except in the main bedroom where he found two empty wine glasses set on a side table next to an unmade bed adorned with lace underwear and a lot of pleasant thoughts. He smiled, re-holstered his gun and went to the kitchen cool box, sprang the door, took out a half bottle of chilled white and a glass, then strolled back out to his vehicle, sat back in the shade, pulled his hat down over his eyes and waited.

*   *   *

Chapter Thirty-five

Construction work can be a tough call; even more so when trying hard not to hammer your thumb flat when both your mind and eyes have taken your focus elsewhere. In this instance the focus was on two pretty girls stretched out on the grass hugging each other; they looked about ready to strip off and climb into bed together. These days some girls have all the luck, and most of them have all the things in the right place to go with it. The one thing most guys needed was money, and a lot of it; more so if it was also in the right place, looks for them are way down on the list. But these girls didn't look as if they needed any guys or any money; seems they had all they needed right there cuddled up in each other's arms. And they sure had the looks; those were way up on the list.

"I guess we should've bought them a six-pack," whispered Josie.

"What! And given my surprise away? We don't drink beer, so who would I have been buying it for, silly? But I think we should leave them to it, honey. Let's get back to the safe house, I don't think they're gonna finish for a long time yet staring at nothing else but your pretty little butt," Brock racked her brows, "that's my special privilege. Anyway, I want them to get finished off today, so we can move in tomorrow. Sound good my pretty, Angel eyes?" Josie voiced nothing; copious tears rolling down her cheeks spoke volumes.

"Don't cry, sweetheart." Maddie hugged her close, held her even tighter.

"You've made me so happy, Maddie."

"Well, let's go and make these guys happy and tell them there's a bonus in it for them if they can finish up today – Deal?" She smiled into Josie's pretty blue eyes, the radiance emitting a soulful innocence that would be a sin to lose. Brock did her nose thing.

The Ford was slow to eat up the miles on an easy drive back to the safe house, but what the hell, there seemed no rush. There's not much point in hurrying to get somewhere when there's no real reason to hurry to get there in the first place. Life had changed a lot for Brock; she'd slowed down and eased back into a lower gear. She loved it and loved everything she could possibly love in it. And one thing, in particular, trumped all else.

"Let's treat ourselves, find a cosy place to have a good meal and celebrate your birthday present. We've got a nice bottle of wine here don't forget."

"It's not my birthday for another three months, Maddie."

"Well okay then — let's celebrate my birthday."
"When *is* your birthday?"

"Whenever I want it to be — today sounds good," she shrugged a smile, "Why not?"

"Okay, Maddie. You win. Let's look for a restaurant."

"Thai, not cholesterol," said Brock.

Fifteen minutes later raising a cloud of dust, Josie pulled the Ford onto the dry-stone parking lot of the Mekong Delta: an inviting Thai restaurant out on the edge of city limits. The sun, still high in the sky at mid-afternoon, suggested it would be the late lunch menu they'd be looking at; although Brock was pretty sure the same menu would be good for all day and well into the night.

Inside the Mekong, the set-up was tasteful. Overseen with sensitivity in mind to ensure no table could be encroached upon by any other. At the entrance, dwarf trees and greenery rose high as a whale spout from large terracotta pots, scrolled with a discreet smile from a fat oriental gentleman, projecting a warm welcome to further captivate an audience, who were already without doubt enchanted by the surrounding ambience. High bamboo screens, lit by soft lighting ensured an intimate atmosphere, along with a heavy dose of privacy. Water cascaded over a fall of carefully-arranged but natural-looking rocks into a small manmade stream trickling through the restaurant. Complete with rustic wood bridges and live Koi-Carp, it served to transport the customer into another world. Exotic ethnic artwork from Thailand, radiating in gold leaf over vibrant colours, hung from bamboo-clad walls. Sitting cosy under the false bamboo-hung ceiling, wooed by soft ethnic Thai background music: an eastern mode over a chanting pedal-point, the girls could easily have been in Thailand itself. The only thing missing to complete a visual sense from the Mekong peninsula would be the red Khmer Rouge headbands for the staff; a failing which was no bad thing, mused Brock.

Josie pondered the menu, wondered at first if she was holding it the right way up; the Mekong was a long shot from Skinny's Grill! Soft eyes smiled across to her benign innocence. Brock leant forward and relieved Josie of the menu.

"Let me order for you, sweetheart. I promise you it won't be a burger."

Brock enjoyed the feeling of being in a different world, far away from her usual environment of violence and death. It allowed her to forget for a moment about how many lowlife scumbags she had killed, and how many had nearly killed her. *Put it behind you, Maddie. Times are changing. Don't rock the boat!*

The waitress shuffled soft steps across from the kitchen; a pen hovered over her pad as she turned to Brock, who apart from her emerald eyes looked as if she could've easily owned the place.

"We'll start with the Mekong Thai platter, then, the talay-ruam for both of us, we'll share a dish of khaw-suay, and end with a dish each of kanom-mor-gaeng. And would you open our bottle of wine for us please. Thank you."

Resting her elbows on the table, Brock nestled her chin on clenched hands and stared a passion across to a very pretty, but confused face.

"What have you ordered for me, Maddie?"

"Thai burgers," Brock joked. Josie shook her head, stared back with the look of a scorned imp.

"I promise you'll enjoy it, sweetheart. If not, we'll stop off at Skinny's on the way back. I hear they do a great line in popcorn." Josie's smile was soft as a cuddle from an ermine-wrap; she purred as she poured the wine.

"Were you born in Thailand, Maddie?"

"Mm-mm," Brock shook her head, "no, my mother was from there, but my father was from the West. They're both dead now, but they did leave me enough to buy my apartment, well – some of it anyway. But no, I've never been to Thailand, much to my regret. My mother was a good cook; I didn't follow in her footsteps," she shrugged, smiling at the irony.

"What about your father? How did they meet?"

"He played piano on the cruise ships, my mother worked on board as a chef. I guess it's how they met. My father loved jazz. He taught me to play the piano before I could walk." She took her gaze far off into the distance, then turned back to Josie. "They both died when I was sixteen, which is when I became a cop. I guess I needed security from somewhere."

"How did you keep such a secret about the cottage?"

"Grady – he helped me. He set up all the moving guys, the construction and security. He's a star."

"Why didn't you use Bugsy for the security?"

"As far as anyone knows, Josie, I don't exist anymore. Don't forget, I was blown to bits by a car bomb. Your name is on the title deeds, and we have a fifty-fifty contract with my name hidden deep as a silent partner," she blew a soft kiss across to Josie, "I didn't want anyone to know the house was anything to do with me. I think we are safe now and will be forever when Grady runs Yungen down. He's getting close now. Don't cry, Josie."

The waitress broke the moment, shuffled Thai-style steps across the room with the wine, two glasses and the starter.

"No chopsticks, Maddie?" asked Josie, wiping her eyes, hoping to hell there wouldn't be.

"No, honey, they're for noodles, and we're not having any of those. Use a fork and a spoon if you want; it's okay, but don't lick the plate," she added with a smile.

Outside, dusk fell in a measured silence while they relaxed in the restaurant until well into the early evening, sipping wine and drinking Jasmine tea from a glass fully stocked with floating things resembling flowers and sea kelp, which *en masse* looked as if it should also contain tropical fish. But most of all – they drank up love.

"I could never pronounce it, but I've never tasted anything as good as the seafood dish. And the pudding was awesome."

"I knew you'd enjoy it, honey. Now thank god we don't have to go to Skinny's. Come, let's go. We've got some packing to do. I'll drive, you've been drinking."

"So have you…" Brock flashed her eyebrows:

"Yes – But I've got a gun and a licence to kill!"

*   *   *

The main beams from the Ford shone bright into the *porte-cochère*, lighting up a black SUV parked under cover as Brock pulled in close behind it. The suspension in the SUV eased as a heavy figure wearing a light grey fedora sprang the door and stepped out onto the driveway.

"Hi Grady, how long have you been here?"

"Not too long – I arrived three or four hours ago; been trying to call you all afternoon. Was gettin' a little worried there, Loot. Where'd you go?"

She smiled, went over and gave him a hug.

"We went to the new cottage."

"Yeah, I figured as much. How'd it go?" Josie stepped forward to answer, hugged Grady and smacked a kiss on his cheek.

"Thank you, Grady."

"You're welcome, sweetheart. I'd do it all again for another of those hugs and kisses."

"How was it this morning, Grady?" asked Brock.

"Let's go inside. I'll tell you all about it."

An upholstery spring struck a high note as Grady lowered his two-twenty pounds onto the long-suffering sofa. The sun had disappeared round the globe, re-arming for a further assault at daybreak, leaving the ambient evening temperature still hot and humid as an athlete's arm-pit taking the flag at a triathlon. Beads of sweat leached across Grady's brow, ran down his nose, dripped off its tip and gave his already sodden shirt the Chinese water torture.

"Why don't you take off your jacket, Grady? Or if you want we can sit out in the back garden, it's a beautiful evening. Go ahead; I'll bring out a chilled bottle."

The moon, a couple of nights away from full, provided the perfect backdrop for romance, but tonight none was in mind; 'maybe later,' mused Brock. She filled three glasses, passed one to Grady and sat back in the swing seat. Josie cuddled in close next to her. Crickets and frog song chanted and burped in the shadows, filling the evening air thick and colourful as the paint on Van Gogh's Starry Night.

"So, tell me – how'd it go?"

"Well, we pulled in Rodger the dodger – Leighton-Smith, or rather we pulled him *out* from a spunky bed warmer – a comforting gift I'm sure his wife didn't buy him for his birthday. This girl wouldn't have to worry about hittin' her nose first if she walked into a wall on a dark night that's for sure." He drained his glass and leant forward for a refill.

"Leighton-Smith had a lot of dope hangin' around but I don't think he's the top man. I still think Yungen's out there somewhere but nobody's singin' yet. Cerrino the police chief might be a good touch. He had an incontinence problem when we pulled his collar, so he may talk. They're all sittin' havin' lunch with their fingernails in hotel Black Rock VIP suite as we speak, along with another half-dozen high profilers who'd have a tough time findin' their morals at the bottom of a cesspit. They're shakin' in their boots, Loot, and not lookin' forward to tomorrow for sure. But now at least they've got one bed they can all draw straws for," in a mock toast he raised his glass. "I did get a lead from Cerrino's cell phone. He had a K H in his call contacts. My guess is it could be for Karl-Heinz. My guy checked it out, but it's a burner and didn't register any calls – as I thought it wouldn't, so I wouldn't want to blow his cover. I'm hoping he'll call. Then we may be able to track him down. My guys are onto it. Tomorrow we hit the scum line a little lower, pushers and runners. There'll be a lot of canaries bustin' a gut to fly away from that particular cage. We may well come up with somethin' useful. So, that's about it, Loot."

"It's Maddie, Grady – Maddie or Brock – It's not *Loot* anymore."

"Sure thing, Loot." She closed her eyes, black locks brushed gentle on her shoulders, wished she had a grape to throw.

"How's the team, Grady – Good?"

"Top class, no enemas needed when they burst in through the door – but I'm sure missin' you, Loot."

"I miss you too, Grady. . . Big time." She blinked a powerful passion through damp eyes. They sat in a stilled eye contact, each immersed deep in their private thoughts and memories as they savoured the sweet sounds of a starry night. Relaxed back in a cocoon of social affinity they finished off the bottle, laughed too loud then pulled the cork on another. Life was good.

The rising moon turned from yellow to a pale blue. Grady stood, stretched his arms and hugged the girls. He thanked them for the evening, said his farewell and strode out to his SUV. Alone now in deep shadow from the moon, he turned, stood and stared sad eyes back to the safe house. His face turned from a visage of pleasure to a doleful frown. He slid in behind the wheel and drove a slow track back to an empty apartment; a lone soul in search of a miracle drowning fast in a cooling sea of lost hope.

*   *   *

Late-evening light glowed in a soft blue hue under the smiling moon as it crept up high into a cloudless sky sparkling with stars. Slumped back in the swing seat, Josie cuddled Brock's head lying mellow in her lap, slow-twiddled black locks around her index finger. They both wore nothing other than a wristwatch and a contented smile. Josie stared down into emeralds, Brock stared up into eternity. The crickets and frogs continued to chant and burp out their same old tireless songs; it didn't sound as if they were about to throw in the towel and hit the coda anytime soon. Life was perfect for some in the windless still of the night, and why not?

"Do you think we *will* be able to move house tomorrow, Maddie?"

"Yes, I want to, it's time now, we have to get on with our lives. I guess we'd better go and pack, we've got an early start in the morning." Brock sat up and rolled off the swing seat. "How about that, Grady left his hat here." She flipped it onto her head and cuddled Josie into the house.

It had been a good day for Brock. Her countenance glowed bright as Venus in the moonlight.

Chapter Thirty-six

The aroma from fresh paint fell way back in the running as the scent from *Wild Rose* streaked past the post and took the chequered flag as the two girls staked their claim at the cute single-bedroomed cottage. Built with a mixture of grey stone, timber cladding, and stucco walls under a shingle roof, the cottage was small but cosy as a feather-down pillow. The land it stood on was spacious, well-kept and tranquil as a small country park without the intrusion of tourists. A rolling carpet of close-cut grass stretched down to a stand of fir trees, setting the southern boundary to the rear of the property. Set under pines on the east side, a small feather board summer house offered sanctuary for the romantics. A well-groomed secret garden set out in a maze ringed with shrubs and greenery, stood private and cute as a kitten cuddled up on a fireside rug. Cradled under the house veranda, a swing seat upholstered in a floral embossed ivory-coloured canvas held two naked bodies' cuddled tight, drinking wine and savouring love in the shade of the scorching sun. Sexually nourished, they swung together in perfect harmony, two souls joined in an affinity that would leave them forever unable to enjoy contentment without the presence of the other. Timeless sounds echoing through still air from vintage Miles Davis, trumped the frogs and crickets.

"How did this all happen, Maddie – was it always meant to be?"

"I guess it's just life, Josie. Things always hit you crook as a curved ball when you least expect it; sometimes good, sometimes bad. Nothing at all happens the way it should when you plan for it. I for one know that truth only too well. The moment I first laid eyes on you I knew I would never want to live without you. I have never felt an emotion so strong before with anyone else in my life, not even close. There was a magic I can't explain; a magic turning from lust to a deep love. I guess it's something very few can find, and to their detriment never get past the lust." She stared into blowtorch blue eyes and soft kissed honey lips.

"I'll love you forever Josie … that I promise you."

*　　　*　　　*

Burning a torrid path westward, the morning sun topped up the bronzing on two naked bodies as they lay sunbathing on fresh-cut grass. Privacy was a big bonus afforded to them in the cute cottage. If money could buy you anything, seclusion was high up on the list.

"I feel so sad for Grady. Maybe we should ask him round for dinner; don't you know any nice ladies we could pair him up with?"

"No-one I can think of Josie. I've always been a little short on friends. You're sure to know more girls than me. What about Grace?"

"Grace is a lovely person but she's no beauty queen, and doesn't aspire to be."

"Grady isn't looking for miss bikini body 2047, he's not the kinda guy who needs a trophy chick, far from it. He knows his limits. He wants someone kind and funny he can cuddle up to and love."

"Okay, then why don't we invite them both round for dinner. Let's make it a house-warming party and see what clicks."

"What a cute idea, Josie. Okay, you call Grace; I'll call Grady. Let's try and make it a date for tonight."

Grady picked up on the third ring.

"Hey Grady, how you doing?"

"I'm good, Loot. What's up?"

"Got any plans for tonight?"

"Well let me see – I've either got a dinner date with a twenty-year-old Russian ballet dancer suffering from a serious nymphomaniac disposition, or an evening playing chess with a blind Japanese Sumo wrestler with a severe flatulence problem; but I can't make up my mind which one would work out best for me. Why do you ask?"

"Okay Groucho, put them both off until tomorrow night and come on over for a house warming with us and a few friends. And don't bring a present, just bring yourself." She waited through a long pause before he spoke soft words:

"Thanks, Loot. I'd appreciate that very much."

"Okay, see you for pizzas at seven – I love you, Grady."

Josie fixed up Grace for drinks and nibbles at seven but thought it might be a little too obvious with only the four of them.

"Grace is good for tonight, Maddie, but why not make up the numbers and invite the major and his wife over, and perhaps Jackie Olsen."

"Yes, I thought about that, but I don't think it's such a good idea. I want to keep work separate from pleasure. I'd love to invite Jackie, but it's holiday season and I'm sure he'll be busy in his bar. So let's make out we invited some other people but something came up and they couldn't make it. But don't mention any names, let's keep it intimate." She smiled a passion through her eyes at Josie:

"Okay, we'd better go on over to the cute little store and stack up with frozen pizzas, wine and some more cheeses; and maybe a tub of ice cream or two, and how about some fresh strawberries?"

"Well how about firing up the barbecue for Grady, I bet he'd enjoy a good steak," suggested Josie.

"Yeah, good idea, sweetheart, would Grace eat barbecue?"

"I guess so. Working at Skinny's there's not much else on offer – apart from popcorn."

Brock dropped a foxy look over imaginary glasses:

"Best we don't mention popcorn!"

At six-fifty-five the buzzer sang out. Brock sprang the door. Dressed in a powder blue suit over a midnight blue silk shirt with a silver tie and blue suede loafers, Grady held out a bottle of champagne.

"I know you said not to bring anything, Loot, but I picked this up out on the driveway," he shrugged a silly smile: "Seem a pity to run it over." She soft punched his chin, hugged him close. He took off his fedora, pulled his cuffs down and stepped inside. She looked at the bottle – expensive!

"Thanks, I should've guessed," she took the bottle. "Come through, Groucho, you can help Josie fire up the barbecue. Oh, by the way, her friend is coming over so be on your best behaviour."

"I'm always on my best behaviour, Loot; apart from when I'm awake," he beamed a smile slick enough to smooth a circuit judge, "anyone else comin'?"

"I invited a couple of others, but it was too short notice so it didn't work out. I was going to call and ask if you wanted to bring your Sumo wrestler friend; thought he could give us a cabaret turn and blow out the celebration candles for us. Anyway, now you got a double helping of beefsteak. Grab a beer from the ice box on your way through."

Five minutes later, Grace pressed the buzzer. Brock called out from the kitchen.

"Can you get the door please, Grady, I've got my hands full."

"Sure, no problem."

Brock looked through the window, dropped a wink and tweaked her nose. Josie smiled. Grady sprang the door.

"Well whadda you know — the popcorn guy!" said Grace as the door opened.

"That wasn't me, it was my twin brother – I'm the quiet one in the family."

"Josie warned me you'd be here."

"And you still came?"

"I was kinda curious."

"Well come on in and be curious over a glass of bubbles," he held out his hand, "the names Grady, and I'm cookin' tonight."

"That would be the food I hope … I'm Grace, pleased to meet you." She smiled, shook his hand and stepped inside.

With the ten-cent tour and pleasantries in the bag, Grady popped the cork, filled four flutes and raised his glass to Brock.

"To one very special lady and her very special partner; may they live long and be forever happy." Brock blushed, damp eyes looked down to the grass, wished she had a grape to throw.

The evening passed by as idyllic and pretty as a flight of Flamingos across a southern skyline at the break of dawn. They laughed a lot, drank a lot, ate too much and looked forward to the replay. Grace spent most of the evening splitting her sides laughing at Grady's stories laced with Groucho innuendos. The more they drank the closer they got. Eventually, she got up, and to hell with it – she sat on his lap. It was without doubt a genial relationship bubbling hot as steaming porridge in an army field canteen from the word go. Brock cuddled Josie on the swing seat – Mission accomplished.

The smiling moon got high along with the party guests. Frogs and crickets chanted out their lullabies and called the close on a steamy night. Grady stood, thanked everyone for a great evening and looked around for his hat as a starter.

"I got an early one in the morning, Loot. I'd best be off now."

"I'd better be going too," added Grace.

"I don't think you better drive, honey, I'll give you a lift home and I'll pick your car up later," offered Grady.

"Forget it Galahad," said Brock, "the only place you're going is the sofa – and Grace, if you want, you can sleep in the summer house. There's a bed and bathroom in there. I wouldn't want either of you to drive, we've all drunk far too much and it's too dangerous to take the chance. Let's not spoil a beautiful evening, guys."

"Okay, suits me. Thanks, Loot. I gotta get up real early and leave for Black Rock around six if it's okay," said Grady.

"Well make yourself some breakfast before you go, but please don't make too much noise. Josie why don't you fix up Grace in the summer house, we'll clear away in the morning. Okay, goodnight guys, thanks again for a great evening." Brock stood, blew Grady a kiss, retired to the bedroom and collapsed back spread-eagled on the bed. She closed her eyes on a good day.

At the break of dawn, Brock woke to the aroma from frying eggs and bacon. Soft voices migrated from the kitchen. Josie, already awake, spoke soft to Brock across the pillow.

"I think Grace has cooked him breakfast; and I doubt very much he slept on the sofa."

*   *   *

Chapter Thirty-seven

A '*Cheshire cat*' skulking in shadow, flea-bitten feral and filthy, was far from smiling. The '*magnificent seven*' dressed in riot gear, armed and dangerous had invaded its alleyway, which functioned as a stinking back passage for the waste of humanity in more ways than one. Overflowing trash cans, empty liquor bottles, skins of cast-off gossamer latex discarded after a brief moment of desire by the amorous and the desperate, left an ugly footprint in an ugly society. But nowhere near as ugly as the ominous collection of disposable hypodermic syringes tossed aside by the walking dead. The sad few no-hopers using the alley would be well gone by now at zero-seven hundred hours, apart from those strung out and on their way to heaven, but more than probably on their way to a further hell.

Grady's team laid a small explosive charge over the lock on a heavy steel door at the back exit to the Honey Pot Club. The ram would've been useless: the door was designed to open outwards. An ear-shattering explosion rocked the neighbourhood. Startled birds flooded the sky as the door, shrouded in a cloud of smoke, shuddered open on rusted hinges. The SWAT team, led by Grady, flooded into a cavernous, dank, uninviting room, empty apart from a lone figure cowering in the shadows. A sad figure who made his last mistake in a very short life as he drew a gun. The unit swept through the building swift as a hot flush at the menopause. Moving along a first-floor corridor, they tailed stun grenades into a squalid parade of dank rooms offering nothing more than the smell of stale sex and a light wallet.

It was still early, footfall was light. Stragglers were lined up against the walls with their hands up and their pants down cursing the taste of honey. The main bar was as empty as a hollow thought, except for cleaning staff which, clutching mops and broom poles, didn't look much of a threat. The SWAT team ransacked the office and nailed the door shut as they left.

Below, in a large underground parking area, the squad met with heavy resistance. A workforce busy unpacking crates had swapped their crowbars for guns. Grady's Streetsweeper took out the overhead lighting. Lead flew in the half light, filled the air full as Kallah confetti at a Simcha wedding. In the chaos, Grady ordered tear gas and stunners to be deployed, pulled his mask down over his face and pumped heavy gauge shot out into the madhouse mayhem.

As the tear gas kicked in, gunfire slowed and ground to a standstill. Grady soft whistled victory into his mask as the sound of coughing eclipsed the sound of gunfire. Apparent light beamed into the dank smoke-filled room. A desperate hand had sprung the rear doors to afford a hasty exit for those without masks frantic to leave. Outside in the street, six agents from Grady's team stood to welcome them with open fire. No prisoners were taken. These people were lowlife scum eradicated to the hell they deserved.

Through a veil of thinning smoke in the warehouse, a sinister sight came into Grady's focus. Stacked amongst the packages of dope, weed and whatever else could incite human misery were enough small arms, explosives and R.P.G launchers to equip a small army.

Indifferent to any sense of compassion, the SWAT team lined up the dead in the street outside the Honey Pot Club in a stark reminder for anyone who sought a similar vocation to realize not everything was sweet as honey in such a sordid place as the Honey Pot Club.

Grady ordered body bags, the blood wagon and trucks to transport the confiscated goods. Then stood his team down and drove a slow trip back to the concrete hotel VIP suite at Black Rock.

*   *   *

A small windowless room offering nothing more than a large dose of dispirited mirth, was sparse-furnished with two steel chairs and a steel table bolted to the floor. In a shaded corner, a rusting bucket was set below a dripping faucet. Dank grey walls and a glow from a low-wattage light bulb hanging from a concrete ceiling offered back nothing cheerful. The only bright thing in the room was an orange suit – it contained Roger Leighton-Smith. Cuffed and dressed in leg chains he shuffled with the similar guise of a sad individual who hadn't quite made the bathroom in time after an over-indulgent night of gourmet excess at the curry house. He certainly didn't welcome the sight of Sergeant Grady Da Silva as he slunk into the room.

Placing his hat crown down on the table Grady took the seat opposite Leighton-Smith and sat back with folded arms. Soft-whistling his tuneless melody he spoke a smug message through narrowed evil eyes. Leighton-Smith moved with an awkward stance on his chair, tried to maintain composure. It was a lost cause. Then the whistling stopped. Grady played his lower lip, massaged his chin and said:

"You stink, Rodger! I'll have to see if we can't get you fire hosed down."

"Fuck-you – You're dead meat. You're gonna fry same as your bitch of a stinkin' partner did."

"I wouldn't go mouthin' those sort of things round here asshole. The lady was well liked, especially by me. You and your low-life scum might not have cared much for what she stood for, but if there's one thing to set your mind at rest when I beat the shit out of you – the Lady sure didn't stink. That's now your sole fuckin' prerogative – Asshole!"

Leighton-Smith swallowed the thought and choked on the outcome.

"Wanna spring me some names? Tell me where I might find your boss, and talk to me about the Honey Pot an' who runs it…?"

"Fuck-you asshole, all I got to say is – you're dead meat!"

"You talkin' brave as this Rodger makes me think you've got the cavalry comin' over the hill blowin' bugles an' whistlin' Dixie up your asshole."

Leighton-Smith glared back a silent, *'you wait and see… Asshole yourself!'* Whistling his soft, improvised atonal melody, Grady stood, walked round the table, spun Leighton-Smith round in his chair, bent over him and breathed heavy into his face:

"Now I'm not gonna' waste my breath askin' if you had anything to do with Lieutenant Brock's death, because there ain't enough room in here for your fuckin' Pinocchio bullshittin' nose, to grow that fuckin' big." Leighton-Smith drew a deep breath and spat full into Grady's face – It was not a clever move. The punch Grady threw could have floored an elephant. Leighton-Smith flew across the floor spitting blood with serious damage to his jaw. He would have gone a lot further if there hadn't been a wall in his way. Grady dragged Leighton-Smith up by his hair, swung another heavy punch leaving Roger the Romeo dribbling capped teeth down his quivering chin. Leighton-Smith gawked around the room, dazed, trying to focus on stars buzzing circles in his vision. Grady bent and ran cool water from the faucet, wiped his face clean, flattened his hair back, set his hat on his head, straightened the brim and pulled his cuffs down straight. As he strode across to the door he spat down at the sorry sight of Leighton-Smith.

"I demand a lawyer!" lisped Leighton-Smith drooling and spitting blood down the wall.

Grady stopped, turned back with a look of disdain.

"Okay, asshole, how about I go an' dig up your old buddy Ludo Mertz, unless of course you want to join that fuckin' piece of crap rottin' away in his shithole in the ground. Which *can and will* be arranged believe me. Sleep tight, Rodger, I'm sure it's gonna be a hell of a lot easier for you now you won't have miss big-tits tuggin' on your dick to keep you awake all night." Grady walked out and closed the door on Leighton-Smith.

Outside in the hallway, two prison guards stood to attention at the sight of Grady's imposing demeanour; his reputation had preceded him. It had become obvious he would be a good person to please. He ordered the guards to put Leighton-Smith in a single cell away from the other prisoners and to make sure no one sees him leave the interrogation building. Then he called up his orderly to fetch a stretcher and a bloodied sheet from the medical centre and take them to the interrogation room.

In the recreation room, Grady waited for a game of pool to finish before choosing one of his team, who stood a similar size to Leighton-Smith, and told him he had a dead easy job for him. Grady led him into the interrogation room, laid him on the stretcher under the bloodied sheet and told him to keep as still and quiet as a clandestine lover holding his dripping dick in a bedroom wardrobe. Then, he called in two of his team as stretcher-bearers, laid the plan out and buzzed for the prison guards to bring in Cerrino.

When Grady heard Cerrino dragging rattling chains behind a worried mind along the corridor, he told his team to go ahead and carry the stretcher out of the room as they let Cerrino in. As Cerrino walked into the interrogation room past the *corpse,* his jaw dropped open; then dropped all the way to the floor when he saw Grady sat back in his chair grinning as he spun the suppressor off his fifty-calibre. Wide eyes of terror stared down at a shock of fresh blood running down the wall in the corner of the room, adding a sinister complement to the sickly grey paint on the walls. Cerrino dreaded what was on offer.

"Come in Mister Police Chief Cerrino. Sit down. Let's have a little chat."

A wet patch blossomed at Cerrino's groin.

*   *   *

The top floor at the office block enjoyed a clear view over Black Rock, and a long way far beyond. Grady knocked on the door displaying a teak board stamped with the name: Major Randolph Falconer etched in gold over a black background.

"Come in, Sergeant. At ease, sit."

"Thank you, Sir."

Decor inside Falconer's office was exactly as you'd expect. Artefacts from military history complemented with paintings of skirmishes throughout the ages hung on show around the walls. It was obvious he'd served his country well and had all the flags, medals and tee-shirts to prove it; and was very proud of it.

"I'm very impressed with your progress so far, Sergeant, congratulations."

"Thank you, Sir. I wouldn't have been able to do anythin' without help from Miss DuBois, an' her de-codin', Sir."

"Yes, I'm sure; she is a very valuable asset. By the way, have you been in touch with the lieutenant and Miss DuBois at all, Sergeant?"

"I saw them yesterday, Sir; kept them up to speed, same as you asked me to."

"Good man. In their new house, I gather."

"Yes, Sir, they both seem very happy. And some good news, Sir: there's word going round in the cesspit of humanity, that the Lieutenant is definitely dead now. So we can now assume she's in the clear, and with any luck no-one else will be looking for her. Although I suggest we still keep her well under cover until we hit Yungen."

"Yes, quite right, Sergeant – you've read my thoughts. Have you gleaned any further information about Yungen from your interrogations?"

"Yes, Sir, but it seems Yungen is keepin' as low an' slippery as a slug's asshole, Sir."

Falconer choked out a small chuckle. "Yes, quite, Sergeant – I don't think I could have put it quite so eloquently myself."

"They're tough nuts to crack, Sir," said Grady. "Yungen seems to have a powerful hold over them, but from where – we still don't know but I believe it must be somewhere nearby in the uptown beach area. We've scanned the whole area with a fine tooth comb, but so far have come up with nothing. I think I may have cracked the police chief. He's a weak link in their chain; but along with the rest of them, he's terrified of Yungen. I'm still working on him, although I'm not too sure he knows very much apart from where to pick up his money for the police protection he affords to the dope dealers. I'm certain he doesn't know where Yungen is holding out. I've put him in a single cell and will work on him again tomorrow, Sir."

"Good work, Sergeant. Is there anything else?"

"Yes Sir: I think we should beef up security around Black Rock."

"Is this to do with the arms cash you uncovered earlier today, Sergeant?"

"Yes Sir. Also from a gut feeling I get from the interrogations we've been carrying out."

"Very well, Sergeant. I shall heed your good advice. We will double the guard and put Black Rock on red alert."

"I also feel we should transfer the prisoners to high-security, Sir; let them have a taste of the Calcutta Crypt. It may well loosen their tongues."

"Very well, consider it done. Thank you, Sergeant, if there's nothing more, may I wish you a pleasant evening. And well done again. Good hunting tomorrow, I'll look forward to your results."

"Thank you, Sir."

*   *   *

Three nubile girls, bronze-tanned with their chastity covered by not much more than bright red lip gloss and a broken promise to the bewildered, played *au naturel* in the condo's plunge pool under the palms. Stretched out under bright sunlight on a pink sun lounger with a serious shot of bourbon clutched in a sweaty hand, the condo owner at the Havana Beach complex took no notice of the erotic expanse of naked flesh flaunted and readily on offer right in front of him. As a middle-aged, balding slob with a fat girth, which had long since obscured his vision to the lower part of his anatomy — an area he'd always assumed to be little more than a plaything for pretty young girls to find amusing for his own pleasure, with not a thought that the power of his fat wallet on the low table next to him was their real magnet. Under normal circumstances he would have taken the bait; but today he had other things on his mind – for he was the owner of the Honey Pot Club.

At ten-forty on the bright sunny morning, a tall heavy set figure in a broad-brim Panama set above a light tan suit over a cream shirt, a silver tie with a red stone pin and a heavy bulge under his left shoulder strolled lazy in cream loafers across the pool deck. Mean eyes narrowed when he lifted black wraparounds and moved across in front of Palmer to take his sunlight. Robert 'Bunty' Palmer sprang up in his seat, spun his head round for security guards.

"Don't bother Blubber-man, they're takin' a nap! Put some clothes on, I'm takin' you for a little ride."

"What are you talking about, don't be ridiculous, who the hell are you?" bleated Palmer.

"I'm your worst nightmare, fatso; an' you're coming to see Herr Yungen," said the big man, "an' he won't want to see you lookin' like a sack of shit." Palmer's face tan bleached from its sun-burned bronze and changed to a panic-struck blank white. His jaw dropped onto his chest, and worried eyes grew wide as a working girl's legs on a busy Friday night.

"Don't be ridiculous; I've been speaking to him yesterday. What could he possibly want with me? He didn't say anything about this," pleaded Palmer an octave up from his normal pitch.

"Maybe it's about some sticky business down at the Honey Pot club. Seems he's pretty mad about losing some of his possessions he'd left in your care – Move some blubber, Fatso."

Pleading an assortment of prayers, Palmer was frogmarched past the three naked nubile nymphs fresh out of the pool with arms draped around each other's shoulders. Grady, enjoying his ruse emptied the cash from Palmer's wallet into the pool, smiled at the girls and said:

"Now don't you girls go spoilin' my fun and tell me you're all called, Grace!"

The SWAT team bundled Palmer into an unmarked black SUV. They weren't careful about him not banging his head on the door jamb. With a lump in his throat to match the one growing on his forehead, he sat shoulder wedged between two heavies on the rear seat. He glared out in both terror and bewilderment through dark-tint windows. Had he been a religious man he'd have been down on his knees.

Sat in the front passenger seat eating a banana, Grady scrolled through his messages, sent back a *hello* to Brock.

"Where are you taking me?" whined Palmer, with a pathetic voice in the mimic of a nasally impaired character from an old Bugs Bunny show.

"I'll ask the questions, Blubber-man; just make sure you don't slip up." Grady tossed the banana skin back into Palmer's lap. Bunty rode the rest of the way in cowered silence, then, dropped his jaw and pinched his bowels tight as they drove through the iron gates into Black Rock.

*   *   *

Chapter Thirty-eight

With his tongue stuck out dripping saliva, the expression on Police chief Cerrino's face underlined the fact he would not be answering any questions today or any other day. His orange suit had been torn into strips and knotted together to hang himself from the steel rafters in his cell. Sat back on the bed board quiet-whistling his tuneless melody, Grady pushed his hat back on his head, folded his arms and stared in up despair at the pathetic lifeless corpse, leaching urine down from its feet to a puddle on the floor. He took his focus up to Cerrino's contorted face strained tight in a noose. Bulging blood-red eyes glared out in terror, even in death. Grady found it hard to believe one man could spread so much oppressive fear and tyranny, powerful enough to force another to take their life in a non-religious environment, for no other reason than to maintain a silence. Maybe in Cerrino's case, it was nothing more than to save him the exposure and shame of a trial – Who knows? Some choice!

'Well he's sure quiet now, and under this reign of terror it didn't look as if anyone else is going to talk either,' mused Grady. He stood, patted Cerrino's cheek, gave his corpse a gentle swing, left the cell door open and walked out into the sweet scent of clean fresh air.

Stretched back in his office chair with his feet on the desk, Grady sank a cool beer to help peruse the next crop of lowlife he'd be rounding up in the following strike with his team. It occurred to him he would need a lot more space to hold them in custody; although he didn't expect to glean much from them, being further down the chain and not much more than gofers, lackeys and lemons, in it only for the quick and easy buck. He organised transport to transfer the captives now held at Black Rock to the Calcutta Crypt. If the island couldn't break them, then nothing would. Not one of these scumbags was anywhere near as tough as Jute Malone, and yet she'd cracked in the end. He buzzed through for Palmer to be brought in for interrogation.

*   *   *

"Bunty! That sounds a little pansy to me, Blubber man; it's the sort of name a little girl might give to her favourite dolly."

Palmer gawped around the interrogation room, decided to get wise.

"It was a nickname I had at school: I was a little plump back in those days."

"Was…?" questioned Grady, chuckling at the paradox.

"Well, let's see if we can't thin you down a little, or shall we leave that to your old buddy Herr Yungen to organise – Where is he, Palmer?"

"I don't know – nobody does."

"What about Leighton-Smith."

"No, he's nothing more than the money man. He does what he's told without question, same as the rest of us."

"So how do you contact him?"

"We don't. He contacts us."

"How …?"

"By scrambler phone; we have to change and dispose of the SIM card after every call."

"So how does he pay you?"

"We get paid in cash through Leighton-Smith."

"So who's financing Yungen?" Palmer shrugged his shoulders, shook his head but looked guilty. Grady let it ride.

"Okay, so what's he planning?" asked Grady.

"Isn't it obvious? He wants power – all of it, and he'll use any means possible to get it, and what's more he's been using you guys to help him to get that one very thing."

Grady swallowed a hard thought, stood and walked round the table, bent and spoke close to Palmer's ear:

"So why aren't you terrified of him, everyone else seems to be?"

"I am, don't kid yourself, but I figure if I talk, then maybe I can cut a deal – it's dog eat dog in the gutter morals of this world. You and I both know that; only the smart guys survive. As far as I know, you don't have anyone on the inside so maybe you could do with someone — someone with as much kudos as me perhaps?" Grady massaged his chin; let the thought sink in for a while. Maybe Palmer *could* be some use after all. He smiled to himself, sat back on his chair and thought: 'honour amongst thieves' – what bullshit!'

"What was his plan with the arms cache we found at the Honey Pot?"

"I don't know, but if you ask me he's planning to take you by force."

"No kiddin' — with whose army?" Grady chuckled through a screwed-up face. Palmer took the floor:

"It's not difficult to persuade people who have no hope or purpose in life to believe there's gold at the end of the rainbow. There are a lot of people out there eating up conspiracy theories by the bucket full. And there's a whole shit-load of them down in the O-Zone waiting for their curtain call. All they need is a strong leader for the flood gates to open. There's fuck all else for them to hope for down in such a filthy shithole." Palmer sat back in his chair, folded his arms and stared smug at Grady.

'*So it's not only about drugs, it's something far more sinister,*' mused Grady playing his chin.

"Okay, blubber-man, maybe we *can* do a deal. You find me who it is financing Yungen, and you'll walk out of here a free man; no comebacks, you have my word on it. It'll be my guess Leighton-Smith would be a good place to start. He must know something. Find out what he knows and you might save him from a whole lot of grief, along with a get outta jail free card for yourself. You'll have to go along with the ruse for a while, or else someone will guess you're in on it. I'll make sure you don't have too much grief at the Crypt." Grady stood and held his hand out to Palmer. As they shook on it, Grady swung a left at Palmer's nose, grinned a smile as he watched blood pour down Palmer's face.

"Sorry to have to tickle your nose, Bunty; but if you leave here smellin' of roses some one's gonna' smell canary . . . I'll be in touch!"

*   *   *

Burning down a wrath hot enough to curl toes on a rhino, the mid-summer sun glowing in the backdrop of a crystal clear sky had yet to gain enough height to radiate its full intensity. A spread of dawn dew over a budding landscape had long since vaporised back up to the starting post, leaving a scorched terrain exposed to the elements. With the ambient temperature already well up into the high nineties, life was as hot and humid as a stripper's G string in a Zanzibar clip-joint.

Way up in the sky, a skylark sang out a sweet song – pretty, but out of tune with an event occurring in a different biosphere below. Shaded under his new Panama, Grady squinted in bright sunlight, stopped whistling up a bad song and sipped on a cold beer. His hair ruffled as a warm breeze light as a new-born's sneeze, whipped up a mess of dust raised by the conga shuffle from an orange-clad group in tight-legged stagger-chains shambling slow across the dirt to an armoured coach. Chugging out blue smoke on tick-over, the grid-windowed coach was all set to take them on a trip; and not a very pleasant trip to be sure. Bunty Palmer anchored in chains, dragging along at the back of the line looked as superfluous as an unnecessary case of excess baggage on a budget holiday, but he played his ruse well. Grady smiled.

Inside the coach, a chain ran from front to rear threaded through leg chains at the base of the seats. The prisoners were cuffed behind their backs. No-one was going to move quick or easy. Air-con or the facilities to open a window were both absent. A precaution not only for security but to annihilate the spirit and teach a hard lesson: a lesson they may well one day reflect upon about how soft it was now compared to what was coming.

Sweat drained off brows, leached through orange overalls and gathered in pools on pressed steel seats. With both hands cuffed behind their backs, there was very little the incarcerated could do except to scratch their backsides. Life was unbearable; but nothing compared to what they were headed for after choking dust through a miserable road trip, followed by a short ferry trip across to the island: a dismal home to nothing other than the Calcutta Crypt, and a very heavy dose of undiluted grief and misery. As losers in a rough game they'd won a first-class, one-way ticket to a hell for the condemned soul.

Two armoured combat vehicles escorted the coach to the ferry quayside. The short trip of half a mile across the water would be received on the other side by the Island Security Force. Stood at the water's edge Grady's team of twelve, before they would leave, stood alert on the quayside to ensure the incarcerated were securely ensconced on the island.

The ferry spewing black exhaust smoke, aptly named 'Retribution Express,' chugged a slow course with its woebegone cargo through shimmering still waters on its voyage to the Crypt. Grady, sitting high in the armoured vehicle, pushed up his combat cap, popped the top on a bottle, and whistled Dixie.

One hundred yards out from the shoreline, a rocket-propelled grenade powering low through the air found its target at the waterline in the starboard beam of the ferry's wooden hull. Shock waves sent burning debris flying high into the air. A thick black cloud billowed from the hull, enshrouding a sad day.

Seconds later two more RPGs struck their targets in quick succession. Their second target was the coach – a sitting duck on the deck. The third RPG tore open the stern of the ferry. Heavy gunfire from scrubland sprayed the SWAT team as they scrambled for cover. Two roof-mounted Heckler and Koch fifty-calibres from Grady's team pumped lead back into an armed group of terrorists revealing themselves behind fading small-arms gunfire in the surrounding scrubland. In the melee, Grady ordered cover fire for the two armoured trucks as they powered through scrubland, raking lead at the enemy. He led the first truck in a pincer movement; figuring attack would be the unsuspected, but more favoured route than defence. Well-equipped but poorly trained, the terrorist group succumbed to their lot after a brief but bloody battle. Their cause lost, but their purpose absolute. No-one would be left alive to talk.

At Grady's call to cease fire, the tang of cordite and a strong stench of death under a hot sun was the sole invader in the stilled silence. Still gripping the fifty-Cal tight, Grady scanned the area. He saw no movement from the bloodied corpses cuddling death in the dust. There were no survivors.

Hungry seagulls returned to the scene wailing as they circled overhead reminiscent of a flock of scavenging vultures. The thought of a free meal from the cadavers of sixteen terrorists lying dead in dusty scrubland was a grim coda in a sad chapter. It wasn't only the seagulls who thought they were in for easy pickings on this day.

Grady looked out to the stricken ferry, gunnel washed and listing at twenty-five degrees. Then watched helpless as the coach, burning bright and billowing black smoke slow-rolled over the gunnel and tumbled into the sea. He could do nothing except listen to the screams. The coach floated half-sunk for a few seconds before the rear end rose up and the whole thing took a slow dive into the depths. A chopper appeared hovering overhead dropping life rafts and life vests in a hopeless gesture.

Grady's prospects for any further interrogations had gone down with all hands.

A body search of the terrorists revealed weapons, cell phones, I.D cards, cash, two-way radios, including a small VHF handset collected along with anything else of any use. The terrorist's bodies were stripped and left to rot where they fell in the dustbowl of a barren wasteland, decaying in the sun under the hordes of blow flies and a worthless promise to the dispossessed. Mange-ridden wild dogs, hesitant in the wings, gathered en masse to feast. After which, it would be left to the vultures, rats and maggots. These people deserved nothing more, they were terrorists, left now as a stark reminder to others with a similar agenda; as once were captured pirates left hanging by the neck in public places three hundred years before in a previous civilised society. Not much has changed over the years – so much for progress. *'Fuck progress!'* mused Grady. He shook his head in disgust.

Two of Grady's team were killed, and a further four were wounded, two seriously. Hidden under bracken, two of the four vehicles used to transport the terrorists sat smouldering in flames. The remaining two were loaded with any arms confiscated and would be driven to Black Rock. Grady scanned around at the dead bodies and burning carnage surrounding him. He worried his lower lip and weighed up his choices – He dialled Brock.

"I need you, Loot…"

*   *   *

Chapter Thirty-nine

At the coda of a heavy workout on the Steinway, Brock ran nimble fingers up the chromatic scale, fingered a soft low A in the bass and raised her wine glass as the doorbell sang out a semitone higher in B Flat concert. She knew who it was; she'd been waiting for him. Clutching her wine glass, she walked over and sprang open the front door.

"Come on in, Grady – hungry? Josie's heating up pizzas in the microwave; you must have a psychic stomach."

"No not psychic, Loot, let's just call it sick. But dinner with my favourite ladies," he clucked a heavy tongue, "how could I resist?"

"It's good to see you Grady. Are you Okay?" Stood silent he spoke nothing vocal, but she could read a heavy message in his eyes. She stroked a warm hand across his cheek, tweaked his ear and popped a finger on his nose.

"Okay, first off we'll eat, then you can tell me all about it. By the way, you forgot this." She tossed him his grey Fedora and tweaked her nose, "your lucky mascot." He flipped it on his head, smiled a thank you and looked a picture of the Grady she always knew and loved – Her very own lucky mascot.

"Come; let's go sit in the garden – wine or beer?"

"A cool beer sounds good, thanks Loot."

"Okay, go take a seat, say hi to Josie, I'll grab you a beer."

Brock shielded her eyes as she strolled out into the low sunlight. Grady, with his back to her, sat in a white cast-steel garden chair talking to Josie. Brock came up behind him and draped her arms round his neck and dangled a beer in front of his eyes.

"So tell me, Cowboy – what's going on?" She turned and settled into the swing seat, cuddled up against Josie, pulled her in close and sipped white wine waiting for Grady to speak.

"It was the same as old times, Loot. We walked straight into it. These guys weren't there to rescue the scum we captured: they were there to kill them. It was nuthin' more than a ploy to stop them from talkin'," he shrugged, looked to her with a plaintive smile. "They came from nowhere. How in the hell did they know?"

"Okay, Grady – so then who did know?"

"Me an' the Major as far as I know, an' I can't believe it was him – no way?"

"No, me neither. How about your guys, they must have known something?"

"Mm-mm, no, not until we were well on our way they didn't. As far as they knew it was a routine escort. They weren't told the destination. So the timings all wrong there . . . Couldn't have been them; those guys are all handpicked." She smiled at the ambiguity, 'trust no-one, live longer,' she racked her brows, sucked her teeth.

"Yeah right! – And the prison guards at Black Rock?" Grady thought deep. Nodded his head slow, worried his chin and realised his shortcomings. He didn't speak.

"Okay, so check them out first. Start with the newest recruit and work back from there. Check out any married guys spending a lot of money on new cars, fancy clothes, guys fixed up with hookers, those sort of things; and most of all – drugs. How many are we talking about?"

"Six guys as far as I know," he replied.

"Okay, check who was on the rota before you made the move, and work back from there. If we can find the snitch, we might be able to trace the contact to Yungen."

She stared across to him. He didn't meet her eye, but looked down to the floor and stroked his chin.

"There's somethin' else, Loot, Yungen's recrutin' up from the O-Zone. The terrorists we took out were all from down there. It ain't only about drugs anymore, it seems that was nuthin' more than a smokescreen. It looks as if he's plannin' a full-on *coup d'etat* and wants to take over here in the A-Zone. An' there's plenty of lowlife scum down there willing to follow him and grab a piece of it. With the ass outta their pants and not a buck to scratch their backsides with, they ain't got nuthin' to lose, Loot. All they need is a strong leader. And Yungen fits the bill big time." Grady spread out his hands, tucked his head into his shoulders. "I don't know, Loot – this is all getting' a little above me. I'm way out on my own flounderin' around in deep water here." He looked to her with a plea in his eye. She returned with a warm smile and did her nose thing.

"Ok-ey, eat up your pizza, Grady. I'll tell you what we'll do: I'll come down and help you check them out. But I don't want to be involved with any field work, guns, or anything which could compromise me in any way at all. I'm through with it. I mean it. I won't do it, Grady, I've had enough. I will come and help you, but only if it's totally secure. And I'll bring Josie, I won't leave her here on her own until this is over – Deal?"

"Deal – thanks, Loot!"

"It's Brock, or Maddie, Grady. Not, *loot* anymore. . . It's Maddie."

"Okay, Loot." He ducked to miss the olive as it flew over his head.

*   *   *

The ambient silence, pure as polished gold, was intruded upon by the cricket's soft buzz at a steady pulse rate of sixty beats per minute, setting the perfect tempo for the meditative mind. Wrapped in Brock's arms on soft duck feather-down, Josie breathed out sweet air through honey lips, cute as a new-born fawn. A soft radiance from the full moon glowed down a tender spotlight, shining bright as the winning numbers on a lottery ticket. The rich ambient light, showering their bodies through open blinds on a cloud-free night, lit up the bedroom window panes as if it were daylight.

At thirteen minutes past two in the morning, Brock was still wide awake, couldn't sleep. This hour of the night she knew was never a healthy time for fifteen rounds with a heavy dose of retrospect. She hated what she'd promised, realising now how much *Jack* had been an anaesthetic to salve her conscience, if not her sanity. She wished he were here.

Josie stirred. Her eyes flicked open. She felt the pain, stretched out and whispered sweet words soft and tender:

"Maddie – are you okay? What's wrong, please don't be sad?" Brock's eyes welled, she couldn't say – wouldn't.

"It's nothing, sweetheart. I'm okay. Go back to sleep, Honey." She turned and kissed Josie passionate on her forehead. Josie cuddled in tight, whispered close into her ear.

"I love you, Maddie. Please don't go away from me."

"That's my problem, Honey. I can't, and I don't want to." At times she wished she could transform back to the life of the cold-blooded killer: a force so dominant in her past life without a conscience to keep her awake at night, and *Jack* to warm and comfort her off to sleep. Back then she had no real reason to live but had never really thought about the *why*. Now she had the reason and the why, and it hurt; it hurt deep into her soul. She held Josie tight both in her arms and her soul with a long-dormant passion she had never before thought possible.

She nestled Josie back down into the sheets and slipped out of bed, poured a glass of wine and wandered out into the garden. Sat alone on the swing seat, she gazed up to the smiling moon, made a wish and sipped at her wine, but wished it was *Jack*. Josie crept out after her, wearing nothing else but a loose shirt and a warm smile. She looked angelic in the moonlight as she cuddled in tight to Brock.

"I'm sorry I promised to help Grady, sweetheart. Poor guy… I should have said no."

"I understand, Maddie. He needs you, we both do," she held her tantalising gaze on damp emerald eyes. "Won't you come and play some piano for me — please."

Brock smiled into the pretty face of pure innocence and bounced her brows:

"I guess music will always be the antidote to salve the soul!"

*   *   *

Chapter Forty

Josie's Ford cut a path through a fine mist rising from sun-baked asphalt following a brief shower of summer rain. Cruising at a lazy pace, the girls made the short drive to Black Rock in less than fifteen minutes arriving at nine-fifty-five. Security was tight. Staring in frustration, Brock sat waiting for her credentials to be checked at the closed barrier into the National Security base. The gate check guard sprang out at the double from the security booth with his face glowing red, and it wasn't from the sun. He stamped his foot down hard to attention with a force strong enough to have kick-started a military cargo plane. His fervent salute, had it not terminated quivering at a half-inch before his forehead but had gone the whole hog, would've put him flat out on the floor. He looked straight ahead as he barked out in the robotic voice akin to misguided authority:

"Major Falconer is expecting you, Sir! It's the top floor at the large white building, third on the right, Sir!" He held his salute as he raised the barrier with his left hand. Brock drove through into the 'Tiger's lair' at Black Rock. Her heart sank heavy as a lead weight without a safety net all the way down to the bottom of a deep dark hole. Falconer was there to meet her, he held out his hand.

"Lieutenant Brock, always my pleasure. And you too Miss DuBois. Come; let me show you to your office."

Through a further bout of security, breezed past with ease at the sight of the Major, and then up one flight of stairs, the office was the first door on the left. LIEUTENANT M. BROCK C.S.F. was lettered in gold on the door panel. Rather than fill her with pride it sent a shiver down her spine. Grady took his feet off the desk as they came in through the doorway.

"At ease everyone," said Falconer. He pulled chairs out for the ladies then stood alert in front of a board of surveillance photos and a large map. He drew a deep breath and held court:

"It would seem Yungen has disappeared into thin air, not that he was ever in evidence in the first place. Such a pity we don't even have a recent picture of him. Anyway, Intel has scoured the whole area and has so far come up with nothing of consequence. So, it leaves me to believe he's not anywhere here in the uptown beach-side, so I can only assume he is hold up further out in the suburbs," he drew a circle with his finger on the large wall map. "So, I've wound down the search in the uptown area, and stepped it up in the suburbs. Sergeant, perhaps you would show us the things you confiscated from the terrorist group yesterday, there may be something of use there." Grady emptied two bags onto the bare pine wood fold-up table stood against the wall beneath the board of surveillance photos. Cell phones, I. D.s, two-way radios, empty wallets, keys, and a bottle opener shiny as the bell press on a whore house, rolled out onto the table. Any weapons captured were stored in the armoury.

"The cell phones have all been checked. Most showed personal in-house calls, a few to call girls and escort agency numbers, nothing solid to go on," explained Grady. "The few valid I.D.s we collected are all from the O-Zone, Sir. So there's nothing much here of any use at all I'm afraid."

"Yes. Thank you, Sergeant." Falconer worried his jaw. Josie reached out and picked up a small handheld radio, studied it in her palm. She flicked through the pages in her notes, ran her finger down the pages as she turned them, then stopped and gate-crashed a conversation.

"I know where he is!" she held up the VHF radio: "he's on one of the super yachts out in the bay. I couldn't make any sense of something I was trying to de-code, but now realise – it's because it wasn't *in* code. VHF 83 didn't mean anything to me at all, not until I saw this." She lifted the tag on the phone. It read *VHF Marine Radio*. Brock snatched up the desk phone and ordered a line through to the harbour master. After a brief wait she gave her I.D. security code and asked for information on any super yachts riding at anchor. In the silence she wrote notes on a call pad, asking for phonetic spelling for one name alien to her. Before closing the call she asked for the owners' names of the super yachts, but knew the call would be a dead end, revealing not much more than a long and useless page of un-listed corporate owners. She hung up and turned to Falconer.

"Okay, Sir," she began: "there are three vessels currently at anchor in the harbour as we speak: 'The Lady Sharon'; 'Easy Living'; and ... 'Usuthu'. I'm not quite sure how to pronounce the last one, Major." Falconer's eyes lit up, he grinned deep, slow-nodded his head. As an armchair military historian, he knew it only too well.

"USUTHU!" he roared, "the Zulu war cry, howled out by Zulu warriors as they went into battle during the Zulu wars in the late nineteenth century. By God, Lieutenant, there's our man, I'd put money on it!" Falconer looked across at Josie, wanted to kiss her but shook her hand and his head instead.

"Well done miss super sleuth, DuBois."

"Grady, haul in the prison guards one at a time; I have an idea," said Brock. "Where is the interrogation room? Come, take me, let's go?" She stood and paused, looked open-mouthed to the Major with a silent question. He gave her a gentle smile and said:

"It's okay, Madeline, I'll mind her."

Sat in straight-backed steel chair comfort, the first guard in the interrogation room said bless you, Sir; thought she'd sneezed when she said Usuthu. The second kept his body language slack with a blank face pure as fresh winter snowfall. The third sat in a slouch, shrugging, looking around for a window. But there wasn't one. He stared at his watch instead. Brock's intuition kicked into gear. She spoke to him slow, almost as if she already knew the answer.

"Tell me what you know about Usuthu." Taken by surprise a flush flooded across the guard's face. Turning red and ruddy as a moth-balled playhouse curtain closing on the first act to a limp applause, his face spoke volumes. He muttered nothing audible, but his spirit and body language howled out a strong Hallelujah chorus to the telepathic. Brock didn't take her eyes off him as she said:

"Search his room, Sergeant." Grady cuffed the guard to the chair before he left. With total disdain, Brock stared at the guard. He avoided her gaze, said nothing. She spoke with evil eyes:

"I'm sure you're well aware of Sergeant Da Silva's persuasive interrogation techniques. So – if you want to save your teeth if not your soul, you'd better answer some questions for me before he comes back." His eyes went to the sides of his sockets but avoided her gaze full-on. He moved around in his chair, desperate as a man preparing to take a jump from the ledge of a very tall building.

"How long have you known Yungen is on Usuthu?" she asked.

"I want to cut a deal," he said. She folded her arms, sat back, shook black locks, spoke slow: "No deal! Tell me what you know before the sergeant comes back. I'll ask again – how long have you known Yungen is aboard Usuthu?"

Loud shouting migrated from the hallway, doors slammed, he trembled, took a deep breath, a dark patch began to flourish at his groin. He started to talk.

"Fuck this," he whispered to himself, dragged a wet tongue over dry lips and pulled his hand down his face.

"He comes and goes. Usuthu anchors for maybe two or three weeks at a time, leaves for a while, then comes back again and re-anchors."

"Where does he go?"

"I don't know."

"How many are on board?"

"I don't know," he bluffed.

She stared a wrath through the silence, then, said: "Wrong answer − I'll ask again only once, motherfucker." Green eyes now turned evil. "How many, are on board?"

He heard approaching footsteps out in the hallway; wild eyes similar to a match point ball at Wimbledon volleyed in red lids.

"Four crew, no more, just four crew."

"No security?"

"No, none, only the crew."

"So I take it: there would be five in all on board – Correct?" He nodded the affirmative to her.

"So why no security?" He shrugged his shoulders opened his eyes wide and looked gormless.

"Tell me – Is there a little girl on board?" Grady walked in through the doorway as she asked the question. He held up a small VHF he'd found hidden in a locker in the guard room. He tossed it down onto the desk, then with a hard hand slapped the guard round the back of the head and sent him face first into the stone wall, taking the chair with him fastened to the cuffs. Grady picked him off the floor by the scruff of his neck and growled into his face.

"The Lady asked you a question, shithead, and she wants to hear an answer, and so do I, so speak up or else I'll take you into the crapper and turn you into a fuckin' lavatory brush."

"Yes, yes – there is a girl. But I don't know nuthin' about it. I'm only the contact man."

"So you feed him information − correct?" she asked. Grady breathed fire down the guard's neck, held his shirt tight in a choke hold turning his face red, popping out his eyes similar to organ stops at the climax of an over-enthusiastic Sunday service. He nodded, gurgled, couldn't speak.

"And I take it you told him about the prison truck yesterday?" she asked. Wild eyes didn't answer, went blank. Brock stood, went to the door, didn't look back.

"Okay, Sergeant. He's all yours."

She walked out of the room and closed the door behind her soft and quiet, winced at the terrified screams behind her as she strolled along the corridor and out into the sweet smell of fresh-cut grass.

In a slow stroll across the lawn, she enjoyed an all too unfamiliar but brief moment of solitude similar to those reclusive moments she spent at her keyboard. If only life was as simple . . .

Josie sat with the Major drinking coffee, enjoying small talk in the Covert Security office; but in truth Falconer was digging deep, trying to uncover Maddie's intentions for the future. He turned to the window. Outside he saw Brock sauntering a slow, sultry ballet across the grass lawn. He buzzed his secretary to bring another cup and didn't take his eyes from Brock until she disappeared from view in the porchway below.

Brock two-stepped up the stairway, followed the aroma from fresh ground coffee and into the even sweeter aroma from *Wild Rose*.

"Heidi's on board Usuthu," she announced in triumph as she walked in through the doorway. Falconer sprang into red alert, picked up the desk phone, played the keys, shouted orders into the mouthpiece and turned to Brock.

"I've put Usuthu under twenty-four-hour surveillance," he enthused, "we must act fast but not so fast as to harm the little girl. I would imagine Yungen has a safe room hidden somewhere on board. So, we must approach this with the utmost care." He turned to Brock as she spoke:

"We are also told there are only four crew members on board, Sir, and no security. I personally find it a little difficult to believe."

"Yes, as do I, Lieutenant," the Major stroked his chin, "unless of course – he's so super confident we won't be looking for him aboard a super-yacht, which could well be the case. Then again, I suppose an armed troop wandering around on the deck of a super yacht would certainly arouse suspicion," he raised his brows, looked to Brock: "It could be he's playing a ruse?" Falconer disappeared down a deep well into deep thought, worried his bottom lip with his thumb and forefinger and then said: "We can't take any chances and storm the ship. It would be a dangerous move and detrimental to the little girl. We will have to be a lot more discreet in our approach so let's not rush into things. If he was going to harm the little girl I'm sure we would have known about it by now. So let's assume she's safe. At a guess, I would think she's being kept alive for a hostage situation. So let's not spook him." Deep in thought, he worried his chin and stared out the window. A nasty thought clouded Brock's mind. *'What is it about windows that they need staring at,'* mused Brock. She shook her head as the reminiscence of bad thoughts invaded her psyche.

"There's a private supply barge feeding the yachts, Sir. Perhaps we could use it for a surprise attack?" offered Brock.

"Yes, good idea, Lieutenant," he slow-bounced his head, "it certainly sounds feasible, unless of course the crew on board the barge are also in Yungen's pocket?"

"I'll get Sergeant Da Silva to check it out, Sir. Perhaps he should requisition the barge," said Brock.

"Yes – yes of course," agreed Falconer, "I'll work out a plan of attack with the Sergeant and his team. I did think about taking Yungen at first light tomorrow, but in retrospect as a priority I feel we should afford complete safety for the little girl and suggest we wait a further twenty-four hours and hit him first thing on Sunday morning. It will be the perfect day to put him down on his knees. In the meantime, I'll put Usuthu under a twenty-four-hour close surveillance."

"I want to be there on Sunday, Sir. I feel I owe it to Heidi. After all she *is* my responsibility and wouldn't be there if it wasn't for me," said Brock.

"Very well, Madeline, but I will not allow you on board Usuthu under any conditions until the situation is totally secure. You and Miss DuBois can accompany me with a small backup team on board the harbour master's launch. I can assure you both: you will have the utmost security at all times. Now if you would excuse me, I need to go and check on the Sergeant's progress. I will keep you informed of any changes we make as soon as I know anything more. Thank you, Madeline, and to you too miss super-sleuth DuBois."

He didn't click his heels as he left.

*   *   *

Chapter Forty-one

"Let's not go back home yet, Josie. How about we take a drive out of town, I need to get rid of this nasty taste in my mouth."

Josie swung a left, took the coast road south out of Black Rock in light traffic and suggested they take a late lunch.

"How about the Thai place again?"

"I guess you enjoyed it there didn't you, sweetheart? Okay, it's good for me also, let's go." Stretched back in her seat, Brock closed her eyes and let her body relax; she felt drowsy after a bad night of interrupted sleep and the trauma of Black Rock. Josie drove slow and steady, pretty much the same way she spoke:

"The Major pumped me about you, Maddie. He was very discreet in trying to find out how you felt about Covert Security, and what your plans are. But I knew what he was after, so I kept changing the subject."

"Good girl – He'll be Okay, I'm not so indispensable, and anyway, he's got Grady now, he couldn't do better than him. I'm not going back, honey, I promise. I'll find Heidi, and then it's over for me. I've made up my mind. We've found Yungen and cleared out the drains while we did it." She closed her eyes and sighed, "It's a clear board for the Major now."

"What will you do with Heidi?"

"There's not much I can do, sweetheart. I'm certainly no mother and don't want to be. If I can get her to safety, it will be good enough for me. But I don't know, I haven't really thought it through. Hell, it must be tough being blind. I guess she'll find some new foster parents, she's a cute kid. Maybe the Major can find something for her, he must have a lot of contacts, many more than I have anyway. I want the easy life now, sweetheart, just you and me and no-one else," she smiled across to Josie, "so let's take an easy day tomorrow, maybe we should take a trip out somewhere, have a lazy lunch someplace quiet, sit out in the sun, or maybe we should just stay in bed for the whole day, cuddle up and drink wine," she bounced her brows at the pretty girl.

"Sounds good to me, Maddie."

"Which one …?"

"Take a guess."

"Cute kid!"

The parking lot at the Mekong Delta was already half full at mid-afternoon in the heat of a lazy summer day. As a popular place in a fine setting with good food and stunning décor, the Mekong was a magnet for many. The rustic seating had a deceptive look but was feather-down plush and not the sort of thing you'd want to get up from in a hurry. As a bonus, the pristine bathroom shone bright as guardsman's boots and smelt sweet as the fragrance from a patch of honeysuckle. What else could one wish for?

The cute waitress shuffled across the restaurant floor in a tight two-step as if she'd had her ankles laced together since birth, she was obviously accustomed to life as a female in the Far East. She was short, but a good shape; not always easy for a small person. Under a prime cut of custom-made raven black hair, her wide smiling face was ageless and attractive; an aspect not uncommon to those from the Far East. She carried her countenance well along with the menu. Again, she went straight to Brock.

"Let's do an early dinner, Sweetheart. What do you fancy: fish; poultry; curry; noodles, whatever? How about King prawns? You can have a King prawn burger if you want."

Brock tweaked her nose. Josie gave her *the look*.

"No, you choose again Maddie. Although I must say the King prawn dish does sound good. Maybe let's give it a try."

Brock turned to the waitress:

"Okay, kung-preow-warn and a dish of khaw-pad for us both please and a carafe of red house wine. But first off let's have the Mekong Thai starter." She handed back the menu to the waitress, smiled and said: "Thank you." The waitress scratched notes on her pad, bobbed her head and two-step shuffled off through the saloon doors. Not two minutes later she came shuffling back out beaming a wide smile above a carafe of red on a dragon print ornate tray. She was in for a good tip; she not only knew it but well deserved it.

"I love it here, Maddie. I was thinking . . . how about we open up a Thai restaurant and wine bar on the Bay. Upmarket stuff — I could run it for you. All you would have to do is play the piano in the bar – but stay well away from the kitchen." Brock chuckled, loved her enthusiasm.

"It's a great thought, Josie, but so is coming up on the lottery. Setting up a lucrative business takes serious money and a lot of it. I don't have anywhere near enough cash."

"But you know all about Thai food, Maddie. Just look at this place, it's buzzing and it's still early yet. We could get sponsors or investors, maybe even the Major might be interested. It would certainly keep him off your back." Brock smiled wide, stared into those pretty blue eyes and slow-shook her head.

"You are so cute, Josie. I promise you I'm not going back to work there. After Sunday, and Yungen has been nailed and I can get Heidi back safe and sound, I'm out of it, that I promise you, Sweetheart. But thinking about it – yes, maybe a Thai restaurant with a piano bar might not be a bad idea. I could live with that. Perhaps we could get Jackie Olsen to come in with us and run the bar. I'm sure he'd love to move out of his down-market flea pit out in the suburbs." She beamed a smile across to a cute and beautiful face, "dreams are what life is all about, Josie; and dreams are one of the few things in life still free. Keep it up, Sweetheart, there's not much else on offer going free!"

"Grady could come in and keep order," enthused Josie to keep the pot boiling. Brock tweaked her nose.

"Well, he's sure had a hell of a lot of practice. Okay, honey, here comes our food."

The sun went down in a similar burning blaze of glory as the six-hundred. Venus rushed in to take first place to light up the night sky. Frogs and crickets hailed their pedal-point fanfare welcome as Brock buzzed the gates open. Josie nudged the Ford in through the gateposts, settled into the cottage driveway under the rising pale moonlight and cut the motor. It had been a good end to a bad day at the office. But it wasn't over yet.

Brock jumped into the shower and Josie jumped into Brock. They cuddled for a while, then got serious for a much longer while, and after an even longer while than both of those whiles put together, they ended up out on the swing seat, naked, sexually nourished and drinking red wine in the moonlight. Right now life was sweet and simple, and it was all theirs. Brock was determined she'd keep it that way.

*   *   *

A rosy glow from soothing rays cast from the early morning sun sneaked through the east side bedroom window, lighting up Brock's face, springing her eyes open wide. It looked to be a good day. She didn't stir but laid still in reverie staring up at the ceiling, slow-warming to the idea of a Thai restaurant. The concept of a piano bar sparked positive thought, more so when she considered her options: running down drug dealers, rapists, paedophiles and anyone else who behaved putrid as a mess of erupting boils on the asshole of humanity; and, having to dodge a hail of lead while she was at it. As an option, it was as enthralling as the offer of a discount bungee jump in a third-world funfair. If the restaurant idea worked out she might even learn some culinary skills. It couldn't be as difficult as all that!

Then a thought struck her: to get up early and make a surprise breakfast for Josie.

With the stealth of a Siamese cat prowling a hungry bird pecking for worms on fresh-cut lawn, she slipped out of bed and tip-toed through into the kitchen with a plan to make a breakfast omelette. In her thirty-two years she had never cooked a meal in her life. Food for her was always bought from a diner, a take-away, or served up in a canteen, never from her own culinary efforts. These days it was frozen ready meals courtesy of a microwave, but she figured an omelette couldn't be too difficult; after all it's only fried eggs cooked in a pan, what could possibly go wrong?

Her boiled eggs as a starter didn't work out too well so she decided to try an omelette; it sounded a hell of a lot easier. So, how many eggs would it take to make an omelette she pondered; six would sound about right she assured herself. So she cracked six fresh eggs into a skillet on the stove. Now she was getting creative and cut a slab of cheese into blocks and threw in some tomatoes, olives and a chopped onion into the mix for good measure; then, she sprinkled on salt and a healthy dose of pepper — simple. She did think of adding a banana and shredded coconut for a taste of the exotic, but passed on the idea. Smug with pride, she fired up the hotplate to full, gave her creation a stir and waited, and waited, then waited a while longer until it started to bubble.

She set a table for two and made coffee while her *chef-d'oeuvre* bubbled and popped away on the stove. It smelt delicious but didn't look anywhere near as enticing as any omelette she would have bought in a diner; but what the hell? Then it started to smoke.

In a mild panic, she turned off the stove and sprang open a window to let the smoke escape, but the smoke billowed and turned black as the skillet caught fire. Overhead, a smoke alarm howled and screamed out a warning. She took hold of the skillet but couldn't pick it up: the metal handle was too hot. She turned to grab a damp towel, peering through the smoke, she saw Josie leaning against the door jamb, slow-clapping.

"Maddie – what *are* you doing?"

"I'm making you some breakfast, as a surprise."

"I hope you're not expecting us to *eat* this?" said Josie, scowling down at the congealing mess in the pan.

"I did try and boil some eggs but after fifteen minutes they were still so hard. I'm sorry, sweetheart; I guess I'm not very good at cooking." Josie grabbed a wet towel, picked up the skillet and threw it out into the yard, then opened more windows and fanned the smoke out in an effort to stop the smoke alarm howling. She folded her arms, shook her head, leant back and chuckled at Maddie:

"What *were* you thinking, Maddie?"

"I guess I was getting a little excited about the Thai Restaurant idea. I thought I should have a go at cooking. I've never cooked anything before in my life."

"Promise me you won't try and cook anything ever again," said Josie.

"I promise – I think I'd better jump in the shower. I smell of smoke."

"Thank heavens for the microwave. You go and take a shower, Maddie; I'll make you an Omelette."

"You're a star, Josie. I have to admit: this tastes a hell of a lot better than mine might have done," said Maddie, ploughing her way through a Spanish omelette.

"I can't believe you've never cooked anything in your life; how come?" asked Josie.

"I've never had to. I've always used diners and take-outs. I guess as a little girl my mother being such a good cook spoilt me. She was a hard act to follow, so I never bothered. Sorry – I *can* make a good coffee though."

"Yes, with the machine. Stick to what you know, Maddie. You can sure *cook* playing the piano!" Josie sat with her elbows on the table and gazed blowtorch blue across to Brock.

"Okay King Alfred, what shall we do for an encore today after you've nearly managed to burn the house down?"

"I thought we could maybe give Jackie Olsen a visit: check him out for your Thai restaurant idea," offered Brock.

"Okay – or maybe we should do what you suggested last night."

"Which was – remind me," said Brock, draining her coffee cup.

"Lounge around in bed all day drinking wine?" Brock smiled into those electric blue eyes, racked her brows, pushed her chair back, walked round the table, pulled Josie up out of her chair and kissed her passionately.

"Okay, you win Angel eyes. I'll pull the cork, you go and get naked."

*   *   *

Chapter Forty-two

At six-fifty-five on a humid, overcast Sunday morning, scavenging seagulls seeking a free meal circled, swooped and pleaded for morsels as Brock pulled the Ford up to the harbour master's office and parked alongside a mess of lobster pots, rusted chain, and coils of fraying trawl warp at the fishermen's pound on the waterfront. Out on the distant horizon, a fleet of trawlers making a westward course back to harbour with their night-time catch were escorted by a flock of screaming gulls seeking nutritional gratification.

A light warm breeze ruffled Brock's hair as she stepped out onto the quayside. She closed her eyes and breathed in the salty bouquet of a marine environment, her mind drifted back to the blissful days of solace she enjoyed at Echo Beach, her eyes welled.

Falconer, in his stock leather jacket, stood vigilant by his Jeep. With his stone face stern enough to warrant further rock drill work at Mount Rushmore. He warmed as he focused on Brock. Forever the true gentleman the major stepped forward, pecked Brock's cheek, held the door open for Josie and led them both on board the harbour master's launch. Four of Grady's combat troops fully armed, two medics and the harbour master's crew of two, stood ready on board at full alert. At thirty-eight feet in length over a broad beam with a spacious saloon, the harbour master's launch offered plenty of room for comfort; but comfort was a far cry from their purpose today.

Mike Nichols, the harbour master, two months short of retirement, smart-dressed in Navy blues and footwear with a dazzling shine in serious need of a volume control, looked ready and fit for another full tour of duty. He saluted Major Falconer aboard and shook the girl's hands.

"Thank you both for coming," said the major to the girls, "we will sit offshore and observe from a safe distance.

Surveillance has not shown there to be many hands on board Usuthu, so it looks as if the Sergeant's Intel report may well have been correct. We have acquired the original deck plan from Usuthu's builder, but at over twenty-five years old, it could well have been altered, so let's not get too complacent. Sergeant Da Silva and his six-man team are circling offshore in the supply barge, with the helmsman at gunpoint, as a precaution." Falconer handed Brock a small two-way radio. "Here Madeline, you can keep in contact with Sergeant Da Silva. We shall not be using the harbour master's open channel on VHF, as it's not a secure channel, so we can never be sure who is listening in. But please, I beg of you both, keep well out of sight and under cover at all times, and most of all, please do *not* go out on deck under *any* circumstances," pleaded Falconer.

With a granite jaw, he turned to the harbour master:

"Right skipper, cast off if you please. Let's nail the bastard!"

The powerful marine engine gurgled at low revs as the H.M. launch set a lazy course around the Lady Sharon, then made a slow turn astern of Easy Living. All was quiet, as would be expected at a few minutes past seven on a dull, overcast Sunday morning. A gentle off-shore breeze lifted cat's-paws across the surface of the bay. Sea birds glided lazy circles high in the thermals. The sole sound above the low burble from the water-cooled exhaust of the H.M. launch came from the soft purring from the on-board generators of the super yachts, set to run continuously over twenty-four hours every day to pander to the whims and fancies of the elite few, relaxed back in untold luxury and comfort; and no doubt still fast asleep.

"So far so good," said Falconer with a comforting grin. Then stern lips spoke into his hand-held.

"Cobra-One to Cobra-Two, are you receiving me, over?"

"Cobra-Two, loud and clear, major – over." Brock mellowed at the sound of Grady's voice permeating the airwaves.

"Cobra-One to Cobra-Two, are you ready, Sergeant – over."

"Cobra-Two, affirmative, ready as we'll ever be, Sir."

"ACTION STATIONS... LET'S TAKE THE BASTARD!"

With the skipper still at gunpoint, Grady set the supply barge at low revs and moved out from behind the Lady Sharon, making a slow passage across to Usuthu. He bought the low-decked supply barge up into a light wind towards the stern of Usuthu and drew alongside the super yacht. The barge nudged heavy rubber buffers against Usuthu amidships on the port side. A somnolent crew member near the end of a night watch ruffled lifeless hair as he rose from his seat at the intrusion. He leaned over the rail on the upper deck and spread his hands in silent question. An answer to his mute enquiry came as seven heavily armed men grappled the hulls together and flooded on board Usuthu. He drew a gun, but before he could use it a red dot appeared on his forehead and the back of his head exploded in a fine red mist. His body, thrashing arms and legs flailed backwards on the impact and made a bloody mess on laid teak decking; his gun barrel cold.

The ensuing battle under the prowess of surprise was brief but bloody. None of the crew on board Usuthu was prepared for the attack. Large windows in the main saloon rattled by automatic gunfire shattered and rained down in crystal shards into the blue waters of the bay. Heavy gun bursts and stunners flashed bright, blazing throughout the cabins in the low light of an overcast day.

In less than six minutes the assault was all over. As the gunfire ceased, a stilled silence pervaded through the smoke and cordite-laden atmosphere. The gratifying sound of victory hung in the air crooning sweet as the mellowed strains of a dulcet melody. Angry seagulls returned circling high overhead singing out their mournful, 'Klee-ew, Klee-ew,' in what sounded a rapturous applause to some, but to others, they would hear nothing again for all eternity.

Observing events through binoculars, the major saw Grady signal the *all-clear* from the upper deck. Grady's voice permeated the airwaves:

"Cobra-Two to Cobra-One – target secured, Sir. Over"

"Cobra-One to Cobra-Two – casualty report if you please, Sergeant, over."

"Cobra-Two – all good for us, Sir; a few minor injuries, nothing serious, over."

"Cobra-One – report the target status, over."

"Cobra-Two – five dead, Sir, Yungen blew his brains out before we got to him, over."

"Cobra-One – and the little girl?"

"Cobra-Two – negative. No sign of her, Sir. She's not here, over."

"Grady this is Brock – Have you searched the whole ship?"

"Affirmative, Loot. She ain't here; maybe she never was, but we'll keep searching." Brock turned to the Major,

"Could we go on board now, Sir? We may be able to help turn up something."

"Yes okay, Madeline, but first we must wait for fifteen minutes to allow the team to make a complete and thorough search. And then we can go on board, but not until I've made sure it is all one hundred per cent secure for you." He held her shoulders and looked in empathy down into those damp emerald eyes, "I'm so sorry, Madeline. Sad to say, I fear this outcome was inevitable."

Fifteen minutes later the H.M. launch motored across the bay and came up into the wind alongside the supply barge. Two combat troops made fast the lines and secured the launch. An N.S.F medic alert chopper flew in and hovered overhead. Falconer sent the rest of his team on board Usuthu to help make a thorough search of the ship.

Grady's team carried out the dead. They laid them on the side decking and covered the bodies with sheets ready for body bags. Grady appeared at the blown-out window in the upper deck saloon. He looked down to Brock, spread his palms and shook his head in despair.

"Okay to go on board now, Sir?" pleaded Brock. Falconer, stiff-jawed but reluctant, nodded the affirmative. Brock hugged Josie tight, held her in tight arms and stared with a deep passion into those blowtorch eyes.

"It's over, Josie – No more!" She sank her head into Josie's blond locks and dropped tears of relief onto her shoulder. "Wait here with the Major, Sweetheart; I'm sure it's not a pretty sight on board. I'll need to see for myself if there's any sign at all to prove Heidi was ever here, or any evidence to where she may have been taken." She hugged and kissed Josie with a yearning desire, smiled thanks to the Major, went out on deck and climbed on board Usuthu.

Grady met her on the portside deck, talked awhile then took her up to the bridge deck where Yungen had blown his brains out. With a mess of blood and grey matter splattered across the front screen and over the instrument control panel, it didn't look a cosy place. Then again, anywhere someone would choose to blow out their brains might also not look too cosy a place. But who knows? Maybe it did to them, or maybe they didn't bother to think about it before committing themselves. Life can sure be a bitch!

"Did you search everywhere, Grady? The engine room, lockers, store rooms."

"Yeah, the whole ship, even the chain lockers. As I said, Loot: I don't think she was ever here. I'm sorry – it's my guess she's dead; the bastard probably killed her out of spite."

"Did you find a cabin that looked as if it could be a little girl's cabin, a little blind girl's cabin?" she asked.

"No, nothing at all, Loot, not even close – I'm sorry."

"Okay, thanks, Grady. So I guess now we'll never know," she conceded.

"Maybe, or maybe not," he said "Someone out there must know something; maybe the money man, and he or she will be keeping down low as a Dachshund's bollocks, you can count on that."

Grady led the way through into the upper deck saloon. Broken glass, splintered wood, blood and shell cases tainted a grim story on the wall-to-wall thick white pile carpet. The heavy tang of cordite hung in the air. Brock shook her head, looked across to Grady, gave a soft-eyed smile and said:

"Well done big guy, I guess we finally did it," she soft punched his big square jaw and did her nose thing. They spoke a silent message with their eyes. Brock relaxed her grip on the big man's hand and moved across to the blown-out window. She smiled and waved down to Josie standing on the aft deck of the launch. She blew down a kiss from her wide smile to pretty blue angel eyes. All was good. At last, it was over.

Under the droning from the chopper hovering overhead, Brock never heard the false panel sliding down in the wall behind the bar, or saw a lone black-clad figure step out in the shadows. A shot rang out; Brock jerked forward, reached out to nothing as she spun and fell to the floor rolling in agony onto her back. In an instant, Grady had spun round and emptied the four shots left in his Streetsweeper to the sound of the shot. His gunfire flash lit up the silhouette of a figure in a black ski mask, dressed all in black in the dim light. Heavy shot from Grady's weapon tore through the bar front, sent a mess of splinters and glass flying into the air. He checked as the assailant jerked, rolled back and slumped down behind the bar. He threw his empty gun in fury into the shadows, knelt down to Brock and cradled her head in his hand. She'd been hit in the back and was bleeding badly. He felt her warm blood running through his fingers as he cuddled her body. A crimson pool leached into white pile behind her. He hollered out in anguish;

"NO MADDIE. PLEASE, NO! MADDIE – NO!" He bent down over her, took her in his arms, spoke soft, almost in a whisper, shook his head and cried . . . "No, Maddie – please, no, not now, no, no... no please God. . ." Grief-stricken he cried, dropped his head. She slowly opened her hand; he covered it with his own. She tried to smile, but her eyes filled with tears as she heard screams from Josie below. Grady's own hot tears flooded down onto her beautiful face. He bent and softly kissed those honey lips he'd never known, for the first and last time. He took in her breath as she breathed out; it was to be her last. Emerald green eyes smiled up to him, then, glazed over, and closed forever.

Behind, deep in shadow, the assailant rose slow, fired up as the mythical Phoenix rising from the ashes. Black-clad and bloodied in Kevlar, the gravely injured assassin limped and slunked a bloodied trail across thick white pile towards Grady, who now lay crouched down, grief-stricken, cuddling in his arms the one and only true love of his life. Hovering overhead the chopper howled. Shouts from below drowned out by screams from Josie wailed up from the lower deck. In his grief, Grady could hear none of it. The assailant cast a long shadow from a dark place and snuck up behind Grady.

Heidi Traudl Yungen, nineteen years old, the only child of Karl-Heinz Yungen, had now no more need to wear the dark wraparound glasses; not with her twenty-twenty perfect vision. Her evil eye drew a bead along the barrel of a Glock 17, down to the back of Grady's head. Her cute little index finger having teased out so many a sweet song, was now cuddled around a trigger – and now no longer so cute.

"Drop the weapon – Now!" Came a shout from afar – But too late. Heidi squeezed out a final swansong for Grady before her body jerked and rolled away in a hail of heavy gunfire.

Grady never heard the shot allowing him to fulfil his lifelong promise to his one and only true love – To take Madeline Brock off to a very special, sacred place; a place far, far away – into a distant empyrean paradise.

*   *   *

Chapter Forty-three

A brief wash of late summer rain left dampened grass glistening bright as emeralds across the manicured grounds surrounding a small wooden chapel and private graveyard, set in the seclusion of a woodland copse of oak and pine trees on the Falconer estate. Inside the chapel at noon, the soft sound of birdsong, the mood solemn, Maddie was laid out in her open casket, bordered with a cherished spray of white roses. The stirring wealth of emotion throughout the chapel brought tears to the eyes of all present. Cloaked in a shroud of white silk, she looked beautiful, even in death; for now she was at peace. A wild rose had been placed in her hand across her heart. A small select crowd gathered behind Major Falconer, who had desperately tried to control his emotions, but had lost the battle as the beautiful ballad 'Blue in Green' by Miles Davis whispered its dulcet melody from somewhere in the background. Struggling to hold back tears on a stern face, Jackie Olsen gripped the lectern tight. Damp of eye, he howled out a long and powerful eulogy for his friend; read not from a script, but straight from the very depths of his heart.

High in the sky a skylark sang. A mystic ray of sunshine in a dull day shone down through a break in a cloud, sending a shimmering shaft of light through stained glass to light up a lone figure stood back in the shadows. Pretty blue angel eyes streamed floods of tears down over a beautiful face; a face swathed with the scent, of 'To a Wild Rose'.

*   *   *

Epilogue

Many tears I've cried for those days of splendour
when we walked in arms on golden sand,
sowed sweet seeds of love in our secluded wilderness,
pledged our troth beneath the smile of the silver moon,

My devotion to you was a love supreme,
such true love before, I have never known,
for it to be so fragile, I could never dream,
such thought in torment, would turn my heart to stone.

But now, my true love you've been taken . . .
In my solitude dark days of grief grow long
without your dulcet lips to comfort me
under a lazy sun, or the smiling silver moon.

My empty world, soulless without you
has bled my aching heart dry.
But my sweet love, to you this I promise,
my heart will bleed no more.

So for you my one and only love,
as I watch the summer sun take its final curtsey,
I will kiss your gun and come to you,
and we'll walk forever on golden sand . . .

Josie, x